ISBN-10: 1492935077

This is a work of fiction. Names, characters, places and incidents either are the products of the author's imagination or used fictitiously.

Cover Art Design: Lukasz Z

For more information on this series, author or bonus content, please follow the author at:
Series Website: **www.operationenduringunity.com**

Other stories by Richard Peters:
Shock and Awe (Operation Enduring Unity II)
The Surge (Operation Enduring Unity III)

The Unreasonable Man (Sci-Fi short story collection)

Dedication

This novel is going out to all my brothers and sisters in every branch of the military. All those that answered the call to serve without ever asking, "What's in it for me?" Especially to the families of those that never made it back. Dead but never forgotten!

To my endlessly patient wife: I really do love you more than my computer!

Table of Contents

- Table of Contents ... 3
- Prologue ... 4
- Part I ... 6
- Chapter 1 ... 7
  - *November 8th* ... 7
  - *10 November* ... 8
  - *Two months later* ... 9
  - *Inauguration Day* ... 12
  - *In the Midnight hour* ... 13
- Chapter 2 ... 17
  - *St. Augustine, Florida* ... 17
  - *Gainesville, Florida* ... 18
  - *Tallahassee, Florida* ... 19
  - *Downtown Gainesville, Florida* ... 20
  - *Washington, DC* ... 21
  - *Jacksonville, Florida* ... 24
- Chapter 3 ... 26
  - *Somewhere over the Okefenokee Swamp (Southeast Georgia)* ... 26
  - *Camp Blanding, Northeast Florida* ... 28
  - *Camp Blanding Airstrip* ... 31
  - *Tallahassee, Florida* ... 34
  - *Camp Blanding, Florida* ... 37
- Chapter 4 ... 42
  - *Context* ... 42
  - *Washington, DC* ... 43
  - *Orlando, Florida* ... 46
  - *Los Angeles, CA* ... 47
  - *5 February* ... 50
  - *Manhattan, NY* ... 52
- Chapter 5 ... 55
  - *Washington, DC* ... 55
  - *Tampa, Florida* ... 56
  - *Lake Butler, Florida* ... 59
  - *Starke, Florida* ... 59
  - *Atlanta, Georgia* ... 65
- Chapter 6 ... 68
  - *10 February* ... 68
  - *12 February* ... 70
  - *Homestead ARB* ... 71
  - *17 February* ... 73
  - *20 February* ... 74
  - *Ocala, Florida* ... 79
- Part II ... 85
- Chapter 7 ... 86

    Mobile command post a few miles inside Florida 86
    USS Gerald R. Ford, 50 miles East of Daytona Beach 87
    Lake City Municipal Airport 90
    North Florida 98
    Keystone Heights, Florida 99
    I-75, just north of Gainesville 104
    Sunny Skies over Florida 107
Chapter 8 110
    20 miles NE of Lake City 110
    East side of Lake City 113
    North Side of Lake City 125
    High Tide 126
Chapter 9 130
    15 miles north of Lake City 130
    Los Padres National Forest, California 131
    7 March 134
    Ocala, Florida 134
    Bama 139
Part III 142
Chapter 10 143
    9 March 143
    10 March 145
    Huntington Beach, California 146
    Daytona, Florida 149
    Great Divide 151
Chapter 11 153
    Nellis Air Force Base, Nevada 153
    Fort Bliss, Texas 158
    Bombing Vegas 160
    Check 162
    And Mate 164
    Trouble 166
Chapter 12 175
    20 March 175
    22 March 178
    New Game 181
    Sacramento, California 184
Chapter 13 188
    1 April 188
    Fort Myers Beach 190
    15 April 194
Acronyms/Slang/Terminology 204

Prologue

November 7th, 20soon

All the waving red, white and blue bunting had a slightly nauseating effect, when stared at long enough through a 13 power scope. John Randall raised his cheek off the rifle's stock and forced a ragged breath. He even managed to blink. The damn debate moderator kept droning on longer than expected. Well, after a month of planning another minute couldn't hurt. Any moment he was going to make history.

From nearly 400 yards away and 4 stories high, he could still hear the idiotic cheering fire up again. When the beaming face of Senator Dimone came into focus a relaxing wave of finality dampened his adrenaline fire. That rich tool was about to make the last speech of his perverted presidential bid.

Ah, but first he must shake hands with his opponent, Speaker of the House Terry Scott. *The only real man on that stage.* John felt a brief flash of regret. He wasn't a complete psychopath. Deep down, he knew this isn't what the congressman meant by: "Enough talk, it's time for action!"

But all those long hours spent volunteering and canvassing for the congressman's campaign seemed so trivial, when stacked against the billion dollars poured into his challenger's various PACs by unknown donors. Remembering how every spare moment of the last year of John's life, so lovingly invested in trying to save his dear country, could be so casually brushed aside by some corporatist conspiring brought the rage back.

While no one would confuse John Randall for a true sharpshooter, firing a box a day of .30-06 for a month on a 500 yard range sure builds confidence. He slid the window open and took up as comfortable a position as he could out on the sill. Just like in the movies. He was even dressed head to toe in black.

The reassuring weight of his semiautomatic rifle, bought without a paper trail from some gun show, relaxed him as much as noticing the wind dying down. Perfect conditions. Shifting his weight, he savored the God-like sense of power from his perch. Randall drank in the grinning face of his prey at the other end of the scope…perhaps a moment too long.

With his left eye shut tight and his whole world focused on the golden clasp of that $1,000 power tie, he failed to notice some Secret Service agent a few feet from the target clutch his earpiece and shout.

He sure noticed the chest caving impact of an alert counter sniper's round ripping through his left lung a split-second later.

The well-practiced, gentle squeeze on the trigger became a rather untidy jerk. His body raced the spent casing to the ground, but he felt no regret. Savoring the fresh scent of decisive action and sweet gun smoke gave him a greater sense of peace than people would expect from someone drowning in their own blood.

*

Congressman Scott wondered what kind of political stunt this was when someone yelled "Get down!" and his opponent shrieked like a girl. The pieces slowly came together when the *craaack* of something split the air, followed by his screaming rival falling backwards.

It all became crystal clear when the round missed the senator, struck a flagpole behind him and ricocheted through the base of Congressman Scott's neck instead. With the vertebrae shredded, he was dead before his body hit the ground. But even so, his disjointed head still made a comical bobbing motion closely imitating his "Together, we can!" advertisements…all in front of the live, primetime coverage cameras.

Millions of voters watched their hopes die in high-definition detail. Thousands of filthy rich campaign donors saw a huge investment vanish faster than any stock market "flash crash." Hundreds of other politicians witnessed the entire political landscape turn upside down. A half dozen television networks observed their ratings skyrocket. Regardless of what each saw from their unique perspectives, they all drew the same conclusion: whether they liked it or not, violence was now *the* decisive force in American politics. It was a lesson none would soon forget.

Part I

"Society was cut in two: those who had nothing united in common envy; those who had anything united in common terror."
– Alexis de Tocqueville, Recollections on the French Revolution

Chapter 1
November 8th
New York City

"That isn't news Chris. It's just a rumor–at best! You can't run that!" Christopher Atkins shrugged his shoulders as he poured his sixth cup of coffee. He had surprisingly little self-consciousness. "That's why it'll be aired as an 'unconfirmed report,' and why you're going to get me some other sources."

Jessica let go her indignation long enough to give into curiosity. "Me? Why do you want a financial correspondent to report on a political story?" Her boss gave one of his rare smiles. "Politics, finance–if you really think there's a difference nowadays, then maybe you're in the wrong line of work."

Jessica snatched her purse and stormed out, only to throw it back at the tacky faux-leather chair she abandoned. "What I mean," she crossed her arms and began with more patience than she felt, "is how can anyone prove overnight that Senator Dimone was behind the assassination of his rival, huh? It's just mudslinging at its worst. It's that sort of gossip politics any loud mouthed dick can cover. I don't see how I can add any value." She finally sat down with a satisfied grunt.

"Your value comes precisely from *not* being one of those loud mouthed dicks. No other news outlet is giving this official coverage. By giving these allegations a fair hearing, by examining the facts involved, you can add that edge of legitimacy that'll turn readers from the competition."

"What damn facts? That's the one thing these claims are short on."

For the first time he took his other eye off the TV in the corner and gave this skeptical blonde his full attention. Not a good sign. He never notices a woman unless he wants something from her.

"Jessica, do you think a newspaper, even one as old as ours, runs on facts? It runs on advertisement and advertisement runs on getting attention. In the TV age we had the edge by offering more detail than the boobtube. Now, in the internet age, we're even getting whooped on that front. All we can offer is speculation or scandal, same as them, but from a respected source. Or even better, speculation about a scandal. Let the reader make up their own mind."

He tsked tsked. "Jesus Christ, when did you get so naive?"

Instead of slamming her head against the brick wall of profitability, she changed tack. "My readers aren't going to care after the election results come in tonight. It's the hot topic at the moment, sure, but the outcome changes nothing. What does it matter who's president anyway? Congress is still going to sit on their collective do-nothing asses. The figurehead occupying the Oval Office is small change."

"Jessica, this has nothing do with the individual candidate. This, like everything else, is all about money. Do you have any idea how much has been spent on these two men? Add in the PACS on top of the direct donations and we've got over a billion dollars for *each* contender. Do you really think people, especially the power brokering type involved here, are just going to write off a billion dollar investment without a fight? I don't know how it'll all go down, but my gut says the real campaign is just starting."

"I'm telling you, this is going to be an epic story. And it's going to happen with or without you. Are you going to be a part of it, or just watch on television like everyone else?"

As disgusted as she was, she was still a professional.

"When do I leave?"

***

10 November

The experts on the bi-partisan panel were in top form. Each talking head was carefully screened to ensure only the most radical pundits were available. Any hint of moderation got you a "don't call us, we'll call you." The producer's last minute change to the lineup, by replacing that boring constitutional law professor with a more media savvy ex-politician made the difference. Ratings were up a good 2 points higher than expected.

"The election results are not unconstitutional or even without precedent. As I wrote in my new book, the *Dark Side of Power*, available at all major retailers, it's happened twice before in American electoral history. In 1800 and 1824, neither candidate won a majority in the Electoral College. In accordance with the 12th Amendment, the House of Representatives chose the next president, just like they'll have to do now."

The debate moderator didn't bother pointing out that no one claimed the election outcome was either unconstitutional or new. It wasn't his job to keep the talking heads grounded. Only to keep them arguing. He stoked the coals some more. "So, a Republican will be chosen by the Republican majority in Congress and the Democrats just have to take it?"

A disgraced former congressman gesticulated the loudest, which meant he got the camera close up. "Absolutely not! Senator Dimone might not have won the electoral majority, but he received far more votes than Congressman Pierce. This is the defining moment of our age. My fellow Democratic colleagues have a mandate from the people to make sure the fascists can't steal this election like they have so many others. We'll fight tooth and nail for the honor of our democracy!"

An ultra-conservative, ex-politico turned reality TV star grabbed the spotlight. "*Really*? That's exactly why we need to have faith in our real leaders not to let these iddy biddy communists derail the democratic process. The government has been lying and spying for 8 years now. I say it's time for freedom to stop dying and time for them to start crying!"

The debate moderator wasn't sure what the hell she was talking about, but it got a standing ovation from the audience regardless. He tried to give her time for another sound bite when the unthinkable happened. Despite his reputation as a kook, the old Libertarian masquerading as a Republican dropped some buzz kill bombs.

"This whole thing is a moot point anyway. This decision won't be decided along party lines. The Republican majority was always pretty slim. The swing votes will be coming from the dozens of incoming congressmen. By the Constitution's rules, only the new Congress gets a voice. This all-important vote will be their first taste of power. You can bet the outgoing politicians will be bitter, and oh boy, how! They'll do whatever they can to influence this historic decision they legally can't make. Mark my words, this will be a 'corrupt bargain' the likes of which our country has never seen. Democracy will be the loser, regardless of who wins the White House."

The moderator was totally unprepared for this onslaught of reckless logic. He expected the old man to babble on about gold or the banking system or something. Thankfully, the producer in his control booth was always ready. He cut the uncomfortably accurate "crazy" man's mike and switched the camera to the conservative, but feisty ex-vice president. The audience went back to cheering or booing while the experts became even more provocative. The show was saved.

***

Two months later
2 January

Jessica kept her smile and pretended not to understand the congressman's not so subtle sexual innuendo. This was her fourth interview with a House member in the last week. She was getting used to the gentle harassment by now. Her curves and not being part of the usual Washington reporter crowd greased the wheels of exclusive access. The downside was looks and novelty attracted these Type A personalities like buzzards to road kill.

"That's nice, sir, but let's go back a bit. It's just that many people are shocked to see the House select Congressman Scott's running mate for president. Pierce is a Libertarian after all–this would be the first 3rd party president since the 1850's. During the campaign you yourself spoke, shall we say…critically, about him. You accused his deceased predecessor of selling out the party. I think my readers are interested to know why the sudden change of heart."

The young man's well-rehearsed lines still came off naturally. He was good, she had to give him that much. He tore his eyes from her legs and poured on the dimples. "In times of crisis, our leaders must put aside partisanship bickering and do what's right for the country. A grand compromise has been reached which looks after the interests of both parties and best serves the American people. If only Senator Dimone would understand that and respect the will of the people. His continued illegal challenges are an affront to democracy and are dangerous attempts to usurp the lawful transfer of presidential power."

Jessica let him drone on about the other candidate for a few minutes. You couldn't interrupt an interviewee of this caliber. The whole thing was a masterful display of public oratory. He stayed 100% on message, never deviating from the talking points and buzzwords his media people focus grouped, yet was still somehow able to turn a display of "bipartisanship" into a diatribe about the opposition. Impressive, even if it gave no real information.

"Yes sir, all of your colleagues have given me the same reasons–verbatim. I was hoping you might be able to speak more…frankly. With all due respect, this is your first term. You've been in office barely two weeks. You don't have the, ah, political entanglements of some veteran members. Far from losing any political capital, you stand to gain the respect of the nation if you could shed some light on the behind the scenes negotiations that went on."

The politician's handlers were trying their best to kill her with their eyes. One flapper came over and whispered something in the frowning man's ear. Her interview style might be effective with executives in the business world, but it was an incredible breach of political protocol. A Washington reporter's job is to either push an agenda or to help push the interviewee's agenda. Relentlessly pursuing facts was far more shocking than spouting conspiracy theories. As great a social faux pas as showing up to the interview naked.

Jessica wasn't stupid. It was clear she'd crossed some invisible line. She swiftly changed course to what was surely a safe subject. "Perhaps we can come back to that. How do you respond, sir, to the Supreme Court's ruling that the House's candidate of choice is ineligible for the presidency?"

Back on familiar and prepped for ground, he wasn't so shy. "First, Mr. Pierce is not a 'candidate.' He is now the legally chosen

President-elect of the United States and will be sworn in later this month. The House of Representatives is the only government body empowered to select the president in the event of a hung Electoral College. The 12th Amendment to the Constitution is clear cut and not open to interpretation."

"But Congressman, it is the Justices' job to interpret the Constitution. They didn't simply decide the House chosen successor is ineligible. The Court ruled that the Republican National Convention failed to properly nominate Pierce in those hasty hours between Scott's death and Election Day. They have firmly and definitively stated that, due to this technicality, Senator Dimone is the rightful winner of the election.

"According to them, this isn't a constitutional question at all. As such, Congress has no say in the matter. If you look at the opinion polls, nearly 30% of the population believes them. A further 40% agree with the current president's call for new elections and only 30% think Congress should choose the next president."

The righteous indignation in his voice seemed genuine. His deviation from the carefully defined talking points was further proof. He shifted his wry bulk in the "statesman" padded leather chair. Not to try to dissemble, but to appear calmer than he felt.

"This isn't about poll numbers. I know it might sound trite to you, but I came here to clean up Washington. Whatever supposed corruptions some people accuse us of, that's small change compared to what the Court is trying to pull off. A tiny cabal of nine old, unelected judges is blatantly defying the will of the people and their *elected* representatives. They are mounting a historic direct challenge to democracy in this country."

Jessica wasn't so easily swayed. "Some would argue it was the historic levels of corruption among our elected representatives that forced the Court to act."

One of the staffers couldn't hold it in any longer. "Who? The same people that published a 3 page conspiracy nutjob peace about Dimone ordering the assassination of his rival? You ran that on the cover of the largest paper in the country and, when the FBI finished their investigation, you buried the retraction on page 30 something between lingerie ads! Where was your vaunted investigative journalism there?"

Jessica blushed deeply, and not from anger. For a change of pace, it was the congressman that spoke up and defended her. "Cut the camera off. Look, I understand. There are realities, whether in business or politics, that force us to compromise our principles sometimes. No one here is a saint. Politicians need to do some unsavory things to stay in office so they can make a real difference later. Don't smile; we do more good than bad.

"And you news people need to do the same, if you're going stay in business long enough to expose real corruption. It's a screwed up world we live in. Sure, the game's crooked, but it's the only game in town." He looked about as close to a normal human being as a politician could.

"Here, and it should go without saying that this is way off the record. If this gets into print your entire paper will never have a chance to report inside the Beltway again. Usually, I wouldn't want to see Pierce President of the United States any more than the Supreme Court. But the cold reality of the current political situation is that the only way to break the gridlock in Washington is to get some fresh blood in there. Someone that everyone doesn't hate yet.

"By caving in, we've already won the key legislative points on our agenda. That has already been hammered out by both parties' leadership as part of the Grand Bargain. If we had gone with Dimone, we would have seen another four years of hopeless legislative stagnation. The political ill will would be unrepairable."

A staffer tried to shut him up and Jessica tried to pump him for more questions, but he kept going. Some of that idealism and energy from the campaign trail seeping back into his voice.

"It may be the stereotypical 'smoke filled backroom deal,' but that's the only way to make progress nowadays. I don't mean just more convenient, but the only way. Come on, you're in the news business. You know the effect those cameras have on people–instant radicalization.

"But it doesn't have to be so hopeless. We're on the verge of a renaissance in American politics. You've seen how things have been. If Pearl Harbor had been hit this year, we never would have declared war. We'd still be debating and accusing each other of this and that while the Japanese occupied California. Our legislative system is a joke these days. But we have finally figured out how to break the logjam. How to usher in a new golden age, and this black robed mafia wants to throw away all that progress."

He sprung out of his chair and shook his head. "I'm sorry, but that cannot be allowed. I tell you all this because I want you to understand when you're spinning your coverage. Congress and the American people have little to lose and everything to gain. No matter how things turn out, the presidential succession won't be decided in the courts this time. It's with us or in the streets, and wouldn't you prefer an orderly, even if distasteful election, to mob rule?"

If the entire interview the cameraman secretly obtained with his hidden digital recorder been aired, people probably would have been relieved at his honesty. Since the chief editor decided to run with a few cherry picked blurbs, the context was thoroughly lost. Of course, that didn't matter nearly as much as the massive increase in sales generated by the headline: *"Congress has nothing to lose and everything to gain" by defying Supreme Court.*

***

20 January
Inauguration Day

    Pierce's swearing in ceremony on the Capitol steps was probably the worst in history. It was downright embarrassing. More a SNL parody than a display of political power. Naturally, no one from the Supreme Court was there. Even the lame duck sitting president didn't bother showing up.

    The president's term in office ended at noon, but he didn't seem ready to go anywhere. He had no legal support, either in the House or with the Courts. Not a leg to stand on. Only his party's slim majority in the Senate kept impeachment at bay. But those weekly votes to start the impeachment process gathered a few defected senators every time. By this point, it would take just a couple of his supporters changing their minds to lose the majority, and his job.

    The only thing keeping those senators on his side was public opinion. The president had always been popular and, now playing the "wise old statesman" role, his public support skyrocketed. While it wasn't terribly disturbing to the assembled congressmen, the president's absence spoke volumes to those watching from home.

    There were also no military bands or other traditional trappings of power. The Armed Forces, upholding a long tradition in America, were careful to stay apolitical and give no appearance of supporting any individual politician. Not a single uniform could be seen within a mile.

    The security staff's decision to limit the audience to a tiny, prescreened group of second tier VIP's made things even worse. The Capital lawn wasn't even a quarter full. The media kept panning over the small crowd and made as much a fuss over the embarrassing turnout as how not a single representative from any foreign embassy showed up. The wind lashed icy rain against those that did attend. Their cringing glumness made for great TV.

    The cherry on top of this shit sundae was having the actual swearing in done by some retired Chief Justice. The idea that seemed so full of rich symbolism when planned in the office came across weak and pathetic in practice. This deeply hunched, 80 plus year old in an ill-fitting suit was missing that indefinable something lending authority to a robed Justice.

    They gamely carried through with the ceremony anyway. Most commentators, comedians and those bothering to watch it live had a blast with the show. Others took in the pathetic ceremony of weakness and counted up the opportunities.

Pierce's handlers wearily tallied the opinion poll results in real time. Their career prospects sinking as fast as the numbers. Finally convinced, they made some calls to their counterparts at the White House and in Senator Dimone's campaign office. They'd pushed brinksmanship as far as they could and probably further than practical. Time to make a deal. While they still had some public support left.

***

*In the Midnight hour
Washington, DC*

The Big Three quasi-presidents huddled around a giant conference room in the White House. Tieless and sleeves rolled up, they looked busy. Around them orbited twenty assistants, top lobbyists and no-title "advisors" doing the heavy lifting. Whenever they worked something out amongst themselves, they whispered the details into the Big Man's ear. Seconds later the idea could be formally proposed.

While the leaders of the three sides put the finishing touches on their long anticipated deal, an aide wheeled in a large television. No matter how hard the president tried, he couldn't escape that damn idiot box. He glared at his excited chief of staff.

"You better be right that this guy is worth the interruption. I can't possibly imagine how the ranting's of Florida's governor can be more important than this meeting."

His top staffer shook his head. "Take a look, sir. It was a surprise announcement. We've already missed the first few minutes of it, but you won't believe what he's going on about. As far as we can tell, he's dead serious! I don't think he's acting this time." He flicked the television on and caught the fat demagogue in mid speech.

Governor Rhett sported a bright red power tie and a comically oversized American flag pin. He nearly came close to pulling off the FDR fireside chat effect in his replica Oval Office. The symbolism was lost when he opened his mouth.

"*Now, ya'll know I've never been a fan of the Washington regime. I don't reckon I'm alone in that respect. But today, we're far beyond simple disagreement over policy. Our supposed leaders, of both parties, have shown how utterly inept they are.*

"*Through their petty, childish bickering, they've shut the government down for all practical purposes yet again. Every year the same games. They've devastated our economy, put millions out of work and made us the laughing stock of the free world. This madness ends today! It's time to get this country back to work. Time to climb back in the saddle!*

"Who's going to get us there? Washington has a credibility gap so wide you could drive a truck full of lobbyists through it. In this leadership vacuum, it's time someone stands up and leads by example. That's the responsibility the great State of Florida now has to assume. Not for the first time, and probably not the last time."

Everyone laughed except for Senator Dimone. He had carried Florida by a wide margin in the election, for what little good that did him. Pierce yawned and reached for another cup of coffee. "Is this shit for real? Are we being put on by some YouTube pranksters?"

The president even grinned. "It's legitimate, alright. I don't know why you're surprised. This crazy governor is in your party. Now you see the nonsense I've had to put up with for years!"

"Those rednecks down there don't have parties—they just want to have fun. They'll swim against any popular political current for the enjoyment of being a pain in the ass."

"There comes a point where you can't trust them any longer. When the regime routinely and unapologetically violates the Social Contract. All this talk about 12th or 20th Amendment issues are just smoke and mirrors. The typical legalese you expect from Washington fat cats trying to hide their crimes. But ok, I'll play along. They want a constitutional precedent—well, I'll give 'em one. Right between the eyes! What about going back to the original Bill of Rights?

"Let's remind those self-obsessed lawyers that: 'The powers not delegated to the United States by the Constitution, nor prohibited by it to the States, are reserved to the States respectively, or to the people.'

"That's clear as day. When the central government can't get their act together, it's up to the states to protect their own interests. The people have to step up and show these Washington elites how to do their job. That's why, in accordance with the official election results of Florida, We the People have chosen Senator Dimone as our next president!" The camera cut to the flag-waving crowd surrounding the statehouse.

It took a minute for the applause outside to die down. How he attracted such a huge audience at nearly midnight no one could understand. Other politicians gawked on in envy. His long reputation of being intentionally provocative always insured a ready crowd whenever he felt like doing some grandstanding. This was no small advantage for a politico.

"Settle down. I know, I know. I'm excited too. It's time for us to wrestle democracy back from those rich special interests in DC. The first step is to get those criminals out of there. Effective immediately, all federal offices in Florida will be shut down. All federal workers are furloughed until the Administration gives up their illegal hold on power, Mr. Pierce renounces his cockamamie scheme to seize the White House and President Dimone is sworn into office.

"Any federal bureaucrat that fails to comply will be considered a traitor to the Constitution and subject to detention. To enforce the will of the people, I have called up the people's watchmen—the mighty Florida National Guard. Our brave

men and women in uniform stand prepared to restore the honor of America by any means necessary!"

Except for those confused and incredulous "brave men and women in uniform," most of the state cheered. Governors in other states were infuriated that their Florida counterpart beat them yet again to central prominence on the national political stage.

Within hours, a dozen states would follow through with similar proclamations. These Jonny-come-lately's wouldn't get the media attention Florida bathed in. For them, it was only talk. Who would go so far as mobilize troops to back such a bluff, like Florida promised? No, there was only one show worth watching.

In a corner of that large meeting room, Senator Dimone conferred in whispers with his handlers. One of his people showed him some hasty poll results. Results so fresh the pollsters were still on the phone with some of the interviewees.

The sitting president ignored Dimone's team and lectured the room. "Ok, what an interesting show, but it changes nothing. His symbolic actions are blatantly illegal and won't stand up in court. Just like all of his stunts. Let's get back to work. We are agreed then, yes? Dimone will bow out of the race and Pierce will take over. After his first term, he will not run for reelection and will throw his support behind Dimone four years down the road.

"The Senate will also fast track all of Pierce's appointees in exchange for help with certain legislation Dimone sponsored, well, you two already worked out the details there. And, of course, I will end my term immediately. Tomorrow morning." He seriously looked relieved when he added, "Thank God, this stuff won't be my problem anymore!"

No one was really satisfied with the arrangement, which showed how great an 11th hour compromise they hammered out. With all sides pissed off, it must be a fair deal.

Actually, one person in the room could still smile. Senator Dimone stood tall, rolled his sleeves back down and tried to hide his excitement. His entourage followed suit.

He purposely avoided the term "Mr. President" as he looked him straight in the eyes. "Sir, in light of the current situation I cannot, in good conscious, ignore my responsibilities to the American People. I'm afraid I will not abdicate my duty to assume the Presidency upon your removal from office."

"That's not going to—"

Few people interrupt the president, but Dimone did. "I've been invited to attend an emergency impeachment vote, which will likely turn out differently than the previous ones. I hope there are no hard feelings; this is nothing personal. It would be big of you to attend the swearing in ceremony tomorrow."

The president was not so easily shaken. "Come on, you can't hang your hat on that rhetoric. Governor Rhett talks a good game, but some games aren't about talk. Something he hasn't figured out yet. That speech was a plateful of warm disaster with a side dish of stupid. We have a deal that you agreed on. It's time to end this self-imposed crisis and get the country back to normal!"

"Then follow the will of the people and resign, sir. You've already split our party; stop this stubbornness before you split the nation. I await your decision. Good night, gentlemen." He and his people left without another word.

The other two supposed presidents continued arguing inconclusively throughout the night, ignoring everything going on down south. The only thing they agreed on was to have Congress officially extend the president's term an additional week. It at least held off the legal grounds for the president's impeachment. Still, all they did was kick the can down the road until they could figure out what to do about Dimone.

Few in Washington paid any attention that night to the swamp rats down in Florida. Let them play their games. What could it harm?

Chapter 2
Florida National Guard Headquarters
St. Augustine, Florida

Within 24 hours of the governor's supposedly "historic" announcement, hundreds of National Guard troops fanned out throughout Florida to "lock down" high profile government offices. Being a Saturday, calling up the men wasn't easy, but the part-time soldiers still rapidly and efficiently carried out their senseless operation. The Guard colonel running this circus nearly burst with pride. Not over his soldiers, of course, but over his exceptional leadership skills and farsighted planning.

For such a self-centered man, he did have a gift for guessing what made other men tick. He instinctively knew which subordinate leaders needed to be fired up with pep talks about defending their freedom from tyranny. He sweetly reasoned with the quiet skeptics that someone had to keep the mobs at bay and protect federal lives and property. The scared, he buoyed with assurances of how quick and bloodless this deployment would be. The veterans groaned at that bad luck curse, but they soldiered up anyway.

He alone made the decision to fully equip and arm each man as if this were a real campaign. What a striking figure he made giving a rousing speech while personally helping to distribute live ammo to his confused troops. If only those pricks at the Pentagon could see him now.

Colonel Beauregard never forgot all their conspiring to keep him from being promoted to general or all those bullshit accusations and then easing him into the Guard when he refused to take it quietly. Oh, he was going to show all his imaginary enemies. Once this silly crisis passed, who would be the most famous, soon-to-be general in America?

It didn't matter much that the governor, let alone anyone in his chain of command, had ever given permission to launch this "mission." Patton had it right: "Audacity, audacity, always audacity." Fortune favors the bold and all that.

Since he was some type of Caesar/Patton reincarnated hybrid super leader, it required ever larger feats of daring to maintain his ego's sense of self-worth. What else could a man like him do when presented with such a unique opportunity?

His leaders asked themselves a similar question. Telling him to stand down was an embarrassing admission of losing control, if not signaling outright defeat. The news clucked over hordes of anti-government protestors, already fired up by the governor's rhetoric, hitting the streets with even more fury after the Guard call up. In the high octane, low responsibility world of American politics it was better to be seen as crazy than weak.

While privately cursing him, state politicians and senior Guard officers fell over each other publically praising him. They all tried even harder than the last to claim credit for forcibly shutting down the "illegitimate" government. To millions of sympathetic viewers they offered a positive, realistic chance to halt government overreach. To millions of others, this unified front offered a shocking glimpse into the flaming abyss of anarchy. To the soldiers being thrown into harm's way, the whole thing seemed like bullshit…not that anyone would ever ask.

***

21 January
Gainesville, Florida

A dozen or so policemen did their best to keep hundreds of near riotous protestors from storming the IRS office downtown. They were only mildly surprised at how fast the crowd formed, even so late at night. It was a university town, after all. The kids were always protesting against something. Facebook and free time were a powerful combination. It sometimes seemed they could organize as adeptly as the police and twice as fast.

The cops found the speed of the National Guard's response really impressive. Without being called, a platoon of five Guard Humvees came growling towards them. They bypassed the packed roads by rushing through the park. An enormously welcome surprise to the overworked lawmen, at first. When they ignored the crowds and began taking up cordon positions on each end of the building, the officers were downright perplexed.

The senior officer jogged over to the one soldier who wasn't holding a rifle at the low-ready. "That was damn quick, but if you guys are supposed to be taking charge of this mess, why didn't anyone tell us?"

"We're not taking charge of anything except this building," hollered the officer. After a glance at the policeman's cocked head he added, somewhat quieter, "Look, I don't know what the hell we're doing here. We were told to 'secure this building,' whatever that means. So that's what we'll do."

If it was possible to show suspicion and hope at the same time, the cop did it well. "So…that means you'll help clear out these assholes then, right? We've got these 'flash mobs' popping up all over town. As you can see, we're stretched pretty thin."

"Negative. I have no orders to that effect. Our job is to make sure no one gets in. What happens outside is not our problem."

"Come the hell on, man. Most of these people are only on the streets because ya'll are out here. I've never paid much attention to all this political crap and honestly don't care one way or the other. But, if we don't stop this crowd…I don't want to think about that."

The LT chewed his inner lip while not so surreptitiously glancing at his platoon sergeant. Whatever order he passed back to the LT was invisible to the cop. At last, the lieutenant nodded his head. "Ok, I'll give you a section, about half my men, just long enough to push this crowd back. Make it happen, Sergeant."

*

Tallahassee, Florida

Governor Robert Rhett could not be enjoying himself any more. He had the frigging President of the United States on hold while he chatted with Senator Dimone's senior staff. How many people could say that? Not even those highfalutin' Beltway insiders could get away with this. But now the president was the one having to show some respect to good 'ole Rhett.

The president wasn't the only one waiting in line, but he'd answer him next. Probably. It was a prestigious phone queue, after all. A round dozen billionaires and key Congress people also waited their turn to bend the ear of the man of the hour. Not bad for the guy the president once called at a Correspondent's Dinner, "The worst thing to come out of Florida since West Nile Virus."

Some would say it was too early to pour a celebratory drink. Metaphorically and literally, since it was still morning. That was no skin off the governor's back. He was on top of the world as he filled up his second Southern Comfort. Kicking up his alligator skin heels, he snipped a cheap cigar and swiped a mess of leaves off his prodigious belly. He could afford better, but he'd always loved the raspy rawness of these cheap Haitian knockoffs.

No sooner had he hung up with Dimone's crew, with an impressive goody offer on the table, did his secretary point out that Pierce's people were waiting. Well, time to get a competing offer. Guess the president could wait a little longer.

His staffers came back and forth while babbling excitedly about some federalization order. Whatever. The Guard already served their purpose. They helped make him a player in the big game. Nothing that lame duck president could do about that now. As a matter of fact, why waste his time talking to him anyway?

He spent the rest of the afternoon ignoring the repeated calls from the Administration; he invested that time in more lucrative pursuits. While carving out a thick slice of power from the baking political pie, he only half paid attention to the news on the streets. He sideways watched, on mute, the crowds supporting their "brave governor." He never noticed they seemed willing to offer more than just moral support.

*

Downtown Gainesville, Florida

"If you ask me, we're pointing our weapons the wrong way. 'Ought a level this place to the ground. You know, what we…"

A calm, but venomous voice came from below in the Humvee and cut the gunner short. "Ain't nobody asked you shit, Private. Now, shut your trap and scan your AO! If I catch you fucking off again I'll ram that 240 so far up your ass you'll need to release the safety to take a piss!"

The young soldier managed to eek out a "Hooah, Sergeant!" before the NCO disappeared back to whatever pit of a hell he came from.

He didn't have long to seethe over it. With half the platoon trying to ride herd on that mosh pit in the parking lot that left only 2 men covering the entire north side of the building. He hurled his water bottle at the giggling driver below just as a bright light exploded further down the block.

"Ah, shit! The news people are here. Wherever they set up shop, trouble always follows." Sure enough, moments later a large group of howling and shoving youths came jogging around the corner. Chased out of the parking lot moments earlier by bayonet-wielding guardsmen, they weren't exactly in the best of moods. With the exciting thrill of cameras on them, the mostly drunk crowd whipped out their wittiest quips. Some shouted for the two nervous guardsmen to shoot up the building, some screamed "go home," and others had the far less practical advice to "go fuck yourself, GI Joe!"

Someone flung an empty beer bottle in the general direction of the IRS sign. The shattered glass seemed to spark some type of collective decision in the crowd. They began launching a barrage of rocks and bottles at the IRS building as the driver called for backup on the vehicle radio. The chastised gunner weighed the risks of firing off a warning shot when a couple of older, almost homeless looking guys broke off from the crowd and dashed straight for the building's entrance.

A flick from the homeless anarchist's Zippo lighter crystallized the gunner's thoughts. He let go of the machine gun and aimed his M16 for a point a few feet ahead of the outstretched arm.

Thankfully, the target stood on soft grass and only a few yards away. Little chance of having some bystander endangered by a ricochet. The sharp *craaack* of his fire shocked the would-be bomber as if he'd been hit. The idiot let the Molotov cocktail fly in what should have been a hilarious and girly way. The comedic value dropped considerably as he accidentally sent it sailing through the Humvee's rear passenger window and showered burning homemade napalm on the gunner's boots.

Seeing his buddy shriek and bolt out the hatch, literally with heels of fire, pissed the 19 year old driver off to no end. In a couple of quick strides he slammed the butt of his M16 into the gaping jaw of the stoned looking arsonist. Whipping his rifle around, he covered the arsonist's other pals—unlit bottles still in hand. He snarled: "Drop it, motherfuckers, or I'll drop you!"

The glare from the Humvee bonfire behind him limited his range of vision, but the light from the excited camera crew frantically panning back and forth caught his eye. "Ah, hell…" he murmured as the camera obviously zoomed in for a close up.

Despite never seeing combat in his short enlistment, the soldier hit the ground first as the ammo in the Humvee cooked off. That saved his life and would have been a good example for the obsessive cameraman to follow. Instead, he tried to catch the action of the stampeding crowd. His camera missed the real action of the belt fed ammo *rat-a-tatting* in the fire. Busy as he was videotaping the other folk dying, he missed a great vantage point when 3 rounds struck him in the chest.

The young soldier high-crawled over to the wounded wannabe Pulitzer Prize winner and tried to stop the bleeding. He couldn't suppress a grin at the man's stamina as he shoved the camera into the soldier's face with his last dying breath.

***

22 January
Washington, DC

"Mr. President, you should see this." An aide cranked the volume up on the TV as the president wearily slumped into his chair.

"…*are graphic and not suited for all viewers.* The fearsome silhouette of a soldier in the shadow of something burning screams at the camera: *'Drop it, mother (*beep*) or I'll drop you!'* The scene cuts to civilians running from the sound of machine gun fire. A flaming orange tracer round catches a fleeing young woman in the back. The scene cuts out with a grunt from off-screen and the camera falling to the ground. It comes back briefly to show a blood stained lens and a close up of some grinning soldier hovering over the dying cameraman. An extremely sadistic looking grin in the dim firelight.

"The previous video was obtained by our local NBKR affiliate in Gainesville, Florida. The video-taker bravely gave his life to bring us the truth of what Governor Robert Rhett is doing in Florida. We cannot, as yet, confirm whether the governor personally gave the order for his soldiers to open fire on unarmed demonstrators or if his men were just following his general order to 'shut down the Federal Government.' The only thing that's certain…"

The president was on his feet instantly. "His soldiers? His men?!" He slammed his fist on the side table. "He doesn't have an army! That's all part of The Army!"

"Get me Governor Rhett on the phone, now! No more excuses, no more games. I've put up with a lot of crap from that blowhard and his party for 8 years, but he's gone too far now. This political grandstanding is getting out of hand. I want to know exactly what he really wants." A young aide happily loped out the door. Never had he seen the Boss so riled up.

He stabbed a finger at the tight-lipped four-star general sitting quietly on the sofa. "General, since the federalization order, those men are under your command. What ideas do you have to stop this nonsense?"

Before the general could answer the president's chief of staff chimed in. "Obviously, the federalization order is not enough. It makes us look weak and highlights our slackening support. We need a show of force. We must get some Regular Army types on the ground there ASAP. We need to get out ahead of this thing or the press will eat us alive."

The general waved his hand dismissively. "If this is a political battle, then why am I here?" No one seemed to hear him.

The president scratched his prematurely graying head for a moment. Another aide, one of his political research people, jumped in. "It's not without precedent, sir. Eisenhower did the same thing in Arkansas back during desegregation. Their governor called out the Guard simply over black kids going to school. He had huge popular support, before Ike put his foot down and sent in Regular Army troops. That strong reaction changed the whole moral character of the desegregation effort. With a quick, bloodless military deployment he accomplished what the Courts couldn't."

The president stared around the Oval Office at the portraits of his predecessors. He paused between Washington and Lincoln, trying to remember who came in between. "Eisenhower, hmm…now there's a president not easily forgotten."

His longtime chief-of-staff knew he had the president hooked. Loading his most reasonable voice, he zeroed in for the kill.

"Every minute this pompous ass defies Federal authority makes you look weaker. The Senate is pressing ahead with the impeachment–that's not a stunt. Every day brings more desertions to Dimone's wing of the party. Even with the sudden House backing, you survived the last floor vote by only one ballot. Strong leadership now is the only chance you have to ensure your legacy." *And not to mention saving my career in the bargain. Who's going to hire an ex-staffer from the disgraced former president?*

The general stiffly sitting on that strange green sofa wasn't exactly known for his sense of humor, but even he had fun. "Gentlemen, excuse me, but are you really suggesting we invade Florida? Tell me, how many tanks should I send into Disney World? Come to think of it, maybe it wouldn't be so hard. I bet we already have a thousand marines in South Beach partying it up right now."

The chief of staff crossed his arms and tried his best, which lasted all of 5 seconds, to stare the general down. "No one's talking about invading anywhere. Just a show of force. We're upping the political ante to the point where the governor can't play anymore."

No one thought it was possible, but the general narrowed his eyes even further. "Once you have armed men facing other armed men, it's no longer politics. This is an extremely dangerous game you're suggesting. It's too easy to spiral out of control–didn't you just see the news!?"

The young assistant came back in without knocking. "Sir, Governor Rhett's office claims he suffered a stroke and is in the hospital. He's supposedly in critical condition. We managed to track down the lieutenant governor, but, well…he's, um…he's on line 1, sir. It's probably best if you talk to him directly." The president raised an eyebrow even as he reached for the phone. "Well, at least we can finally talk to someone."

"Hello, Mr.….? I'm sorry? I didn't get that. You're breaking… Where are you calling from? What are you doing in China while all this is going on!?" The president shook his head. "Well, how soon can you get back to Florida? Who's running things in the meantime?" Another staffer wrote a quick note for the president.

"Wait…no, he's not out of the hospital yet. Fine, I'll play along. Here's what we know. He's had a stroke and is out of commission for the foreseeable future…Governor. Now, I want to know how we can turn this craziness off. I'm sure the ex-governor kept you in the dark about many–pardon me?" His amused exasperation turned suddenly darker.

"No, that's exactly why you need to get back as soon as possible. How can you not be interested in…now wait one God damn minute! I'm not impeached! I'm still your president, you son of a— hello?! Hello!"

No one wanted to be the first to speak. Not even the chief of staff. Strange, because the president was the type of leader who liked to let his subordinates duke it out. He usually weighed in only after ideas survived the first contact with their opposition. That's when he'd step in and, in the words of a predecessor, "be the Decider in Chief."

An advantage of this "never proposing anything" leadership style is that your staff can mercilessly dissect bad proposals without fear of offending the head honcho. The key to getting recognized in this environment was having great ideas—there wasn't any ass to kiss. The boss never voiced an opinion until after your thoughts were already clear.

It was a sign of his stress and worry that the president stopped starring out the window and made up his mind. He didn't propose anything or attempt to provoke any further debate. He made his decision.

"People, I understand exactly what we need to do." Striking that election-winning stance and intelligent grin, he realized how presidential he looked in front of that famous Oval Office desk. But there wouldn't be any cameras around for this.

"My staff will work with Congress and find some legal grounds for direct intervention. General Jacobi, your mission is clear. I want federal troops occupying the major Florida National Guard bases by tonight. We will remove any chance for them to commit further atrocities. I don't want to see any fighting and under no circumstances any bloodshed, but we must have our men on the ground physically controlling the situation inside of 12 hours."

The general thought only a politician could consider that order "clear." Still, he said the same thing every senior American officer ever said to their civilian leadership when given one of these impossible missions.

"Yes, sir."

***

23 January
Jacksonville, Florida

"Who's your source again, Major?"

"My wife's cousin, sir."

The Air National Guard wing commander still had humor left to smile. "We really don't have time for this." He turned back to his cappuccino and the day's emails.

The fighter pilot wasn't about to back down so easily. "I know it sounds weak, sir, but he's a senior maintenance technician at Fort Bragg. He wasn't just passionate when we talked; he was exact. Five C-130's, escorted by eight F-22's, would make up the first wave. Their goal is the big base at Camp Blanding. A second flight will hit Tallahassee 2 hours later because they didn't have enough transports available immediately. A third flight will –"

"Hold it! Take a breath, Major. Between you and me, I don't care either for that asshole in Washington. But it'll all be worked out in the courts before too long. Now, go on back to your duty station. We need to stay alert for real threats, not fantasy. Contrary to the rumors, I can assure you the president is not trying to take over the country and he's sure as hell not going to attack Florida. Dismissed."

A slightly nervous radar operator chimed in before the pilot left. "Sir, we've got a large flight inbound coming over southern Georgia. 5 C-130's and 8 smaller, somewhat stealthy craft."

Hairs prickled on the wing leader's neck, but he didn't give over so promptly to paranoia. "Call Moody AFB and find out what's going on. I want the name of who screwed up and didn't send us the flight plan."

Another officer tapped the radar screen with a satellite phone. "I've been trying, sir. I've called every Air Force base in Georgia. No answer. Same over the radio. Equipment's working fine, but no one wants to talk to us."

"Check the gear again and keep trying!" He grabbed his phone and called the personal numbers of a few senior officers up north. None answered.

Another tech ripped her headset off and bounced out of her chair. "Sir, the FAA just declared a no-fly zone in a 50 mile radius around Camp Blanding. No other details."

All eyes were on him. He had the authority to launch air defense craft. Who above him did? The president and governor were both calling each other madmen. Shit, he wasn't a lawyer. He was a simple soldier. He had to make some type of decision. With that much firepower bearing down on them, even doing nothing was doing something. Whatever he did, he'd be picking a side.

Not one known for hesitation, libertarians usually aren't, the Wing Commander made a call without too much delay. He knew full well where his responsibilities lay, even if loyalty was becoming a fuzzier thing. The craziest order of his life, but someone had to do something.

"Ok, we've identified possible bandits. Scramble the Alert Flight. Intercept, try to divert, harass if necessary, but they will not go weapons hot unless they get a direct order from me. No exceptions, not even in self-defense."

Chapter 3

23 January
Somewhere over the Okefenokee Swamp (Southeast Georgia)

"Colonel Anderson, I gotta tell you one more again. In my 15 years in uniform, from Afghanistan to Syria and everywhere in between, I ain't never seen a more half-assed, hare-brained operation."

Not many people could talk to the battalion commander like that and even fewer would try, but Command Sergeant Major Brown wasn't most men. The lieutenant colonel sighed. "I'm not terribly excited about this myself, John, but at least we have the element of surprise."

The Mississippian spit into his empty Dr. Pepper bottle. "Fuck surprise, sir. I'd rather have artillery! I mean, I've seen some political shit, but that pencil dick from the White House staff telling me which weapons I can bring on a mission takes the cake! Rifles only, no heavy weapons? I couldn't do anything about the big explosive gear, but we were pretty selective about defining the rest of the weapons."

He gave the frowning colonel a wink. "Don't worry, sir. I followed those orders to the T. No 'heavy weapons' came with us."

He turned to the side and shouted down the rows of paratroopers: "Ain't that right, boys! Who's got a weapon that's too heavy?" A dozen machine guns and grenade launchers pumped in the air. Twice as many men grabbed their crotches and cracked dick jokes.

The colonel, quite used to these excessively macho displays of self-affirming aggression among the yeomen class of landed freeman infantry, simply ignored them. "Sergeant Major, that's why I leave the details to you. Frankly, you are correct in your assessment of the tactical situation. We have no air support–no inorganic fire support of any kind as a matter of fact–and at least a 4 hour lead time until the rest of the brigade conducts a movement to contact. Not to mention that the, ah, less than transparent rules of engagement will present many command and control challenges. It is my intent –"

The sergeant major slapped him on the back. "You *must* be nervous, sir, if you're getting all technical War College on me. Don't you worry none. We'll secure that airfield and ammo dump right quick and then curl up like a masturbating porcupine until reinforcements get there. That'll make the rules of engagement pretty simple: Stay out of our way or pay."

The last was delivered as a yell and rapidly picked up in a "Hooah" chant from the rest of the company. The pilot's "20 minutes till drop zone" announcement only heightened the war whooping.

*

Fifteen miles behind them and a couple higher up, two much more subdued Florida Air National Guard pilots switched on their radar sets. This electronic equivalent of a warning flare did not go unnoticed. Guided to their intercept by ground based radar, the interceptors surprised the hastily thrown together federal task force which lacked such support. Surprised or not, two pairs of F-22's flying escort for the cumbersome transports peeled back and roared head on towards the interference.

Over the open Guard channel a Key West twang could be heard laying down the law.

"Unidentified aircraft, you are not authorized to enter Florida airspace. Return 'mediately to the nearest federal airfield or you will be considered hass-tile." In the face of all that high tech death racing towards him, the bluff sounded pretty impotent to the ANG pilot. To the thousands of people listening into the unencrypted channel, he came across as deadly serious.

The Air Force section leader still couldn't believe just how far off the reservation these nutty Floridians had gone. His slow Texas drawl didn't disguise the anger he felt.

"All Florida Air and Army National Guard forces have been federalized by order of the President of the U 'nited States. As the senior federal officer on the scene, I order allll National Guard elements to immediately stand down and return to base." Not without a little showmanship himself, he couldn't resist tossing in a little white lie to up the stress factor. "This is your first, last and only warning. Lethal force has been authorized."

The ANG flight leader never paid much attention to all the talk on the news about the president trying to play dictator. Politics wasn't his thing, but he started to believe the stories now.

With a combined closure rate of over a thousand knots the two sides didn't have much time to make up their minds, or even to bluster further. Years later, historians would passionately argue about why the threat receiver light began blinking on the lead F-22. Provocation or malfunction–it really made no difference. Even explicit orders on both sides to avoid firing go out the window when you believe your ass is on the line.

Training, reflex and perhaps a dose of fear took over when the warning bulb flashed. Without any further confirmation of an attack, the Air Force flight leader uncovered his fire control safeguard and let a Stinger heat seeking missile fly towards his opposite number. His well-disciplined wingman followed suit without a second thought.

Barely two miles away is practically knife fighting range for modern jets. At that speed, the missiles reached their targets in less than

4 seconds. There wasn't a point, or a chance, in evasive maneuvering. The guardsmen didn't even have time enough to fear their oncoming death. They did have just enough time, at least, for one of the F-15 pilots to snap shot off a return missile before becoming a thousand flaming missiles his self.

All the US fighters passed easily out of the oncoming Sidewinder's engagement envelope before it had a chance to arm. The five heavily loaded, slow moving C-130's a few miles further along were a different story. The fire and forget missile acquired a target and proceeded to avenge its atomized master.

*

Lieutenant Colonel Anderson stood straight and tall and addressed his command team. Well, as near as possible for a man with 200 pounds of parachutes and gear hanging off of him could. "So, it's agreed then. After the complete loss of Charlie Company, we won't physically occupy the ammunition holding area. Two platoons from Alpha Company will secure the entrances and engage anyone entering or leaving. The rest of the battalion sticks to the original plan to take and hold the airfield. Questions?"

Considering the situation, he was surprisingly calm. Of course, dealing with disaster is always easier than sitting around waiting for it. Especially from an officer's point of view. Once things went to hell, screwing up further didn't reflect so badly upon you. You didn't have to strive to live up to some idealized standard. Simply pulling your unit through the ordeal makes you a hero.

Command Sergeant Major Brown's focus laid with much more prosaic concerns than his career. 96 of his boys, not even counting the Air Force crew, just died without a chance to fight back. That's not something a man like him could shrug off to bad luck.

Pointing at the radio man, he clarified the only part of the plan that interested him.

"That's a hot LZ. Ya' make it damn clear that everyone knows the ROE just changed. Positive ID is now all you need to engage. If they got a weapon, they're free game. No complexities, no exceptions. I want every man briefed in the next 5 minutes and I want confirmation from each platoon sergeant."

The young radio operator didn't have the courage to defy the sergeant major by glancing at the colonel to confirm the order. The best he could muster was five seconds of hesitation to give his leader a chance to speak up. To give anyone a chance to speak up. No one did.

So, he followed his orders.

Power Games

***

Camp Blanding, Northeast Florida

PFC Donaldson cursed as he soaked himself yet again with the supposed "deep woods" bug spray. "This shit's about as useful as my Guard enlistment," he murmured for the tenth time.

Just another big city boy from Michigan seduced by endless Miami Beach music videos, he convinced his parents that only the University of South Florida could provide that quality education they were always going on about. And, for the first couple of semesters, the 19 year old managed to live the rap star life in bikini heaven while making (barely) the grades needed to keep the folks off his back.

At least, that was before the interest rates doubled on his student loans thanks to some weird federal legislation. His father was "very proud" how he finally found a part time job to help out, but that between his mother's medical bills and the loan's new costs, they had to "make some tough choices."

Lucky to have found even a minimum wage job these days, he jumped at the instate tuition reimbursement incentive the National Guard offered. With the ink still wet on the papers he called his father to tell him not to worry. For just one weekend a month and two weeks a year, the Guard would "pay for his future."

Turned out, he lied. He wasn't even out of basic training when, as part of some complicated "deficit reduction deal" in Washington, the state lost most federal contributions that helped fund the National Guard. Barely able to provide basic pay to their guardsmen, Florida wasn't about to pay for his education in addition–contractual obligation or not.

"Fuck!" He swatted, too late, at another stinging something. How could a swamp be so alive in January? Winter is just a word in Florida. It was cool getting sun burnt on New Year's Eve, but now it's getting ridiculous.

When that dumbass of a governor called up the Guard, Donaldson tried to weasel out, naturally. That's when the stick-up-the-ass, ex-active duty NCO on the other end of the phone mentioned his contractual obligations. He saw now how sassing off about government contracts being binding only one way explained why he was guarding the access road entrance to a fucking swamp on a Saturday night!

"Son of a bitch!"

The older specialist looked up from his porn magazine at the stressed out skinny kid hovering around him. "What the hell, man?"

Donaldson ground his teeth and reached into his shoulder pocket. "Just thinking about shit. Here, I'm going to burn one. Keep an eye out, Hough."

"Ok, but do it back in the tree line. If the on-duty NCO catches you, it's both of our assess."

About 10 yards away, in a slight depression surrounded by high scrub Palms, he finally felt safe from his real enemy: God damn sergeants.

It wouldn't be the last time smoking saved his life. No sooner was he out of sight than the specialist heard something moving around in the dark. He naturally assumed the worst–that the NCO of the guard was trying to sneak up on them as part of some "gotcha" game.

Spc. Hough sprang into textbook action. He shut off the shack's interior light, swung his M16 to the high ready and lit the road up with his pivot mounted halogen searchlight. He expected to hear a shout of "well done, soldier!" Or, at worst, a "what took you so fucking long?"

"Contact, 11 O'clock!" surprised him as much as the two controlled pairs coming right on its heels. The ballistic plate in his vest was designed to stop 1 hit, maybe 2 if lucky. With this many rounds striking him center mass at close range, the body armor didn't have much value.

PFC Donaldson's heart stopped at the burst of fire. Training told him to take advantage of his lucky position and engage the enemy in flanking fire. His gut told him to run like hell. Some small, rarely used part of his brain spoke up with much more practical advice: *Keep calm, don't move, you're vastly outnumbered!*

With all the noise around, the crickets suddenly halted their incessant orgy. He noticed for the first time how dangerously quiet it got at night without the bugs. Convenient, since he couldn't see much from his scrub palm redoubt anyway. The new voices clarified the situation just as good as seeing it.

"Clear!"

"Only one of them on duty? Fucking National Guard amateurs!"

"Does he need a medic? Maybe he's not–"

"Ha! Way too late for that. Shit, he had a weapon, man. I mean you saw it, right? What was I supposed to do? The ROE are clear, he had a weapon…"

"Enough of that shit. You did well. But now the whole fucking camp knows we're here. We need to get back to the ambush site at the other gate before their QRF gets moving. Police this mess up and let's go!"

Donaldson waited a good 5 minutes after it was dead quiet again before going back to the guard shack. His buddy's body lay untouched. Well, almost. Someone emptied his ammo pouches and his rifle was missing. So was the shack's radio.

At least they'd forgotten the backup phone. The warning light exploded. Thank God it had no ringer.

For the first time ever, he was glad to hear his sergeant's voice.

"Rock on! You're still alive. Listen up, things just got real. Enemy airborne came in about 15 minutes ago and they're crawling all over the place. We've lost contact with the airstrip and they seem to be picking people off left and right. You hear anything, shoot first and ask questions later. QRF is heading your way, so don't shoot at the Humvees! They'll reinforce your position. We need to hold the AHA until we can get the ammo and heavy weapons out, is that –"

"Sergeant, look, they've already taken the AHA. They hit us here a few minutes ago." He finally admitted it to himself. "Hough's dead and they got our radio. I'm alive. I, uh, I got lucky."

The NCO on the other end didn't miss a beat. "No time for that now. You made it; that's all that's important. What is the enemy up to?"

Donaldson brought up the 4x power ACOG scope on his rifle. He couldn't make out detailed shapes in the dark, but movement was clear enough. "I think they're setting up an ambush site between the north and east gates. They can hit anyone entering either from there plus cover the main road."

"Are they now? Want to ambush my QRF?" Donaldson could have sworn he heard a purr over the phone. "You know, there's an artillery battery that was out doing some night fire training earlier. I wonder if they still got a few rounds left. Where is the enemy *exactly*, Private?"

"Um, along the reverse slope of the safety berm. Straddling the access road about 300 meters northwest of my position, maybe a 100-200 meter front." The fear in his voice finally gave way to adrenaline. "At least two platoons, but not a full company. I think they're trying to dig in."

"Do you remember how to call in an artillery fire mission, Private?"

Donaldson went pale thinking about this latest failure. "Ah, not really, Sergeant."

"Don't worry about it, kid. You just did. Find some cover. Danger close!"

*

Camp Blanding Airstrip

Thump, thump, thump, thump, thump, thump!

The barrage in the distance hit all at once, but you could hear the distinct explosions if you listened carefully. Alpha Company's CO was not easy to make out on the radio over all the small arms fire and shelling.

"Roger. That was 155 art…casualties…enemy…about company strength, over."

Lieutenant Colonel Anderson's tone held the calm and clarity that only someone not under fire could. "Gator 6, this is Eagle 6. In your assessment, can you disengage and fall back into cover in the AHA, over?" Silence from the radio, but the steady stream of semi and full auto fire in the distance told the story.

Sergeant Major Brown practically hopped up and down. "Damnit sir, we've rounded up enough loose vehicles here and no one has made a move to retake the airfield. We could get a company over there to help fast."

Lieutenant Colonel Anderson frowned. "They're almost 2 kilometers away. Our lines of communication are far too tenuous, even with mobile resources. Our force is spread too thin as it is. I can't risk dividing it further. Doctrine calls for fire support…XO, keep pestering higher for that close air support! No more excuses from them. Make our situation crystal clear."

To his credit, the colonel didn't waste time with "might have been's." Nor did the sergeant major bother with "I told you so's."

The radio came back to life before either could speak. An older voice called this time.

"Eagle 6, this is Gator 3-7, over."

A platoon sergeant? The colonel knew the answer even before he asked. "This is Eagle 6. Where's Alpha 6 actual, over?"

"Gator 6, he's KIA, break…near as I can tell, I'm Alpha 6 now, over."

"Gator, Eagle. Can you disengage, over?"

There wasn't any hesitation. "Negative, Eagle 6. Too many wounded to move and too much open ground to cross anyway, over." The firing appeared to die down somewhat.

"Gator, Eagle. Can you hold your position, over?"

Again, no hesitation. "Not for long Eagle, break…they've already flanked us and are in the AHA in large numbers, over." The sergeant major looked contemplative for a change.

"Eagle 6, they're keeping us pinned down until they get the Bradley's loaded with ammo. It won't be too much longer until they're done. When they come, we got nothing to stop them, over." The colonel chewed on that for a long time, all while fiddling with his VMI class ring.

"Eagle 6, this is Gator 6. Did you copy my last, over?"

The radio operator clicked the mic on and tried to answer. Anderson grabbed it back. "Roger, Gator 6. I copy…break…break…the surrender of your command is at your discretion, over."

Brown snatched the mic. "Wait one, Gator 6."

Voice barely above a whisper, he growled to the enlisted men: "Let me talk with the Colonel alone." The two enlisted melted away fast. Even the XO found somewhere else to go.

"Don't you fucking dare, sir! You make a command decision right now. Don't force a junior NCO to make that type of call to save your fucking reputation. Man up and tell them to…" he had to spit the word out, "fucking surrender, or tell them to die to the last man, but it's *your* responsibility, not his."

Someone burst away with a SAW on the far side of the perimeter, towards the highway ringing the field. M4's joined in a second later…not all as outgoing fire.

The battalion operations officer came back. "The Guard's just probing the perimeter, sir. Trying to define the battle space. Don't worry. We have tight 360° security."

Anderson finally spoke up. "Little good it does us when they have armor and artillery."

The XO finally stopped his perpetual scowling. "We're working on that, sir. They promised us a few FA-18's are being scrambled. It'll take them nearly an hour to get on station here and you'll have to personally approve every strike, but it's something."

The sergeant major needlessly kept pushing the forward assist button on his M-4, an old nervous tick of his. "They don't have an hour. Minutes, tops. Make a call, sir. I'll back you either way."

Anderson stretched out his hand. "Am I allowed to communicate with my command now, Sergeant Major? If you don't mind, I'd like to be in charge of this unit for a minute."

"Hooah, sir."

The colonel never broke eye contact with him as he took the mic. "Gator 6, Eagle 6, over."

"Gator 6, over."

"You are authorized, correction, you are ordered to surrender your element to the enemy, over."

"Say again, over?"

"This is Eagle 6, you heard me. You've all done a fine job, but there's nothing more to be accomplished there. This is not Afghanistan. I'm not going to throw any more lives away over this crap, over." The radio was silent so long the colonel thought he'd lost another leader. The curt reply spoke volumes.

"WILCO, out."

The livid executive officer waved the Sat phone in disgust. "They called them back, sir! Straight from the president! He overruled Headquarters. Only explanation was some bullshit about not wanting to 'escalate' things. That fucker even relieved the General for refusing to obey."

Brown dropped back on a knee. "So? I knew that promise of close air support was too good to be true. Fuck it, we didn't have the fast movers before–we haven't lost nothing."

"No, Sergeant Major. I don't mean just them. I'm talking about the rest of the brigade! Our follow on relief, the Tallahassee task force–everyone! They cut us off. We're ordered to hold in place until further orders. Oh, and avoid taking or inflicting casualties!" To the open mouthed faces gathered around he added, "I swear, you can't make this shit up!"

A familiar, clanking whine far too close cut off the bitch fest. A short salvo of 25mm HE rounds landed harmlessly in the middle of the airfield. Things just went from bad to screwed.

A nearby soldier, valiantly but comically warding off the hulking Infantry Fighting Vehicle with his under barrel mounted grenade launcher shouted: "Sir, the lead Bradley's waving a white flag."

The colonel clasped his hands behind his back so no one could see them shake. "About time! I thought they would never give up." What an amazing effect one lame joke could have on so many men with so little hope. By the time Anderson stood in the middle of "no man's land" and saluted a full bird Florida colonel, the quote had been passed everywhere along the 300 man line. Growing more defiant with every retelling.

*

"Sir, that proposal is unacceptable." Lieutenant Colonel Anderson took off his K-Pod as well. More for the opportunity to slide out of the oven for a moment than as a show of trust. Even a winter night in Florida was hot for a Maine man. The armor and helmet added a good 15 degrees, easily.

"I grant you our present situation is unfavorable, but if necessary, the gloves can come off. I will designate this entire base a Free Fire Area and call in the full weight of my air support. We have accomplished our primary objective of occupying this air field to prevent additional atrocities. We haven't advanced further out of concern for inflicting unnecessary casualties, but we–"

The Guard colonel, who hadn't even bothered to put on his IBA, literally slapped his knee laughing.

"You're something else, all right! I wish I had you on my staff back in Afghanistan negotiating with those assholes!" He paused to savor his opposite number's sour look.

"Don't bullshit a bullshitter. We're all using the same frequencies and the same COMSEC. You don't have any mortars, no anti-armor ability, no reinforcements coming and sure as hell no air support." His smirk disappeared as iron crept into his voice.

"All you've got is blood on your hands, a president who abandoned you and 300 outgunned, outnumbered and surrounded men. Internment is the best deal you're going to get. You have one hour to talk to your officers and see what your superiors think. If they'll even bother communicating. They seem quite willing to wash their hands of you all. Remember, that hour ceasefire is a gift. Professional courtesy. Dismissed, Colonel."

Anderson didn't even offer a half-assed salute in reply.

***

Tallahassee, Florida

Attorney General Francis Pickens hung up the phone in confused disgust. Half an hour wasted arguing with various staffers at the White House and all he could get was a promise that "someone will call you back." They still didn't believe the governor was really in the hospital and incommunicado. They were like a dog with a bone, trying to get back in touch with him. It was even harder for them to believe that the dithering moron of a lieutenant governor wasn't interested in stepping up.

Pickens sure didn't have a problem believing either. About the only thing surprising with the governor's stroke was that it hadn't dropped him years ago. The heart of anyone who drinks and smokes that much was essentially a ticking time bomb. And his number 2 was just the high-school dropout, hillbilly brother of some major campaign contributor. His hardest assignment to date centered on representing the governor at monster truck rallies. They only stuck him on that China trade trip to give time for the sexual harassment allegations to blow over.

Florida sure needed some strong leadership in this vacuum and that's what he was trying to give. He made the decision to expand the Guard call up to protect every federal building and he personally ordered those senior federal workers to be placed in protective custody. In some cases they'd saved them straight from the hands of lynch mobs. But somehow, this all came off as provocative to DC. "Escalations" that idiot White House staffer called them.

He'd even held a press conference explaining it all. Or tried to, at any rate. Never before had he seen such a polarized press corps. They kept shouting him down trying to outdo each other with more outlandish questions.

He couldn't even secure the attention of that egotistical dipshit in charge of the FNG force at Camp Blanding. While the attorney general was nominally the commanding officer of the state guard, during times of crisis the senior professional military officer on the scene took over. At least he would return Pickens' calls, even if he then ignored all the orders to merely contain the paratroopers and try to avoid any further bloodshed.

Pickens wanted to sack the man so badly and had the authority to (probably), but wouldn't that create its own set of problems? Would firing the most senior officer willing to stand up to the Feds destroy the Guard's cohesion? Thereby removing the only real bargaining chip he had. Or would those strange military people ignore him and carry on with their business, in effective staging a coup? Would Washington interpret the action as a peace overture or weakness? There were too many damn unknowns and things kept happening way too fast. If only he could have a little time to think!

Pickens weighed whether to fly out to Blanding and personally oversee the operation or not, when the former governor's chief of staff interrupted and let himself into the office. It was the first time he'd seen a smile on that jowly face all day. Now he laid it on pretty thick.

"Hey, Picky, I've got some good news for a change." The attorney general bristled at the nickname. For years there wasn't anything he could do about it since the fat man was an old college roommate and hunting buddy of the governor. Well, he also couldn't do anything about him now. It was a shame that this prick's expertise and inside knowledge were needed during this crisis.

But as soon as things settled down, oh would this Bubba be out on his ass fast. Don't let the door hit you on the way out, type of out. The chief of staff assumed Pickens' smile was because he enjoyed the nickname. The douche took a seat, unoffered.

"I just got off the phone with Senator Dimone's campaign manager. They want to set up shop down here. In Orlando, to be exact. Well, fleeing for his life from the mad dictator or some such craziness is how they're spinning it. I've already chartered a plane to pick him up and promised on your behalf to grant, get this, 'asylum!' " He couldn't get enough of his own wit.

"The senator's staff will be calling any second to hammer out more details. I wanted to be the first to congratulate you."

"On what? This just complicates everything even worse. I'm doing all I can to keep things from falling apart here, and now this asshole wants to use the anarchy in the streets to score a few publicity points against the president. He's one more headache I don't need."

The staffer looked shocked. "I guess…you haven't had time to think this through. Step back a second. You just got bumped up to the big leagues. That was the governor's whole plan and you've succeeded where he failed. We're no longer a chess piece in this game between the Washington elites—we've picked a side! We're no longer a prize they both have to compete for—we can tip the scales in the senator's favor. Or anyone's, for that matter. We're both the audience and judge!"

"Think about it. Previously, you had the senator up against a corrupt Congress and tyrannical president but backed by the Supreme Court. The quintessential 'People's Champ,' but before you came along, he was just an idea without a host."

"Like a parasite," chimed Pickens dryly.

"That's what I like about you, Picky. Even throughout all this you keep a sense of humor. Well, call him whatever you want, but they'll call you the People's Champion. If we can convince a few of the Justices to 'flee' as well, the opposition's public support will collapse lick split. Take a look at the polls, man! The Supreme Court's opinion ratings are higher than the president and Congress combined! Which horse are you going to back?"

The attorney general hated to admit it, even to himself, but that was a damn good point. What a huge chance he had here. They both forgot the fact that this wonderful opportunity was made possible only through the unwilling sacrifice of so many lives. Well, they didn't completely forget. It was just that their egos were so large as to assume they could fully manage the situation and prevent any further bloodshed, while somehow still orchestrating victory. Like so many "great men" throughout history, they were terribly wrong.

*

Camp Blanding, Florida

Lt. Colonel Anderson had never held a council of war in his entire career. Nonetheless, he felt it was the noble thing to do. Straight out of Xenophon's playbook. Despite a 200+ year legacy of defending democracy, voting was a rather un-Army tradition. He naturally assumed the council would be a mere formality that could add a touch of romantic flair to the history books.

It was soon obvious why democracy is nicer in theory than practice. When he put the simple yes or no question to the assembled captains, first sergeants and lieutenants of what was left of 2-6 Infantry, he received votes for 4 different courses of action. Despite the situation, he marveled at how the "party affiliations" lined up by ranks.

The captains were willing to throw in the towel. The young, unbloodied lieutenants wanted an Alamo-style last stand and the first sergeants wanted to try a breakout. His normally conservative XO held the minority opinion to join, in his words, the "rebels" and march on Washington. He was less than half joking.

50 minutes of arguing only solidified their positions. As for the opinion of the junior enlisted men, out vigilantly maintaining the

perimeter, no one asked or cared. They kept their ideas in heated, but pointless debate amongst themselves.

The first rays of dawn slithered through the pines when the colonel finally noticed something strange. "Where is the Sergeant Major? What's he doing that's more important than this?"

The Headquarters Company captain looked thoroughly puzzled. "He's with the scout platoon, sir."

"Ok…and where the hell is my scout platoon?"

"They're out probing the enemy's cordon for weaknesses, sir. The Sergeant Major said you ordered…ah, shit!" It wasn't a cuss of anger, but one of hope.

The colonel knew the rest of the story even before his personal phone vibrated–the ammo dump was the only place the CSM wanted to go all night. On a whim, he put the phone on speaker.

"Hey sir, damn good job! Keep buying us a little more time. Maybe 15 minutes and we'll be back."

"Sergeant Major, what in God's name do you hope to accomplish? The situation is untenable!"

"It's amazing how easy it is to infiltrate these amateurs' lines at night, sir. Especially when you wear the same uniform and speak the same language. You know, we're probably overcomplicating things. Bet we could march the whole damn battalion right out under their noses! He haw!

"Anyway, Santa Claus is a comin'. Got us about 3 dozen AT-4's, 6 Javelins and even a mother fucking TOW! We didn't get enough vehicles for everybody though–didn't want to draw too much attention. Just enough to get us and our goodies back there."

"Hold where you're at, Sergeant Major. We're surrendering, effective immediately. There's no honor left in this anymore, and I'm sick and tired of this damn debating!"

"What the hell, over! I'm telling you, sir, it's a clusterfuck back here. The Guard's got a dozen different units running around–each thinking they're in charge. With some heavy weapons to hold the Brads at arm's length, hell, they'll probably fold with one big push. We could, at a minimum, break contact pretty easily. Maybe steal some civilian cars in town. It's only about an hour drive till the border –"

Anderson cut the phone off and stood up. He dropped his K-Pod and shed his IBA. The cooling kiss of only warm air wafting over his heated, sweat soaked body made him sigh. Florida winters were always mild, but this year was insane.

"It's over, gentlemen. Collect your units' ammo and stack arms. Battalion formation here in 10 minutes. I still want every sensitive item accounted for."

Everyone was on their feet now, but all the rest still in their battle rattle. The XO began shaking, his hand unconsciously dropping to his sidearm.

"Robert, I can't believe you're betraying us as well. I, ah, I think we need to discuss your ability to retain competent command."

The captains moved to the colonel's side. The first sergeants reached some private agreement with a shared glance and took a step backwards. The lieutenants uniformly had a deer-in-the-headlights look.

By his reserved standards, the colonel lost control. "Major, is it even necessary to point out how out of fucking line you are? You have just relieved yourself of your duties." He drew his own sidearm, though without aiming it anywhere. "Now hand over your weapon or I'll take your rank too!"

The oldest first sergeant nodded at the other enlisted and stood at parade rest. "Sir, I have a suggestion. How about letting us slip out in small groups? If you go parlay with them, for just a little bit longer...I mean, it's still half dark. Like the CSM said, they're disorganized. The officers and senior NCO's will, of course, stay behind and keep up the masquerade while the rest of the men break contact by squads. I think we could get most of the boys out that way." He strived for the missing words. "That would be the most honorable compromise, sir."

Like a true professional, he always listened to a NCO's advice, but like a true officer, he then ignored it.

"We've had enough of this every man for himself shit tonight. We fight as a unit, we die as a unit and, in this case, we will survive as a unit." He raised his sidearm to the low ready. "If anyone has a problem with that we can begin summary field Court Martials!"

The XO flipped open his holster cover unnoticed, or so he thought. The colonel's 9mm flashed dramatically straight up. His warning shot was almost anti-climactic. Whether it was the therapeutic effects of letting off rounds or just impotent rage, he couldn't stop there. He let off 3 more shots into the air.

*

Leaning over the engine block of a utility Humvee blocking the road, a righteously pissed off young Guardsman jumped at the sound of gunfire. No official word had come down yet, but he heard from a medic buddy that his cousin died fighting at the AHA. It was bad luck for everyone that he was just moving on to the anger phase of grieving when shots rang out from somewhere over at the air strip.

He didn't care enough to bother telling the difference between an M16 and a pistol. Nor did he touch the radio or wait for an order. He ripped off a solid 15 round Rambo style burst from his SAW, more or less in the general direction of the sound.

Two hundred meters away, a paratrooper lying in a shallow, hasty foxhole answered the wildly far-off shots with a perfectly placed round from his M320 grenade launcher. Guided by the small laser range finder attached to it, he dropped a range perfect shot right over the truck's hood. The 25mm flechette grenade popped barely 2 feet in front of the target's face. The gunner's battle buddy didn't have a chance to return fire. He was a little too pre-occupied dragging his partner's headless body behind the Humvee.

An ironic calm seemed to radiate from the skirmish. Action, so long delayed, left everyone in a thousand yards from the explosion unsure how to take the initiative. Well, almost everyone.

FNG Colonel Beauregard wasn't sure himself who had the initiative, but he knew who had the artillery. He issued a string of long awaited orders. For the first time in this busy night he strapped on his body armor. Noticing the quiet around him, he added a little heat in his voice.

"What the hell are you waiting for Captain? You heard me. Execute the prepped fire mission." Keeping the order in familiar, safe military terminology sanitized the thought enough for the young Fire Support Officer to suppress his doubts and obey.

"WILCO, sir."

Unlike most of the guardsmen under his command, Beauregard didn't find it hard to believe the president was trying to seize complete control of the country. A megalomaniac himself, the political chaos gripping the nation presented an obvious opportunity to grab power. He was even in the same party as the president. Were he in the White House, he wouldn't have hesitated to do the same thing.

Hell, the only thing that pissed him off was knowing that Guard officers from an opposing state would probably never rise high in the new regime. If only he'd been approached personally to assist with the coup, well…that's not how it happened. Being on the other side, his only route to power and fame lay with being the man that decisively halted the dictator's ambitions.

None of this meant anything to the men he so poorly led and even less to the battalion of US paratroopers on the receiving end of his massed artillery. Not one known for noble gestures, the hour cease fire he granted was spent arming and sighting his 18 heavy 155mm howitzers and the 8 lighter, but faster firing 120mm mortars. The next hour would be spent killing more Americans than died in the First Gulf War.

The men of 2-6 Airborne gritted through 3 end-of-the-world volleys before they realized that time and ammo were on the enemy's side. There were no senior leaders left to order an advance. Colonel Anderson and most of the unit's core leadership were powwowing in the exact center of the incoming Steel Rain, apparently trusting too much in the armistice. They hit the dirt at the first whistle of incoming, but there wasn't much cover around. None would get up again.

Still, you didn't need an officer to point out that the only way to survive the hell storm around them was to close with the enemy as fast as possible. If they could get close enough, maybe they could fight their way through the scores of armored vehicles ringing their position. It was more a collective hope than a plan, but in the absence of heavy weapons, hope was all they had.

The survivors began bounding forward by squads and fire teams, laying down thick suppressive fire as they went. That subtlety didn't last long. The overwhelming urge to get close enough to the surprised guardsmen, to get out of the hammering artillery kill zone, culminated in an old-fashioned charge. With a collective shout of "Airborne!" heard even over the artillery and machine guns, they surged forward all across the perimeter. Their "wild" firing was not only intense, but incredibly accurate. These were some of the Army's most experienced troops, after all. Elite men with a narrow mission and only a few hundred yards till revenge.

They almost made it.

The scout platoon charged down a dirt back road towards the maelstrom. The fear of missing the big fight, of letting their brothers die without them, was a horror worse than the slaughter itself. Everyone rushed to the battle except the sergeant major. He stopped his Humvee and contemplated the tracers, all the same color, in the distance.

Despite the personae he'd cultivated for years, he wasn't all balls, no brains. You didn't survive the things he'd been through or climb so high in the ranks without having a good sense for which battles to pick. With the single TOW missile launcher on the Humvee's roof he couldn't make much of a difference to the disaster ahead.

Brown spent all of thirty seconds wondering where a single antitank missile could have the most impact. He chose his battle. In the confusion gripping the base and the rest of Florida, no one bothered stopping a lone Humvee heading north towards the border.

Chapter 4
Context

"Yes, that's correct Dave. We're just getting confirmation that the last of the president's handpicked storm troopers have been captured. However, as you can see, they wreaked incredible destruction before the authorities could subdue them."

The curvy, angry blonde waved a microphone over her shoulder while the unbiased camera followed. The rows of body bags and several still burning vehicles in the distance were context enough for millions of stunned American viewers.

Twenty feet away a hot, snobby brunette provided context for her studio. "Yes, that's correct Tom. The local militia claim to have finished massacring the rest of the US soldiers. We still don't know why they attacked the president's peacekeepers, but as you can see, this is Governor Rhett's view of a New America."

The rows of body bags and several still burning vehicles in the distance confirmed the suspicions of millions of other stunned American viewers.

Thirty feet further, an older reporter for a local news channel offered depth, context and reasoned analysis based upon the facts he could corroborate. Everyone changed the channel. His producer went into damage control mode and before too long sent him to find and harass, correction, interview the new widows.

All these wild rumors flying over the internet and television, not to mention the straight up insanity pouring out of the radio, should have been easy to disprove. Problem is, retractions are simply not that profitable. The truth has slim margins. Any pangs of journalistic integrity the media suffered from were washed away by the never ending flood of ever greater provocations and senseless violence. If you aren't first with a story, you're last.

In theory the three omnipotent 24 hour a day news networks, with their deep corporate pockets, should have been able to offer unprecedented insight into the nationwide crisis. The reality, like it had been for so long in America, was that none of the big three would dare cover the story from a slightly different angle than the competition. Too much risk the viewer might change the channel. All their resources could only be focused on a single common narrative at a time.

Three networks, but only one slice of the story at once. And a new chapter in this shitty saga broke seemingly every hour. Little wonder so many people were disgusted with the superficial, ADHD coverage of the "mainstream" media and turned to the "alternative" media outlets.

That's right. Millions of Americans were now getting updates on the most important and complicated events affecting their lives from the most respectable news source they could find…the Goddamn internet.

***

27 January
Washington, DC

Self-proclaimed President Pierce's smile lasted long after the last camera was shooed out of the Oval Office. The sitting president's smile fell apart before the door even shut.

"Wipe that smirk off your face. My resignation might help you, but you're still a long way from sitting in that chair." Already tired of the formalities, he leaned back on the *Resolute* desk and folded his arms. "How do you plan to fight the Supreme Court, Senator Dimone and the whole state of Florida? The rebels need to be dealt with –"

Pierce came around the desk to admire the view. He laughed the president silent. "My God, man! What rebellion? Why should anyone have to fight? Four years without having to campaign has really left you out of political shape, hasn't it? According to the Supreme Court, your VP will be forced to resign as well. That drops the ball on the Speaker of the House.

And who do you think was appointed this morning to that vacant role? We'll sidestep the Supreme Court ultimatum and congressional stubbornness by following the letter of the law. That will give us a legitimate president until we can hold new elections. And I'm sure being the man who prevented a civil war won't hurt my campaign!" He turned back to the president.

"That only leaves our runaway senator friend. Once you're out of the picture, he'll no longer have any illegitimate foe to demagogue against. A rebel without a cause. His popular support will fade away as quickly as it came. As for his financial backing, well, I've already approached Dimone's biggest financiers. They aren't interested in throwing good money after bad. I know exactly what they want and find it an acceptable price. It's a bit funny how they're willing to sell him out so cheaply. They'll settle for even less than my own supporters. Maybe I'm in the wrong party!" He was excited as a schoolboy, while the president just shook his head.

"Anyway, with Dimone defanged, I'll offer that calculating attorney general running the show in Florida a face saving way to come back into the fold. Another notch on my belt as the hero that brought this country back from the brink. I don't know why you never thought of it. You've dealt with harder political problems over the last 8 years; why were you stumped by this one?"

The president tried hard to hold the disgust out of his voice. "You think this is some sort of political campaign? Do you have any idea of the social and economic forces aiming to subvert our democracy? The struggle we're facing is probably harder and even more dangerous than the Civil War! Those rumors about holding 'independence referendums' out west are real. We as a nation are on the verge of the greatest fight in our history, and I don't know how to stop it!"

Pierce still kept his perpetual grin on, but his voice held no humor. "No sir, I'm afraid it's always been you doing way too much fighting. You, by staying in power beyond your term and using military force to defend that position, have not only created this crisis, but made it worse at every turn. The only real threat to democracy that needs to be dealt with is you."

The president's eyes burned for a fight. The soon-to-be president backed off. "Ok, I know it's not as cut and dried as all that, but you know how these things work. Come on, the people need a scapegoat. 500 dead soldiers on both sides is not something we can pass off on an overzealous subordinate. 'We need to hold someone's feet to the fire.'" Pierce grinned harder at his favorite campaign slogan.

"Not to worry though. This is politics, nothing personal. I'll pardon you in a few months when things settle down. As part of the healing process. Sure, we'll have to let Congress haul you up for some televised grandstanding hearings, but that's all."

Pierce wagged his finger. "Your biggest problem will be all those pissed off soldiers and the families of the fallen. If I were you, I would be spending these next few months reinventing myself as the greatest and most generous veterans advocate around. Have your handlers talk to my PR people; they are great at this stuff and will help with all the details. To help show there's no hard feelings."

The president ambled away from the desk and over to the Lincoln portrait on the far wall. "You know, they–Buchanan and even Lincoln at first, thought the same thing back then. That the growing southern rebellion was just political stuntery and could be countered by other political games. They failed to take decisive action until it was too late to stop the war from happening." He hung his head.

"My mistake wasn't sending in the Army, but rather calling them back. I lost my nerve and now I seriously doubt the military will follow me again. I don't dare to push them and find out. You should learn from that mistake.

Dimone has bitten off more than he can chew. From everything we can tell, what's happening down South is turning into an honest to God secessionist movement. If you don't rip this tumor out now, the demonstrations spreading around the country will only be the beginning."

Pierce sat slowly, almost hesitantly, in that famous office chair. "Good God! Are you listening to yourself? After so long sitting here you are starting to think you're Lincoln or something. Your paranoia and stubbornness sparked this whole catastrophe. What you so casually shrug off as 'political games' can put a halt to this senseless violence without another shot being fired!"

Leaning back, Pierce relaxed even deeper in the plush chair. "Perhaps it was too much for you to handle, but I've got this whole situation in hand. By the end of today, this crisis will be a footnote in the history books. Not some type of damn civil war you seem so hell bent on starting. I'll–"

KADUSH!

In the movies, people outrun the explosion and jump to safety or something. The human mind simply cannot process the threat an explosion represents fast enough to do any good. The president did not blink, speak or react at all until several seconds after he was blown literally out the door of the Oval Office. Pierce, gesticulating in front of the window, wasn't blown away…just blown apart.

The president had no direct experience with explosives. Still, even he thought it was strange how the blast radiated in a narrow cone from the punctured, bullet-proof window and left most of the room unscathed. One bomb, one kill. If only all military operations could be so sanitary. As he slipped out of consciousness, he was impressed by how beautiful a surgical strike could be–when properly carried out.

*

After the impact Sergeant Major Brown nodded and dropped the radio missile guidance control box. He climbed as casually as could be back into his stolen pickup and drove away without a backwards glance. The TOW launcher stayed in the bed of a second borrowed truck, exactly where he fired it from. Except for wearing gloves while handling the equipment he wasn't terribly worried about covering his tracks. Obviously, he'd be caught one day. Just not today.

He launched his baby from the Thomas Jefferson memorial parking lot, across the tidal basin from the Washington Monument, right after closing. At a distance of 2.7 km the launch site was well outside the Secret Service's enhanced threat security cordon, but still easily within range of the antitank weapon. For a half-baked revenge scheme, put hastily together on the road and relying on radio news reports for his intelligence, it went pretty well. By the time the Capital Police discovered the launcher he was a good 20 miles inside Virginia and whistling Hail to the Chief.

He was thinking that maybe he'd head back to his base, have a couple homecoming beers with his buddies who must think he's dead and then go make the local MP's famous in the morning. Those plans changed when he pulled over for gas in North Carolina and saw a TV. The president gave an impromptu press conference from a hospital bed somewhere. Maybe he didn't look too great, some burns and superficial shrapnel injuries, but the bastard sounded strong and lucid. Humbled but defiant, said the broadcaster. His ratings spiked a good 10 points within hours.

Brown hadn't yet worked out the details, but instead of heading home he pointed the truck towards that dangerous hellhole he swore he'd never visit again. He headed back to sunny Florida.

Outside of needing more gas and a quick burger he made only two more stops along the way. At a bank and then a gun show.

***

28 January
Orlando, Florida

A nervous, plain clothes State Trooper opened the hotel room door for a relaxed attorney general. Senator Dimone mumbled hello without looking up from the television. A pudgy man in a sweaty suit stepped away from the air conditioner, hung up his phone and extended his hand. The grip was surprisingly firm. "Governor Pickens, thank you so much for accepting my invitation. I think together we can make quite a difference to your cause."

"Please, call me Frank. Remember, I'm not the governor. I'm just a simple civil servant trying to maintain neutrality and law and order in the wake of the real governor's criminal actions." He smiled even brighter and pointed at the distracted senator.

"Or…a brave, Constitution loving freedom fighter standing up to tyranny. We'll have to see how this plays out."

The unnamed man, you don't need introductions in the political world when you've financed as many campaigns as he had, laughed heartily and put his arm around the attorney general.

"I like you; damn if I don't! Oh, I think we can do business. You see, you forgot the third option. How about going down in history as a loyal and high-ranking member of the new administration? With a presidential pardon for all so-called "crimes" committed in the name of defending the Constitution?"

The attorney general gazed around the hotel suite that was larger than his house. "Well, I've never been a history buff. What would this high ranking position pay?"

As he so often did, Senator Dimone ignored the conspiring around him. He had two televisions sitting side by side to monitor. Each tuned to a major liberal or conservative network so he could compare the slants in real time. You don't get to be a five term senator without having an intuitive grasp of popular opinion. And right now popular opinion scared the hell out of him. The only point both sides seemed to agree on was that the time for compromise had passed.

He interrupted the acting governor and Him. "Don't you think we're escalating this too far and too fast? After the assassination we don't enjoy the rock solid public support you think. A lot of people still believe we were behind that, despite your advertising blitz. I mean, look at this footage. Just look at all these people pouring out of Florida. The only ones coming in look like militia nutjobs!"

The Forbes "Man of the Year" finished fixing a drink for their guest and rested a well-manicured hand on his shoulder. "You can't see the forest through the trees! Don't lose your nerve on me now. We have them on the ropes. Look at all these demonstrations–nationwide! Hell, even in the president's home state! The Administration's support is crumbling around them. People weren't even this fired up during the campaign."

He waved at the press release on the table. "It's political theater, that's all. How's it any different than when you shut down the government over a budget dispute? You do whatever it takes to force the other party to negotiate. It's time to turn up the heat." He was almost sexually excited.

"The president is barely standing. One strong push now and he'll fall fast. Not to mention all those congressmen that fought against his impeachment. I even have it on good authority that two of the Justices will be retiring this year. All of this is too much stress for them. Good God, man! Don't you realize what's at stake? Stay the course now and our party can control all three branches of the government in one fell swoop! We're making history here. Don't piss that chance away over a few dead soldiers! How many have died far more pointlessly? Honor their memory by making sure they didn't die in vain!"

Senator Dimone was as enraptured as a school child. "Christ, and I thought I was a cynical, calculating son-of-a-bitch. But when you're right, you're right. Let's do it then. Get it over with. Close the border and all the rest, but we have to play this carefully. No one else gets hurt, clear?"

They were so enthralled with the fun little details of their plotting that no one noticed one of the State Troopers step outside. As an ex-marine, loyalty ran deep with him. Sometimes though, disgust runs even deeper. He called an old buddy from the Service he heard was doing something for the CIA nowadays.

***
1 February

Richard Peters

Los Angeles, CA

Sophie put the final touches on her picket sign as her father finally muted the TV and sauntered into the kitchen. "Honey, for the last time, don't go out there with all those hippi…" he changed tack swiftly when she stabbed him with her eyes, "all those protesters. This isn't like anything I've ever seen before. I mean, this could be worse than Rodney King."

She sighed and rolled her emerald green eyes. "We've been over this a hundred times, Dad. How can I sit back and let the president take over the country?! This is a coup! It's like something that would happen in Africa. Do you really want to see America run like a 3rd World military dictatorship?"

It was her father's turn to overdramatically roll his eyes. "Come on, you don't believe those new political advertisements, do you? I raised you smarter than that. For every one calling the president a dictator there's another one calling the Floridians terrorists and secessionists. Don't get involved. I'm begging you baby, please." For a moment the pleading in his voice almost swayed her. Unfortunately, a moment is not enough to hold a nineteen year old's sense of righteousness at bay.

A horn blared outside and cut off the growing battle. She girded her already short brown hair into a tight ponytail and snatched her world changing signs. "Ben's here! I have to go. Look, we'll be safe. I'm just trying to raise awareness, that's all. Seriously, I'm not some type of revolutionary! Love you, daddy. Bye." She was out the door while he still fantasized about putting his foot down.

She kissed her boyfriend and slid into his hybrid with her other friends. They left the suburbs and headed downtown like any normal weekend. They stumbled into a police barricade a good mile from where they intended to meet up with some college classmates. That should have been the first clue that things were bigger than they imagined.

Onward on foot they went, joining in with whatever group happened to be marching on that block. They chanted with the unemployed, cursed with the environmentalists, laughed with the gays– it was a great time with the regular crew. However, closer into town they began noticing new actors. The themes changed from broad social issues to narrow political ideas. In contrast to the always present protestors, the people here voiced disturbingly specific complaints. Most ominously, they also had narrow and clear objectives.

Around the next corner they took, a well-dressed and mostly middle aged group demanded the president's impeachment. In the blink of an eye they began cussing and shoving against a strikingly similar looking group demanding the arrest of so-called "traitors and murderers." The youngsters were so enraptured by the sight of what could have been their parents fighting in the street like teenagers that they ignored the random gunshots in the distance. Even the faint whiff of burning plastic and oil was chalked off as just the smog.

The police were nowhere to be seen. In fact, throughout the city, they were spread thin on the ground. That was partly due to the sheer size of the unrest. But the call up of Reserve and National Guard personnel didn't help–a large fraction of local cops were also weekend warriors. Perhaps the single biggest drain on resources was the run of the mill criminals. From teenagers organizing "flash mobs" at stores to armed gangs clearing out banks, everyone seemed to be taking advantage of the situation. Hell, at that moment someone was stealing Ben's car a mile away.

During this chaos the media stuck to their predefined narratives. Demonstrators on their smartphones, especially the young, gaped open mouthed at images of cops elsewhere in the city rounding a corner in formation. They pumped out tear gas and bean bag rounds into the crowd as if paid per shell.

The image cut off for a moment and came back with several of them firing live rounds at someone off screen. Unarmed protestors, according to the newscaster. Some bright boy at the studio had the award-winning idea to superimpose the president's voice from a recent speech promising: "To do whatever it takes to bring back law and order."

There was no mention of the surprised gangbangers who, in panic at a wall of police officers trumping towards them, fired wildly at them. In the rush to be the first with something different, the media had no time to explain such subtlety. The job for the police only got harder, but with every drop of blood some news outlet grabbed an extra "2 share." When the governor deployed the already mobilized National Guard, and Congress authorized limited use of federal troops as well, the media practically orgasmed.

Sophie had a change of heart when a separate phalanx of cops came within sight down the block they were trapped on. "Come on Ben, let's get out of here." Her boyfriend glanced from his IPhone to her and back again. Gone was the self-righteous bravado he was so well-known for. "Okay, maybe you're right."

He tried hollering for their friends but they were all surging forward with the crowd of other youths. Sophie and Ben would have been caught up in it too, if she hadn't shoved him into a nearby burger joint, one of the few stores still open. When tear gas canisters flew past the windows and their eyes watered, they didn't hesitate. The two bolted out a back service door and onto a parallel street.

They continued this half mad rushing through alleyways and random open businesses until they finally hit a quiet street away from the trouble. A *too* quiet street, in fact. They rushed to a bus stop and checked the schedule. Only 2 minutes to wait. They shared a laugh of relief. It never crossed the minds of these suburbanite children that public transportation might be slightly interrupted by such wide scale civil unrest.

It took a moment for the pair to notice there was no traffic on the road, or even anyone on the sidewalk. Well, not completely true. A clusterfuck of skinheads (the grammatically correct term for more than one) stood over a barely moving, dark-skinned kiosk owner across the street. They were staring up the block with their arms full of booze and cigarettes. Sophie followed their gaze.

Two dozen locals solemnly marched this way. From the Indian gas station clerk with a double-barreled shotgun to the Hispanic furniture store owner with a Berretta, not one of them looked like they were in the mood to talk. Which was just as well, because neither were the punks.

The only thing more shocking for her than the shooting was that no one got hurt. The wannabe NAZI's weren't exactly expert marksmen, even the few of them that weren't drunk or high. And for their part, the locals were way too excited and fired wild and high. For most of them, it was the first time ever firing the gun kept for years behind the counter. Had she been at home watching this on television and not close enough to smell the powder she would have had a good laugh. At the moment, her sense of humor was stretched thin.

About two minutes into the Looney Tunes version of the OK Corral the cavalry arrived. The skins scattered as two Humvees blocked the road and a squad of soldiers dismounted. That should have been the end of it, but some of the punks decided to shoot blindly behind them as they ran. A lucky shot from a spraying Uzi struck a soldier in his bulletproof vest. Fine or not, the close call pissed the troops off…and changed the rules of engagement. The professionals soon silenced all the crazed shooting with controlled pairs from their M16's.

It was simply bad luck that Ben had shaved his head in support of his passion-of-this-week charity: cancer survivors. It was also bad timing when he pushed Sophie to the ground just as a dying skinhead dropped his weapon nearby. To the young soldier searching for targets through the limited visibility of his gas mask, it sure looked like another asshole reaching for a gun.

All Sophie would remember was her boyfriend's head exploding as he tried to protect her. Before she blacked out from screaming, she saw two of the president's henchmen, in the heat of the moment, high-fiving over their victory. She never noticed the unit patches on their sleeves were from the California National Guard.

Power Games

***

5 February

The cemetery was busy for a Monday. To be expected after three days of rioting put down only by a massive deployment of state and federal troops. There was too much business happening too fast for the funeral homes to stagger the ceremonies. Some would have to go on at the same time. Even if that sometimes created damn awkward situations.

Sophie couldn't understand how her boyfriend's mother could be so sympathetic with the other family nearby. That young soldier being laid to rest over there helped kill her boy. Oh, he might not have pulled the trigger, or even been in the same unit, but in Sophie's eyes, he was just as guilty of killing Ben. Another hired gun for the rich.

The wind direction was horrible. Every time she heard their minister mention something about the meek inheriting the world, she would catch a "defending our freedoms" from the other funeral a hundred yards upwind. The rival preaching would have disgusted her…if she wasn't already sick with anger. She couldn't even focus on the family and friends in front of her standing up to say a few words. Her cold gaze kept drifting over to those flashy uniforms laying the casket in the ground. The folded flag, the whole shebang—so much for a thug!

The poor girl couldn't even get a good cry in. She wouldn't allow the enemy the satisfaction. Sophie tried to force that strange *E*-word from her mind, but it wouldn't leave. She was a rational, partially college educated modern woman. Her social consciousness ran deep—borderline hippie, her father would say. But she had seen where that gets you.

All the talk and singing in the world seems kind of naïve when the rich bastards have an army to do their bidding. If only there existed an army that fought for the regular people. Of course, she assumed, that would be a contradiction in terms. Regular people had to fend for themselves.

When the 21 gun goodbye blasted off, she was the only one in her circle that didn't jump. The melody of gunfire inspired her more than any Bon Jovi song. Her rage ashamed her, but not enough to forgive. Not by a long shot. She thought she knew what hate meant, but then came something that made her lust for vengeance seem mild.

Those Westboro Baptist Church nuts were at the cemetery, but she hadn't even noticed before. A curtain of bikers and other volunteers kept them separated from normal people. That was until the ceremonial shots rang out. With the cordon momentarily distracted, the freak show somehow slipped through that human wall and stampeded towards the soldier's funeral. The four psychopaths waved their antigay and anti-American signs like battleaxes as they charged into the grieving family.

There were no cameras around. Too much going on all over the state for the media to be everywhere at once. Maybe that's what drove these protestors over the edge. The church members didn't just enjoy attention; they lived for it. Perhaps they didn't feel so insane when in the spotlight. Maybe it wasn't even as complicated as that–they weren't exactly stable to begin with.

At any rate, they halted around the coffin and screamed incoherently about how "God hates fags" and this poor boy was somehow going to hell because of it. No one stopped them immediately when they began spitting on the casket, because no normal person could have ever imagined such a scenario. The fallen soldier's father recovered first from the shock. He released his nearly apoplectic wife and ploughed a meaty fist into the face of the closest freak.

A female protestor looked aghast. "You can't do that! This is freedom of speech!"

Another Westboro member unzipped his pants and pissed on the coffin. "Yeah, that's assault! You're going to jail. You have to respect different opinions. We're going to sue you people for all you're worth! Fag loving Satanists!"

The last semblance of civilization left the assembled friends and family. Even the bikers hung back in fear. For a few minutes, that cemetery turned into Rwanda.

An old uncle yanked the peeing man back and slammed him head first into the ground. Others ringed him, kicking wildly. He wasn't even unconscious when the sweet young widow of the desecrated soldier snatched his fallen sign, yanked down his pants and literally shoved the thick wooden post up his ass.

From grandmothers to teenagers, everyone got in on the action. Even the minister whipped his cursing, elderly Westboro counterpart upside the head with a thick leather Bible. Almost no one's hands were bloodless…or feet, for that matter. Of course, it was a different story when the police arrived. A hundred witnesses swore the four unarmed, mutilated bodies had attacked them.

Obviously, a simple case of self-defense. The two cops first on the scene saw the crazy signs and remembered when they tangled with these assholes before. They both shrugged, took statements and let everyone go. The cops had far more pressing matters to attend to.

Sophie took careful note of the whole thing. For years, no one had ever been able to do anything about these insane religious fanatics. More than a decade of lawsuits, court injunctions and physical threats only emboldened them. But with a little direct action, these people permanently removed that thorn in the ass of humanity. Unfortunately, that was the only lesson she learned this day. But she learned it well.

***
*2 February
Manhattan, NY*

It was a scary time to be rich and successful. There's something about having everything that makes you worry about losing it all. It was also that incredible wealth, that ability to live in a different world, which made it so difficult to comprehend their irrational poorer brethren. So many of these prestigious Ivy League Alumni were scions of wealthy families–old money, to put it mildly.

Since they had never experienced having nothing, they couldn't fathom the frustration and sense of hopelessness the lower classes struggled with. Let alone understand how when you have nothing, you have nothing to lose.

A room full of conservative minded money managers set around a television watching the near anarchy in the streets and the true anarchy in the marketplace. All their technical models and analysts weren't worth a damn in a market controlled by headlines. How do you short Armageddon?

Still, confusing as things were, you didn't rise to manage billions in assets by being the type that just reacts to events. That they would do something was a foregone conclusion. The only question was what. They'd already poured hundreds of millions into various PACs and campaign contributions. Those investments weren't panning out. They were paid, and paid obscenely well, to think 3 steps ahead of the news and 1 ahead of the competition. It was their job to identify future trends when they existed as just rumors and isolated events.

Of course, you didn't have to be Warren Buffett to realize that the politicians were losing control of the situation. The trick was trying to determine who would be controlling events when the dust settled and how best to influence them.

With the politicians riding the waves of popular opinion, the highest court being ignored and even the military seemingly impotent there was an obvious power vacuum. The only thing clear was the next president would be chosen through force, not the ballot box. Even if the current president went through with his promise of holding new elections, the opposing party and millions on the streets promised to "stop him." There was only one way to accomplish that…and it wasn't in the courts or chambers of Congress.

One of the men stopped reading the proposal and cleared his throat. "I don't know. I have serious doubts about the effectiveness of this investment. Come on, I trade derivatives. Frankly, I don't know the first damn thing about running a militia. Maybe we should stick to the PR campaign? That seems to be shaping public opinion our way."

One of the most ruthless females shook her head at him. "How many votes does a million dollars' worth of advertisements buy us? Who really knows? Now, how many votes does a million dollars' worth of guns get us?" She paused long enough to assure everyone's attention. "All we need." Several heads reluctantly nodded.

A futures trader waved at the TV. "We can't afford to be so naïve. The traditional political process died along with Terry Scott. This violence at the polls is going to happen regardless of what we do. Too much is at stake." He added the magic words for this crowd. "I just want to make sure we get in on it during the startup phase. If we don't, the competition will." He tried to sound funny, but he was dead serious.

"This is an emerging market. We could be locked out pretty quick if the other guys dominate it. And the consequences are a little bit more severe than missing our bonus targets."

A famous bond manager spoke up. "The competition? Things are worse than that. The takers are trying to turn America into some type of socialist paradise. It's everything Ayn Rand warned us about. Cynical as it sounds, we have to defend ourselves."

There weren't any further holdouts.

The great irony about using anonymous PAC money to recruit, train and arm a paramilitary force to "help ensure the constitutional transfer of presidential power," is that it's perfectly legal and even tax-free. Not that taxes would be much of a worry if they were successful. Simplifying the tax code, at least for job creators, would be a top priority.

In a 50th floor office across the street their liberal counterparts met and reached similar conclusions. Major conglomerates around the world also independently realized the realities of the new business environment. Most of them were apolitical and saw themselves merely responding to the threats around them in the most cost efficient way possible. Regardless of motivation, the results were the same.

Some would hire private security contractors to defend their interests and others would help fund existing "constitutional protection" groups. A few founded their own private armies to have a chip in the new political game. Regardless of the method used, the nation would never be the same.

The random violence gripping the country was such a mild danger compared to the much greater threat entering the arena: corporate sponsorship.

Chapter 5

3 February
Washington, DC

"Mr. President, I must caution again that these are preliminary findings, at best. It's only been a few days—so much can still change. Just because the serial number matches the Florida Guard's armory records doesn't mean the weapon wasn't stolen recently. Perhaps in the chaos at Camp Blanding?" The head of the FBI looked more embarrassed than conciliatory.

"Between the so called 'protective detentions' of federal law enforcement personnel in Florida and the sealed borders, we're finding it rather difficult to get cooperation with this investigation."

"And fingerprints or any forensic evidence?" asked a junior aide, almost absentmindedly.

"Well, quite a few, as a matter of fact. All current members of the Florida Guard…" Several aides nodded and moved on to other matters. "Again sir, you shouldn't base any course of action on what's really circumstantial evidence."

Another aide rushed in with something Oh-So-Important and bumped the FBI chief out of the way. This wasn't his first time in the situation room. He'd seen the Administration pissed at him and pleased with him, but he'd never seen them uninterested in what he had to say. He caught a glimpse of a draft speech on the table. There'd been a few memos generated by his office with the same subject, but this just wasn't in the same league. He couldn't suppress the chill in his bones at seeing that one magic word repeated multiple times. *Terrorism.*

The director tried to catch the president's eye, but he was deep in quiet conversation with someone from the CIA and several new generals. He didn't recognize any of them. There'd been a hell of a lot of personnel shakeups, resignations and transfers out west or overseas, among the senior military staff since the Florida fiasco last week.

Working his way closer around the big table, he caught a "…very high confidence, sir." over the humming voices. The president whispered something about wanting to see a "target package" and then spun around suddenly.

"Yes, I heard you Steve. But our course of action has been set by the rebels' other provocations." The Director raised an eyebrow at the R-word. While it was bantered about by some news organizations, this was the first time he heard it from any official source.

"Sir, I understand your frustration, but please be careful with such catchphrases. They can influence your staff's thinking and have a habit of becoming policy."

"It's a simple statement of fact. I'm afraid I don't have the time now to give you a run down. Watch the speech tonight. That will clarify everything."

"Sir, with all due respect, when is the chief law enforcement officer in America left out of the loop on a matter of so-called terrorism?"

One of the new generals answered while the president tried to form a diplomatic answer.

"When it's a military matter."

A staffer rested a hand gently on the FBI chief's shoulder. "I'm sorry sir, but you'll have to leave. We're about to start a classified briefing. Essential personnel only."

***

5 February
Tampa, Florida

Ever since the genius politicians closed the border, the state of Florida was on a war footing. There seemed to be an armed man behind every Palm tree. That paranoia grew as much from internal threats as from fear of Washington's response. According to the opinion polls, ¾ of the population supported the acting governor and Senator Dimone. So many people so fired up, it was a classic case of the tail wagging the dog.

Of course, in a state of 19 million people, that left millions of potential agitators. Within their own borders existed an enemy far more numerous than the combined Federal Armed Forces.

You also had to reckon with the Floridians' love of lawlessness just for the fun of it. For every IRS office burnt or ransacked during the first few days of heady "freedom," a local county tax collector's office went the same way.

Still, like most things in Florida, it was only for show. The "closed border" was one of the most active in the world. By conservative estimates, a quarter million people crossed every day. Mostly headed north to get out of the way of the oncoming storm, but a surprisingly large number coming south looking for trouble.

Another crumbling aspect of the facade was the local politicians that weren't onboard with the program. Especially from communities that benefited heavily from federal spending. For the most part, Tallahassee followed the time honored political strategy of just ignoring them. This whole stunt was supposed to be for show anyway. Any attempt to punish the local holdouts would give the enemies of Florida, naturally defined as Senator Dimone's political opponents, proof that they weren't such a united front.

In this game of high-stakes chicken, a war of explosive bluffs and rapid fire sound bites, the slightest perception of weakness is a battle lost. In retrospect, this same facade of steely resolve scared so much of the country and guaranteed a heavy handed response. Like so many accidents, it seemed like a good idea at the time.

Just act invincible a little while longer. Keep consolidating your base support while the other guy's split. An old strategy, but effective. They saw the president's extreme blustering as desperation. The more they provoked him, the more rope he had to hang himself. Of course, the harder they pushed, the more his actions appeared justified. Welcome to the surreal world of American politics.

This Council of Governors here in Tampa should have been the centerpiece of the grand theater. They weren't off to a great start. The name itself was a misnomer. Only a handful of governors came themselves and not even every state bothered to send a representative. But none of the organizers were getting bogged down in such technicalities.

They kept their eyes on the big picture. On all that really mattered–how the show looked on television. The décor, the pageantry, the marching band and the laser light show were all so over the top as to make Kim Jong-un look humble.

This desperate gamble was the biggest sign for Governor Pickens, head honcho after his old boss finally passed away and the lieutenant governor resigned overseas, that maybe he wasn't backing the winning horse after all. The president's backers definitely had deeper pockets and weren't shy about reaching in.

Their advertising blitz numbed the mind. They didn't bother spending marketing money in Florida; why compete with Dimone's money in a state that was already lost? Instead, they showered the swing states in their cash. It was working, too. While Florida became more radical, the polls everywhere that mattered swung slowly but steadily in the president's favor.

That's why they needed success in this meeting so badly. If they could flip just a few sympathetic governors, the president's hold on power would collapse. Only a mass movement, or something perceived as popular, could rattle the Administration's power tree. One rough shake and he and all his cohorts would come tumbling out of their clubhouse.

Conversely, Dimone stood on the ground with no real tree of his own. This get together was the best and maybe last chance to show the legitimacy the senator's campaign so badly needed. It also wouldn't hurt his own standing. Pickens didn't try to suppress his self-satisfied smile as he counted all the network cameras crowded around the convention center's entrance. The senator and company liked to treat the governor as a useful fool. Well, who outmaneuvered whom?

Senator Dimone is going to be the last to arrive at his own party. What a smooth move from Pickens to convince Dimone's PR team to slip the governors of California and Washington into the senator's motorcade instead of the boss. Those two were by far the most famous and prestigious guests. Their presence ensured instant and major media obsession. Riding in Dimone's limousine, they would draw the network attention first, helping to bolster the senator's national leader credentials. They were the opening act for his grand entrance.

The key detail Pickens left out was who, of all people, would be the smiling face welcoming them to the Freedom Convention? While the senator rode along behind them in an unmarked SUV and a little too late for the big show? He beamed harder and fiddled with his American flag label as the motorcade drew within sight.

A quick whoosh could be heard over the humming crowd. He did briefly see the missile's flaming tail, though his mind wouldn't register the fact until he dreamed about that night in agonizing detail. After the black cloud cleared, the strike's precision was immediately impressive. The laser guided death ripped Dimone's limousine into two twisted pieces and left a small crater in the road…but caused practically zero collateral damage. No physical collateral damage, at least.

The motorcade's security detail had kept the dangerous crowds and suspicious traffic at a safe distance. Which just made their principal an even more inviting target for the Reaper drone cruising 5,000 feet overhead. She would continue to circle for another half hour and use a variety of outrageously expensive sensors to confirm that the senator did not survive the attack.

Dimone knew a photo op when he saw one. Despite the wrenching of his stomach he sprinted from his place in the rear of the convoy straight towards the fire. The moths and their cameras fluttered in from the convention center. Casting about for the best response, he began performing CPR on a fallen motorcycle cop. The officer's pleas that he "only had the wind knocked out" were met by more vigorous pumping and awkward attempts to kiss him.

Just as the policeman drew his service pistol to finish what the drone couldn't, another cop stepped in and "relieved" the politician. Dimone fired off that world famous grin and shouted "he's going to make it!" at the cameras. Neither of the popular governors or their driver were so lucky.

300 miles northwest at Eglin Air Force base an Air Force general, provisionally promoted after his predecessor refused to carry out the mission, congratulated an unhappy pilot sitting in a souped up Xbox video game console. A junior officer peeked in and meekly suggested he should turn on the TV and, by the way, there was a rather pissed off White House staffer on the line.

***

8 February
Lake Butler, Florida

Despite the supposed lockdown, Sergeant Major Brown didn't have much of a problem moving around. The stolen out of state truck didn't draw as much attention as he worried it might. The cops appeared to have bigger worries. He grabbed another beer and studied the notes and photos he accumulated over the last few days.

The least wounded survivors of his unit had been moved to a minimum security prison not too far from the original fighting. A prison just a few miles down the road from his hotel room.

Getting detailed inside knowledge of the detention center was incredibly easy. The guards might have been hardnosed civil servants, but the Corrections Department relied on an army of minimum wage contractors for all sorts of tasks. An entire weekend spent in local honkytonks, 500 bucks in direct bribes and probably as much in free booze, got him everything he needed to know. He looked over a copy of the guard duty roster, detailed maps, the week's schedules of everything and pages of miscellaneous tips. Man, he wasted his career in the military–should have joined the CIA.

Nah, spying didn't interest him, but human intel was crucial to his mission. This secret transfer of his people to an unknown location in the morning was pretty interesting. He'd already scouted the route they would take to the interstate and cleaned his weapons. He'd even run through some drills. The prepping was finished.

Time to end his little vacation and get back to work. War was his profession, and he was damn good at it.

***

9 February
Starke, Florida

The State Trooper driving the lead car swore under his breath as they hit a traffic jam. All that careful route planning thrown out the window by some random accident. Damn drunks! He fought the temptation to flip on the siren and blow through. No good, he had orders to keep a low profile. He looked over at his partner. "You found a new route yet?"

"Well, the quickest way to the interstate is to go back two lights and cut through the industrial side of town. Hmm, probably set us back only a couple minutes. I better call the Guard anyway and let 'em know we'll be late."

The driver flashed the blues to clear space for a U-turn. "I still don't get why we need a military escort to drive these guys to Georgia. We have enough manpower to stop a lynch mob, even if people found out who we have back there. Seems like a waste of money to send troops."

His partner hung up his phone. "Speak of the devil. They don't want to wait for us. They'll meet the convoy on the way. If I didn't know any better, I'd think they don't trust us. Damn amateurs." He radioed the change of plans to the prison bus and follow-on car.

The driver grinned conspiratorially as they turned off into much thinner traffic. "We ought to ditch the soldier boys. Just take the cargo to the border ourselves. Man, I think the president is a socialist asshole, but he ain't a dictator. That's all a bunch of bullshit. Getting the Guard involved in this mess just provokes people. Makes everything more intense than it needs to be."

His partner threw up his hands. "Maybe, but…hell, I don't know. You hear his speeches…Well, you can't argue the fact he's still in power weeks after his term ended. That's suspicious enough, to me. Anyways, you're right that this Guard commitment is stupid. Just politics. The governor wants to give these prisoners back as a goodwill gesture, but not so gently remind the president that we're still ready to fight. Trying to negotiate without showing weakness. You can at least respect what he's trying to do."

The driver shook his head. "And we're stuck in the middle of their pissing match. Well, at least it's easy overtime!"

"A lot of overtime, if we keep hitting every damn red light." His partner sighed as they came to another halt.

Behind them, a black F250 inconspicuously closed the distance. Sergeant Major Brown had fantasized about building an IED. He'd fought against insurgents long enough and captured plenty enough devices to figure out how to reproduce a decent one. But no, too much could go wrong. He decided to keep things simple. Except for helping guide the convoy through the warehouse district on a weekend, to reduce the risk to bystanders, he didn't do anything to the route.

One last minute hiccup to fix. He gently sideswiped some random minivan in the next lane. The infuriated driver pulled over and called the cops, while trying to get the license plate of this hit and run asshole. After a last scan to make sure no other civilians were around, Brown hit the gas in his trusty stolen pickup and bore down on his prey. He had nothing against the police. What he had to do truly saddened him. But they were big boys. They chose which side to join. Life wasn't pretty for John, but it sure was black and white.

Both State Police cars were stopped a comfortable distance ahead of and behind the packed Florida Department of Corrections bus. The little convoy also waited in the right lane, rather than trying to block all traffic. Perfect.

Style wasn't Brown's strong suite. Filmmakers would find his brute force 'tactics' boring, but no doubt they were effective. He stayed in the left lane and slowed down casually as he approached the light. Just as he pulled abreast of the rear police car, he crushed the breaks.

He already had the side window rolled down and his semi-automatic shotgun rigged on a sling…pointing at a preplanned, slightly downward angle. With 20 rounds ready in the drum, all he had to do was reach over and tap the trigger one handed.

The two bored uniforms glanced up at the truck in time to see the last muzzle flash of their lives. Brown let rip 8 rounds of double-aught buckshot into the unarmored car below. Refraction from the shattered windshield and protection from their bulletproof vests stopped many of the 64 pellets, but not enough. Some still hit something vital. The driver's head blew wide open. His partner lived a few minutes longer, but he was clearly out of the fight.

Three seconds later, Brown sped forward 20 yards and locked the sling into the next firing position. He repeated the well-practiced maneuver with the DOC's bus driver and his backup man. 2/3rds of the enemy dead in 11 seconds. Brown wasn't pleased. It hadn't taken longer than 9 seconds in the dry runs. The gun smoke assaulted his senses and watered his eyes. Strange, because that had never happened before. He ignored it and focused on the tactical problem in front of him.

There were two possibilities he'd planned for. He couldn't expect the lead vehicle to sit complacently and wait for death. Either they would jump out and fight or speed away from the immediate kill zone and dismount under cover. He had a strategy to deal with each eventuality. When he saw the car spurt forward, but leave behind one shooting officer, he laughed. Of course the enemy didn't get the memo about his plans. Oh well. "Adapt and fucking overcome," he muttered.

He dropped his head down and surged the truck forward. The on-foot policeman easily dodged the blind pickup. He emptied his magazine into the vulnerable driver's side door during that brief moment as it swept past. Only 5 feet away, impossible to miss.

Once past the angry cop, Brown downshifted and aimed for the U-turning car ahead. Stripping out most of the cabin's interior and mounting that cheap steel backing behind the console and doors was a damn good last minute call. At the time, he thought he was becoming a Nervous Nelly in his old age. The "armor" wouldn't stop a rifle, but it did the trick against these 9mm handgun rounds. Sometimes paranoia comes in handy.

He passed out of effective pistol range before the other officer reloaded. The cop ahead misread the situation and assumed this guy was trying to escape. He stopped his turn and stayed in his vehicle to block the road. He should be excused for that fatal error. His previous experience with armed men revolved around trying to catch them. Total war was something new.

Brown rammed his "deer scraper" grill into the tire on the police car's lightest end. The squad car made a screeching, bouncing, nearly complete 360° turn. He'd cut out the airbag in his truck before the fight, so nothing got in the way of yanking the quick release strap for the shotgun and redeploying it out the driver's window. The sergeant major emptied his last 4 rounds through the barely conscious officer's windshield and airbag. The cop slipped into the next world without a clue what caused it.

Brown calmly exchanged the Saiga-12 for an AK-47 knockoff in the cab and dismounted. He absentmindedly put two in the chest and one in the head of the other State Trooper charging towards vengeance. Mopping up done, he massaged his aching ribs with one hand while scanning for new threats. All clear. He began to flash a thumbs up to his men back on the bus, but then felt fear for the first time today.

Smoke poured out of the bus's cabin. He dashed in as fast as he could to help. Nearly there, his nose dripped. He finally recognized the mild sting of tear gas. One of the guards must still be alive and is gassing his troops! He brought his rifle up to the high ready and prepared to finish the job he started.

Only a couple of yards from the door, a familiar grumbling behind him changed his plans. Without looking back to confirm, he veered left and slid to cover behind a brick sign for some manufacturing company. Just in time.

Less than two hundred yards past his wrecked truck four green Humvees raced this way. They must have seen him dive in here. Hell, he was the only moving thing around. They probably weren't shooting because they couldn't be a 100% sure which side he was on. Time to remove any doubt.

He took careful aim from the prone and popped the lead gunner in the neck. Don't look for their reaction—react first! He sprang to his feet and dashed behind a semi-truck parked nearby. By the time the other three gunners responded and lit up the whole area Brown crouched 20 yards deeper in the parking lot. The long trailer didn't provide much proper cover, but the concealment was enough, for now. He smashed a glass door from the locked building behind him and slipped inside.

Escaping from sight and direct danger gave him a chance to flank these National Guard fucks. The idea for one man to take on twenty was insane, but what else was he supposed to do? The shouts of his trapped brothers in the smoking bus steadied him. He faded deeper into the sprawling network of warehouses and shipping offices.

The lightly armored Humvees halted within 50 yards of the stranded bus and fanned out. Gunners and drivers provided over watch against the lost sniper while the dismounts swept the area. The bus wasn't a threat; they were all about to be released anyway and knew it. The problem lay with this vigilante or whatever this deadly crazy guy was.

The sergeant major's half conceived strategy was to overwhelm one of the Humvee's and turn the machine gun on the others. Maybe it could have worked, maybe it was suicide. Either way, he never got an opportunity to find out. His stealthy approach on the farthest away truck wasn't sneaky enough. The dismounted driver heard gravel crunching and spun around before Brown could plant his K-Bar into the terrified kid's liver. He beat the surprised guy to the draw, at least, and put two messy rounds through the guardsman's head first.

Had the truck's gunner simply snatched his backup rifle he would have easily finished off the exposed and unprotected sergeant major. In the heat of the moment, he took the time to swivel the turret ring around, hoping to perforate this asshole with his M240. Brown dashed forward and below that limited plane the machine gun's spindle could depress. He shoved his rifle through the open driver's door and into the standing gunner's crotch. The man above scrambled to navigate the weird angle of shooting straight down with his M4 when this psychopath literally shot his nuts off.

Brown captured himself a Humvee and gun alright, but what a Pyrrhic victory. Before he could clamber into the turret the other guardsmen opened up on him. They knew full well both their compatriots were dead, and they weren't about to let that go. Brown took cover behind the armored Humvee while hundreds of rounds gradually chewed it apart. He fired blindly around the fender from time to time, but more as a "fuck you" than resistance.

It was a good 10 yard dash to cover. No doubt about it, he'd gotten himself thoroughly pinned. Like a fucking amateur, he let his passion control his actions. Only a matter of time until they flanked him and taught him a final lesson. Hell, exposed as he was, they only had to move a few dozen yards to get a better firing angle. All his extra gear sat uselessly back in his pickup truck. He counted the rounds in his last magazine. Not much he could do about that now.

Brown half-sat on the steel bumper and wiped some blood from his face. His or someone else's? Doesn't matter–stay focused. He gurgled piss warm water from the nipple of his Camelback, wishing he never quit smoking. The shooting around him picked up. Suppressive fire. The enemy was on the move. Maybe he could see them coming and take one or two more with him. Fuck it. They say your status in hell is judged by the size of your entourage. He aimed to be a bigwig when he got there.

The whole time the sergeant major played Rambo, the smoke pouring out of the bus only increased. The tear gas canisters he accidentally triggered in the slaughter fest were part of that, but not all. The cloud was too dark. Those nonlethal devices created a fire in the cabin, as they so often do when used in confined quarters. Now, that small fire shouldn't have been such a big deal. There wasn't so much combustible material in there to begin with.

But there were plenty of combustible fumes pouring in from the ruptured fuel tank. Not all of that shot went straight through the target. They ricocheted all over the place. This, as well, shouldn't have been a problem. It was diesel after all and not flammable…at room temperature. After being heated for 5 minutes by the fire though, things got considerably more dangerous.

When the bus finally exploded, Brown's heart stopped, but he didn't. He took maximum advantage of that brief opportunity when the soldiers thought they were being attacked from the rear. He dashed 10 yards to the nearest lot, vaulted over the low fence with one hand and got out of sight without a single shot following.

He paused long enough to twitchingly take in his men, trapped in the locked prison transport, burn alive. Downwind of the inferno, the soul killing stench of burning hair and oily flesh consumed him. In his long career, he'd seen some shit. But nothing like this.

He checked the rifle's magazine while his stomach lurched. 7 rounds left. What could he do? The hardest thing he'd ever done in his life was turn his back then. It wouldn't do his boys any good for him to get captured. Well, nothing would do them any good now. His legs were cement, his joints rusted, but he kept on pushing. He ran until clearly out of danger and then kept going. The adrenaline kept the pain at bay better than any pill.

To say anger propelled him was wrong. The burning heat inside him could not be expressed in words, but it could be expressed in action. No mere man escaped from the scene. That was a nuclear bomb running loose in America.

*

The suggestion by some investigators that a lone wolf attacked the convoy was considered nonsense, at best. Others saw it as a blatant cover up. A single assailant didn't kill nine armed policemen and soldiers and then murder all the prisoners. Obviously, the rebels slaughtered these defenseless detainees to send a message to the president. One congressman after another promised that such atrocities would not go unpunished.

For their part, no one in Florida's command structure knew what the hell to make of the massacre. Why would the president send in a Special Forces rescue team after the prisoners were being turned over? There was only one possible explanation. The president must want to send a strong message that he didn't need to negotiate–he could just take what he wanted.

To the opposition leaders that was proof enough he'd gone way beyond political posturing. Full blown dictator mode. The president, or at least his followers, truly wanted to seize permanent power. It terrified Dimone and his cohorts. When they realized that the great big game just got real…well, they were tempted to throw in the towel. They probably would have too, if they had lived in a world immune to public opinion.

If the speed of headline events had been pushing them along too fast before, after the massacre the train went totally off the rails. That simple initial press release from some clueless Florida bureaucrat stating that 30 federal soldiers perished during a routine prison transfer could not have been more inflammatory.

Since there were no reporters there to speculate on things, the facts of the attack were gathered quickly and leaked even faster. Everyone received the same information without spin. Unfortunately, the facts alone don't always lead to the truth.

State officials were reluctant, at first, to admit they had tried to give the men back. Who wanted to appear weak when things were coming apart? That tightlipped strategy was all the proof that the pro-Fed media needed to run wild. For their part, the Federal Government's contradictory statements and general confusion as to what the hell was going on proved their culpability in the bloodbath.

While everyone blamed everyone else, only one thing was clear: assassinations and atrocities were just the beginning. Fewer people cared everyday who became president. The big national debate was over how to get revenge. How to change the system to keep this craziness from ever happening again came in second. But who should be president? Who cares!

Americans aren't quick to collective anger, but once they've committed to something, they are unshakable. They must see it through to its dreadful end.

***

Atlanta, Georgia

"Brothers and sisters, this isn't a matter of politics. This isn't some squabble over legal technicalities or any other mundane human affair. This is a matter of good versus evil. As believers and as

Americans, we don't serve any one man. We serve the Lord of Righteousness. God is our master and liberty our reward. But in these dark days, God is ignored and freedom threatened. Are we to sit idly by while the Forces of Darkness consume our great land?"

The well-known preacher was in top form and not even warmed up yet. His "aw-shucks" demeanor wasn't intended to hide his oratory mastery, but accentuate it. From his tone to the practiced pacing and power gestures, he kept the congregation hanging off every word. Whether they believed it or not, no one could just simply ignore him.

"What would have happened if Moses, or Thomas Jefferson, had just thrown up their hands? If they had said, 'I'm not a political man. I don't want to get involved. It's not my fight.' My dear friends, I haven't seen such a worthy fight in all my life! Not since the days of the Apostle Matthew has the light of Truth been in such jeopardy! The wolf is at the door. The devil is trying to extinguish this world's last flame of freedom with the cold, dark waters of tyranny!"

He shifted focus away from his congregation of 2,000 and towards the cameras reaching out to a million more. His tone softened. "I'm not saying that *that* man in the White House is necessarily the anti-Christ, as foretold in Revelations. He may be just laying the ground work. An unwitting agent of the Prince of Darkness. I don't know; the devil has not yet revealed his self. What he has made clear, however, is his ultimate purpose." He carefully built up righteous fervor.

"In order to begin their reign of hell the forces of evil must destroy the only nation standing in the way! Not since the time of jack-booted Nazi's have we been so close to the abyss. With 'wars and rumors of wars' abounding, you could argue that we are indeed approaching the End of Days. But why? Why, I ask you, must it be so? God warned us about these End Times, not to scare us, but so that we might fight for Him! That we might make ready and avoid this great calamity." Tears welled in his eyes.

"I hope, nay, I must believe that my beloved America, God's great gift of freedom and righteousness to mankind, cannot be beyond redemption. That we will not go easily into that dark night! That we will honor the memory of our forefathers that stood up to the last king America had and cried in one loud voice: Give me liberty or give me death!" He stabbed that black Bible into the air like a sword.

"Whether you are saved or not doesn't enter the question here. Even a non-believer can love freedom. But, as Christians, we have a special commandment from our Lord to defend liberty. The only thing necessary for evil to triumph is for good people to stand idly by. Will you do nothing? Fathers, look at your families. Mothers, look at your children. Do you think the gathering clouds will storm somewhere else? Do you really believe the Devil, or the ordinary variety of opportunistic evil men always following him around, will just leave you alone? That your loved ones will be magically safe? That they will take everyone else's freedom but yours?!"

His tightly controlled showmanship slipped with the raw passion in his voice. The display of human weakness only heightened the effect of his words. No one minded how far he deviated from any widely accepted religious doctrine.

"But, my brave brothers and sisters in faith, we are not alone. Nay, the Lord of Hosts is on our side. He promises to protect anyone who will believe in and stand with Him with all the righteous fire of Heaven! We can and we *must* drive the forces of evil and corruption back to the depths of Hell where they came from. He will carry the battle for us—we must only have the courage and the faith to stand with our God! From Genesis to Revelations, the Bible has always had a clear message: good can triumph over evil, if only the good will act!"

The standing applause wasn't universal. Several parishioners wordlessly slipped out. Some stormed out more dramatically and still others passionately argued with the person next to them. The fierce ovation and screams of "Amen" and "Hallelujah" from the majority drowned out those dissenters though. The preacher took the time to catch his breath and compose himself. He gave that trademarked humble grin.

"I can see I'm preaching to the faithful here! So, you're probably wondering what, exactly, should I do? Well that, you warriors of Christ, is a personal matter between you and God. He calls each to serve in different ways. Pray on it. Search your souls and accept His calling, even if that doesn't fit with what you want to do." His fatherly tone became more thoughtful.

"There are those that are now simply refusing to pay their income taxes, refusing to help finance evil. It's a small, but powerful and growing movement. There are others, like those brave stalwarts of freedom in Florida who believe now is the time to directly take up arms against tyranny. The movement out west to cut out the cancer of corruption and form a new government grows stronger every day. Which is the most effective method? I'm not sure. I just know God works in mysterious ways. Fact is, anyone resisting the enemy of Justice and Liberty, in even a small way, is my brother or sister and worthy of my respect."

"What's clear is that the time for wailing and gnashing of teeth has past. It is time to gird ourselves with the righteousness of God in faith and seek battle with the foes of Light. As Christians and as Americans we owe it to our God, our forefathers and, most importantly, to our children. One day, my not yet born grandchildren will ask me, 'Grandfather, what did you do during the Second

American Revolution?' And I'll proudly look them in the eyes and say, 'I'm why it's called a revolution and not Armageddon!'"

This wasn't the only preacher, priest, rabbi, mullah or "guru" proselytizing against the government. Across the country, thousands invoked similar messages, even if to smaller congregations and without television coverage. However, since this was America, no consensus opinion could be found. For every religious leader speaking out against the government, another passionately called for a vigorous defense of democracy. Those few calling for peace and moderation were, in the eyes of friend and foe alike, supporting the government.

Even the Pope's numerous addresses for peaceful dialogue and vague pleading that both sides respect the rule of law and democratic processes were considered provocative. Naturally, each side read between the lines and found what they believed in his words. Pro-government sects hyped his "support" and the American Roman Catholic church, already at sharp odds with the president over his previous political stances, were deeply offended. Before too long they would finally follow through with their years of threats and officially break with the Church.

Whatever each side called it–a war for freedom against tyranny, protection from anarchy, justice for a thousand different sins or plain old fashioned devil fighting–the one common theme among them all was that this war…would be a holy war.

Chapter 6
10 February

Reni's Redneck Yacht Club might of made great barbecue, but they made a poor Checkpoint Charlie. That iconic photo of the historic standoff over the I-95 Bridge on the Georgia/Florida border should have been hilarious… and not so goddamn scary.

When the last federal employee angrily crossed the border a National Guard Humvee followed behind them and blocked the bridge. The gunner, with all seriousness, pointed his **.50** cal machine gun at a federal M2 Bradley on the far bank. From a distance, he looked full of deadly resolve.

The only resolve he held, as he stood there shaking in fear, was to abandon his weapon and dive into the water below if the Feds moved so much as one inch forward. This shit was insane! He wasn't about to piss his life away over some publicity stunt.

The impression on television was a bit different. Despite the violence and rhetoric, quite a few people still viewed the whole "Florida crisis" as one great big joke. At least, before today. Those powerful video images of resolute soldiers squaring off across no-man's-land raised long-forgotten ghosts in the older generation.

The footage even shocked many of the disconnected youthful skeptics. An entire young generation that didn't remember the passions and stakes of the Cold War had no personal frame of reference for this new danger. In many ways, that left them more susceptible to the propaganda from both sides. They lacked the anti-rhetoric inoculations the older generation spent many painful years accumulating.

Which was a shame, because it wouldn't be the middle-aged called upon to settle this issue on the battlefield. One thing truly hadn't changed over the years. Despite all the hi-tech toys, war was still about old men talking and young people dying.

But perhaps things wouldn't get so bad. Millions of people rushed to Google who their congressperson was for the first time. Most House members' websites were shut down within hours by what amounted to a denial of service attack. The Washington branch Post Office had to rent a warehouse for the overflow snail mail. Those slightly better connected or better at research kept an army of temp workers trapped on the phones for days.

The US House of Representatives weren't famous for their moral courage or strong leadership to begin with. The shocks from the last few months were way too much for those poor lawyers. In their entire careers nothing had ever really been expected of them, but now people were demanding bold, genuine leadership. This was sure as hell not what they signed up for!

Between the reluctant withdrawal of Florida's 27 member congressional delegation, several of them on key committees, and the untimely death of their two most famous and forceful members, the House was in an incredible state of disarray. Worst of all were the special interests. Sensing the shifting center of political influence, they rerouted the river of lobbying cash to flood state legislatures and various "grassroots, community based organizations." Which was such a sweet term that ignored the armed nature of these civic minded citizens.

Change in general is scary, but such extreme change is petrifying. As if they didn't have enough internal problems, the Supreme Court even declared open season on them. The new Congress and every piece of legislation they pumped out, no matter how mild or innocuous, was labeled unconstitutional by those old bastards. Usually the Executive branch shouldered the burden of wrestling with the Judiciary, but now the Legislature was supposed to play that rough and tumble game. Legally speaking, there was no legitimate president to hide behind. Those delicate flowers had no experience with this new leadership role. It just wasn't fair!

By this point they truly needed a president–any president. Republican or Democrat, it didn't matter. Just someone to nut up and make the hard decisions. Most importantly, someone to shoulder the responsibility of decisive action. That R word was as scandalous and shocking to these professional politicians as a flasher was to a maiden. It disturbed them to their souls. Their entire carefully constructed understanding of reality was under attack. Apparently, the only bipartisan force powerful enough to make these children agree on anything was mutual fear.

As tempting as it was to give in to the courts and just go with Dimone, they couldn't. That probably wouldn't end the crisis and it surely would be political suicide. No good way to spin a decision like that–it would be total surrender. The new Supreme Court appointed administration would ride roughshod over both parties.

Such a betrayal of their constituents after so much blood had been shed and radical passions aroused could not be forgiven. In this political environment, compromise was weakness and there was simply no tolerance for weakness with so much at stake.

That's why it shouldn't have been so surprising when Congress exercised their 20th Amendment power to select the president. They voted nearly unanimously to maintain the current Administration "until such time as new elections could be reliably held." Better to stick with the devil you know.

It didn't help Senator Dimone's case that he had long since alienated whatever potential allies he could have had in the House. It also seemed so logical to punt this politically radioactive football to a lame duck president whose career was already dead.

Logical, but dangerous. Scarier than the violence in the streets, or the so-believed "rebellion" in Florida, was this worrisome concentration of power and purpose in the hands of a man who had nothing left to lose but his legacy. Power might corrupt, but purpose kills.

***

12 February

The first combat action of the Florida Campaign actually took place over the Chattahoochee River on the Alabama/Georgia border. An A-Team from Florida's tiny Special Forces Group pushed a zip-tied and gagged drawbridge operator through the dark Pines. These Afghanistan veterans were having too much fun playing the insurgents.

Following President Dimone's orders, they were doing everything they could to slow down the federal military buildup along the border. That sterile order, decided upon by politicians sitting around in plush, air conditioned offices, resulted in some unsanitary actions in the field.

"Damn, he looks pissed. Ha!" One of the youngest plain clothed weekend killers gave the prisoner a gentle shove. "Would you rather us have left you sitting on the bridge with 300 pounds of plastic explosive? You wanna die that bad? Well, the day's still young; unlike you. We'll move faster without your old ass."

The master sergeant running the show almost told the new demolitions expert to shut the hell up. He let it slide, for now. The harassment might be a tad unprofessional, but it did help keep things quiet if a detainee wasn't 100% sure of your intentions. Besides, it was important to stick with the rednecks-blowing-random-shit-up cover story. Good neighbors shouldn't destroy their neighbor's infrastructure. But who knew what a bunch of crazy hicks might do.

The tied up old black man, a Vietnam veteran himself, failed to pick up on the humor. All he heard was some dumb cracker joking about shooting him and the head honcho looking contemplative and then smiling. For the first time, he stopped being angry and began to worry. They hustled down some deer trail a good half mile from the rail bridge and only heading deeper into the Pines. Not much around in the way of witnesses.

A familiar whistle in the distance didn't distract him, but stunned the rednecks like a gunshot. "Shit, since when the fuck are the trains early!" one shouted. The head Bubba, who strangely enough had a Chicago accent, issued an order.

"Two minutes to det. Blow it now. Right now or they won't have any time to stop!"

The Lynnrd Skynyrd T-shirt wearing asshole behind the prisoner hauled out a familiar looking green device from his cargo pants. He turned one key and began taking a knee like the rest of the squad. Two of his teeth went flying when he took a bonus knee to his face from the old man on the way down. The barely conscious redneck lost control of the armed detonator. It sailed out of his hands and disappeared somewhere in a stand of blackberries along the trail.

Several soldiers scrambled into the bush after the little box, cursing at the thorns, while two more dived for the old man. He hadn't shown such flexibility since his wedding night, but somehow slid his tied hands up under his butt and out front before they reached him. It was an awkward grip on the fallen man's M4, what with both cuffed hands on the handle and butt stock pressed against his chest, but he managed. Style wasn't important at arm's length range. He flipped the selector to 3 round burst, what was full Rock n' Roll in his day, and grinned as the first hillbilly took it all in the chest.

He might have had just enough time to swing a few more degrees and take out the second fellow, if Mr. Busted Nose behind him hadn't drawn his sidearm and blown the old man's brains out. The gunshot barely stopped ringing when they heard a distant explosion, followed by a seemingly never ending screech of steel on steel. A battalion's worth of M1 Abrams tanks just went swimming…along with 45 drivers traveling in a cabin car.

The master sergeant muttered something about "fucking Murphy" and chucked the now pointless detonator at the demo expert. The rest of his team vainly slapped on 6 pressure dressings to their wounded man. They didn't stop until well after the medic rose up and shook his head. It slowed them down, but of course they took his body with them.

The dead civilian they left. His unarmed body, shot in the back of the head, would later be chalked up as yet another terrorist victim. The old man, never a member of the NAACP, still became their poster child. Already a strong supporter of the president, the organization grew practically militant over the coming weeks.

***

15 February
Homestead ARB

Pickens couldn't get comfortable in this new office. The never ending window rattling from reservist F-16's doing "touch and go" training maybe contributed to that. Witnessing rhetoric give birth to desperate action played a larger role. He popped another antacid tablet and grudgingly wished he could be as mellow as the senator, or president, as he called himself nowadays.

"You seem so damn relaxed, for a man considered public enemy number 1 by half the country. Your government is trying to kill you, yet there you sit, planning how to staff your new administration. You're either the most optimistic man I've ever met or the craziest!"

President-proclaimed Dimone ignored the incredulity in his compatriot's voice and gestured at the television. "You should be relaxed too. Because this is the end game. That they're resorting to raw military force shows they've lost control and are out of viable political options."

"Or they don't see this as a political game anymore," Pickens snorted.

"Come on, don't play the country bumpkin. You know damn well what this is all about–you even helped start it. It's all showmanship. As long as we stay strong, as long as we keep preparing and looking dreadfully dangerous, they'll back down. We just need to keep our war face on. It's always been a question of who's going to blink first."

"I don't know. All the normal political calculus hasn't been serving us well lately. Wouldn't you say?" He gestured at the federal general giving a press conference on TV. Looked just like the press briefings for the Iraq invasions, except this map was much more familiar from postcards.

"Ok, then look at it this way. We've passed the point of no return. At this juncture, it's fame or famine. Either prison or the presidency, and not many options in between. When you're face to face with a bull, all you can do is grab 'em by the horns and hold on tight!" What an odd reference for someone who'd never been within a hundred yards of a farm, let alone any bulls, to make.

"And if they do attack, despite your confidence? All our military people are convinced the best we could do is hold them off for a few days, and even that would require a lot of luck. What's the point?"

"Governor, power isn't defined by how many guns and bombs you have. It's about how many people are willing to sympathize with you. The more they push the more radical our support becomes. The harder they fight, the stronger we get! That's why Al Qaida is still a danger today, even after having their top 5 leaders killed 10 times over."

"So…we're like Al Qaida? God, I hope the press doesn't quote you on that one! You sound just like the president." Dimone dismissed his half-serious joke.

"You know what I mean. Armies can be wiped out, charismatic leaders can be killed, but a popular idea will raise fresh, larger armies and produce new, smarter leaders in perpetuity. The Brits slaughtered one Minuteman army after another for years, but they kept coming back. Tougher, smarter and larger every time. Righteousness can't be destroyed. Persecution only emboldens it." Dimone didn't sound like such a tool when speaking off the cuff.

"If you want directly relevant examples, just look over the border. The Georgia legislature has condemned us in the strongest possible terms, but the people there are on our side. We canceled the sabotage campaign after that first screwed up mission, but our neighbors are doing a hell of a good job without our help. Look how much they've hampered the Army's response. We haven't done anything to encourage them. That's just the power of an idea.

Dimone refused to make eye contact. "I'm not excited by how all this turned out. I hoped we could succeed without any violence. Unfortunately, that mad man in Washington is hell bent on war. The only option we have is to stand up against him. At this point, our followers demand it. I wonder if we could even back down if we wanted to."

Upon closer inspection, Dimone did have a slight tick in his left hand. He kept drumming his fingers while muting the volume, just as the president made yet another public appeal to him to end this madness.

"If they do come, we don't have to win. Just slow them down and show that force has a chance to stop the president. Our real support isn't here; it's with all those millions of moderates around the country, especially out West. Once they see the lengths the Administration is willing to go to defend their illegal grip on power, that'll be their undoing. What happens on the battlefield here…"

A pair of jets made a low-level fake bombing run over their heads and drowned out his words. Pickens wasn't sure if the senator was delusional or a genius. For better or worse, he'd find out soon enough.

**

17 February
California

Sophie went down hard as a 200 lb riot-armor clad policeman wrenched her own shield out of her hands and smashed it right into her face. On the ground, she at least had the sense to fight from where she landed instead of getting back up. Even with a sports cup, that same officer nearly fell over when she shot out a long leg and caught him in the groin.

When she finally rose, she didn't run back to her V-shaped phalanx trying to push through the police line. Nor did she head back to safety away from the enemy. Instead, Sophie gave a banshee scream and flung herself at the knees of the other officers in the line. Armed only with youthful rage, she didn't get far.

Two burly men still pummeled her with plastic baseball bats well after the instructor blew her whistle. The rest of the "strike team" and "police officers" reluctantly lowered their plastic weapons and shields.

"What the fuck are you doing, girl?" The female instructor yanked her up by the pony tail. Despite a bruise on her cheek and tears in her eyes, Sophie's voice still held defiance. "Kicking ass, ma'am!"

The older woman grinned, despite herself. "Not out of formation you're not." She waved for the rest of the students, OPFOR cops and similarly armed BLUFOR protestors, to gather around. "You've all heard me say it a thousand times this week. You never break rank! That's the only edge the fascists have on us–they fight as a unit."

Her eyes burned the faux cops. "If we're ever going to smash their lines, if we're ever going to show the Man and his lackeys they can't just gas and club their way into power, we have to match their Gestapo discipline with our own iron discipline!" She took a breath.

"It's my own damn fault here. What the hell was I thinking putting a 100 pound girl on the skirmish line? Miss Kampbell, you've got the fighting spirit, alright, but it's wasted in this course. Non-lethal, dynamic protesting is not your style." She grinned knowingly.

"The type of war you want to wage can't be learned with this program. Why don't you go back to administration and ask for a slot in one of the Proactive Defense Brigades? Tell them Shania suggested it."

Sophie managed to look hopeful, angry and confused all at once, in the way only a teenager can. "The militias? I've never touched a gun in my life. They'll never take me. Please don't boot me out of the class. I just want to make a difference…"

"Damn, girl! Shut up already. They're not putting together a vigilante mob over there. We're building our own army. You're not being fired–you're being promoted. This here is important, but it's just the beginning. When the pigs are routed and the Man calls in his jackbooted thugs, that's where you come in. That's where you can make a difference." She suddenly wheeled back on her class and seemingly forgot about Sophie.

"But that don't mean you'se all can slack off! We've still got to get control of the streets. Masks on! Form up! We're going again."

Sophie spat out a little blood and made her way to the admin office…to look for more.

***
20 February
DC

"No sir, we're not quite ready, but we will be shortly. By the end of the week, tops. That sabotage campaign slows things down a little, but not significantly. We just need to arrange for additional force protection along our lines of communication. The casualties so far have been light, although the loss of material is more frustrating."

Some presidential aide interrupted the general's briefing as casually as he would a subordinate. "Like that Army fuel dump outside of Valdosta, Georgia that blew up for no apparent reason? How many trains have these saboteurs derailed? You've lost dozens of men and hundreds of millions of dollars in equipment…before the invasion has even started! The Joint Chiefs said you were the wrong man for the job."

"The Joint Chiefs are an advisory board and not in the chain of command. Neither are you. I'm in charge of this ridiculous operation and will prosecute it how I see fit. Who the fuck are you anyway? Where do you get off telling me how to do my job?"

Once upon a time, such unprofessional bickering in the situation room was unthinkable. There were a lot of new precedents being made nowadays. In every meeting the usual mild tension between the military and the new age breed of young civilian technocrats seemed to reach new heights. The president shook his head and finally stepped in. He wasn't impressed with the general's performance either, but he had zero doubts about his loyalty. At this delicate time, that was a pearl beyond price.

"General, no offense was intended. We're civilians and used to debating things before taking action, that's all. I have complete confidence in you and your staff. Please continue." The president's smooth lying mollified the general, but the indignant staffer spent the rest of their meeting only half listening while plotting ways to ruin the officer's career. How dare some simple soldier talk to him like that?!

"Yes, sir. As I was saying, I'm confident that we have more than enough resources on hand to deal with any elements of the Florida National Guard that choose to resist. Even these rumored irregulars shouldn't present much of a threat."

The president scratched at a pink spot on his wrist just beginning to scar. "General, I hope you're right. We've made the mistake of underestimating this rebellion far too often. Despite how they're spinning it, Florida is a secessionist state. The problem's not just their terrorist leadership. Look at the polls. If we don't cut that tumor out cleanly, and on the first try, the whole damn country will fall apart." He deep rubbed his temples with both hands.

"I mean that literally, not as hyperbole. California, Washington, Arizona–at least 10 states out west so far are planning to hold referendums on whether to stay in the Union. Or, as their PR people put it, whether to form their own 'legitimate' Federal Government!" The president shoved the tactical map away and pointed at the wall map of America.

"If we don't stamp this shit out now we might never have another chance. Congress has already amended the Posse Comitatus Act. They gave us a 30 day free reign to do whatever we need to. I fear that we don't have a month. Too much is happening too fast. Now, I'm ordering you to use overwhelming force, anything you need, to put an end to this war before it gets started. Do I make myself clear?"

The general didn't exactly look convinced, but he wasn't a fool. "Crystal clear, sir. And that's exactly what we're doing. By any measure, our response is an overkill." He launched into his patient teacher routine as an aid turned on a beam projector.

"As you can see, we're mobilizing a reinforced heavy division for this operation. Of course, sir, we could be ready faster if you weren't so insistent that the Georgia and Alabama National Guards must take part. We don't need them. It's more of a logistical burden to have them on board than anything else."

"We've been over this often enough, General. We have to show the country that this isn't Big Brother stomping on some independent state. I want to head off all that 'states rights' nonsense from the beginning. Showing resolve is not enough–the perception of unity is needed. We have to make it clear that the entire nation stands against Dimone and his rebels. I admit, it is a political decision, but these are the type of politics that have military repercussions." He paused and counted to 10 as he heated up. He got to 3.

"Do you want to have to repeat this invasion over and over with every radical state? Don't you see what's happening out West? Those referendums are not political theater–the people themselves are about to decide whether to end this 240 year old American experiment. Not since World War 2 have we had so much riding on a single operation. We will only get one chance to influence that public opinion."

He got out of his chair and had to pace.

"I know, some of you think I'm losing it. That I'm trying to go out in a blaze of glory and want to take the country with me. Isn't that how some news networks put it? But ladies and gentlemen, this disaster is bigger than any one man. We are way beyond politics now.

"Whenever people focus on a single issue at the expense of all others, especially when egged along by our modern media with its insane advertising pressure and short attention span, then the people are ripe for exploitation by demagogues and all sorts of crazies. Mark my words, if we don't crush this rebellion now, and decisively, things will only get worse. For starters, it means the end of my Administration and everyone in it."

The president already looked older than God, but somehow aged even more in the last few minutes. "If that was the only worry, damn, then I'd resign immediately. God help me, I'm tempted to! But it won't end there. Not by a long shot. Every day Dimone stays in control of Florida the fabric of this nation is torn a little more.

"If they even remotely appear like they might get away with their treason, how many opportunists will jump onto the band wagon? Ultra conservatives, ultra liberals, those two well financed extremes terrify me alone, without even counting the run of the mill crazies America breeds like rabbits. I'm telling you, failure here will mean the end of the United States as we know it!"

The president's Lincoln personae didn't faze the assembled bureaucrats, whether in or out of uniform, but the prospect of losing their careers did. The four-star general smiled as one of his assistants, a real PowerPoint Ranger, flipped to the next series of slides.

"No worries there, sir. We're going to come down on them like a freight train. A reinforced brigade of air assault troops will secure the State Capital in Tallahassee and link up with the besieged forces at Eglin Air Force Base, 60 miles west. For all practical purposes, that gives us control of the Panhandle. At the same time, two light brigades will secure the population center of Jacksonville in the northeast and stage for further advances down the East Coast if necessary." He stood at parade rest, really getting into the groove.

"But the primary thrust is with the bulk of the 3rd Mechanized Infantry division already stationed in Georgia. That's nearly 20,000 men with plenty of armor and artillery. The division will push down the relatively thinly populated center of the state along the I-75 corridor. We plan to occupy Gainesville by the end of day one. A short pause to rest and refit and then we make the final push. The ultimate objective is the provisional Florida capital in Orlando. Shouldn't be any reason to advance further. All totaled, a two day, three at the outside, campaign."

Every general and admiral nodded vigorously. The whole table of white, blue, green and brown costumes were in complete agreement. A rare sight.

"Whatever loyal forces they can muster will have to fight us before we get to Orlando. This is all sparsely populated, relatively dry and flat land. We'll never have to enter the real swamps in the southern part of the state. Everything north of Orlando is decent maneuver country for armored vehicles, in the unlikely event we meet true resistance and have to deploy off the roads. Most importantly, there'll be few civilians caught in the middle.

"Again, sir, this operation will more closely resemble a race than anything else. We plan to avoid any real urban combat. They'll have to come out to us. As far as our sat intel can discern, that seems to be exactly what they're preparing for. The bulk of the enemy's forces appear to be massing and digging in across the interstate, right along the axis of attack."

The general leaned forward to hide his partial erection. "Which is the worst possible strategy an outnumbered force could pursue. Remember sir, the FNG have no real tanks, limited artillery assets and even less of a logistical support train. It's top heavy in infantry, primarily light infantry. Let's face it, sir. How professional can you expect a force that only trains one weekend a month to be? In a stand up fight, they'd never stand a chance. I think they know that as well. At first contact, they'll break wide open. And if by some miracle they nut up and hold their ground…well, that's why they say God's on the side with the heaviest artillery!"

The president skimmed the printed details with little interest. "And their Air Force? They've caused us enough trouble already."

An admiral chimed in. "Well, sir, their air power seems impressive, but we should be able to negate that advantage on Day 1 and with minimum losses to their equipment and personnel."

The president made a sour face. "I've heard all these promises before, but how are you going to deliver this time? How are you going to keep this from becoming another disaster?"

A different Air Force general answered him, but not with his first thought: *By not letting you micro-manage the operation.*

"By surgical air strikes, sir. All their combat aircraft are concentrated on just 5 airfields. We'll crater the runways, without hitting the aircraft themselves or the support facilities, with guided bombs fired from F117 stealth fighters. The laser designation will be provided by UAVs instead of Special Forces operators on the ground. Quick and clean. Minimum damage and even fewer chances for collateral damage, but hideously effective nonetheless. They won't know what hit them. By the time they can repair the fields, the Army will have the insurrection well in hand." His supreme confidence was infectious.

"Sir, they cannot hope to resist for more than a few hours, days with incredible luck. Frankly, I'm surprised they're even trying. If I hadn't seen the satellite imagery of their feverish preparations or hear Dimone's fanatic followers on the news, I wouldn't believe it myself." He shook his head.

"There is one more thing, sir. We really wish you would reconsider the No Fly Zone option. If we went ahead and grabbed air superiority now, while waiting for the ground forces to get ready, we could significantly attrit their maneuver units before the first man crosses the border. We might even break their will to resist before we set any boots on the ground."

This time the president's chief of staff was the one telling the military how to do their job. "No, no. The president is correct that this needs to be a shock and awe type of operation." Someone groaned at that worn out phrase.

"Call it what you like then, but we need to go in there without warning, without preamble. We can't let their media people have time to define the talking points. We hit them like a bolt from the blue and the shock value is even stronger. The perception of the fight will be just as important as the fighting itself."

An Air Force general pleaded directly to the president. "I understand your concerns, sir, but these Rules of Engagement make it more likely that there *will* be a fight. For example, demanding that a two-star general or above personally approve every air strike, regardless of ordinance used or quality of intel, drastically degrades our air power's effectiveness.

"We'll have air superiority early in the invasion. Why not use that advantage to smash any enemy task forces by air? Smash them long before the Army gets within range. We could shut down their artillery and keep any force larger than platoon size from massing to oppose us. The Army would just have to mop up. Even if we can't break their will, we'll have the opportunity to break their ability to fight before they get a chance!"

The president snorted. "Gentlemen, I don't know the difference between a platoon and a task force and neither do most Americans. What they do know is the difference between military and civilian casualties. I don't care if you can hit what you're aiming at 99% of the time. Just one bomb falling short and hitting a school or hospital will undermine the entire purpose of this mission."

Some random civilian aide, who had never served in the military, felt knowledgeable enough to chime in. He had never even met someone who had served before coming to work at the White House, but he still somehow knew all about warfare. "Let's be realistic, General. A soldier face to face with a rebel is far less likely to misidentify him with a civilian than a pilot flying at 300 miles an hour at 15,000 feet."

The general didn't know where to begin explaining that it's usually a soldier on the ground telling the pilot exactly where to drop his guided bombs. Or that officers are too busy to micromanage fire support. They had an elaborate system of target acquisition and checks and balances to reduce civilian casualties. How do you distill decades of hard learned experience into a simple explanation that these kids could understand? He tried hard to find a witty analogy, but hadn't prepared for this. After a few false starts, the president closed off the conversation.

"The American people can shrug off a bombed mosque in some far away land as just 'collateral damage,' but things will be quite different if they see the First Baptist Church of whatever Podunk town crowded with worshipers blown up. Not another word about this; my decision is final. Damn, I can't believe we're even discussing this!"

***

25 February
Ocala, Florida

The attitude inside of Florida's Joint Forces Forward Operations center was even more chaotic than the storm outside. Several dozen personnel, including several civilian contractors and trusted volunteers, alternately screamed, pleaded or threatened into twice as many phones and radios.

In the eye of the storm, some 6 foot tall colonel with a pro swimmer's build attempted to stare down a lanky S-3 officer. For the skinny guy, the big man was just one more bullet point on a long To Do list. He listened courteously, but with little interest, while trying to balance a laptop on his knees, a radio on the shoulder, a satellite phone in one hand and a coffee thermos in the other.

"There is no way the general signed off on that op order, Major. My brigade is the most experienced fighting force you have. We sure as hell proved that against those paratroopers up at Blanding. 70% of my men have at least one combat deployment under their belts and we're at 98% preparedness, with nearly every single combat platform up and running. Yet, you're telling me we're being held in strategic reserve!?

"You're going to let that disorganized militia mob form the center of our defensive line and that joke of a 'Minuteman Brigade' cover the flanks, while keeping us spinning our wheels back in the sticks!? I didn't expect brilliance from a simple *staff* officer, but I expected at least basic competence!"

Gorgas wiped the spittle from his computer screen and feigned confusion.

"That's why we need a leader like you to bolster the line, sir." Major Gorgas intentionally ignored the contribution of the blowhard's unit in order to penetrate straight to the colonel's ego. He kicked it up a notch by lowering his voice and letting him in on the "Big Secret." The great big secret that should have been obvious.

"I think you deserve to know the truth, sir. Those vigilantes aren't expected to hold the line. The Feds will plow right through them. The whole point is to get them to speed down here convinced they won't encounter significant opposition. And that's when you'll strike back. Our best commander, personally leading our best unit must deliver the decisive blow. Just like you so famously did at Camp Blanding. Sir, please, we need you!"

Colonel Beauregard pondered that for a moment. "Well, aren't you a sneaky son of a gun. Ok, if the general wants me there, that's where I'll be. Carry on then, Major." He showed the major a new measure of respect by returning a half-assed salute before strutting off.

Gorgas wasn't the type to mull over confrontations and get all stressed out by them. He built his whole career on smoothing ruffled feathers, pampering delicate egos and just generally manipulating senior officers into actually doing their jobs. All the while being looked down upon as a cowardly staff officer.

To be fair, he was an oddity. The Army tries hard to rotate officers between staff and command positions in order to broaden their horizons. Or to keep them from becoming competent at any one job, depending on your point of view. Gorgas had the dubious luck of always somehow falling through the cracks. Training, planning, organizing, but in his 20 year career, he'd never once commanded soldiers.

The strange thing is he really was combat arms by training—an artillery officer. It was just that at every new unit he arrived in they never seemed to have a command slot available. So, they'd plug him into a staff support role while he waited for his chance. There he would always commit the same mistake: he'd do a good job. Just like in the civilian world, nothing keeps you from being promoted more than being irreplaceable.

That's why he left the regular Army and joined his home state Guard. Pretty much the only chance he'd ever have to make lieutenant colonel someday. Then the president just ups and declares war on his home. Florida needed every leader they could get; surely now would be his chance. No dice. Turns out, building an army from nearly scratch requires a real organizer. And he was the man for the job, or so said everyone who didn't want to do it. He never could catch a break.

He wasn't particularly proud of the militia trick that impressed the colonel so much. That's only a minor game that may or may not pay off. His success in unifying the new Florida Defense Forces is where his pride came from. The real trick was the Herculean task of organizing scores of independent National Guard and Reservist units, with widely varying grades of loyalty and motivation, as well as thousands of civilian volunteers into a somewhat cohesive army with a unified command, control and supply network.

But he did it. All in the span of just a few weeks and with hardly any funding, since the Federal Government wasn't chipping in anymore. Organization might be boring. It definitely wasn't sexy like clever battlefield tricks, strategic surprises or secret weapons. But all those cool things weren't useful, let alone even possible, without an efficient foundation.

From the ancient Romans to modern armies, it wasn't brilliant leaders or super weapons that were dangerous, but rather the simple bureaucratization of war that allowed killing to be so efficient. That's what both won wars and made them so terrible.

It's not the highly skilled, renowned sniper that's the real threat on the battlefield. It's the far seeing planning staff that puts him in the perfect firing position and the well-organized supply staff that ensures he has ample food and ammo. Those paper plans and background support are what makes sure that the war fighter can keep on killing. If a sniper is taken out, a new one could be simply reassigned to take his place. If that discipline and organization breaks down, then the fighters are as good as dead, no matter how well armed and courageous.

Of course, he couldn't claim all the credit. Having General Cooper on board was a lucky break. The man was the closest thing America had to a respected general. The best part was, he hailed from Texas; not just a local hero. Should help to show the nationwide breadth of their struggle. Or so they hoped. If nothing else, his briefing style excited and motivated the civilians.

General Cooper was also the one who demanded a free hand from the politicians to prepare the Florida Defense Forces as he saw fit, and had the guts to keep them from trying to micromanage things. He even sold the idea of *not* taking every halfwit with a gun into the FDF. President Dimone's now famous call to arms rallied close to a 100,000 volunteers in that first week! The politicians, as usual, wanted to take them all without the slightest idea what they were supposed to do. Throw them in human waves at the Feds maybe? Hoping they ran out of bullets before we ran out of idiots?

Just feeding, equipping and paying (well, promising to one day pay) the 16,000 they did take was difficult enough. They were at the point, maybe a bit past even, of optimal efficiency. Any more men and it would be necessary to cannibalize arms and equipment from other units and so dilute the supply chain that the army would be less combat effective as a whole.

He was surprised by the quality of these vetted volunteers. A good 60% were veterans–mostly young vets from America's multiple 21st century wars. They had assigned most of them to outfit a second mechanized infantry brigade. The vehicles and equipment of that unit were courtesy of a sympathetic (or treasonous, depending on your point of view) Daytona-born captain of a massive container ship, who decided to make a short port call in Key West due to unspecified "mechanical problems."

The beaming captain called his FNG brother-in-law and told him to find the highest ranking person he could and come on down South. When the other guy mentioned he was way too busy for games, the captain switched on the video feature of his smartphone and panned over the cargo bay. Hundreds of vehicles, from tanks to trucks, and mountains of ammo pallets filled his mini screen. A complete heavy brigade equipment set, everything except the troops, returning from Germany and in route to Texas was just "requisitioned."

Gorgas organized the rest of the civilian volunteers, virgin fighters but as motivated as you could find, into four light infantry "regiments." About 2,600 carefully vetted men, and a surprising number of women, in each. Technically motorized units, if you count the 500 or so pickups confiscated per unit.

Frantic work done on a few to weld on light steel armor gave some crude protection. A great idea on paper, but the hillbilly tanks weren't all that useful in practice. They soon abandoned the whole idea and agreed the vehicles would be best deployed as battlefield taxis. Speed and not looking so obviously like a threat were the best armor they could improvise. Better to spend the time doing as much hasty training as possible.

Their small arms were a mix of private weapons and whatever could be spared from police and Guard armories. At least almost everyone had a semi-auto rifle and ammunition was plentiful. They were a well-armed posse, but a weak army. But if things went according to plan, these irregulars would never have to fight against the professional soldiers. Their whole mission was to penetrate the enemy's lines and harass the rear areas. He wasn't morbid enough to throw these amateurs up against veteran combat troops.

He did make sure to outfit every regiment with two professional National Guard officers to act as commanding and executive officers. At least one professional NCO was assigned to each subordinate company. Young ex-soldiers with combat experience in Iraq, Afghanistan or Syria were tasked as junior militia sergeants and officers whenever possible. Still, raw civilians with more guts than brains made up 90% or more of each unit.

Gorgas was inflexible about making sure everyone had uniforms, no matter how much Tallahassee bitched about the expense. Maybe just the old-style BDU's, but it was crucial they had matching uniforms nonetheless. It was the best he could do in the short time he had to make them feel like a real army, part of something bigger than themselves.

A couple weeks of training, even as intense as their program, is simply not enough time to instill the levels of discipline, teamwork or confidence necessary to turn a bunch of civilians into real soldiers. To say nothing about teaching them marksmanship, field craft, or tactical drills. At least they were flooded with gung-ho paramedic volunteers. Something the major feared would be important when these regiments were thrown into the grinder.

There was one kernel of luck in this shit pile, at least. Enough civilian police officers volunteered to allocate one to each platoon. Their presence imparted a level of discipline, of professionalism and, not to put too fine a point on it, legitimacy not found in most armed mobs.

The few heavy machine guns, grenades, antitank rockets and other boom stuff the Guard could afford to strip from the regular units were kept centralized in a special company under the direct control of every regimental commander. Not terribly efficient, of course, but it was the best way to guarantee that the weapons and their tiny stock of ammunition would only be used during the most decisive moments of battle.

They also had some experimental weapons, like UAV guidance jammers and Hellfire missiles mounted on ground vehicles, but those were just unproven toys. With some luck they might help a bit, but this fight wouldn't be decided by technology. This battle will be won or lost by rifleman face to face with the enemy. All the other stuff existed solely to make sure those shooters could get in range of the enemy without being slaughtered.

In short, the whole thing was one of the most complicated strategic and logistical challenges in military history, and he almost single handily sweated it down to manageable size. The result? No one gave a damn! The importance and subtle intricacies of flexible organization, relevant training and dynamic control structures were apparently too complicated for these supposed leaders to grasp.

He took some cold comfort in knowing that, if his own side didn't appreciate the sweeping changes he'd made to the Florida Defense Forces, then it wasn't likely the enemy did. How much value would that surprise have? History was full of clever and carefully organized forces being stomped on by the side with more men and artillery.

Speaking of artillery, he waved the supply officer over. His whisper this time was genuine. This one was a bonafide secret. "So, Kamil, have our tropical friends come through yet? I've got 6 batteries worth of ex-gun bunnies on a tight training schedule rotating through the mockups, but we need the real deal. Combat is hardly the best time for initial gunnery practice."

The S-4 smiled. "All 36 pieces were offloaded last night. They'll be trucked off and deployed tonight. Your obsession with secrecy is what's taking so long, but maybe you have a point. I don't know how much the Cubans were paid, but they sent even more ammunition and spare parts than we were promised. Which is damn good, because I haven't been able to find a contractor able to fabricate replacements on such short notice. But we do have some options for self-manufacturing in the future. I found several places not only able, but willing to retool and copy these things, or any type of artillery for that matter. We just need a bit more time."

Gorgas shook his head as one of his phones rang. "I love that you're thinking so far ahead, but if this drags on into a protracted war, we're fucked. We can't hold this thing together for much longer. Everybody's dick is hard now, but that passion fades. And don't forget, we have to pay for all of this eventually. At some point, all these IOU's Tallahassee are throwing around will come due.

No. Three weeks of prep time was a blessing. Three more weeks of waiting will cause this whole pyramid scheme to fall apart. The worst thing the president could do to us would be to do nothing to us."

Part II

"The capacity of the human mind for swallowing nonsense and spewing it forth in violent and repressive action has never yet been plumbed."
– Robert A. Heinlein

Chapter 7

5 March
Mobile command post a few miles inside Florida

The invasion of Florida, or liberation depending on your version of history, began with a whimper rather than a bang. The internet loved to call it the "Wet Firecracker War." No cruise missiles swarmed the state. No rolling artillery barrages or swarms of strategic bombers flattened anything.

A handful of stealth penetrators conducted some ultra-surgical strikes on a few airfields, but far from the camera's eyes. Ferocious tanks with names like "death dealers" stenciled on the barrels and thousands of other armored vehicles surged across the border with safeties off. They slammed right into the rebel's defenses and overran…nothing.

Not a shot was fired. After 20 miles, a reconnaissance platoon made contact with the first FDF position. Perhaps "contact" was too strong a word. This handful of BDU clad old timers, armed with a motley mixture of shotguns and bolt-action hunting rifles, hardly qualified. They fired a single shot, probably by accident, before chucking their weapons to run away faster. Similar scenes were repeated every few miles.

*

US General McDowell drove his staff crazy by his excessive attention to every little detail. He endlessly questioned everything. Hell, he even personally monitored the radios. It had only been 4 hours since the ground offensive kicked off, but his team had spent every second unnecessarily stressed out by their fearless leader.

Not that he doubted the loyalty of his command staff. At least not anymore. Military intelligence carefully vetted every person in the headquarters. The handful of questionable characters transferred somewhere far away, usually overseas. He even went so far as to transfer anyone originally from Florida, of any rank, to units far on the West Coast.

It didn't help the division's unit cohesion to randomly replace hundreds of team members at the last minute, but he couldn't afford any hesitation on this mission. It definitely pissed a lot of soldiers off, to have their loyalty suspected without a chance to defend themselves. Oh well. They'd sort that stuff out after the fight.

The real problem rested with his whole figurehead position. His large staff handled the details, while he was responsible for…well, everything. It was his job to be the scapegoat if things went bad. It's frustrating when everyone above him held him accountable for things he had so little control over. All that responsibility, but so little direct power.

Now to be fair, their commander spent every second of the invasion being harassed by his higher ups. A round dozen senators and congressman invited themselves to tag along with the invasion. Most of the associated riff-raff following the Army, from kooks to celebrity kooks, his troops could keep outside the perimeter with little trouble. Regrettably, the politicians were immune to weapons. They ate up his day with one unreasonable demand after another. The White House had already called 3 times to add more contradictory commands on top of the confusion.

At any rate, the sheer size of the federal force should give room enough to make mistakes and still ensure victory. The amateurishness of the resistance helped as well. They cleared out every little sniper or roadblock lightning fast, without suffering any casualties. The Air Force apparently even delivered on their promise of grounding the Florida air wing. Not a single hostile aircraft was spotted all day.

The only frustrating part was that so little had been seen. The last aerial recon reported Florida's main body digging in around Ocala, in the middle of the state. Uplinks to the spy satellite that should have passed overhead an hour ago to give him the enemy's latest position were somehow cut. His Air Force liaison officer tried to explain several ways this high-tech state might've pulled off such a stunt, but the general wasn't interested.

High winds and some suspicious radio interference caused problems with his UAV component as well. Two surveillance drones already lost communication with their controllers and were assumed lost. Just one more blind spot.

The president even decided, for whatever brilliant random reason, that his long range reconnaissance patrols were unnecessarily risky. Since he was forced to pull them back, the Army resorted to old school methods for operational level recon. How wearisome to wait for a recon flight to fly overhead and the photos to be analyzed, but really, it shouldn't matter in the long run. The exact location of the enemy couldn't change the overall strategic picture. The rebels were trapped on a peninsula and vastly outnumbered. What chance did they have?

*

USS Gerald R. Ford, 50 miles East of Daytona Beach

The gunnery sergeant never saw mutiny on the high seas before, but he'd always fantasized there'd be more swashbuckling and less, well…sitting around. Clearing out 30 or so redshirts simply relaxing in the hanger bay and refusing to load any ordinance, or let anyone else do anything, was work for a pissed off chief petty officer. Disciplining lazy seamen shouldn't be his problem. How demeaning to send two squads of armed marines to deal with them! Lame as the mission was, he still had a reputation to maintain. So, if this is what the captain calls a mutiny, well, he wasn't going to let a bunch of squids make him look like a jackass.

He briefly mulled ordering his men to "fix bayonets," but thought that bluffing to gut your fellow messmates for being slothful was probably a weak and transparent threat. Getting whipped upside the head by the Shore Patrol style billy clubs, on the other hand, wasn't an empty threat. It was just a matter of time if they kept up this crap.

To up the mind-fuck factor, because fighting is a matter of psychology and psychology is just mind fucking the enemy into not fighting, if he remembered Sun Tzu correctly, he yelled to his squad: "Too much live ordinance here. Don't shoot them unless you've got a clean shot!"

Several sailors grew pale, while a surprising number looked only more resolved. Not a single one of the unarmed men or women moved however. A small part of the marine's mind could respect that courage, if not their common sense. Some senior petty officer he hadn't noticed before stood up from the hippy circle.

"Gunny, stand down. Everyone, just stand down. Son, I've been maintaining and loading these things onto strike craft since the 1st Gulf War. I know, and you do too, that these bombs aren't half as smart as the manufacturer claims. Never mind how you feel about the president or that other guy, if we drop so much damn fire power as the admiral plans, civilians will die. Our civilians! Goddamn Americans, man!"

"That call ain't yours or mine to make. That stuff is way above our pay grades. Now, you all are relieved of duty and confined to your bunks until further notice. You've got 3 seconds to get your assess moving or we'll assist you the only way we know how." He counted down without any further blustering.

The petty officer stuck out his hand, palm first, as the gunnery sergeant reached "one" and immediately advanced. "Wait, damn it! We always used the excuse that, 'we're fighting over there so we don't have to fight over here.' Well, what excuse do we use now? Do you want to be a part of *this* shit? The only thing our country needs defending against is itself!"

Even through the poker face, it was clear he had a hook in the marine. "Just give us a little more time, Gunny. That's all we're asking. You don't have to do anything except do nothing."

"Time for what?" The other marines could have sworn there was a note of admiration in their sergeant's voice.

A rebel yell in the distance answered him. Whatever siren song of reasonableness the petty officer sang shattered when some other sailors, kids really, catapulted the first 1,000 lb JDAM far out the port side aircraft elevator door and deep into the blue below. They whooped a bit more before grabbing another weapon cart and sending that one flying even further out to sea. It didn't matter that the fuses were removed–this shit was way beyond regulations.

With the marine's sense of order and discipline desecrated, he gave a hand signal to his men. They put an end to the amateur mutiny inside of 5 minutes. Shortly, they had every non-cooperating sailor, man and woman, either in Zip Cuffs or on a stretcher. The captain even came down to congratulate the "brave Gunny" personally on his decisive and level-headed response. Only a couple of sailors had to detour by the infirmary on their way to the brig.

There were less than a hundred non-locked up witnesses to the whole fiasco. Nevertheless, the whole ship knew the story within minutes. Or a version of it at least. The captain decided to extend his news blackout even further. He went so far as to block the ship's internal television, newsletter, bulletin boards–everything. But just like his ban on external news outlets it didn't do a thing to help morale. In the absence of real news, even the wild speculation mills on TV that billed themselves as "news," gossip reigned supreme.

By the time the story reached the engineering decks the death toll had climbed from none to ten. By the time it reached an extremely homesick Floridian engineer in a certain central compartment, the story turned darker. He gazed in horror back and forth between the douche bag next to him laughing his ass off about some chick from Miami getting her skull caved in and the fuzz from the wall-mounted TV. The nuclear reactor watch crew always reveled in their macabre sense of humor, but this time the jokes hit a little too close to home.

Some would claim he was a wannabe terrorist. Others, a hero. The judge at the court martial would later call it the most dangerous and egregious breakdown of discipline he'd ever seen. What everyone failed to realize was he never made a principled decision either way. If you look at it from his limited point of view, what else was he supposed to do?

His family lived in Florida. If the Navy was willing to do all the terrible things the scuttlebutt claimed to their own, what would they do to the so-called enemy? When his chief turned his back, he stood up and shuffled to the center of the control wall. With a shaking hand, he hit a series of giant red "Oh Shit!" buttons. He made neither speeches nor excuses when alarms blared and the rest of the watch came running. After what he just did, words were superfluous. Simply sitting down and staring at the wall stunned his mates enough.

Modern nuclear reactors are equipped with multiple emergency shutdown controls intended to immediately halt a melting reactor core. Now, to avoid lasting damage, they are usually employed one at a time and in only the direst situations. The hasty mutineer simply activated them all at once. These controls were last ditch tools to prevent another Chernobyl, manual overrides in case the automatic processes failed. As such, there was no way to abort them.

The chain reaction stopped almost instantly after little explosive bolts dropped several neutron absorbing control rods into both cores. Not finished yet, the system then dumped a load of boric acid, so called "nuclear poison," into the coolant system. Flooding the coolant tank with seawater as a final touch was really over the top. It would take weeks, at least, and millions of dollars before either reactor could be cleaned, repaired, inspected and safely started up again.

The *Gerald R Ford* was the most modern aircraft carrier in the world. Her designers chose an ultra-reliable, but energy intensive, all electric catapult launching system. Without the endless supply of power from the ship's twin reactors though, her 90 next-generation combat aircraft weren't going anywhere. Until that power plant could be reactivated, this technological marvel was $9 billion and 100,000 tons of scrap metal. Thanks to his own paranoia, the ship's captain got the mutiny he feared.

So much of the US and USN air forces usually stationed in the Southeast were either deployed overseas or sitting on airfields throughout Florida. Besieged as those were, they might as well have been in a foreign country. The powers that be decided to ground them all out of terror that some $50 million plane and a million-dollar-a-year-in-training-costs specialized pilot might be shot down on takeoff by some Bubba with a hunting rifle.

That's why the carrier represented half the combat aircraft assigned to Operation Enduring Unity. Planners at the Pentagon were annoyed to lose so many planes just hours into the invasion, but it was no great cause for worry. They sent warning orders to Air Force units outside the Deep South to be ready to deploy in support, but no assets were actually moved.

Aircraft weren't supposed to play such a high profile role in this fight as in most operations. With the repressive rules of engagement, it seemed close air support was as tightly controlled as tactical nuclear launches. Besides, all their intelligence assets were positive that no any enemy aircraft were able to take off. What was the point in spending so much money to move unnecessary planes anyway?

***

Power Games

Lake City Municipal Airport

General McDowell couldn't sit still any longer. Everywhere he looked government troops secured one sensational success after another. All federal forces except for his command, God Damnit! From his perspective, he deftly and methodically advanced his unwieldy horde into Florida. He crushed any minor resistance encountered with decisive and overwhelming force. Everything he could do to avoid unnecessary losses, to civilians as well, he did. No matter how long it took.

To the bigwigs around him, though, he plodded slowly and ineptly down the center of the state against little resistance, with no politically necessary spectacular successes to show for it. Their greatest accomplishment so far was capturing Lake City, some evacuated little town in the middle of nowhere, and only 60 miles from the border.

Conversely, the rival East Coast Task Force took Jacksonville by H-hour plus 2. The news hailed their commander as a hero for so swiftly relieving the surrounded naval base and liberating a city of a million people; all without a shot being fired by either side. His live interview, explaining the intricacies of his tactical brilliance, was interrupted by an even greater triumph to the west. Tallahassee had fallen.

Which was the worst possible news of all. McDowell always hated that impudent ass from VMI who commanded the Panhandle Task Force. Sure enough, the general watched from his aid's tablet as the prick reached new heights of grandstanding. Ever the showman, he must have planned this well before the invasion kicked off.

The other task force general posed on an M1 tank turret, in his spotlessly clean full battle rattle, and surveyed the "brutal battlefield" around him. He wore every ribbon, badge and medal from his Class A dress uniform attached to the body armor. A light machine gun rested casually under his broad shoulder, the belt removed from the ammo box and looped impractically over the weapon. His unit's standard, carefully shredded by some staffer to appear "battle worn," waved defiantly from his left hand. The stub of an unlit cigar in the corner of his mouth completed the ensemble.

To other soldiers, the man looked ridiculous–borderline disrespectful even. To the millions of civilians watching on television though, he came off as some awesome fusion of Chuck Norris and John Wayne. Raw, pure Americana baddassery personified. The camera shook with the operator's excitement. These were career building, history book type shots right here. Oh, but the show was just getting started.

Someone had removed the Great Seal of Florida that usually flew over the dome of the Capitol building. In its place, they raised a massive 25' x 40' American flag, confiscated from some used car lot, on a brand new pole. The crane doing the heavy lifting would later be photo-shopped out, but the four soldiers struggling, Iwo Jima style, to guide the flag into place would stay in.

Just as the cameramen and producers were practically orgasming in their pants, four F-15's flashed by in a perfectly synchronized, high-speed flyover. Better than the Super Bowl. Some singers were already recording country songs about this. The already cheering crowd roared louder and spontaneously sang the Star Spangled Banner. With mostly the right words even. A million flags waved hysterically–tears and hugs were passed all around.

General McDowell became physically sick. Even his professional staffers were pissed. The senior senators and congressmen in the tent with him shook their heads in disgust at the general they foolishly decided to ride along with. His second in command hung up a satellite phone, frowning.

"Was that the White House again?" The general didn't make eye contact with anyone.

"Yes, sir. They want to know what the holdup is. I told them you were inspecting the front and it would take a bit to transfer the call. I suggest we –" One congressman in the corner couldn't stand it anymore.

"Are you going to keep hiding from the enemy like you do from your president? You were supposed to represent the sharpened heart of the liberation force. You outnumber these rednecks several times over, and they're not even fighting back! What more opportunities do you need? You could end this war today if you would only have the courage! If you were half the leader…"

The senator didn't need political instincts to realize it was time to shut up. The general's murderous glare made that clear. This fabulously rich man had never been close to physical danger in his entire life, but something in the soldier's suddenly loose stance told him he was just one careless word away from serious bodily harm.

No one, of any rank, spoke for an uncomfortably long time. At long last, the general said the one thing no one expected.

"Ha! I think I finally figured it out. We have been drastically overcomplicating this operation from the get go. I see it now. This whole 'last stand' of the enemy is just a stunt. The politicians on the other side are exactly like ours. They want one great big glorious battle to show their resolve and bring the other side to the bargaining table. We've been treating this like a real military operation and forgot it's all a damn game. A deadly game, but bullshit just the same." He spoke louder, so that the whole tent could hear.

"Let's see how they like it when the pawns move on their own. Where's my G-3?"

A grinning colonel leapt up, notepad in hand. "Ready, sir."

"I need you to organize a FRAGO. We're going to push south as fast as possible along every major road. 3rd Brigade will continue down the interstate, secure Gainesville, and then Ocala but stop before making contact with the enemy's main body. 1st and 2nd Brigades will move east and west of them. I want them broken down into battalions, companies even, if necessary. Whatever will enable our troops to cover as much ground as fast as possible. They need to move as quick as they can and then some." His officers looked skeptical, but the general only looked more thoughtful.

"Yes, speed is the key. We've about 5 hours before sunset. I want Orlando surrounded by dinnertime. If we set up our FOB here in Lake City, we can leave the slow support trail and most of the vulnerable artillery, engineers and air defense assets in one safe, central location. Slimmed down to pure combat power, the maneuver units should be able to make it. Yeah, that's the key. We need to own as much real estate as possible by nightfall.

Come morning, the enemy will be left a lonely island in a sea of federal troops. Tomorrow we'll push on to Miami. In 48 hours these rebels will be an army without a country. What choice would they have but to surrender? Maybe some little negotiation, but they won't have any good bargaining chips. Total victory, without the big bloody battle these ghouls want so much. That's the goal. Work up the details, Colonel. I want our people moving in 20 minutes."

To his credit, the general fostered an open debate atmosphere among his command staff. No one was afraid to challenge the boss. "Sir, that'll leave us terribly vulnerable. Our reconnaissance has been badly hindered. I mean, there are gaping holes in our intelligence profile. We don't know for sure that all the enemy's strength is waiting south of Ocala. If we move as rapidly as you envision, our units won't be able to support each other. Our greatest strength is numbers, and we'll be giving that away."

"You vastly underestimate the superiority of our men and equipment, Colonel. Troops on the offensive enjoy a formidable morale boost. No, we'll have no problems overcoming any little surprises the enemy might be able to muster. Come on, gentlemen. We're talking about weekend warriors and untrained civilian levies, not real soldiers." A few heads nodded around the tent.

"As long as the bulk of their forces stay concentrated while we're dispersing around them, then any temporary success they have anywhere else won't change the final outcome. We just have to adapt and overcome. We're wasting time, everyone. Get our boys moving!"

A great commander realizes the key to high level leadership rests with knowing exactly the capabilities and limitations of his unit. He will make sure that his command is simply never placed into a position where victory isn't likely. A poor commander knows his unit's strengths and weaknesses as well, but assumes that by some force of his will and/or his own tactical brilliance he'll somehow always be able to generate victory under any circumstances.

The former is a craftsman who carefully shapes the project in a way that can be managed with the tools and resources at his disposal. The latter believes that a square peg can fit into a round hole with enough force and determination. That physics is merely a matter of morale. In the rare occasions where he's successful, both the peg and hole are usually left permanently damaged and useless.

The first peg to be flattened was the Seventh Cavalry squadron. Those 500 men lead the 1st Brigade's mad charge south along Highway 41. They advanced in parallel to the main thrust on the interstate, just a few miles east, but might as well have been a hundred miles away. There was no coordination with any other unit. The troops were as fired up about the race as their commanding general. Everyone wanted to be the first into Miami. Liberate all those beach bunnies.

Now, a cavalry squadron is basically a slightly larger, faster moving and armor heavy battalion sized task force. The mailed fist of the modern battlefield. Their specialties are so-called "reconnaissance in force" missions. Using a battalion of 27 M1a2 TUSK tanks, the cutting edge Abrams mod with all the bells and whistles, 39 equally souped up M3 Bradley's, an armored mortar platoon and 6 armed OH-58 Kiowa helicopters all as a light recon force was just the type of gentle, subtle touch the Army was famous for.

Their organic Kiowa air support drew first blood. Flying in 3 pairs, each a mile apart and several miles ahead of the Squadron, they enjoyed a bird's eye view of the enemy. These were small and old helicopters, first seeing action in the Vietnam War and practically obsolete. Just like old soldiers, though, there's a reason they're still kept around. They'd proven themselves deadly.

At the I-75/ Hwy 41 junction in the middle of nowhere, four green and brown FDF M1's unwisely deployed on top of the overpass. The open location was perfectly situated to cover the east/west and north/south approaches. It was just too tempting to have an elevated field of view in a state that was so hopelessly flat. A perfect firing position to engage the enemy at maximum range.

Perfect, except that maximum visibility cuts both ways. Those 16 ex-soldiers manning the recently requisitioned tanks didn't seem to notice how silhouetted they were. No one noticed the long range missiles fired from the low flying scout helicopters that blew the armor platoon apart until far too late. Every man on that overpass had been out of the Army for several years before rejoining the Minuteman Brigade. They struggled to readjust to tactical thinking. Hopefully, when they died, they went to a better place that didn't require such attention to detail.

The scary thing was that the antitank missiles on the choppers were mere accessories. Even destroying a fair fraction of Florida's armor in a matter of seconds was merely a fun bonus project. Only after their million dollar thermal imaging sets, mounted on a mast above the rotors, displayed scores of poorly camouflaged armored vehicles in the strip mall behind the overpass and in the surrounding woods did the crews activate their scout platforms' primary weapon: the radio.

Normally, a few magic words spoken into that black box would bring down the wrath of God, delivered in the form of fast movers or massed artillery. But these were far from normal times. With the general's maniac demands to reach the next town by yesterday they were operating well outside the range of artillery support.

Those guns were still sitting 20 miles north in Lake City and not going anywhere. As for air power, well, no one even bothered forwarding air support requests higher. No mission would ever be approved in this built up civilian area. Instead, miles back, the Squadron's commander methodically redeployed his company sized Troops. He was going to have to do things the messy way.

One of the Kiowa's hovered in place a little too long while examining some strange road work. The old highway must of had some potholes freshly repaved, judging from the heat signature. After all the route clearance operations they'd flown in Afghanistan, none of the crew believed in coincidences. But just as the gunner clicked his radio on to report the possible mines, a Stinger missile lanced out from the roof of a Travelodge half a mile down the road. The pilot dumped all his flares at once and dived for the deck. He damn near made it.

His wingman raked the source of fire with a .50 cal. Too late to save the flaming Kiowa, but it at least made them feel better. After confirming there were no survivors, the other birds fell back to cover the flanks of the advancing ground element. With the goals of finding the enemy, determining his strength and general disposition completed there wasn't much point in risking themselves now. It wasn't their job to make the final kill.

That job fell to the 3 advancing cavalry Troops now moving from column formation and spreading out over a mile front. Like a well-oiled machine, the battalion moved as one. The mortars, accurately directed by a pair of forward observers, began softening up the enemy's position. Most of the tanks, centered along the highway, set up a base of fire to pin down and distract the defenders. They carefully covered the rest stop and surrounding woods and farms in overlapping fields of fire.

All the while the infantry, out of sight to the defenders, swung wide to the east to flank the enemy's position. There were some dry(ish) swamps and a small stream to wade through before they could take the enemy in enfilade fire. The ever present Kiowa's protected the attacker's flanks and rear, as well as kept an over watch out for any enemy surprises. No West Point professor could've dreamed up a more textbook perfect deliberate attack.

That's why it was so shocking when things stopped going by the book. The lead Abrams disappeared in a cloud of asphalt and black smoke. When it cleared, the 72 ton vehicle looked fine, except for the flames pouring out of all 3 hatches the crew should've used to escape. Another one crossing through the grass parking lot of some tiny deep woods church lost the left track and the exposed commander's arm to another mine blast. A third explosion on a side road broke another tank open, as well as two of her crew.

Simultaneously, enemy artillery–not mortars but real life 155mm howitzers–started counter battering the hell out of the mortar platoon. All 4 motor carriers, caught in the open, were destroyed or otherwise knocked out of the fight in the first two volleys. Thankfully, the enemy guns moved on to some more important and distant target soon after.

The speed and accuracy of this shit storm implied they had an artillery locating radar involved. Somewhere out there it detected their outgoing rounds, backtracked them to the source of origin and fed that grid to the enemy's hungry guns. All in less than 25 seconds. One hell of a useful tool that the Feds also possessed…way up north.

You don't become a cavalry trooper by being the dithering type. Without any higher level guidance, each Troop rammed their vehicles off the crowded roads and into cover. Crushing quite a few pine trees, farm fences and the occasional armadillo in the process. Finally, with a little maneuver room and partial concealment, they could pick out targets. Of which there was no shortage. Javelin and TOW antitank missiles seemed to be blossoming from behind every rooftop and parked car ahead.

Now, tankers enjoy the protective cover of friendly artillery as much as the next soldier. They just don't stress so much when it's not available. If the enemy is in sight, a tank's 120mm smoothbore cannon is fire support enough. The radio world became deathly quiet as up and down the line each vehicle commander, regardless of rank, "fought his track." From the Squadron commander to the most junior NCO, they were all busy shouting targets and directions to their gunners and fine tuning movements to their drivers.

The dividends of countless hours practicing and drilling spoke for themselves. In less than 10 minutes, they had systematically disabled every exposed enemy vehicle and set every building on fire, including both gas stations in a series of beautiful explosions. For good measure, any potential enemy firing positions also received bursts of .50 cal and 25mm fire to discourage resistance.

The squadron's flanking force finally got around Olustee Creek and began pouring their fires into the surprised enemy. Well, not nearly as surprised and disoriented as the Squadron commander hoped. Either way, with the main infantry force engaged, it was time for the base of fire to get in closer. He calmly received the slant reports from his subordinates and dispassionately adjusted his line accordingly. From long training, he didn't dwell on how few of his men were still able to move forward.

He left his sergeant major to organize the casualty evacuation and let his gunner engage at his own discretion. Fun as he had getting his hands dirty, someone still must lead the unit. He checked up with his Troop commanders. Two of whom were only a few minutes into the job. Cav leaders led from the front, but what an expensive motivator.

No time to worry about that now. He made another fruitless call for close air support and was told to "wait, out." Knowing the only air assets around were running low on fuel and would have to leave station soon, he committed the five remaining Kiowa's to provide direct fire support for his dismounts and accompanying Brads flanking the enemy.

He nearly dropped the radio when he heard that sudden, fast ripple of artillery and mortar fire. The Cav lieutenant colonel knew exactly what that meant. He should, because it was standard doctrine. Final Protective Fire. As a basic component of any defensive line, it was simply a last ditch wall of fire. A pre-planned line covering each side of a unit at skin-scorching range. It was proof that the enemy was at last being overrun.

An FPF fire mission has priority over all others and is considered a "net call order." In other words, when an FPF is heard over the radio net, every receiving fire direction center in range drops whatever target package they have and lays in all available fires on that grid. The FPF can also include a "dead man's switch." If communication with the unit being overrun is lost and not recovered in the time allotted, the fire mission's target is shifted to the unit's last known location.

When you encounter that type of Steel Rain, the only logical solution is to push on hard, before a forward observer refines the fire plan more accurately. Get out of the kill zone and close with the enemy as fast as possible. Of course, that same WWI style charge is only slightly less suicidal than standing still and watching the fire storm waltz towards you.

Not an easy choice to make, but then again, that's why it's an all-volunteer Army. Without hesitation, platoon leaders recalled their dismounts into the still firing Brads. Six dismounted eggs in one steel-clad basket had a better chance of survival than alone with the thin Kevlar eggshells they wore.

The Brads leapt forward at max speed through the shrapnel clouds, and surprisingly made it almost painlessly. One IFV was rocked by a near miss which threw a track off. The crew could only sit there helpless and praying as more rounds thumped around them. The only vehicle that took a direct hit was one that had hung back in "safety" to provide covering fire.

Seconds after kickoff, a 100 pound HE artillery round detonated against the weak turret armor of that over watching vehicle. It didn't so much blow the track up as simply disintegrate the Brad. What happened to the three men inside is best not described. They at least died instantly, even if the bodies could only be ID'd by DNA testing.

By the time the infantry were through the "fire line," they weren't about to stop. Most of the enemy force had already extracted themselves, leaving a mixed company to cover their withdrawal. Without artillery or aircraft support, the cavalry had few options to catch the retreating enemy. So, they didn't try. Instead, they focused all their energy into slaughtering that rear guard. Considering how many causalities they'd suffered, they were incredibly honorable by letting the wounded surrender, even if no one else.

When the shooting finally paused, only 10 Abrams and 20 Brads were still fully functional. All of the low flying Kiowa's miraculously survived the artillery barrage, even if two were forced to land. They were so badly damaged they'd probably have to be blown in place. Almost 200 men dead or seriously wounded in just half an hour.

Every building around the intersection was either flattened or burning. Despite the damp air, a wildfire raged nearby. It would eventually consume hundreds of homes, since no fire departments would operate around here for days. One of the overpass spans had even collapsed and they would still be discovering bodies from both sides for hours. With the damage suffered to the Cav unit, this would be their first and last combat operation of the campaign. But this peg jammed into this grid square. Whatever that was worth.

***
North Florida

Along a 50 mile front, the same scenes were being played out. In order to satisfy the general's desire to flush out the enemy as quickly as possible, the brigades split into individual battalions and, in some cases, operated independently down to the company level. That strategy sure covered a lot of ground astonishingly fast, but was the worst way to meet a concentrated, mobile enemy.

Despite being outnumbered almost 3 to 1 on paper, the consolidated Floridian Minuteman Brigade usually achieved the numerical edge in any given tactical engagement. A platoon wiped out here, a company ground down there–it all adds up.

Now, the various federal leaders soon recognized the self-made trap they stumbled themselves into–they were pros. But it took time, way too much time, to extract and consolidate their far flung forces. Disabled vehicles had to be towed or blown in place. Wounded had to be cared for and a hundred other non-combat related chores needed attention. One federal chess piece after another was chewed up piecemeal and rendered combat ineffective by an enemy they, in theory, outnumbered and should have been able to steamroll by lunch.

The only thing worse than their small elements blindly rushing into the enemy's waiting concentrations of troops and tanks was the enemy's huge artillery park. In addition to their known brigade of self-propelled howitzers, these Floridians somehow pulled a bunch of 122mm artillery pieces out of their asses. The field of guns had been spotted by air hours ago, but there was little that could be done, at first. In a modern war, the 36 old towed D-30 artillery pieces should have been considered obsolete.

Survivability of howitzers in the age of aircraft and artillery spotting radar is a factor of how quickly those guns could be moved. Official doctrine called for a "shoot and scoot" strategy. Rarely would they fire more than three volleys from the same place. By all rights, the slow moving Cold War relics should have been effortlessly removed from the equation.

However, in yet another case of the government's penchant for inflicting self-injury, the two primary tools for dealing with such sprawling artillery parks were not allowed in theatre. Long range MLRS and/or air dropped cluster bombs were the best ways of sanitizing large areas of poorly protected targets. Both weapons were considered too dangerous to civilians and were consequently banned from the operation.

Even more conventional aerial bombing was forbidden. The guns were conveniently located in zones the Feds labeled "Restricted

Fire Areas." Those RFA map overlays blanketed large swaths of built up civilian areas where only direct fire weapons could be used. The Army always practices safe war.

Never mind that the local police already forcibly evacuated bystanders from the area, or that the weapons stuck out like sore thumbs in these suburban neighborhoods. No one in the White House or Pentagon was willing to allow wanton destruction of civilian American property. An easy decision to make, if you're far away from the howitzers and their constant rain of death.

The Feds were intentionally fighting with one hand tied behind their backs. Much to the soldiers' frustration, the rebels apparently never got a similar memo. They appeared to be fighting for keeps. As soon as the FDF noticed the Army spreading itself thin, they threw anything and everything they had, or could buy, borrow or steal at the enemy. Unlike the Feds, they fought with little regard for civilian casualties. Everyone had a chance to get out of the battle zone already. With their back against the ocean, they couldn't afford such niceties.

The only thing not working in the rebels' favor was their own side. In addition to the quasi-regular militia forces they funded, at various times and places thousands of other self-organized irregulars would show up to join the fight…not always on the side of Florida. Even when they were fighting against the Feds, their amateurishness and lack of oversight usually caused more harm than good. Some armed gangs also tried to take advantage of the confusion. Random attacks on their rear area convoys and the need for extra security guaranteed the FDF would not be able to complete their hoped for encirclement.

*

Keystone Heights, Florida

Of course, the going wasn't so easy for all the defenders. The Feds were, on at least one occasion, able to rapidly consolidate their scattered units in order to surround a larger rebel force. That was the catastrophe recently promoted Corporal Donaldson found himself stuck in the middle of. As Florida's first "war hero," he was one of the few regular soldiers assigned to the recently raised Minuteman battalions. Only a corporal, but he found himself the de facto first sergeant of Charlie Company, 3rd Minuteman battalion. An honor originally exciting, but now one he desperately wished he never accepted.

Things went great, at first, as disasters usually go. His mechanized infantry battalion stuck together and managed to slaughter one enemy scout platoon or company element after another. That success far exceeded their wildest dreams about simply repelling the invaders, but it also helped make them reckless. Their excited battalion commander pursued the enemy far too intensely. As if he could somehow whip the whole Army singlehandedly.

He ignored the carefully crafted strategy of bleeding the enemy dry. In his wild hunt for more low hanging fruit, he wound up getting the whole battalion surrounded and trapped in some sleepy little town east of Gainesville. They were in old school Florida; still looked like the frontier days. Donaldson expected to see a cowboy riding a gator at any moment. How many of these ancient locals witnessed the last time Yankees and Rebs squared off?

Worst of all, to Donaldson's admittedly narrow point of view, is that his precious ass needed to be sacrificed to get the battalion out of danger. That was the type of crap people expected from a hero. In the commander's desperation, he decided his best option was to send Donaldson to probe the tightening noose around them, to find a weak link in that lethal chain. Unfortunately, they found one. He half hoped they'd hit a solid wall and be forced to fall back immediately. Then someone else could do this bullshit.

Corporal Donaldson led a crack platoon of...well, anyone willing to follow him. With surprisingly little trouble, the Brads roared through the enemy's dismounts outside of town and kept on going a good mile. The speed with which their IFV's penetrated the thin screen of federal infantrymen, busy fortifying their positions, without drawing a single shot from a heavy weapon buoyed their spirits. No enemy armored vehicles in sight. Donaldson decided to turn around and retrace their steps, killing anything in the way. He fantasized about rolling back into the rebel command post and leading the charge out of the enemy's eggshell thin perimeter.

They burst right through the enemy's line, alright, but they soon found out it was just the first of many. The second pass through the enemy went differently. Half a mile short of friendly positions he heard a double *whoosh, whoosh* as he rode with his head out of the turret. Even 50 meters back, he felt the mild concussion as two AT-4's ripped into his lead Bradley.

He had a great gunner, thank God. While Donaldson hesitated, he laid the coax machine gun on the source of the smoke trails and suppressed the hell out of them. Some other vehicle's gunner hit another unseen enemy rocket man just as he squeezed a third anti-tank rocket off towards Donaldson's track. Being shot at the same time you're firing tends to throw off your aim a little. Donaldson felt the heat on his face as the rocket missed his turret by two feet and kept on flying.

The close call snapped him out of his dithering. Time to nut up and do something.

"Dismount! Action, right!" Donaldson left his capable crew to handle the vehicle while he dived out the back ramp to fight with his men. He wasn't a great leader, he was way too junior for his post, but he had one fundamental down–always lead from the front. That alone made him at least an okay leader. When he was on the street he waved at his dismounts and gave that old, magic infantry motto: "Follow me!"

As he plunged headlong into the thick pine woods along the road, he didn't look back to see what they were doing. No need to, everyone was behind him. They jogged in a loose skirmish line for about two hundred meters before he called a halt. Taking only a few seconds to determine that his rapid firing vehicles back on the street still seemed to have the enemy pinned down, he organized the men around him.

They bounded towards the enemy dismounts, which, judging from sound, were probably still 400-500 meters ahead. By an incredible stroke of luck, Donaldson and his men somehow surprised the enemy. Just a few minutes more and they'd pay. He only had 3 fire teams–12 men total, but showing up uninvited on the enemy's flank is always a "force multiplier."

They were just about to make contact when a series of explosions back on the street shoved Donaldson's stomach into his throat. Through the trees, he couldn't see anything. He tried to raise any of the crews on the radio. You didn't have to be fucking Napoleon to realize that without a base of fire, a flanking attack against an enemy of unknown size is a mistake. Blessedly still unnoticed by the enemy, he called back his guys.

The mission, his mission, was a failure. To his credit, Donaldson adapted to the situation pretty quickly and without too much self-recrimination. He wasn't an officer; he didn't try to salvage his reputation with unnecessary aggressiveness. He did the best he could to sidestep the enemy and slowly work their way back to friendly lines. About 10 minutes later, friendly's made it to them.

You can imagine his delirious relief to hear a Brad clanking in from the north. He ordered the survivors of his unit to hold their position while he hopped out of the bushes to welcome their reinforcements. He slowed just as he emerged from the tree line and saw the smoke column up the road marking the remains of his unit. The guilt and shame of losing most of his platoon so easily slowed him down. He paused to light a smoke and shake the shame off.

The federal troops in the track a few feet away were curious as hell who this new dude was. Not one of their guys. All their dismounts had taken off in the other direction. You had to be careful since the enemy wore the exact same uniforms and, for the first time in over 150 years, spoke the same language. Well, anyone that's shouldering his weapon can't be that much of a threat.

The flick of his cigarette lighter finally calmed the crew down and made the gunner relax his grip on the coax machine gun. Who would attack them with a cigarette in hand? The battlefield here happened to sit exactly on the boundary between 3 separate companies, so there were a lot of friendly strangers running about. The track's commander dropped down into the cabin to open the rear ramp and meet the new fellow.

Donaldson was pleased to see a regular guard platoon leader when he slipped through the ramp door. Thank God, their main body must have finally linked up with them. That meant his mission was no longer needed. He excitedly explained where the rest of his unit was hiding and what little he knew about the enemy's location. Donaldson idly wondered why the guy looked so confused.

If it was strange how the LT's eyes widened when he looked closely at the unit insignia on Donaldson's shoulder, it was downright insane when he whipped out his 9mm. The frightened corporal grabbed the man's gun hand while telling him to calm down and take a breath. There was no reason to worry. It will all be over soon. The LT was, by this point, freaking the hell out. He fired fast and wild at this rebel psychopath who'd infiltrated his track and wanted him to calmly accept death.

Donaldson fell to the floor with this shooting nutjob on top of him. The LT's body, while doing everything it could to kill him saved his life by shielding him. Blasting away with a high velocity weapon inside of a sealed metal container is a dangerous game. Each of the dozen rounds ricocheted multiple times off the deck or ceiling. Donaldson couldn't hear when the rattling finally ended. It would be several minutes before his ringing ears would stop hurting and any sound came back. He only noticed it was over when the guy on top of him mostly stopped moving.

Shoving the twitching body away, he wound up puking into the cavity that used to be the back of the LT's head. The sight of so much vomit mixed with brains and blood only made him heave harder. He spun around to take his eyes off that horror, only to see the driver's cleaved open face grinning back at him. The poor bastard must've crawled into the crew compartment to see what all the fuss was about. Dry heaving by this point, Donaldson dashed up the turret to try and get some fresh air.

The gunner's riddled body blocked his way. The poor guy had taken his IBA off to move more freely about the cramped turret. Sitting behind several inches of sloped armor, he must've felt pretty safe. The gunner died so fast he barely had time to regret that call. The man's body slouched over both the fire control switch and turret traverse lever in that tightly packed turret compartment. Donaldson didn't need to hear anything in order to feel the 25mm auto cannon blasting away uncontrollably. He yanked the gunner off the controls and finally got his head out of that hellhole.

And right into a new hellscape. The other three tracks in the platoon were shredded. They had taken up firing positions in a rough circle around their commander and weren't ready for their own platoon leader to open fire on them. Not one member of the other crews managed to get out of the flaming death traps in time. The shocked dismounted survivors were being mopped up by the rest of Donaldson's men.

Donaldson's previously dejected troops could not have been more gung ho and motivated after an example like that. Watching their skinny young leader calmly waltz into the mist of the enemy, fucking cigarette in hand, slaughter an entire track's crew and then wipe out the rest of the platoon's vehicles singlehandedly was the most badass, Audie Murphy style shit they'd ever seen. They weren't just going to sit back and watch–they wanted a piece of the action.

For his part, Donaldson still didn't know what the hell was going on. It was hard to wrap his mind around the idea that some of his brothers in arms could turn traitor. He didn't mention it when he grabbed the radio mike, though. Who would believe him? Instead, he called for fire support on a large enemy force moving towards them from the south. He switched the radio to preset channel 4, which was his battalion command frequency. As luck would have it, on the captured federal radio, those settings happened to be the Fires net…the direct line to the artillery.

Several miles away a thoroughly confused fire direction center busily plotted a fire mission. The terrified young soldier calling for support was using an unknown radio call sign and had an odd reference point to the target. But the map had these particular grid coordinates free of friendly forces at the moment.

Since the Department of Defense had temporarily shut off the GPS network just a few minutes ago, to deny its access to these surprisingly high-tech rebels, the artillery were forced to rely on more old fashioned methods to keep track of friendly forces. In this swirling, running fight even a few minutes delay in updating a unit's location could falsely show a unit miles from its real position.

In normal circumstances, they would have double checked with the appropriate battalion headquarters. But these were far from routine times. Besides, the artillerymen weren't immune to the desire for action. This unknown unit was one of the few in range to receive fire support. The chance to save a platoon about to be overrun by this surprise enemy force was overpowering. The mission was approved and rounds flew downrange in record time.

Needless to say, with the federal artillery busy shelling their own side, the Florida breakout went relatively smoothly. A perplexed

Corporal Donaldson received the first battlefield commission since Vietnam on the spot by his grateful colonel.

*

I-75, just north of Gainesville

By modern standards 1st Brigade stuck together like a phalanx down I-75. They left most of the cumbersome support train back at FOB Lake City, but even this "light" force still consisted of over 500 tracked and wheeled vehicles loaded with more than 2,000 men. All rolling down a single interstate. The convoy sprawled out easily 5 miles, even when taking up both north and southbound lanes and the median. Sometimes less than 4 miles spacing, if the lead elements were forced to stop.

Which happened practically every other mile. One ragtag militia group or another tried blocking the way or sniped from the side of the road. Quick problems to deal with, but they paused the entire advance each time. Though not all at once. When the lead elements suddenly halted the column to clear whatever ineffective resistance the militias threw up the rear kept going. They were too far back to even hear the firing ahead. This miles long accordion effect was as dangerous as it was hilarious.

The danger didn't come from the constant hit and run attacks. Only one soldier had been slightly wounded in nearly 2 hours of stop and go fighting. Whereas the Feds recovered dozens of militia bodies. They might not be able to pin the enemy down into a big standup fight, but at the rate they were bleeding them dry, there wouldn't be anyone left to fight in Orlando.

Not that the Army hadn't swooped up a surprising number of prisoners, but that only slowed them down further. It sure didn't provide much useful intelligence. Some of these combatants weren't even from Florida. Much less have a clue where the FDF main body lurked. A few didn't even know they were firing at federal forces; thought they were rebels. What a clusterfuck.

1st Brigade learned a hard lesson from the 2nd and 3rd Brigades' messes. They wouldn't scatter themselves in small units across half the state. No, far better to stay a giant armored steam roller flattening anything that dared to get in the way. A ferocious, invincible desert tan camouflaged can of whoopass just waiting to be opened.

Their aircraft above finally reported something of real intelligence value. Florida's only fully professional brigade wasn't 60 miles further south racing to get to Gainesville ahead of the Feds. Apparently they were already inside and waiting. The Fed commander relaxed at the news. He was never pleased with the great plan to merely pin down the enemy. His force had the edge and he ached to use it. Their brigade was a bit larger, armed with the latest equipment and their men better trained. Unfortunately for the government troops, the rebels knew a few ways to exploit a compacted target. Terrible ways that do wonders at leveling the odds.

On the outskirts of Gainesville the fighting seemed to die down. This far south, well outside the carefully defined "battle zone" the police evacuated, large crowds lined the streets to enjoy the show. Some waved signs welcoming the Army and others suggested less pleasant ideas. The random sign plugged some local fast food joint or end of the world religious message. Quite a few people brought picnic blankets and beer coolers.

All and all, it seemed like a pretty normal 4th of July parade. Except that these weren't ageing Korean and Vietnam era vets. The alert and fit young men, reeking of oil and gun smoke, were better suited to a movie than a small town patriotic fair. That's what attracted the crowds in the first place. And that's what disappointed them when nothing happened.

Then, exactly like a film, the "building context" lull in the story ended and the action began. It was sad, but not surprising, that those civilians with the best view of the show were the first to die. Had the strike been guided by a live observer seeing all these bystanders, then it likely would have been called off.

Fortunately for the FNG, but unfortunately for the civilians, the whole thing had been preplanned on a map. No chance to stop the inevitable. Half a minute earlier and 20 miles deeper south, a battalion of rebel HIMARS artillery rippled off their entire arsenal of 108 GPS-guided rockets. Each of these telephone poles carried 404 DPICM sub munitions.

The computer controlled distribution pattern ensured almost all of the 40,577 bomblets blanketed a front only 100 yards wide and nearly 4 miles deep. Even after the 7% dud rate, which was twice as high as the supplier claimed, one bomb still exploded every 5 square yards.

Each little cylinder contained an embedded shaped charge warhead. When it struck the thin roof of a vehicle, the small bomb detonated in a fashion that sent 65% of its explosive energy in a narrow downward cone straight into the engine compartment. Or, as was too often the case, the packed crew compartment. If one failed to strike a vehicle and hit open pavement or grass instead, the devil's firecracker bounced back up to waist height before exploding–sending shrapnel in all directions.

For those civilians either fortunate or foresighted enough to watch from a safe distance, the entire column disappeared in a never ending popcorn string of explosions and smoke. Witnessing such a large force seemingly annihilated in seconds was so far beyond their level of comprehension as to be biblical. Most simply fled as fast they could.

Explosions tend to pump out huge clouds of smoke several times larger in diameter than the blast itself. Hence the perceived devastation is always so much worse than the reality. As the wind cleaned the air a bit, it was clear that the majority of the unit survived in good shape. The soldiers might have been shaken, but drill and discipline stood in for morale well enough. Perhaps a quarter of the unit just died or were seriously wounded. A third of their vehicles were now smoldering hulks or at least immobilized, but the brigade reacted as if this happened all the time. That discipline prevented complete annihilation.

Lining up in column formation might be the quickest way to move a large force around, but it's the worst way for a large force to fight. As the FNG advanced in a long crescent, most of their weapons could concentrate on just the tiny forward section of the enemy's Conga line. Conversely, only a fraction of the other federal fighting power could hit back at any given time. Whether an ancient Greek phalanx or a modern armored force, that was a wet dream for one side and a horror for the other.

The Florida brigade slowly encircling and devastating them was primarily a Guard force, but they were backed up by a single Minutemen armor company. Working side by side with the active duty guys motivated these ex-military types. Earning the respect of your peers is as great an inspiration in the heat of battle as patriotism.

The rebel track commander grinned like a wolf as his swift loader shouted "Up!" and his skilled gunner hollered "away" barely a second later. They were a damn good team already. Less than 5 seconds after he ID'd their slow moving Feddy counterpart as a target, his boys sent a sabot round on its way.

And what a way it went. Almost as soon as the shell blasted out the 120mm barrel the round split apart. The plastic sabot shoe allowing it to fit inside the big gun spun off and left only a tiny depleted uranium penetrator hurtling towards some tan spec in the distance. That little rod aiming to kill a hulking main battle tank was barely an inch in diameter and 31 in length. In this case, size really didn't matter.

Kinetic energy, or killing power, is a result of mass times velocity squared. With the smallest possible surface area to reduce friction and molded from the densest alloys known to man, this was the most advanced spear imaginable. Thousands of years of chemistry and physics focused on improving the human lot were on terrible display in this "silver bullet."

The tank's expensive fire control computer augmented the gunner's skill. His shot led the target vehicle perfectly. The thin penetrator struck the crawling enemy Abrams over 2,000 yards away dead center in the side of the turret…at 5,700 feet per second. At that speed, the kinetic energy easily dwarfed the explosive warhead of an anti-tank missile. By the time the non-explosive munition worked its way through the tank's nearly 1 ½ feet of laminated armor and breached the crew compartment the rod was coming apart. Which was fine, since the kill had already been made.

The dart didn't just disintegrate into ordinary shrapnel. Heated depleted uranium burns when exposed to oxygen, much like magnesium. Essentially napalmed shrapnel. As if that wasn't nasty enough, hundreds of white-hot shards from the tank's armor also shot inside as well. The interior anti-spalling Kevlar lining helped keep all these burning splinters from ricocheting…but only after they ripped through flesh and bone.

The driver, alone in a separate sealed compartment, made it out without a scratch on him. Instead of running from the burning track, as normal people would do, he did what a soldier does. He clambered onto the smoking turret, tore open a hot hatch and hauled the barely breathing loader out.

As an extra safety design feature, the Abram's cannon rounds are stored in a separate compartment at the rear of the turret. In the event of an explosion, the compartment was designed to funnel the blast up and away from the vehicle and crew. A useful feature…if you're inside. The driver had just dragged his buddy out the hatch when the fire reached the ammo closet and the world ended under his feet.

Above them, a company of 6 armored Apache gunships, each dangling 16 Hellfire missiles and packing 30mm automatic cannons, picked their targets from the rebel smorgasbord. Time to level the playing field. The crews didn't know they themselves were targets until three disintegrated in a blaze of glory. The rest scattered and would be recalled back to base without ever firing a shot.

Even higher up, a pair of Florida Reserve F-16's, equipped with their cutting-edge look down, shoot down radars rippled off Sidewinder missiles at the defenseless helicopters below. The choppers weren't their primary mission. They slaughtered the Apaches en passé, without even deviating from their assigned objectives. These $18 million ultra-advanced, Terminator-style frightful killing machines were simply "targets of opportunity" to the enemy's air force. Casually swatted out of the skies like so many mosquitoes.

*

Sunny Skies over Florida

Across several hundred square miles of sky above, dozens of federal and National Guard aircraft duked it out for air superiority. More streaked in low and fast, each trying to drop several tons of high-tech, high-explosive ordinance on the poor damn ants below. Florida's surprisingly large and advanced network of ground based anti-aircraft weapons also began showing its full strength.

To make matters worse, in order to limit unnecessary losses, the Air Force's protective screen of fighter aircraft had long since been scaled back to a bare minimum. It seemed a logical precaution, since all of Florida's combat aircraft were successfully neutralized in the opening air strikes.

The first sign that the Feds' intel was less than accurate were several volleys of long-range AMRAAM missiles slamming into their scattered Combat Air Patrols. Apparently, the enemy dispersed their aircraft far better than expected. The rebel's victory wasn't cheap, but presently the Guard's surviving F-15's secured local air supremacy. It might be short lived, since more Fed fighters were scrambling from Georgia and even some of the recently "liberated" air bases in Florida, but the next hour would be hell on the defenseless federal soldiers below.

For the first time since World War II, a large American ground force lay naked to enemy aerial bombardment without a single friendly fighter around. They didn't even have much in the way of anti-aircraft weapons, since most of the division's air defense assets were busy fighting for their lives up north. The rebels made the best use of this short term advantage despite their limited resources.

This aerial counterattack involved more than just the Reserve squadron of F-16's dropping cluster munitions on any clump of vehicles they could find. It was even more intense than the battalion of AH-64's fanning out into pairs and providing direct fire support to units in contact. General Cooper, whether from luck or an uncanny feeling of the battle, shoved everything that could fly into the fight at the exact moment the enemy's advance ran low on steam.

One slightly modified Florida C-130 even tried its hand at carpet bombing. Unfortunately for everyone concerned, they were never given an opportunity to practice the mission beforehand. All 40 five hundred pound, unguided bombs rolled off the transport's back ramp at far too high an altitude. They did nearly as much damage to the retreating guardsmen as to the federal infantry battalion close on their heels. Still, the shock value of encountering a threat not seen in generations threw the Army, to put it mildly, off stride.

What started out as a vast race had long since devolved into a grinding, running slugfest. After the shocks from the air, even that trickle of momentum faded fast. General McDowell's grand plan was shattered as hopelessly as the morale of his scattered soldiers.

It is difficult to envisage the vast space modern mechanized battles take place in. Between elaborate communications systems and seemingly endless numbers of fast vehicles, small units today can effectively cover an area so large that one platoon could not even hear the shots of their brother platoon.

A single brigade in the Civil War might've barely occupied a mile long front when deployed for battle. Even unopposed, they'd be lucky to march 20 miles a day. This 21st century version here in Florida effortlessly strung themselves out over 50 square miles and advanced in just half an hour over what their ancestors covered in a day. The flipside to this breathtaking capability is the short reaction time leaders have to avert disasters.

While the astonished command staff up in Lake City hastily reconciled this surreal turn of events with their fantasies and tried to whip up a new plan on the fly, things only got worse. The more the situation worsened, the narrower their tunnel vision became. From general to lowest clerk, their attention was fully tuned to untangling the forward units and bringing their exposed support assets under the air defense umbrella at FOB Lake City.

The Air Force's steady warnings about a significant militia force advancing from the east towards that same logistics center and their own command post weren't taken too seriously. Only with the enemy minutes from town did anyone react. Finally, the division's command staff absentmindedly deployed their only reserve battalion to screen their exposed flank and deal with this nuisance while the big brains focused on the "real war."

Chapter 8
20 miles NE of Lake City

1-6 Infantry Task Force raced east along Interstate 10. Racing, by the standards of armored vehicles, meant a convoy speed of 45 mph. Even at that breathtaking pace, they were less than 15 minutes away from the I-10/US 90 junction. Once they could occupy the intersection they'd cut off those small, retreating Guard units coming from Jacksonville and annihilate the militiamen pouring in from the coast. And slaughter they would–they were loaded for bear.

Even running in both directions of travel the unit couldn't be all seen at once. The 30 M2 Bradley IFV's, 14 M1 Abrams tanks, dozen M113's, including a mortar platoon and 20 some odd trucks and Humvees bringing up the rear were still spread out over a mile. It was an impressive site to behold. And beheld it was.

As soon as the battalion entered the bottleneck of the Osceola National Forest, a series of spotters began making cell phone calls. The most lethal of which came from a forward air controller perched in a forestry fire watch tower. Without even setting down his cappuccino– Starbucks, not instant, he wasn't in the fucking Army–he ran the prey's speed and location through his hand held computer. With a few short code words over his radio he ordered death as casually as regular people order a pizza.

Fifteen miles further east, an assortment of 16 prop-driven Cessna's cruised at tree top height. They resignedly acknowledged the targeting information and began climbing as fast as mechanically possible. Each had been hastily modified to carry and fire, with somewhat reasonable accuracy, 4 Hellfire antitank missiles.

These top of the line and hideously expensive missiles, as well as their targeting accessories, were in plentiful supply thanks to the politicians. When the governor requisitioned the large stock of advanced ordinance at the sprawling Lockheed Martin complex in Ocala, Florida business leaders screamed murder. They were happy to contribute to Dimone's campaign, but that sense of civic mindedness disappeared when real sacrifice was required.

Appropriate aircraft were also ubiquitous in a state full of retirees with plenty of time and hobby money. The only things in short supply were pilots willing to fly them. Donating your insured plane to "The Cause" was one thing. Risking your precious, irreplaceable ass something else entirely.

All things considered, these sixteen reasonably competent and mostly sober pilots were an impressive turn out for such a Hail Mary endeavor. Unknown to them, their "suicide mission" became a lot safer even as they popped into radar detectable height and braced for enemy jets to pounce them.

A hundred miles north, the Feds' E-3 AWACS, watching for just such low altitude threats, shut off its powerful radar and dived for the deck–a pair of long range, PAC-2 surface-to-air missiles closing fast on its tail. The giant radar plane had been circling a few miles inside the Georgia border and over watching all of North Florida. No one on the planning staff ever expected some clever NG Patriot missile unit would be so far forward deployed.

The Patriot battery crew on the ground, cut off by the speed of the federal advance and temporarily forgotten by their command, didn't wait to see if the plane and its 22 person crew survived. They packed up immediately, but it was too late. Both the plane and missile crew were already dead despite their desperate attempts to escape. An orbiting fighter spotted the outgoing smoke trail and let rip a HARM missile at the source. The pilot howled when he received permission to follow up his strike with a regular bombing run on the first call. Without the big "eye in the sky" giving him directions, he never saw the real threat below him.

The Cessna armada leveled off roughly parallel with the interstate. Impressively, the amateurs kept a tight formation. The crudely fashioned targeting displays in their cockpits didn't allow for much manual selection. All they could do was point the mini radar in the approximate direction of the mass of targets 4 miles west and 5,000 feet below. With the help of some last minute adjustments from the ground spotter network they rippled off their payloads. Praying that the $100,000 fire and forget missiles had at least some targets within their narrow engagement envelope.

None of the vehicles barreling down the highway noticed the barrage. The barrage of smoke trails blazed only a kilometer away before the first soldiers noticed. A few quick thinkers popped their automatic smoke grenade launchers, hoping to blind the weapons' sensors. That saved a few lives, but there wasn't time to do much about the supersonic missiles homing in on them. Most of the crews never knew what hit them.

None of the giant, 72 ton main battle tanks leading the formation were hit. They all had "low profile" heat kits installed, making their thermal signature drastically smaller. To the mindless heat seeking warheads, they represented a much less inviting target than, say, the Bradley fighting vehicles packed with helpless infantrymen behind them.

A couple of missiles misfired and failed to even launch from the makeshift racks. Nearly half that launched failed to find a target and, of those that did find some prey, several rocked the same vehicle. Nevertheless, the strike utterly destroyed 16 random Bradley's in seconds. 140 men killed or seriously injured without ever knowing what hit them. With far more luck than the rebels had hoped for, both the battalion commander's vehicle and the executive officer's track were shredded as well.

Most of the task force halted and dispersed as much as possible along the road while trying to extract the wounded from the burning, twisted death traps. A 26 year old company commander now found himself in complete command of the battalion with far from complete information. He pushed his scout platoon ahead, backed up by the tank company, while he tried to reorganize the shattered core of his unit.

The advance party encountered the first roadblock only a couple miles short of the objective. Local police and armed civilian volunteers laid down an impressive volume of small arms fire on the lightly armored scout Humvees, but quickly lost their nerve with the first blast from a tank. They scattered so fast the soldiers believed it had to be some type of trick, part of some larger ambush strategy.

The tanks were unwilling to leave the open road without infantry support and were convinced the road ahead was mined or otherwise somehow a death sentence. There was just way too much strangeness happening today. They took up a defensive posture against the unknown and radioed higher for guidance.

The young captain turned battalion commander received the report just after having his second request for air support denied, or delayed as some staff officer said. Apparently, the poor Air Force was spread a little too thin and stressed out. Helicopter support was likewise out of the question until air superiority could be reestablished. Far too many whirly birds had already been blasted out of the sky by the surprising resurgence of Florida aircraft.

The boss weighed his options. Either take the objective by driving forward into a likely dug-in enemy of unknown strength or follow the book by breaking contact, rallying in a safe area and coming back with overwhelming strength. He made up his mind when someone shouted "incoming." A pair of stretcher bearers nearby, and their wounded cargo, disappeared in a cloud of flame and smoke. The whole task force broke contact by companies while the mortar platoon thumped out a smoke screen to make life harder for the enemy artillery spotters.

Less than 10 miles away at the targeted road junction a river of rebel reinforcements poured into Lake City unmolested from the east. Two armed civilian "regiments" and a few light National Guard/Reservist companies suddenly entered the equation just when the Feds thought they had it solved.

To be fair, thousands of refugees headed in both directions along the highway, but those semi-organized militia regiments were clearly visible. Miles above them a pair of FA-18's, loaded down with precision laser and satellite guided munitions, circled and reported all they could see. What was so clear to them was not so self-evident to the senior officers many miles away. To give the order to engage and risk killing innocent civilians–American civilians–was a responsibility none were willing to shoulder.

The US military had always been sensitive to civilian casualties, but previously were willing to accept the losses if they took reasonable efforts to mitigate the risk. This would be the first time they would let humanism cripple combat operations. The sad thing was, even this hesitancy, this acceptance of higher military losses in exchange for protecting noncombatants, wouldn't save civilians from having the brutality of war dumped on them.

*

East side of Lake City

Jessica wasn't nearly as excited as her editor. The first armed confrontation between two state National Guard forces since the Civil War might make for exciting TV, but she thought it was a distraction from the real story. Unfortunately, her interviewee didn't agree. Congressman Alfred Eliot was fired up about seeing "the rebels brought to justice" first hand.

So, like a true professional, she ignored her better judgment and accepted his invitation to ride along with him. Representative Eliot was not only one of the president's most vocal supporters in the current crisis, but also an ardent proponent of congressional oversight in military affairs.

"Oversight" was the quote, but Jessica thought harassment might be a better term. He spent the whole day tying up officers with endless questions and accusations. Whenever he came across a military unit standing still he felt compelled to motivate them.

"Onward to Miami!" was his passionate, sound bite friendly rallying cry for every professional soldier just trying to do their job. He wasn't the only camp follower around, but out of the thousands of politicians, celebrities, activists of every stripe and ambulance-chaser lawyers tagging along with the Army, he stood unrivaled in assholery.

Annoying or not, he did possess an uncanny sixth sense for where the action would come from. With all the major fighting further south he seemed to be the only person, in or out of uniform, worried about the mixed Florida Guard and paramilitary force coming from the coast.

The staff at the forward command post, far more interested in the surprisingly stiff resistance encountered by the main body, gently kicked him out. They were all so confident that the Georgia Guard, backed up by US airpower and the bulk of the division's artillery stationed in town, could deal with this rag-tag flank attack.

Congressman Eliot was no military genius, but he did have a politician's uncanny ability to sense weakness and…opportunity. Historic weaknesses and photogenic opportunities. So, with every reporter he could find in tow, he set off for the Georgia command post, wondering the whole way if he could talk one of the soldiers into giving him a gun. No, no. A gun might offend some of his constituents. Did they have an American flag somewhere?

Jessica busied herself by noting down other opportunities on her IPad. She viewed the whole endeavor as ridiculous. Borderline insane, even. Sending 50,000 troops to capture a handful of hotheads seemed the most wasteful and dangerous folly she'd ever seen. And she'd been covering Wall Street scandals and repeated taxpayer funded bailouts for years. Didn't the Brits try something similar way back when? It didn't turn out so well for them.

From the few prisoners and locals she'd gotten a chance to talk to, not one considered themselves a "rebel." They all felt their back was against the wall and had no choice but to defend themselves. They were under attack by the mad president and power hungry Washington elites. How many of these combatants would just go home if the Army did? Half, for sure. Maybe most.

Of course, that's not what her editor wanted to hear. She wrote several variations on that same story, only to find each one rejected. An hour of raw interview footage with dejected militia detainees and confused farmers was edited down to 60 seconds of defiant sound bites. He even ignored the strategy session she was allowed to sit in on and secretly recorded.

Jessica thought the exclusive recording was cutting edge insight into the professionalism and methodology of the Army in pursuing an irrational objective while doing everything possible to avoid civilian casualties. However, the only snippet that showed up on the air was some general's cliché motivational parting remark after the meeting: "Give 'em hell!"

She could understand the competition, even if disgusted by it. The battlefield was crawling with reporters as if a tornado had struck a celebrity murder trial across from the Super Bowl while the Pope was visiting. Once upon a time, that meant to stand out a network had to provide deeper context and analysis than the competition. Nowadays, just shock value alone could hold the channel servers in place. With so much money at stake in corporate news the truth is the first to be downsized.

Even with the gravity of the situation, she couldn't help but smile when they got to Wal-Mart. Or the forward operating base of the Georgia National Guard Task Force as they called it at the moment.

Far from feeling like being occupied, the soldiers were the ones surrounded. Their mini-encampment in the parking lot was ringed by menacing razor wire to keep out most of the protestors and camera wielding gawkers besieging them. It was just dandy that the congressman had a stressed out security detail to keep the crowd at bay while searching for a way into the perimeter. Jessica didn't have such support.

During that short hike to the gate someone spilled a beer on her, another thoroughly lost reporter tried to interview her and someone else shoved a religious pamphlet in her hand while screaming about the Lord's wrath. The cameraman on her hip bought a burrito, hit someone trying to pick his pocket and got flashed by a drunk girl who thought the camera was running. Except for the armored vehicles, a pretty typical Saturday night at Wal-Mart.

The atmosphere in the camp was quieter, but not for the reasons she expected. Four camouflaged men and a skinny, shirtless man knelt zip-cuffed in front of the headquarters tent. A steaming colonel just finished some little speech as the congressman approached. Jessica's cameraman had his own quick instincts. He started filming with a wide lens but left it dangling at his side. Without a sideways glance, the colonel drew his sidearm and shot the cuffed and half-naked civilian through his right temple.

Representative Eliot's gut wrenched and he skidded to a stop. Not from the sight of the gore, but from the realization he personally might have been caught in any camera shot. He relaxed a little when it was clear that the only camera around wasn't recording. He waved for his security men to holster their weapons and began browbeating the colonel without introductions. "Who the hell do you think you are? Your orders are clear that no one will be executed under any circumstances! This is still the land of the free!"

He lost his righteous indignation when he remembered no one was filming. "Shit, Major or Colonel, whatever. Do you know how bad it looks if we start killing these hillbillies out of hand?" The cameraman raced off unnoticed back to the van to upload this soon to be Pulitzer Prize winning "rebel execution" picture.

The colonel finally stopped glaring at the body and holstered his weapon. He spoke as much to the soldiers crowding around as to the politician. "That was no rebel. We caught this meth head trying to pilferage our medical supplies. He scammed his way into the triage tent and stabbed one of my men in the neck when they surprised him stealing morphine. No, gentlemen, this wasn't an execution. That was justice."

He crossed his arms and stared down at the uniformed prisoners. "I wish I could do the same to you. I never expected that my own men would try to sabotage our mortars and then desert. That's worse than cowardice in the face of the enemy, in my book. You all are a disgrace to the uniform you wear and I will personally see to it that you spend the rest of your lives in Leavenworth!"

Inside the command tent his young radioman couldn't see or hear all the details going on outside. He knew several guys had been caught trying to desert or something–the rumors varied. The colonel had stormed off to chew them out while muttering something about mutiny. The gunshot crystallized everything. He wasn't one of those soldiers that hated this mission and joked they were fighting against the wrong side. It didn't matter either way. He tried to stay a professional just doing a job. He genuinely believed in the Old Man. His faith in the boss was unshakeable. Or so he thought.

No one in Florida had ever shot at him, but now his own commander was killing fellow Georgians. Not that there was anything he could do about it. His job was to man this radio and document the reports received. Or perhaps even make a report of his own…

What the colonel regarded as an isolated case of sedition was a rampant disease throughout his unit. Georgians, like most Southerners, were fiercely patriotic. Proclaiming loyalty to your country is easy. Even traveling far overseas to fight other people that hate your land is fairly straightforward for a proud Southern man. To follow an order to kill your cultural kin, and in several cases throughout this South Georgia based battalion, your actual kin, just to show loyalty to a regime a thousand miles away was a different story.

Peer pressure, as much as professionalism, kept the guardsmen in their hasty fighting positions. Now, when that peer pressure turned the other way things got ugly. Some condescending report from the Tactical Operations Center that the colonel had executed a deserter and would do the same to anyone else that failed to carry out their orders changed the whole dynamic. Perhaps, in the heat of battle, the threat of death from your own side can provide a temporary motivational boost. It has the opposite effect if the men have a little time to contemplate on it.

The colonel's personal assurance a moment later that no troops were executed only made things worse. What the hell is going on at the TOC? Were they lying then or are they lying now? Even the men that defended his draconian approach to discipline were put off by the idea of secretly killing your own men. The whole episode left a dirty taste in everyone's mouth.

What started out as a mild heat of uncertainty in the mission and general lack of faith in their leadership reached fever levels with the news from above. By the time the poorly organized Florida Defense Forces began to breach the town, the entire Georgian's unit cohesion teetered on edge. NCO's had broken up more than one fistfight among the junior enlisted men, even while suspiciously eyeing their own officers.

Individually, or in small groups, the whole Task Force soon decided what side they were on. Sitting in the crosshairs, they didn't have the luxury of sitting on the fence and seeing how things played out. The lines were drawn. The only question was who would make the first move?

Things likely would have calmed down and turned out quite differently if the first contact with the rebels came against a different Georgia element. In one of those fateful little mistakes in history, the advance FNG party missed their planned turn. Instead of entering town along a side road, a path covered by a loyal Georgian officer, who hated the homeland of his ex-wife, and commanding a bunch of troops terrified to cross him, they barreled straight into town along the main boulevard.

The company forming the center of the defensive line across that street was commanded by an officer who went to college at the university down the road in Gainesville and even married a local girl. His first sergeant grew up not too far away and his parents still lived there. Almost all of the men had some connection to their neighbor land. From a favorite fishing hole to a sweetheart, no one wanted to kill anyone here. Those few soldiers who didn't care so much for Florida weren't so passionately opposed as to break with their battle buddies.

The gunner in the lead Florida Humvee laughed when he saw an enemy officer appear from nowhere and wave a white flag. Of course he was badassery personified when leaning back with a MK-19 in his hands, but it couldn't be that easy. He nearly pissed his pants when his truck stopped and he got a better look around him. More than a hundred dug-in men and a dozen camouflaged Bradley's all pointed black barrels his way.

Even after they all stood up, dropped their weapons and shook hands with the Florida guardsmen he couldn't stop shaking. Had he ever come so close, without knowing, to such hidden death before? He hoped he'd never find out.

A half mile away, the Georgian battalion commander shook as well, but for different reasons. In his anger he forgot that not everyone was listening onto the battalion command frequency. So, when he put out a net call order to treat any member of Bravo Company as an enemy combatant, even his supporters were confused. The mortar platoon flat out refused to fire on the company. When the colonel threatened to shoot the platoon leader for treason the battalion sergeant major pistol whipped his commanding officer. *Then* things got confusing.

*

Jessica's cameraman wasn't willing to go anywhere. Hell had broken loose around him. This intentional friendly fire was career making footage. Every sullen prisoner a cash bonus, every shocked death mask a magazine cover. It wasn't just morbid fascination that kept him rooted in the parking lot as partially uniformed amateur militias swarmed over the squabbling Georgians. He was a professional and presented with the opportunity of a lifetime. He wasn't going to abandon this golden perspective into a historic moment over worries about his personal safety.

Congressman Eliot was a lot less concerned with history and much more interested in saving his dear ass. Jessica sensed the real story moving somewhere else and followed closely behind his entourage. She hadn't planned to ride in the SUV with him, but one of his security people shoved her into the backseat out of reflex when stray rounds flew overhead. She didn't even have a chance to object or call back to her cameraman before the driver gunned the engine and the Mercedes peeled away from the chaos.

They swung west on the big highway, only a few seconds ahead of a dozen pickups loaded with whooping rebels. Her story eye noticed the mixture of civilian and military weapons, rudimentary organization and the extra antennae masts on the trucks. All that equipment and semi-professional discipline implied a much higher level of coordination between these "rag tag" mobs the Army joked about and the professional Florida Defense Forces. Coordination implied a plan, and plans were dangerous.

She didn't have long to ponder this threat before she came face to face with a bigger one. Chased by rebels who thought the twin black SUV's were leading the charge, the security crew in the lead vehicle headed straight towards the first clump of friendly soldiers they saw. The combat engineers, busy trying to hastily setup vehicle barricades, were shocked to see the rebels so close already. They were amazed at how quickly the militia turned to insurgent tactics. In line with their training, they took cover and engaged the apparent suicide car bomber.

The guards in the second car, ignoring the frantic congressman in the back, were damn good. The driver didn't flinch when the lead vehicle got Swiss cheesed at close range. He didn't hit the brakes or even try a U-turn. He just dropped to a lower gear, banked gently to the right and shot off the road and out of the kill zone as fast as possible. The turbocharged and under loaded "off-road" vehicle still wasn't able to clear the draining ditch completely. They cracked the muffler and the rear fender flew away, but they squealed the SUV behind some seafood restaurant and out of sight in seconds.

There they briefly paused. The driver jumped out and confirmed the rental car still had a few miles left in it. Probably. The shooting on the other side of the fish joint wasn't getting closer, at least. Of course, any closer and they'd be a target. Time to find a way back to friendly lines, if such a thing still existed. The survivors of the private security detail didn't waste a moment to check on their fallen comrades. Bodyguard work is a nasty business. Their leader sighed and nodded at the driver. He pulled out of the back lot unto a deserted side street in search of a quick way west.

Kadush!

A speeding pickup truck sideswiped them immediately. The security chief wiped some of the blood from his busted nose and hacked at the air bags around him with his always handy blade. His field of vision didn't improve much. Some young guy wearing old fashioned BDUs squirmed on his back on the hood of their car. He kept banging his good arm against the windshield and cussing at them. Someone else stuck his head in the passenger side window. The bill of a camouflaged hat bobbed inches from the guard's face.

"Are you allrig–*pop, pop*!" A pair of 9mm rounds from the stunned and startled security man answered him. Blood and brain matter covered the windshield of the other truck. Someone hopped out of the mangled pickup and fired wildly as soon as his buddy's body fell out of the way. The M16 rounds ripped just as easily through the aluminum door as through the organs of the security guard and driver, before flying out the far side and ricocheting off the pavement.

A hysterical Eliot tried to dive out the other side and run for it. Had he done so, he would have been holed as mercilessly as his bodyguards. Jessica saved his life by jerking him back inside and springing out herself. Her long blonde hair checked the militiamen's trigger fingers.

"Don't shoot! I'm a reporter!" She gave her best camera ready smile. "You just captured a congressman! What unit are you boys with?"

One of the pissed off and confused men opened the back door to find a well-dressed, middle aged fellow fiddling with an American flag lapel like a talisman. He cowered in the corner baby raccoon-style and babbled nonsense at the grinning militiamen. At length, he finally spit out something intelligible. "I'm a Republican too! We're on the same side!"

One of the men posing for pictures turned around. "What the fuck does politics have to with anything?"

*

The militiamen rushing headlong into Lake City and ready for their first taste of combat found exactly what they expected: the enemy falling apart in terror by the ferociousness of their advance. Better than a movie. Most of the Georgians either surrendered or jumped into the rebel's loving arms, turning their weapons on their former brothers when needed. The few holdouts scattered or made hopeless last stands against superior firepower.

The small FNG contingent, with their new found allies, were busy mopping up, consolidating their position and trying to find out where in town the enemy was located. They weren't in any hurry to advance. Except for turning their tiny towed Cuban artillery section and the captured mortars on the small airfield, packed with Army helicopters on the far west side of town, they kept to themselves. Such was not the case with the thousands of volunteers around them.

The irregulars, emboldened by their first "victory," fanned out through town. And what a target rich town. Like a tide, they washed over the division's surprised support elements. What little discipline the volunteers possessed promptly collapsed. Each platoon tried to gobble up as much glory as they could, to hell with what the others were up to. To the support soldiers' credit, they neither panicked nor surrendered, and even tried time and again to form hasty defensive lines–without much success. Their hasty fortification attempts were as effective as sand castles against high tide.

The oncoming horde's complete disorganization happened to be their greatest strength. It was less like stopping an enemy advance and more like trying to catch water with your hands. If you covered the streets you found yourself quickly surrounded as they poured through buildings, lawns and alleyways. Whether on foot, in convoys of pickup trucks or in captured Humvees, they were everywhere if you were trying to make a stand, but nowhere if trying to call in an artillery strike.

At one major intersection near downtown several different support teams came together to make a tougher stand. An air defense company and some supply people, armed only with M16's, setup a hasty ambush. They were led by a communications officer and backed up by a platoon of mechanics who brought a handful of real few machine guns. They got the drop on an entire militia platoon obliviously barreling down the highway in their trucks and wiped them out before they could get a single shot off. The platoon following behind them became thoroughly confused and started a heated firefight with some other militia group trying to flank the ambush site.

The defender's exhilaration was short lived. Their laughter died quickly when they took heavy fire from a Dollar General store behind them. Someone else chucked grenades at them from the roof of a Subway. One group of the now surrounded soldiers tried to fall back from their exposed Hemtt's and Humvees blocking the road and into several brick houses across the street.

That sound strategy fell apart when the first soldier through the door took a shotgun blast to the face. The forlorn soldiers hesitated too long when they realized the extent of their encirclement. No doubt about it; they were cut off. Naked in the front yards, unseen rebels cut them down with fire from every window and doorway.

There was no question about the rear echelon soldiers' courage or fighting spirit, but they obviously weren't combat troops. These narrowly trained specialists didn't know the first thing about the organized shifting of fire, bounding and covering principles or reacting to a near ambush. As soon as they found themselves surrounded, the common glue of discipline began fraying. Instead of one 200 man unit fighting off the enemy, they were 200 one man units, each basically fighting for themselves. As the battle coalesced around a single point, the rebel's need to seek the safety of numbers gave them a level of rudimentary organization that was an edge in this kind of fight.

Encircled, outnumbered and shocked by such massive casualties the soldiers were about to cave in. An old mechanic master sergeant gathered volunteers for a final charge that might distract the enemy long enough to allow the other survivors to escape. As he put the final touches on this frantic plan, a sidewall of the enemy's Dollar General redoubt exploded and dropped the roof in. Some nearby drive-through liquor store and its enemy machine gun crew disappeared off the face of the earth in another cloud of smoke and splinters.

A ragged "Hooah!" rose from the soldiers when through the smoke a battery of friendly M109 mobile howitzers could be seen rushing towards them at breakneck speed…about 20 miles an hour. Big, ugly and slow, but those 155 mm cannons providing direct fire support were a beautiful sight. For the defenders, at any rate. The militiamen scattering ahead were less inspired. Another cannon blast annihilated a moving truck full of rebels and shredded everyone within 50 yards.

At a range of only a few hundred meters, each round had enough kinetic energy alone to destroy a vehicle. The 30 pounds of HE packed into each shell was over the top. The artillerymen's .50 caliber machine guns and 40mm automatic grenade launchers, which served as mere backup weapons, chugged away at the enemy. This was no fair fight; they were just kicking someone while they're down. Which was exactly what the Feds felt like doing.

For the first time, the floodwaters parted. The volunteers had never seen such abject destruction and rapid violence in their hilariously short military careers. They didn't have the slightest clue what to do about it. The tide melted away and gave the slow moving death mountains a wide berth. The delay gave the defenders time to reorganize, evacuate casualties and receive reinforcements.

One enterprising rebel tried to take out a howitzer with a captured bazooka. Or what he thought was a bazooka. The Stinger anti-air missile sailed a good 50 feet over the targeted track and kept on going. An artilleryman quickly cut the pissed off shooter into pieces with a machine gun. He never got to see the missile eventually acquire a target and blast apart an Apache gunship coming to back up the line.

The Apache's undamaged wingman clipped a power line in his rush to avoid the debris and any follow up ground fire. Whether thanks to the helicopter's elaborate safety design features, the pilot's skill or just a big slice of luck, they somehow made a fair crash landing.

The crew of the second chopper survived the "landing" only to be drafted by a passing artillery officer trying to organize a scratch counterattack. They hopped into the back of a 5-ton truck full of gung-ho but poorly armed headquarters paper pushers, medics and dismounted supply truck drivers. Part of a large convoy of such hardened warriors. All they could do was shrug and pray some more helicopters could get airborne. Because if this was the best they could muster, they were screwed.

They didn't know that shrapnel from a near miss artillery round riddled the last flight worthy gunship back at the airstrip at that very moment. Not that their aviation commander let such petty details faze her. She kept busy dismounting machine guns from the damaged helicopters and wondered if they could somehow hastily mount rocket pods on the back of Humvees. She had to give up on the idea since she'd already sent most of her mechanics into town to play infantry. All she could do was find a rifle and join them.

The Feds scored surprising success with their hasty counterattack. The rear detachment troops struck back over a wide front and spread their numbers too thin…which worked in their favor. The militia, who moments ago were trying to flank one abrupt hard spot, found themselves suddenly under attack across their entire "front." When a squad of soldiers showed up where least expected, that force became a company by the time the report got back to the overworked and under-informed rebel command posts.

The now bloodied militia regiments, assuming they were about to be overrun, gave a good account of themselves. They retreated, of course, and fast, but fighting the whole way. The nervous support soldiers, some of them firing their personal weapons for the first time since basic training, gained confidence with every retaken block. No matter how many lives it cost.

The decisive point of the battle was fought at a strip mall on Highway 90. After being forced back half a mile, one Guard NCO commanding a militia company refused to budge any further. His regiment's commanding officer sent him the special weapons company and all the fresh men he could dig up. The NCO carefully deployed the MG's in mutually supporting positions and fortified the buildings as best as possible. He even pushed out a few small hunter killer teams of his best men, armed with half their precious antitank weapons, to keep those damn howitzers at a distance.

When the Feds stumbled into the kill zone they immediately pulled back. Their commanding officer couldn't allow that. The whole miraculous counterattack was so damn precarious. Only momentum kept it going. If they ever let up on the pressure, if they ever ceded initiative to the enemy, they'd never get it back again. The rebels were just too numerous.

He tried bringing up his makeshift armor units. Some hidden enemy forward scouts knocked out one of the lightly armored artillery pieces and a M113 armored command track with AT-4's. The rest of the battery didn't get much further. Just before they had a clear line of sight and could level the whole place, the rebels showed off yet another surprise. From somewhere much further down the street a blossoming salvo of Hellfire missiles turned four more M109's and 16 men into flaming pyres.

What shocked the federal commander the most wasn't that the damn Floridians had figured out how to mount an advanced air-to-ground missile onto the back of a pickup truck. Clever, whatever, but how do they have so many of these munitions that they could spare them for the flippin' auxiliaries!

He had no way to know those 8 missiles were all the enemy could deploy in the area. Nor that his rebel counterpart was chewing his lip and hoping he hadn't just shot his wad for nothing. Those tank busters were the last trick up his sleeve. There just weren't enough to kill all the enemy's armored vehicles. If he made a mistake in the timing and misjudged the battle flow, then he had merely prolonged the inevitable defeat.

Apparently, his timing was just right. The commander of the ad-hoc Fed force couldn't risk anymore of his precious guns. The logical thing to do was move them out of the combat zone and let them pound the enemy from afar, as designed.

Unfortunately, they were more than just big guns. They were both the mascot and backstop to this advance. His rag-tag force would fall apart if they saw their only real support flee the battle. He had no choice but to hold them in place. Well out of range of the enemy's missiles and too far to effectively engage the enemy. In this attack, they would play no further role.

So, knowing full well the folly of assaulting a fortified position head-on without artillery or armored support, he ordered his troops forward anyway. As much as he hated to, he scrounged around looking for any more fresh meat he could feed into that grinder.

To his surprise, his troops didn't mutiny at the idea of charging through machine gun fire across open parking lots. He hadn't commanded these people long enough to really know their measure.

The troops on both sides instinctively knew that it was make or break time. The fighting was vicious, confused and, sometimes, even hand to hand. Vehicles and high-tech modern weapons aside, the best way to describe it was…medieval.

At one end of the mall, a petite female MP crossed the last few feet of the exposed parking lot in a headfirst dive, enemy rounds flying inches above her back. She rolled to cover in the crook between the wall around a dumpster and the side of a Domino's pizza shop. Without missing a beat she cooked off her 2 grenades in rapid succession. She lobbed one on the roof and the other through the shattered side windows and into the kitchen, then turned to the man behind her and screamed for more frags.

The man behind her lay face down in the parking lot, a good 20 feet away. As a matter of fact, every other member of her squad laid still or rolled in pain out there. Despite all the covering fire, she was the only survivor of that mad 50 yard dash. Which also meant she was the only one in a position to take the strongpoint.

The lock on the back door of the shop had somehow already been shot off. She inched closer. Men on the roof blazed away at far off targets, despite the grenade, but firing more or less blindly. Without sticking up their heads. At least the covering fire had some little effect. Inside, however, everything was deathly still.

She wasn't fool enough to think her grenade had killed everyone, or even anyone. They were waiting for her pretty little head to pop in there. Well, she wasn't the type of girl to keep a guy waiting. She reached into her web pouches and yanked out the only grenade left: a green smoke for marking purposes. Without wasting another second thinking about how stupid this was she just popped the smoke and rolled it through the door.

The men barricaded inside half expected another grenade, but not this. The sickening phosphorous stink from the deep green cloud disrupted them more than HE would have. They fired blindly at the entrance. Through the ruckus, they didn't hear the MP dash around the side of the building, strut right through the front door, take a knee and raise her weapon.

The SAW is not a preferred close combat weapon. Something lighter with more stopping power, say, a shotgun or revolver would have been a better choice. But you work with what you have. Besides, an automatic weapon firing in long bursts into a 40 square foot space still got the job done. But what a messy job.

Feeling around the 6 bodies, she found all the frags she needed. One by one she chucked them up the access ladder and among the oblivious guys above. She planned to sit back and use them all up–to kill in style. After the third explosion though, the whole north end of the roof, already stressed with nearly a ton of sandbags and way too many men, collapsed and brought the enemy to her. Picking off the shocked and wounded men trying to climb out of the rubble might have been as fair as shooting fish in a barrel–but she loved to fish.

She kept firing short bursts until the belt ran out, long after the last enemy stopped twitching. While loading her remaining 200 round box, the rest of her platoon came rolling in. She'd been so focused on staying alive she forgot all about the point of the operation. Taking this strongpoint on the wing of the enemy's position created a gap in those deadly interlocking fields of fire that the rest of the unit could funnel through.

One of her platoon mates snapped a quick photo of her at that moment of exhaustion. She stood in the rubble, surrounded by more than a dozen bodies, and innocently redid her ponytail. It wasn't the Medal of Honor she would later receive that made her famous, but that "Fucking PMS" photo. By nightfall she'd be an internet sensation.

*

The chaplain said a prayer for the young rebel under him, even while still untangling his bowie knife out of the man's lower intestines. He finally got it loose, wiped the blade on his victim's shirt and slipped it back into his vest sheath. He gave the terrified boy a mercy double tap to the head and then another pair for his fallen compatriot next to him.

That probably wasn't even necessary, but he was a thorough man. The preacher had shot him twice point blank in the chest before the now gutted kid jumped over the cash register and surprised him. Few of these rebels wore any sort of body armor. He even thanked the Prince of Peace for sparing his life by giving him the strength to kill these people. After tactically reloading his M16, he repositioned the rest of his grim flock and waited for the next rebel counterattack.

Things were usually pretty bad if the chaplain was the only officer left in a unit. On the other hand, he was one of the few officers anywhere that still held the respect of the desperate support personnel following him. Whether a result of luck or a side effect of being crazier than your enemy, either way, he had an aura of invincibility. He had protection from On High, and everyone wanted a share in it.

In the shaky condition his people were in, that was all it took to command. But what made him a real leader, one that might just inspire his people to overcome all odds, was he didn't ask his people to do anything he wasn't already doing.

***

North Side of Lake City

The luckless 1-6 Infantry seemed to always just miss the fighting. By the time they were ordered to abandon their blocking position on the wrong side of Lake City, the battle had already moved downtown. That didn't faze the pissed of troops though. It was payback time.

Despite losing a third of their manpower, they were still the largest federal combat force in 20 miles. As they entered the north side of town it was surprising to see the Georgia Guard battalion still active and moving around. The Georgians apparently weren't overrun at all. What was all the fuss about?

While the new battalion commander tried to wrap his mind around that, 4 F-15E's roared in and hammered them from the air. This time it was the large Abrams that drew the attention from a volley of Maverick missiles. The first pass from the fast movers annihilated five of his tanks. The next pass cost two more and a Brad.

As if they didn't have enough problems, the Georgia Guard laid into them with TOW missiles and 25mm auto fire. Apparently, the battalion bumped into yet another ambush. All they could do was begin breaking contact. Orderly, but quickly. At least they finally had something they could shoot back at, even if retreating.

Thankfully, there wasn't a third pass from the Screaming Eagles. Someone up at Division HQ heard the battalion's desperate calls for air cover at the same time and place the forward air controller rattled off kill tallies. It was disturbing how long it took to put 2 and 2 together, but eventually some genius up there decided to halt all close air support missions until targets could be positively identified.

The frustrated pilots, still with plenty of munitions on board, gawked at all those targets moving around below. Maybe they had just whacked a friendly unit, but most of those vehicles down there couldn't be friendly's. After 20 minutes of circling, they watched helplessly as a company of IFV's slaughtered an artillery battalion in town.

By the time the ground based command center finally sent them targets again, it was too late to make a difference. The same scenario was being played out across the sunny skies of Florida. All those war birds could hurt and harass the enemy, but by the time they were finally turned loose the chance to decisively influence the battle was past. That was the exact quote the history books would use to explain the limited role air power played in the entire Florida campaign.

***

High Tide

After one hell of a hard fought hour, the Army managed to painfully claw their way into dominating half the mall. The local's last line of defense was anchored on a Publix supermarket. They were totally on their own now. The small professional guard contingent and their newfound Georgian comrades were busy dealing with some federal counterattack from the north.

Every spare man the militia could scrounge up had long since been shoved into the fight. Far too many fighters in way too small a space–it guaranteed casualties would be even higher than necessary. But unfortunately, safety in numbers was the only way for these amateurs to build the confidence necessary to stand their ground.

There wasn't even any fire support left. The rebel's last mortar and artillery rounds were long since expended. Either shelling the small airport or various other high value targets, the poor infantry didn't rate high enough on the totem pole to get any support back when there was ammo to spare. Now the guns were silent and the Feds' air force did a damn good job making sure no more supplies reached town.

Regional command promised one convoy after another but they all disappeared somewhere along the open road. Where the war birds used to be so hesitant to strike, terrified they might hit civilian refugees rather than combatants driving civilian vehicles, they now took the gloves off. Something about getting their asses handed to them broke down their reserve. The heat of battle tends to bend the iron of ROE. Thankfully, they were only turning up the heat outside of built up areas…so far. They'd yet to drop a single bomb in town despite plenty of observers and opportunities.

The short ebb in the fighting ended with the Feds reclaiming the initiative. They had long since dismounted the secondary armament, automatic grenade launchers and heavy machine guns, from the artillery pieces. Not surprising, considering their supply dump sat in a truck stop only 2 miles away, they had no shortage of ammunition.

Several Mk-19's thumped out an endless stream of 40mm HE grenades into the militia's positions. They were small explosives, but with each gun firing 40 rounds a minute, there were a hell of a lot of them. This mini-artillery barrage cleared the roofs of the occupied buildings, often by collapsing them. Machine guns of all sizes hammered anyone trying to shoot back.

This final push was far better organized than previous assaults. The Feds moved some of those artillery pieces far enough away so they were able to slam some high angle fire on the rear areas of the rebel lines. Ignoring the ROE and hitting anything suspicious paid off. Two lucky shells smashed a bowling alley being used as the temporary militia command center. A few more unfortunately leveled a church being used as a makeshift aid station–for wounded from both sides.

Three small smoke screens blossomed in no man's land a few minutes into the intense bombardment. All three on the right flank of the rebel's line. The defenders took note and concentrated all their suppressive fire into the clouds, hoping to break up whatever assault the enemy had in the works. The exhausted on scene commander even committed his tiny reserve to reinforce that wing.

The actual assault came without much prep work on the far left flank. A line of six hulking M88 recovery vehicles grumbled just inches abreast towards a Lowe's Home Improvement store. The tracked and heavily armored tow trucks smashed through the thin pine trees and high bush on an undeveloped lot between the lines. They blazed away with roof mounted M240's at the rebel's forward pickets, who skittered away like so many panicked armadillos. Just like the little rodents, they were doomed to be road kill.

While the mechanics played tankers and drew attention, a mixed company loped along on foot a few dozen yards behind them. This team was made up of a real scout platoon, a fresh group of MP's and a few loose infantrymen assigned to desk jobs for some reason. Just about all the combat troops that could be rounded up in the rear area.

If they could crack that retail redoubt, even if just a little bit, these worn out rebels would collapse. Behind them came a company of fresh combat engineers ready to exploit the gap in the enemy's lines. The most powerful wedge they could find to drive into that foothold. In the ragged state the militia was in, it should be more than enough to pry them loose from their dug in positions.

The rebel's knocked one vehicle out with the last of their supply of handheld antitank rockets. An overzealous mechanic TC in another one stopped a round with his neck when he stuck his head too far over the gun shield, hoping to get a better look at his targets. Unfortunately, the vehicles didn't exactly do a perfect job shielding the dismounts from fire.

One infantryman went down with a painful gut shot. Another round striking square in the IBA knocked some other guy right off his feet. The body armor saved his life, but that much force still cracked a rib. No doubt, he was out of the fight. The two wounded men took four more fighters out of the battle while they helped haul the injured out of the kill zone.

Messy or not, the assault force crossed the open area and breached the loading dock of the big box retailer in moments. The wide aisles inside made clearing easy. They didn't even suffer a single casualty from the backroom to the cash registers. In less than five minutes the only strong point on the rebel's flank rested in federal hands. In bloody federal hands. The professional soldiers gleefully mowed down the amateur enemy survivors trying to retreat across the open parking lot. Payback was a bitch.

As luck would have it, God was on the rebel's side. Maybe the two dozen Brads growling down the street weren't avenging archangels, but they'd do until the real deal showed up. The high water mark of the Fed counterattack was also their last hurrah.

The mixed Georgia/Florida Guard team finished breaking up the weak counterattack up north less than 20 minutes ago. With nothing better to do and no higher command to interfere, they hauled ass out to the only other source of fighting around. The shocked support troops had broken out so few anti-armor weapons from stores. There simply wasn't any need to earlier–they were supposed to be the only ones with armored vehicles! The few AT-4's they had handy were poorly deployed and even worse employed. Except for a single glancing blow that blew a track off of one vehicle, none of the enemy Brads were harmed.

One company of IFV's raced west down the main boulevard to shred the artillery pieces mercilessly shelling the rest of town. The other company hung around the shopping mall. Their bursts of 25mm rounds or coax 7.62mm killed any camouflaged thing that dared move. In a flash of inspiration that was far from SOP but effective nonetheless, they rammed their 32 ton mini-tanks straight into the enemy's lines. Firing the whole way.

The squad of infantrymen in the back of each track shoved M-4 barrels through the firing ports and added poorly aimed but plentiful 3-round bursts into the fray. Maybe it more closely resembled a video game than a traditional breaching operation, but the results spoke for themselves.

By the time the tracks barreled through the Army and dropped their dismounts a safe distance behind enemy lines, the Feds were thoroughly broken. They had no chance to regain the offensive and they knew it. All around the mall the devastated troops began falling back. Firing the whole time, but clearly bugging out.

That orderly retreat fell apart when the reinvigorated militia upped the pressure and charged their shattered defenses. All the repressed disaster and stress of the last few hours came back in a collective trauma. They surely put up an impressive fight, but they weren't combat troops by temperament. They just weren't used to this *shit*!

The final straw came when the Brads behind them began blasting apart unarmed trucks full of retreating men and women. A few hardcore small groups held up wherever seemed a little defensible and died to the last. Everyone else who didn't have an immediate chance to escape threw down their weapons and raised their hands.

Despite the desperation of the fight and all the bad blood endeared, most were allowed to surrender. The occasional soldier had a smart ass comment to offer the exhausted enemy. It was usually the last thing they ever said. Still, almost everyone that kept their mouth shut and arms high was rounded up safely.

The rest of the militia went full Rambo as they rampaged throughout the collapsing rear area supply and maintenance depots scattered across town. At the airport, some posed for photographs on top of an abandoned Blackhawk helicopter. In a Winn-Dixie parking lot, others spray painted obscene jokes on the sides of multi-million dollar mobile radars. The irregulars even cursed the president who was at that moment saving their lives.

30 miles north, a fresh, brigade-sized task force bore down on the burning town. The Georgia National Guard force couldn't wait to avenge their slaughtered brethren—the details of the desertion disaster in Florida apparently changed a little bit before reaching the rank and file outside of the combat zone. In any case, they were willing and more than able to finish the job the regular Army started.

Fortunately, for the rebels, this president, who had never served in the military and sat 800 hundred miles away from the actors involved, did not trust the Georgians. Desperate to help and reading fragmentary reports, he believed he saw something the generals missed. Determined not to allow the enemy to receive further reinforcements, he called the unit directly. Entirely bypassing the chain of command in his ignorance.

The frustrated brigade, only minutes from Lake City, halted and reluctantly turned around. Their commander's disrespectful, almost mutinous response to the order convinced the president he made the right call. This success, of course, only emboldened the president to "help" further.

Chapter 9
15 miles north of Lake City

General McDowell hadn't been overwhelmed–he'd just been under fire. Now that his command post was far enough out of town that tracers couldn't rip holes in his map anymore he could finally think. Despite the desperate retreat, made even worse with all those civilian tag-a-longs blocking the roads, he somehow managed to get his unwieldy command staff and vehicle park out of harm's way. A shame the rest of the division's support trail wasn't so lucky.

McDowell came closest to sympathizing with the rebels when the president personally called back his Guard reserves over concerns about their loyalty. Which could not have been more ridiculous–their commanding officer was a West Point classmate of his, for Christ's sakes! The combined Georgia/Alabama BCT now streaming back across the border might not have arrived in time to prevent disaster, but they would've given him options at least. And at the moment, that's what he was shortest on.

All the doctrine called for establishing a forward operating base and concentrating his support assets there. It was the most efficient way to supply his combat maneuver units while maintaining the minimum security elements. Lake City had seemed by-the-book perfect. Centrally located, with its own airfield and natural defenses that would channel attacking forces into narrow avenues. Just what doctrine called for, even if things turned out so terribly. Problem was, none of the field manuals held a solution for your own people turning on you or your president micromanaging the battle.

At least his requests for more aircraft hadn't fallen on deaf ears. But the White House's several hour delay, while they debated and dithered and hoped the situation would magically "clarify itself," resulted in the unnecessary deaths of God knew how many federal troops. They were either unable or unwilling to wrap their minds around the air losses he'd suffered. And those were just a scratch compared to the ground casualties. He shook his head and pushed the thought down. It was time to extract the rest of his units.

On paper, it seemed like they were screwed. Scattered, surrounded, cut off and under pressure from every side–things looked bleak. Reality wasn't so bad as that. The rebels holding Lake City didn't appear to have any lust to leave the safety of town and fight out in the open. The Air Force's now regular bombing runs helped to encourage that point of view. As for the regular rebel forces to his south, even after the losses his men suffered he outnumbered them easily 2 to 1.

The enemy had clearly suffered as well. Not nearly as bad, but they were so much smaller to begin with. Their cohesiveness must be nearing its limits. This was more than wishful thinking. Judging by how the enemy's aggressiveness tapered off, and how little interest they seemed to have in finishing his trapped units, they were probably at the end of their endurance as well.

The only success they'd enjoyed so far was being able to concentrate whole brigades against his individual battalions. Like so many senior leaders in the military or civilian world, he just chalked that up to bad luck and ignored the large role he played.

To the general's credit, he didn't cry over spilled milk. He began carefully extracting his maneuver units back north. With dark setting in, they were finally able to break contact with the National Guard forces clinging to them like so many ticks. From what they could tell, the rebels were terribly short on night vision and thermal imaging gear. If only they could be shorter on luck.

Back in town, when watching those armed civilians swarm over his base like a zombie horde, he'd fantasized about recalling his combat forces and stomping them out. It wouldn't take long. As much as it stung, he was professional enough to realize that wasn't the answer.

Those tanks and infantrymen might be too powerful to be overrun, but they sure wouldn't be overrunning anyone else anytime soon. For the time being, he had no way to supply them. And 3 modern brigades needed an endless train of supplies to stay dangerous. The only solution was to get back across the nearby friendly border. Or friendly enough border. They had to regroup, rearm and reorganize as soon as possible. The temptation to step on these irregulars on the way out of state was powerful, but it would have to wait a little.

No, the only logical, sound tactical decision was to retreat, no matter how much that pissed Washington off. He'd already stopped answering their calls. All the insane requests were funneled through trusted subordinates that could stall for time. He would have had his staff tell them he was dead, but then one of those armchair generals might try to take charge themselves. Though, how could that be any different than the current command structure?

***

6 March
Los Padres National Forest, California

Pop, pop, click.

Shit. Sophie had lost track of how many rounds were left. She slid out the magazine, locked the bolt to the rear and rested her peacemaker on the sandbags in front of her. Fighting the itch to stand up, she pushed the oversized helmet as far out of the way as she dared. Her instructor noticed; he catches everything, but seemed to let it go.

He had a bigger annoyance. Everyone else on the line but her still carefully pumped out rounds downrange.

"Why the hell aren't you firing, Kampbell?" Even over all the shooting, he was loud and clear.

"Out of ammo, Sergeant!" That clearly wasn't the answer he wanted to hear. "Also out of targets, Sergeant!"

For a wonder, she caught him off guard. He straddled her firing pit, waved his red paddle at the range control tower and pointed down at her. A second later, all the targets in her lane flipped up, but then all went back down. The instructor looked as close to impressed as that scowling, jagged face ever could.

He blew a whistle. "Check fire! Clear and safe your weapons!"

Range control recocked everyone's lanes but left up the plastic army men each missed.

"I'll be damned. 40 out of 40 and finished 10 seconds before anyone else. Where did you learn how to shoot so well?"

Sophie licked her thin lips, but tried not to look too confused. "From you, Sergeant!"

What type of trick question was that? The instructors loved to trip trainees up with logic traps. There is no right answer. The truth made her look like a kiss ass and he'd sniff out a lie immediately.

Well, the right answer wasn't the point. The whole game is a test to see if you hesitate. Right or wrong, so long as you sounded off good and strong they'd leave you alone. Show the slightest indecision–oh! Then you'd be doing pushups until you puked.

He studied her with something verging on respect while preaching to the assembled squad. "You know what's special about this soldier, eh? She actually listens! See what you can accomplish when you shut your cock holsters and open your minds?"

He smiled wide…something you never want to see a drill instructor do. "Listen up, all you good 'ole boys out there who think you know everything there is to know about shooting, because your 'grandiddy' taught you. Look at these scores. Not one of you shot over 30 out of 40. You don't want to listen to me when I show you the four fundamentals of marksmanship, fine. Maybe you'll listen to her."

He waved his painted ping pong paddle at the tower. "Reload, we're going again. Anyone who misses a single target will be personally coached by this little soldier until you're less of a fuckup. What are you waiting on? Let's go, let's go! Move with a sense of fucking purpose!"

Sophie just received her first promotion. In her NCO's eyes, she moved up from unidentifiable animal shit under your boot to a real human being. After only 3 weeks in this program, she was amazed at how much that respect meant to her. Her heart fluttered at what he called her as much as any of Ben's pet names. It was a word she hated, until applied to her–*soldier*.

With colleges across the state temporarily closed, unemployment approaching 12% and, frankly, so many people pissed off, this private camp bustled. Their free curriculum helped. The shadowy organizers–some new non-profit foundation primarily funded by a LLC, which was itself a daughter company of a shell corporation of an offshore holding company–hired only the best instructors. They even worked out an arrangement with some schools to provide "professional learning credits" to anyone who successfully completed a "proactive defense" program.

Everyone started in a week long dynamic self-defense class. Despite the hype, these classes trained people in a type of civil disobedience closer in spirit and practice to Che Guevara than Martin Luther King and Gandhi. But since the BDU wearing teachers stopped short of issuing firearms, they could still play the non-violence card.

The real purpose of the course was far more than just teaching people how to protest more effectively. Each class was a large-scale recruiting event and actually cheaper, per head, than the US Army's recruiting efforts. Less than 5% of attendees proved enough passion and drive to be invited to join "advanced lessons." The ultimate reward being able to eventually join one of the hip, still-evolving Freedom Brigades. Recruits were also paid, and paid well, to volunteer for these non-profit "Constitutional Clubs." At least that was the name on the tax forms and in friendly media coverage. Everyone else just called them "The Militia."

A pair of National Guard observers conferred off to the side and critiqued them every step of the way. Originally those uniforms were supposed to represent the enemy, but Lordy had things changed rapidly over the last month! Acting Governor Salazar took a more contrarian position to the Federal Government every week. The hotter her rhetoric, the higher she climbed in the opinion polls. Which meant she gave the people more of what they wanted. A strange cycle, but not terribly interesting to Sophie.

Sophie didn't know who paid for all this, nor did she care. In all the clubs and causes she'd ever participated in, none gave her half the motivation as "The Brigades." The friendships she forged out here in the woods would be lifelong. The memories of their hardships still fresh 50 years from now. She was part of something truly important, something bigger than herself.

These freedom fighters had no such impotent goals as "raising awareness." No, their mission was to evoke real change. At the point of a gun, if need be. To not just protect, but create freedom. Next to that sense of purpose everything else in life had the volume turned down.

She hadn't had contact with anyone outside the program in, what? Three weeks now. Some of the other guys were homesick, but she couldn't feel more at home. Her friends back in L.A. thought it crazy that someone so socially conscious would join a paramilitary organization.

Sophie couldn't understand why her civilian friends *didn't*. Putting on the uniform is just another version of civic virtue. And a semi-automatic rifle solves more problems than a picket sign. Those 5.56mm rounds deliver a lot more permanent social justice than any lawsuit. This girl, not even old enough to legally drink yet, wondered how you could expect a fucking civilian to understand something like that?

***

7 March

From politicians to generals, all believed the failed attack in Florida was merely a costly but temporary setback. Just a few days to reorganize and they'd hit back with everything they had. Surely that would be the end of the whole rebel experiment. It was even true. Everyone knew the Floridians could never withstand a further assault.

But that didn't matter worth a damn. The fact they were able to kick the full weight of the federal military back on its heels, albeit temporarily, emboldened millions across the country. What seemed just yesterday a fantasy was today reality.

So many groups, from the truly crazy to regular folk just fed up with the current system, saw new vistas of hope opening. Maybe real change wasn't so impossible. Even foreign nations sensed a new world order emerging from the federal weakness. The battle that cost both sides so much also created opportunities for so many others.

It was a painful lesson that even after Vietnam, Iraq and Afghanistan America's leaders still hadn't grasped. Using the bare minimum force necessary to achieve even partial success gives you the option of scaling up later. Accomplishing just part of your aims with a fraction of your military might was usually enough to bring the other side to the negotiating table. With the implied threat hanging over their heads of what could happen if you fully invested in the project.

On the other hand, failing to achieve total success immediately with overwhelming force caused more than embarrassment. Such a show of weakness became an invitation for further enemy aggression.

Maybe the Feds weren't as obtuse as they appeared. They grasped the new reality quite well. That's what made them so desperate.

***

8 March

Power Games

Ocala, Florida

With the Feds temporarily thrown out of North Florida, you'd expect the rebels to be celebrating and taking a load off. Despite the near hysterical excitement out West, they were far from happy. Everyone in uniform looked around at their shattered, bloodied units and wondered how they were supposed to stop the next attack.

There was too much cleanup and prep work for the next fight to be done. Too much work and, after that disastrous fight yesterday, too few survivors to do it all. In all this crap Congressman Eliot was just a neat trophy.

The Florida Defense Forces didn't have a detention center setup for high value prisoners. Such a need seemed pure fantasy at the start of the invasion. Most of the enemy soldiers they still held were severely wounded–they wouldn't be leaving the crowded hospitals anytime soon. Those few hundred captured up in Lake City were crammed into a football stadium in Tampa. It didn't seem appropriate to shove a politician in with them. None of the militiamen really knew what to do with a captured congressman.

Eliot's almost comical "take me to your leader" demands eventually paid off. He and Jessica bounced around from one field headquarters to another before finally landing at the head command post in Ocala. Getting there was one thing. Getting someone to pay attention to them something much harder. Jessica wasn't zip-tied like the congressman, but she sure wasn't free to move around.

Way back when in J school they cautioned about getting too close to the story. Shit, she thought, I'm smack dab in the middle of it. Any closer and I'd be an obituary. She wasn't terribly worried, mainly just annoyed that no one wanted to talk to her. What she could learn if the guard would let her go anywhere outside this little corner of the convention hall. What her editor would pay if she could get an exclusive from "the heart of the beast."

She gazed with lust as General Cooper intensely conferred with a bunch of his officers only a few yards away. What she wouldn't give to get in the middle of that! She even tried flirting with the guard, but he was far too focused on his hatred of Eliot to be interested in her. She pondered screaming "rape" when a tall, dark sergeant marched up to their glaring sentry.

"Private, can't you see these detainees are hungry? Go get these civilians a couple of MRE's. I'll watch 'em." He unslung his M249.

The PFC looked him over skeptically. "I'm sorry, Sergeant. Major Gorgas ordered me to stay here until he personally said otherwise. I can't abandon my post." His words were respectful, but his tone implied: "fetch your own shit."

It was pretty obvious the sergeant wasn't used to disobedience.

"Private, I don't give a rat's ass what some fucking officer told you! You're in my headquarters; these prisoners are my responsibility. So get your ass in gear!" This buck sergeant, fairly old for an E-5, had an impressively refined command voice.

Every instinct in the poor kid told him to obey, but a strand of discipline held him in place. "Uh, I can't. My orders…" a stray idea crossed his mind and gave him a little more confidence. "Um, what unit are you with, Sergeant? What do you do around here?"

If he thought this strange NCO was angry before, he wasn't ready for this white hot rage. The sergeant jumped right in his face. Curiously, he yelled just loud enough to scare the kid but not draw attention from the command staff on the other side of the large room.

"Boy, if you have to ask, *you* don't belong here! Now, I gave you an order. Are we going to have a problem?"

The private's endurance lasted two more seconds. Fuck it. "Hooah, Sergeant." He left quickly, muttering under his breath about how the left hand never knows what the right hand is doing. He was sick and tired of always being in the wrong no matter what he did.

The moment the guardsman stepped outside, this curious fellow whipped out a blade and rushed up to the now terrified congressman. He cut the plastic cuffs, searched both faces, and spoke to the strongest one.

"Alright lady, take this dude and get out of here, right now. There's a sentry outside the entrance, so stop when he yells or you'll be shot in the back. The important thing is not to come back in here, no matter what you hear. Clear?"

Jessica had never seen such calm, yet focused intensity. She neither argued nor questioned. Just nodded and pushed the congressman towards the door. As soon as they were moving Brown turned and strolled towards the center of the hall. No more time to waste. People were already throwing curious glances at him.

In normal circumstances he never could have pulled off this stunt. The two dead guardsmen in the trunk of his Humvee outside would have been missed much sooner. Even as swamped as these command staffers were, they should've known he wasn't kosher. Could've, would've, should've—too late for all that now.

Major Gorgas caught Brown's strange movements out the corner of his eye. He didn't understand any of it, but he didn't waste time trying to.

"Frag out!" he screamed.

Gorgas dropped the map in his hand and yanked the general to the ground with him. A second later, both grenades detonated. He peeked around the old desk to see this stranger in a friendly uniform take a knee and blaze away with a SAW. No real tactics involved. Just stand in the middle of the room with an automatic weapon and kill everything that moves.

General Cooper was not thankful for the lifesaving. He drew his sidearm with a war whoop and popped straight up to engage this crazy fuck. He collapsed almost immediately without firing a shot, three holes in his gut and a trio of larger exit holes out his back. Gorgas yanked off his own ACU top and did the best he could to stop the bleeding.

Someone from somewhere chucked a flash bang grenade at the killer in the middle of the room. It might've seemed clever at the time, but it dazed those firing back more than it distracted him. The only effect was to allow the attacker a chance to slip away. Brown had shoved ear plugs in before even tossing the grenades; which was probably unnecessary. His murderous focus couldn't be thrown off by some non-lethal toy.

When the defenders could focus again, the enemy was gone. Like a killer dream. In just 20 seconds a dozen officers and key staffers were either killed or seriously wounded. What the fuck?! Someone noticed the side door still swinging. An only slightly wounded master sergeant lead a scratch squad of men out the door after him.

And straight into a bigger fight. That same grinning asshole stood in the turret of an up-armored Humvee and rocked a .50 cal. The master sergeant shoved his guys back under cover when the barrel swung their way. Half inch slugs ripped easily through the brick wall inches above his head. After a short burst, Brown swiveled back to his main target, the other Humvees around him.

He systematically shredded several occupied trucks whose gunners were a little too slow on the uptake. He hadn't planned to make a last stand in the parking lot, but what are you going to do? How long did he have before they flanked him? Despite the big gun in his hands he could only shoot one target at once. Any second they'd figure that out and hit him in the back. All he could do was make it costly.

It didn't surprise him when he heard the truck's doors open below. What a shame the guardsmen were so quick. Time for the big finale.

He stuck his thumb in the pin of his last grenade, which was already taped around a canister of homemade napalm. Just as he prepared to yank it out, he looked down to face his enemy for the last time. A mound of blonde hair stuck between his legs and smiled.

Jessica ignored the obvious erection next to her face. It was already there before she climbed into the driver's seat. "So, you ready to get out of here? Or are you having too much fun?"

She barked at the sobbing congressman to buckle up while she tried to figure out this military vehicle. The steering was simple enough, and even an automatic, but where were the fucking keys? How do you start this damn thing?

Luckily, the diesel's glow plugs were still warm. The engine roared to life when she randomly flipped switches and got to the big green knob on the left of the steering wheel. She had no time to celebrate. Several something's slammed the window next to her. Two big cracks appeared in the armored glass. More rounds hammered the outside of the truck all over. "Go! Go!" was the congressman's advice. For once, she agreed with him.

Jessica peeled away as fast as the heavy truck could accelerate. She sideswiped another Humvee on the way out and nearly ran someone over, but they got clear. The suppressive fire from the gunner's hatch above stopped only when they were nearly a mile distant.

The stranger dropped down, shook his head at the guy in back and clapped the woman on the shoulder.

"Damn fine job! But take this next left; we want to go south." It pissed her off how her nipples crinkled at his touch, but she couldn't stop. When he slipped a loaded pistol belt around her waist and buckled it, steamy breath behind her ear, she was positively…well, excited. She was a modern, responsible, professional woman. There was nothing sexy about killing and nearly getting killed. Why couldn't Mother Nature join the 21st century?

She stayed focused and kept her eyes on the road, rather than on that rugged face. "Why south? It's only a couple of hours until the border if we go the other way."

Brown kept himself busy getting everyone a weapon and inventorying their remaining supplies. He tried hard to avoid staring down that neckline…God Damnit! She didn't even have perfume on. How could the scent of an unwashed woman be so intoxicating? This gal was more trouble than tear gas.

"The whole rebel army is north of us. Believe me. I've spent a lot of time tracking their movements. Everything they got is up there. No one is south of us. What do you say we hit the beach and wait for the real Army to get here?"

She mulled that over briefly and tried to keep things light. "Hmm, and I didn't even bring a bathing suit."

The mental image of her in a bikini made John drop the magazine he was loading. He laughed nervously. He felt like a teenager again. A well-armed teenager probably being hunted by both sides, but right now, he didn't worry. Amazing how tossing a girl into any situation suddenly makes it less disastrous.

He stuck his hand over the radio mount, partly just for the excuse to touch her. "By the way, I'm John." She held his rough hand longer than necessary.

"Jessica. A pleasure. I take it you aren't with the Guard?" Damn girl, she thought, turn the reporter routine off for a second!

Brown changed the subject to something safer, even if more difficult. "Listen, ah, I want to say…I mean, that was some hardcore shit, um…I appreciate your help back there and all, but why?"

She shot him another grin. "You're not particularly good at saying thank you, are you? That's ok, no need to. I see this as more a suicide prevention incident. I'm a reporter and saw the hottest story around," she blushed a tad at her choice of words, "um, was getting itself killed. Besides, you got us out of there safely. Karma wouldn't be pleased if I didn't return the favor."

"Is Karma a boyfriend or…?" Brown tried to stay nonchalant and scanned around the vehicle, even while scanning her intently.

She had such a carefree laugh. "That's a good one!"

He was still trying to puzzle out what she meant by that when their luggage suddenly joined the conversation. "Soldier, on behalf of a grateful nation, I want to thank you for saving me from those fanatics. But now we need to find some way to communicate with the Hill. I'll see to it you are evacuated as well. Oh, and by the way, I don't need this. Could you imagine if a photo was taken?"

"Who are you and what the hell are you talking about?" Brown turned around in time to see the congressman waving the 9mm he gave him right in his face. In typical fashion, the politician ignored the "help's" comments.

Brown reacted instinctively. He crushed the threat's wrist and pushed the gun up and away while trying to draw his own. Jessica reached over, seized his arm and rolled her eyes before he finished killing the suit in the back. "Relax, John. Let me introduce you. That's Congressman Alfred Eliot, from New York's 29th congressional district."

John holstered his weapon, but shoved the other back into the congressman's hand, grip first. "That's how you hand over a fucking weapon. And keep your finger off the trigger unless you're ready to use it!" His command voice even worked on the millionaire in back.

"Well, then. Please do forgive my…unfamiliarity with firearms. I'm afraid I'm not qualified to use one. However, if you get me to a telephone, I'll have a hundred professional shooters here in a hurry."

Brown yanked the pistol away. "Maybe you got a point." Before he could get more pissed off about the idea of deploying soldiers as casually as calling up a plumber, Jessica got him back on track.

She reached behind her head and patted the machine gun turret ring. "I think we should stop anyway. We need to find a different vehicle somehow. This thing might not be special to you, but that machine gun sticks out in polite company." She grinned wide and tried to get a rise out of him.

"We need to find a place to hide your big gun." It gave her goose bumps when he focused all that intent energy solely on her.

"Yeah...sure. Ok, we'll find a phone and a car to steal in the next town ahead."

It was Jessica's turn to be surprised. "Steal a car? Have you ever done that before?"

"Oh, I might've seen it in a movie once."

*

'Bama

Dimone fled Florida in his private schooner minutes after the Feds' initial attack. Despite being the first to run, he still arrived last to the conference. He spent too long trying to get back in touch with financial supporters that no longer returned his phone calls.

Being labeled a terrorist and hunted by half the country didn't faze him. Even being forced to hold a clandestine meeting in a small church in Birmingham, Alabama with his few remaining supporters didn't devastate him. Instead, the passion of his fanatical followers buoyed his soul. Obviously, he stood for truth, justice and the American way. Why else would people follow him so devotedly?

For their part, the various religious, political and conspiracy wackos willing to fight in his name were also inspired. For years they were marginalized, but now here came this mainstream politician needing their help. What better proof they were right about the terrible black/Jewish/UN/alien plotting all along? No one ever said man is a rational animal–he is a rationalizing creature.

Dimone reached out a hand to Francis Pickens, sitting in the front pew. "It does me good to see you, Picky. You're a fine man to stand with me when so many of your compatriots are selling out."

Pickens didn't touch his hand. "Don't flatter yourself. What other options do I have? That puppet state legislature the Feds installed has renounced me and I'm only one notch below you on the FBI's most wanted list. And for the last Goddamn time, it's not Picky."

The wannabe president's gaze already focused on some other guy. This one in uniform. "Ha, good man!" He slapped the runaway governor on the back and went towards his more useful follower with arms outstretched.

"Great to have you onboard, General!" He pumped the uniformed guy's fist, while ignoring the thick facial hair and strange rank on his collar. "You're the first of our brave soldiers I've seen since the invasion! How many of our boys are still able to fight?"

The old man looked confused and flattered. "I don't rightly know what's going on with the Florida Guard. I'm Group Leader Lee Davis, commander of the Southeastern Regional Constitutional Society, at your service, sir."

"The Constitutional…what? Which unit is that?" Dimone was no expert on military affairs but even he thought something didn't make sense.

"Oh, we're not with the regular army, nor do we come from Florida. We've waited a long time for a leader like you, sir. The mainstream, ultraliberal media called us crazy for years, but we always knew there'd come a day when a Beltway insider would get fed up with that nest of snakes! We've been gearing up for a long time, and now we've got the one missing piece. No sir, thank you!"

It took a moment for Dimone to realize this wasn't some sick joke. He shot a "what the fuck" glance at his staff that put this whole meeting together. "I, ah, I think there's been some misunderstanding. You see –"

The bearded man sensed he hadn't made the impression he'd hoped. "Now, I know what you're thinking. This ain't amateur hour. You need real help to throw out those Washington fat cats. Well sir, I'm just a spokesman really. I'm the current executive of the Society's board, but we are far more powerful than this little delegation here." He waved at a motley looking collection of uniforms in the back of the church. Not a single dark face among them.

"We represent a pretty solid confederation of over 80 independent militias in 7 states outside of Florida. Combined, we've got nearly 10,000 armed members and five times as many unarmed sympathizers. Our numbers have swollen in these last few weeks and we're training them hard! Believe you me, sir. We can offer a lot to the Cause."

"Sixty…thousand, you say?" He looked at his staff with new respect.

The Bubba grinned. Finally, some respect. "Oh, yes sir. The South shall rise again and liberate the whole country!"

Pickens guffawed nearby. No one paid him any attention.

He knew the poll numbers well. The South was solidly in the president's camp. Fiercely pro-American; to be expected since they've borne a disproportionate burden of defending it over the last century. All he heard was *only* 60,000 supporters out of 7 states. My how the mighty have fallen.

On the other hand, this force is larger than the Taliban even at their strongest…and look what havoc they unleashed.

Part III

"The time has come when the strongest arm and the longest sword must decide the contest, and those members who are not prepared for action had better go home."
– Stephen Hopkins, after signing the Declaration of Independence.

Chapter 10
9 March
Clearwater, Florida

Major Gorgas personally doubled checked the last truck's cargo. There would be no load manifest for this trip, nor the hundreds like them. No paper trail at all and only the most trusted drivers. Men and women who'd proven themselves during the initial invasion. He had no idea where they were headed. The less he knew, the safer they were. Each driver and the guerilla cell they belonged to were responsible for hiding their own weapons cache.

Maybe some of them would turn around and sell it all on the black market. Maybe some would just park the truck, leave and wash their hands of the whole mess. Still, he was confident that most of the arms and ammo would be squirreled away somewhere. That'll come in handy for the future resistance.

Satisfied that the last ammo dump was empty, he supervised burning all the paper records. The computers had already been scrubbed, just like all the state's Guard records. The central data servers were also destroyed, courtesy of the enemy's air superiority and paranoia. The personnel records, unfortunately, were centralized at the Pentagon. There was nothing he could do to keep the identities of his soldiers a secret. The best he could accomplish was slipping them into the new "underground" or somewhere out of the Feds' reach.

That was getting much harder as the Federal Government tightened their no fly zone and naval blockade noose around Florida. He was pleased to get out just those few hundred guardsmen to safe havens out west. Over two thousand more were accepted by Cuba, and thank God for how many they were willing to take in, but that still left way too many rebels to easily hide.

Unfortunately, there wasn't much chance someone higher in the command chain would be asking questions. The politicians were the first to disappear. General Cooper never recovered from his wounds and most of the rest of the senior staff hadn't survived the relentless Air Force revenge campaign.

Revenge was the only way to describe it. After keeping such a low profile during the invasion, the White House turned them loose to do whatever they could to halt the much feared "rebel invasion." They blasted apart anything of even remote military value. Everything from A-10 Warthogs to B-1 strategic bombers roamed the sunny skies above, looking for vengeance.

Which was the biggest overkill Gorgas had ever seen. They'd pulled off the stand in North Florida by the seat of their pants. A damn miracle the first time and it wasn't something they could ever repeat. The regular Guard forces suffered around 70% equipment and 40%

personnel losses. The irregulars were in nearly as bad a shape. There wasn't a single flight worthy combat aircraft left in the inventory.

To make things even worse, most of what they still had left was tied down maintaining law and order. Armed, self-organized militias and gangs roamed more or less out of control from the Keys to St. Augustine–and not all of them were friendly. Not all of them seemed to have a goal either, outside of simple looting and pillaging. Many of them were preexisting self-styled militias that weren't accepted into the FDF due to one crazy ideology or another.

The pro-Fed groups were frustrating, but the supposedly loyal ones were the deadliest. They were desperate and seemed to think ferociousness could turn the tide. One of the Florida National Guard's last combat operations was against an independent band of pro-rebel "white supremacists."

These assholes didn't have the balls to battle against the Feds directly, but when the fight was over, they had the guts to take over some small town. They went door to door one night shooting supposed "Federal collaborators," i.e., anyone they felt like. Oh, the Guard shut them down before the sun rose. Not a single one of those bastards survived, but vengeance is a poor substitute for prevention.

The ranks of the state's law enforcement agencies and security forces were seriously depleted. Whether from fear of federal retaliation, hopelessness of the cause or simply a desire to protect their families, more and more personnel disappeared every hour. Between the desertions and casualties, they could just barely keep chaos at bay during daylight hours. But the night belonged to the bandits. The once haughty Florida Defense Forces couldn't even hold their own land. The idea of an offensive was a twisted joke.

The whole conflict was never personal for Gorgas until the unrestricted air campaign kicked off. Sure, he was angry in the early days; just like everyone else. The president seemed crazy, the governor was so passionate and everyone around him itched for a fight. War seemed natural. That terrible fever the only solution. They didn't so much decide to start a fight as just stumbled into one.

The simple truth is he had been too busy being a professional doing his duty to really examine why he was fighting. To wonder how far he was willing to go. That was just too complicated a thought to deal with. It was too easy to push down and ignore, what with all the other things he had to do. But when he saw his homeland being treated like some 3rd world shithole so that some asshole a 1,000 miles away could stay in power–well, it got personal.

Despite the partial social breakdown, he had to salvage what he could of his forces. Besides, that gargantuan federal force massing on the border, twice as large as the previous invasion, would be moving soon. They could clean up the mess. He had bigger battles for his enraged and now bloodied veterans.

He was officially deactivating the last Guard units and unofficially breaking them into small, hidden bands while the TV ran live footage of the second and final federal onslaught. He knew that this would not be the last fight. Not by a long shot. While the politicians in Washington, whether in suits or in uniform, jubilantly watched their soldiers storm through the state, Major Gorgas and millions like him decided that the real war had just begun.

***

10 March

The second invasion of Florida was the most watched program in television history. It was also probably the most disappointing for action junkies. The whole "battle" fit easily inside the 3 hour primetime slot, including commercials. In typical government fashion, this time they were ready for anything–just as the enemy gave up. Almost no resistance was offered against the enormous and carefully advancing federal force. The rare exceptions were met by such overwhelming firepower, employed with such flexible ROE, that the Taliban would think they had it light.

While domestic news outlets reached new heights of biasness and speculation disconnected from any remote sense of reality, the foreign news channels were bewildered. The First Battle of North Florida was dreadful enough. Why would there be another one? From London to Tokyo, the deaths of 7,000 Americans in a single day–a Pearl Harbor, September 11th and a couple dozen mass shootings combined–blew their minds. Everyone outside the US just *knew* that after such dreadful violence no one could possibly be interested in any more fighting.

Surely such horrific losses would catapult moderates to center stage. Cooler heads must prevail and this dive into collective insanity would be short lived. The naïve Europeans only knew war through the lens of pointless futility that the history books gave it. Most Asians were more practical minded and lamented how bad for business the fighting was. Much of the Muslim world was excited, either to see the price of oil skyrocket or to see the Great Satan tearing itself apart. They only prayed that the US wouldn't blame them somehow. It seemed only Africa and some parts of South America could understand and sympathize with the American outrage.

They were the only ones personally familiar with the fact that people haven't improved much from the Stone Age. Only the conditions we live in have changed. All our enlightened ideals are just the products of idle time and not of a new environment. The peace and security of civilization allows people the chance to indulge in such luxuries as liberalism, humanism, tolerance and compassion.

They knew too well from painful experience how weak that house of illusions really was. The chill of fear, fire of revenge, stink of paranoia and winds of opportunism are the real natural environment of our species. When threatened, the artificial constructs of society are easily jettisoned for the tried and murderously true ancient instincts. Men might fight and die for those postponed lofty ideals, but the causes of wars are much less complex.

You tell the grieving parents, the shattered spouse, the abandoned children, the devastated siblings or the shocked friends of a fallen soldier that they died in vain. That it was time to put this childish foolishness behind them and just let everything go. Hurry up and get back to normal. You try to shove that terrible genie back in the bottle. Good luck. To the ancient Greeks, it wasn't the wrath of the gods that would be released by Pandora's Box, but the collective anger of humanity–a far deadlier curse than any supernatural being.

Once upon a time, the US waged total war against Japan. Eventually nuking two cities and leveling dozens more with traditional ordinance, all as payback for their killing of 3,000 Americans at Pearl Harbor. For almost the same causalities on September 11th the US waged a worldwide, intensely bloody, generation spanning war to prevent another attack. God alone knew how much death would be needed to calm America's insecurity and assuage their bloodlust this time.

Politicians gave their speeches. Businesses ran their political advertisements. Celebrities and religious leaders endorsed one plan or another. But that was just background noise. The families of the dead were center stage. It was the hysterical wailing from the mother of a slain National Guard fighter and the tear clotted face of his stoic father that provoked action. The heart wrenching pleading with God from the widowed wife of a federal soldier, with two terrified young kids in her arms, aroused just as much rage.

Once you ignore the rhetoric from supposed leaders and listen to the people, the question of why war was inevitable isn't so mysterious. Wars can be pursued scientifically, but their causes are rarely so rational.

***

11 March
Huntington Beach, California

Elections aren't won by convincing your opposition they're wrong. Elections are won by getting your people out to vote, by firing up your base more than the other guy's. Of course, the corollary means keeping the other side's supporters from the polls is just as effective a strategy.

This was the primary rationale behind founding the Freedom Brigades in the first place. The extremely tenuous legal status of these armed vigilantes rested with the fear of other armed vigilantes interfering with the democratic process. In practice, they were mainly used to keep the democratically elected Federal Government from stopping California's statewide Freedom referendum.

The country's most populous state had a long history of passing legislation directly at odds with federal law. Usually Washington looked the other way while the district courts sidestepped the issue and avoided making landmark decisions. Not this time. This was no minor squabble over legalizing pot. This unmistakable and dangerous challenge to central authority could not be ignored. It also would require a gentle approach and extremely delicate handling. So, with typical government finesse, they sent in the Marines.

Sophie didn't feel at home in her new tactical vest or body armor. She no longer sported bruises when she took the heavy gear off, but the weight still felt strange. These new boots weren't even broken in either. The strange Israeli made TAR-21 assault rifle also felt off. With magazine and bolt assembly built into the butt stock, pointy parts of this bullpup design weapon always jabbed into the side of her breast. Not for the first time she was glad they weren't bustier. Comfortable or not, at least she looked impressive.

She assumed that's why these FBI agents kept glaring at her. Some obviously worried, some clearly angry, but all showed respect. To her and her team protecting the polling station, at least. They were far less deferential to the local police blocking their way inside. Had the policemen been alone, yeah, they would have caved into the official pressure. Let the Feds shut the place down. With a dozen soldier look-a-likes backing them up, they were emboldened enough to tell the federal cops to "fuck off."

California's leadership would not tolerate a repeat of the street violence back in February. The Guard stayed on alert, but ordered to stay put in their bases. No sense in inflaming the situation further– might as well give these auxiliaries a chance to shine.

For his part, the president had decided on the soft approach this time to interrupt the plebiscite. He sent whatever federal law enforcement personnel they had in California, from FBI agents to Park Rangers, to try to put a stop to this nonsense. That gentle touch in the face of prepared, armed resistance only further showed the weakness of the president's dictatorial gamble. In politics, as in the jungle, weakness was an invitation for trouble.

Sophie had no way to know why these agents were backing off. Not all of these confrontations around the state were such bullshit stunts like this one. While the cops and Feds traded insults and threats here, in other parts of town they traded shots. A mile away, her sister militia group gunned down a trio of ATF agents trying to arrest them. These might be the first federal causalities of the day, but they wouldn't be the last.

These FBI men received a call from someone. After a quick huddle they just hopped back in their cars and sped off. Not another word spoken. Their abrupt departure even took the gusto out of the small cluster of pro-government protestors across the street.

Sophie's group leader, they weren't yet properly organized into hierarchical units, whistled. "That was damn easy. Look at them run! Talk about voting with your feet!"

Sophie laughed as well. Despite their success, disappointment gnawed on her imagination. Her lust for action, to put all this new training to use, rivaled any longing for a lost lover. How would she react when things got real? That sweet mix of anticipation and fear over her first time only heightened her desire.

When she finally found the chance, about an hour later, to go all the way she had no time to worry. Let alone savor it. Survival was her great orgasm. The rumble of Humvees filled the street, echoing off the apartment complexes around them as if she were in a giant concrete cave.

Those FBI cars came back leading two Humvees full of marines. No one blustered, threatened or tried to negotiate. Time for all that had long since past.

Voters ran every which way to get out from between these groups. Some of the running civilians briefly blocked Sophie's line of fire. She didn't get the honor of shooting first. Who did is a little unclear. Her battle buddy up in their Humvee's turret let rip his machine gun more or less at the same time as the marines. Didn't matter. This was it!

Sophie took cover behind the engine block of some Mazda sedan. She leaned around the fender, keeping her head below the hood, and lined up on the last of a group of bounding camouflaged men. Noticing his body armor, she dropped her aim to his hips and led him just a bit. Sophie took as steady a breath as possible and lightly squeezed the trigger on her exhale, repeating a heartbeat later. The marine's momentum kept him going several strides before his shattered pelvis locked up his legs.

She tried to line up on his crawling head for a finishing shot, but too many rounds ripped up the car around her. A bit distracting.

Sophie waved at a couple of her buddies firing blindly over the hood of their Humvee down the street. "Action right! 3 dismounts in the Walgreens!"

With a more concrete target to strive for, her teammates lit up the storefront and suppressed the hell out of the men inside. She took advantage of the opportunity and dashed to a better firing position. All the while shouting out more target ID's.

Sophie spent the rest of the afternoon far too busy to think about anything but shooting, moving and communicating... and maybe the occasional smile.

*

Daytona, Florida

Brown and his little gang parked their stolen car in a strip mall inside Daytona. The "social breakdown" the radio harped on was difficult to find. Practically all of Florida's cell phone networks were down, for example, but everything seemed normal on the streets. While Congressman Eliot used one of the few remaining paid phone booths in the free world to call home, Jessica and Brown went searching for something to eat.

No one in the grocery store gave his uniform a second glance as they swooped down on the deli. Brown practically salivated when he beheld the smorgasbord ahead. Not the variety found under normal circumstances, what with the embargo and all, but hardly a Third World pantry.

"Alright. No more damn MRE's tonight! What would you—holy shit! 20 dollars for a box of fried chicken?"

The aproned clerk smiled and shrugged. "Supply and demand, sugar."

A clucking sound brought his attention back to the store's entrance. Some denim clad good ole boy pushed two buggies full of chicken cages towards the customer service desk. A trail of shit and feathers followed on the well-polished floor. "Evenin'. Heard ya'll paying 10 bucks a chicky. Got me a whole mess ah eggs too, if yah 'ant 'em."

Some guy wearing a white polo shirt with corporate logo and a Glock 17 in a shoulder holster strolled up, both thumbs in his belt. While an armed guard in a supermarket might be normal in some big cities, around these parts it was surreal. Just part of the new cost of doing business.

"Local sourcing is around back in the loading dock. Please take your wares there, sir."

Jessica laughed and stepped a bit closer to Brown. "I guess demand was just supplied. So, what about a few Cuban sandwiches for our first date."

He cut his eyes at her, suddenly alert. Before he put his foot in his mouth she gently squeezed his arm. "Relax, big boy. I'm just teasing. Let me pay. I'm on an expense account."

The middle aged lady behind the glass counter shook her head and waved at a sign. "Sorry, darling. It's cash only. Barter's available for large purchases. The boss is all worried about the banks and whatnot."

Brown yanked some dead presidents out of his shoulder pouch to get the ball rolling on the subs. "Looks like it's on me then. So much for feminine independence!" He wished he could take back that careless remark as soon as he let it slip. Why is shit always so much wittier in your head? On the other hand, it was a good sign that she laughed at his stupid joke.

Jessica smiled and nibbled the corner of her lip. He wondered if he imagined her whisper. "Oh, don't worry. I always wind up on top in the end."

Her eyes held as much challenge as invitation. He took a chance and slipped an arm around her waist and pulled her closer. For a long millisecond she hesitated on that delicious cusp, only to cave in completely and push against him. Brown decided to go all in. He tipped her chin up and charged those puckered lips.

Just before contact their baggage came bounding towards them while screaming like a kid on Christmas. For the second time that day Brown wanted to shoot the fool, and he had just met him.

"They're on their way! Let's go, come on, please! Let's get the hell out of this hick town!"

"Relax, hoss. Even if the Army crossed the border right now, it'll take the lead elements a day or two to get here." He smiled down at the contemplative woman in his arms. "Hopefully at least a night or two."

"Are you crazy? The military has had a drone watching us ever since I first called. They've got helicopters coming from whatever Air Force base is next to Cape Canaveral. Come on, we're behind enemy lines here." He finally toned it down and lowered his voice, trying to act more natural. "Could you imagine if these hillbillies really knew you-know-what?!" All the other shoppers politely ignored him and his rudeness. Rebellion or not, this was still the South.

Only then did Brown show nervousness. He hadn't planned to go anywhere, too much unfinished business to attend to. Over the air conditioning and background country music he heard *whumping* outside. The three of them rushed to the storefront windows while everyone else ran to the back of the store. The search and rescue team was already here, with a pair of Super Cobras as escort. Brown weighed the impossible odds of taking them down with his rifle out in the stolen car while the other two cheered.

Jessica grabbed his face and pulled him close. Finishing what he started. They came up for air about 10 seconds later.

"Looks like it's my place tonight…" she murmured.

After all this time, Brown was finally trapped.

*

Not only was Sergeant Major Brown welcomed back from the dead with open arms, he was even awarded a Distinguished Service Cross by a new command structure desperate for heroes.

His reluctance to talk about his experiences since escaping Camp Blanding was chalked up to PTSD. The Army intelligence types that debriefed him noticed many discrepancies in his story, but they had bigger things to worry about. Their consensus suspicion was he might have gone AWOL for a while, but after what he did for the congressman, best to let it lie. The official line is: "He's a hero." Why rock the boat?

The FBI team investigating the White House attack matched witnesses' descriptions and some security camera footage to Brown long ago, but that line of investigation went cold when they learned he died at Camp Blanding. Thanks to typical bureaucratic efficiency, none of the investigators would ever learn that the rumors of his death were greatly exaggerated.

Even if they had, they probably wouldn't have cared. By now, all their likely suspects were on the run Florida ex-Guardsmen. Besides, the FBI would be swamped with thousands of other major attacks over the coming years. One more unsolved mystery at the bottom of the stack.

***

Great Divide

It wasn't stagnant wages or growing inflation that pissed people off. What's new? That trend started in the 70's. Ok, the youth of the land lucky enough to go to college were saddled with student debt and had bleak job prospects upon graduation. Frustrating, of course, but how's war going to help? Retirees saw their financial safety blanket shrinking every year and the middle class were assaulted by all of these problems plus onerous taxation to boot. Well, so what? The exploitation of the elderly and the middle class was older than most of the world's religions. Why would things reach a breaking point now?

No, the great divide in America wasn't one over left or right wing politics, social issues or about the economy. It wasn't even over what specific changes should be made, but whether real change was truly possible through the existing institutions of government. It was really a simple question of faith. Who had faith that a new government would screw things up less than the current one?

Oh, there were many people that did believe the president was a wannabe dictator and despised him. There were also others that thought he was a great elder statesman trying to avert disaster. Those were powerful emotions, either way, but neither cause was strong enough for the average person to fight over.

Who was willing to kill and be killed over some damn politician they never met and who would never meet in a thousand years? No one planned on risking their life in combat either for or against the president. He pissed some people off and these unresolved social issues strained already high tensions, but that was all.

No matter how worked up people got, an elected politician wasn't devilish enough to war against or hero enough to die following. While these broad social problems crushed the poor, they just weren't powerful enough to cause the middle class to jeopardize their comfortable existence with revolution. And without middle class participation no revolution is possible.

No, the fighters in this war weren't trying to defend or oppose a particular person or some vague ideology. The broken system that put their backs against the wall was the enemy. The fallen, martyrs. Oh, eventually specific goals would be spelled out, but to start a war passion is, regrettably, enough. In the twisted logic of mass emotion, more blood needed to be shed to ensure that the blood already shed wasn't shed in vain. That's just how people tick.

One way or the other, something had to change. Whether someone believed our existing institutions just needed reforming or it was time to scrap the whole thing and start anew, there was no going back to normal. Too much passion had been aroused. Too many opportunities had been presented and far too much blood spilled to simply go back to the status quo.

From the unemployed to the upper middle class, a depressingly large portion of the population had simply lost faith in the current system. The most common belief held, regardless of your agenda, you had no chance to realize it unless you were either fabulously rich or otherwise "plugged in" to the system. Liberal or conservative, radical or moderate, country folk or city people, even gay or straight–the labels meant nothing nowadays. Money was power and the rest was bullshit.

The majority of the US population were actually on the same page, with respect to the fundamentals. They believed Congress was a nest of snakes and just in it for themselves. The president was an obtuse, ineffectual and perhaps dangerous figurehead, and God only knew what went through the minds of those nearly senile dinosaurs on the Supreme Court. Even the Fourth Estate focused solely on raising the share price of whatever media conglomerate owned them.

Too many people no longer believed the American Government worked for the little guy and gal. The idea itself wasn't new. Just how many people believed it and couldn't stand it anymore changed things. When a society reaches this critical mass, when peaceful petitions of redress are mocked and trampled on by deep-pocketed special interests, violence is the final option left. The only questions being in what form and how much. For better or worse, Americans aren't known for doing things in moderation.

Chapter 11
15 March
Nellis Air Force Base, Nevada

Popular legend would have us believe "the Great Split" occurred overnight. In reality, the slow train wreck shocked no one at the time. It wasn't surprising when the Freedom referendum passed by such a wide margin in California or that equivalent statewide votes passed in Washington and Oregon the next day. Even similar plebiscites being scheduled in the coming week in 12 more Western and Mid-Western states was hardly a startling development. After all, the opinion polls showed majority support in these states when California's acting governor, after the federal assassination of her predecessor, first proposed the idea. That climbed close to 80% in the terrible wake of the first Battle of North Florida.

What shocked observers the most was how promptly the California legislature acted on the mandate to form a "legitimate Federal Government." Within hours they proposed and voted on a sheaf of new laws, requisitions and declarations over, well, everything. Just writing them all up alone should have consumed days. Of course, they did have a lot of help. Thousands of concerned lawyers, in the interest of patriotism and at the behest of the loose alliance of corporations they worked for, volunteered their time to assist with the great project.

Many of the laws were purely symbolic and unenforceable, an old problem for Californian legislatures. In this grand coalition of conservatives, liberals and silly moderates, who had no hard platform other than wanting to "see something change," practicality and common sense were the first to be disenfranchised. With more power only came more ridiculousness.

Those laws were for the protestor's consumption anyway. The real brokers behind the movement knew that money was the ultimate goal. Not for their own direct personal gain, but for the power cash gave. A few pessimistic visionaries were thinking about Cicero's old saw: "The sinews of war are infinite money." Most were only interested in the air of legitimacy deep coffers conferred upon this new government.

At any rate, within 24 hours of California's legislature declaring themselves the acting, but sole legitimate government of the United States, the first federal payroll deductions were redirected from the IRS to temporary state stewardship accounts. The speed with which the state confiscated federal funds and institutions was in direct proportion to their profitability.

It was also surprising how many of the bureaucrats didn't care who they worked for. Not just loyal to the new regime, but straight-up didn't give a damn. Protecting their fiefdoms was all that mattered–war or not.

The IRS was the first to be "re-nationalized," while the Department of Education came in last. No one wanted to touch the Postal Service. They quickly redirected Social Security taxes, but chalked up missed payouts to the illegitimate old government playing politics with the elderly and disabled. The excuses could hold for a while and hopefully direct anger back east, but what a dangerous line the politicians were tight roping.

The elected fools tearing the country apart were simply riding the wave of public opinion. The corporations assisting them just saw an opportunity to shortcut the middleman of lobbying and directly enshrine a few key principals of free enterprise into the revitalized government. And the regular folk celebrating in the streets were excited that someone was finally doing something. So many were giddy with innocent excitement that after years of legislative stagnation something new was happening.

Obsessed as they were with their own private agendas, few of these movers and shakers imagined themselves as secessionists. After they struck such a decisive political blow the Administration's support would surely crumble. The disgraced Congress that supported him must disband and, after new elections, it would be business as usual. Better than usual, since everyone was busy carving out new fortunes and favors in this future America.

Now, before these utopian fantasies could be realized, there was one large element of the old government that needed to be dealt with purely for non-financial reasons. The vast military presence on the West Coast was the great wild card in the game.

The pro-Freedom media blitz of the past couple weeks likely didn't have the intended effect on all those Service members that it had on the general populace. What might sway a civilian into voting one way or another wouldn't convince a professional soldier to betray their comrades. All the advertising in the world couldn't accomplish that.

In the First Civil War, regional identity was a clearly definable thing. The US was a smaller place back then. Not just in land area but in perspective. Most people, unless they were immigrants fresh off the boat or wealthy, had never travelled more than a few miles from their place of birth. You could count on, by and large, a soldier from New York being loyal to the North and one from Virginia, loyal to the South.

150 years later, things were a bit more complicated. In such a highly mobile, deeply intertwined country, which views buying your groceries at Wal-Mart versus Whole Foods a significant cultural difference, something as deep as political allegiance is incredibly unpredictable. How do you gauge the regional loyalty of a soldier who

grew up in some Midwest red-state, went to college in Florida but has been stationed in California for years? And has a spouse from New York to boot?

Hence the delicate gloves they used with the military. Those troops in any base not willing to pledge allegiance to the new government were merely offered a special half-pay, reserve status and ordered to stay home. A gentle way to take them out of the equation.

Attempts to double the pay for those that signed loyalty oaths backfired. Far more personnel were insulted than tempted. Any group that wanted to move as a unit back east was allowed to, but without their arms and equipment. It was all such a logical plan on paper, but messy in practice.

Facilities and hardware were so easily absorbed by legislative fiat, in the politicians' fantasies, but reality was a "no spin zone." Occasionally, victories came cheap. Some bases and units with a large percentage of sympathetic staff simply integrated themselves into the local Guard command structure without incident. Sometimes there was more…push back. In such cases it was safer to let the military work things out amongst themselves. Let the blood be on their heads. And every now and again, there were exceptional cases.

Just such a special problem brought Sophie to Las Vegas for the first time in her life. Of all the military facilities throughout the rapidly growing New American territories, Nellis Air Force Base on the east side of the city might be the most valuable. The base was best known for being one of the Air Force's premier training schools. It was less famous for its primary value to the growing new American government: home to a major nuclear weapons stockpile. Any country can have tanks and ships, but only superpowers wielded nukes.

Technically, this little occupation force could be considered an invading army. Nevada only voted on their referendum today. Their polling stations were still open. It was almost assured to pass, but the results hadn't yet been ratified when the California task force crossed the border. Of course, of all the quasi-legal and outright illegal acts ordered by the new Federal Government over the last 48 hours, the raid should be considered small potatoes. The prize was surely worth the bad press.

This wasn't the first attempt by the new Feds to get their hands on part of the country's nuclear arsenal. But they learned a hard lesson from the first try. As soon as the state of Washington joined the movement a mixed team of guardsmen and State Police showed up at the sprawling naval base in Bangor, just across Puget Sound from Seattle. When the gate guards refused them access, the authorities forced their way in. That turned out to be a terrible mistake.

Security there was far tighter than at most installations, since the base was home to half the US strategic submarine force. That made it the single largest repository of nuclear weapons in the free world. The haphazard breach was not met, as expected, by a senior officer willing to discuss surrendering his command, but rather a Quick Reaction Force of well-armed marines. The loyalty of the defenders to the regime back east wasn't terribly strong but, politics aside, they had a clear mission: Keep those weapons from falling into the wrong hands.

Needless to say, the entire rebel party was either killed or interned on base. Not only did they fail to secure any nukes, the outright aggression lost the support of most of the post. Solidarity with your comrades trumps politics. This well-armed, independently run base next to a major rebel population center was still a thorn in the side of the new republic. One that no one knew what the hell to do about.

This raid would be different. Key agents from the provisional capital in Sacramento, California contacted the brand new base commandant via back channels ahead of time. For a hefty fee, and the promise of a higher rank in the new Air Force, he handed over his base the moment Nevada looked like they would join the cause. The 300 Guard technical specialists and troops in the contingent were along just in case he or any of his personnel had a change of heart. The 50 hand-picked militia fighters were along because nobody had the guts to tell them otherwise.

Those militia folk weren't hastily raised and desperate volunteer forces like in Florida, either. These people were well funded, well equipped and well trained. Originally organized to fight against the state's security forces, they were rapidly becoming an integral part of the budding nation's security apparatus. As privately funded units, they were a hell of a lot cheaper than professional soldiers or overtime working police officers. Which was a great boon for the cash strapped new Federal Government.

The only real point of concern was that their reclusive, but well-connected financial backers insisted on maintaining a separate command and control structure. They had a parallel leadership hierarchy cooperating with, but not necessarily subservient to, the official chain of command. Curious and annoying, but hardly problematic. There were even historical precedents for such affiliated but private armies. These and more were some of the rationalizations the elected folks told themselves to pretend they weren't so desperate.

The Californian Guard commander practiced tolerance, at least. He was firm that "no fucking civilian will get within 100 yards of a nuke," but outside of that, he treated the volunteers as real auxiliaries. Sitting there guarding the outer perimeter around the ordinance bunkers, they felt like part of the mission and not merely a public relations stunt. Not just there to show the "grassroots" nature of the new republic.

Buck Sergeant Sophie snatched a lit cigarette from an older man in her squad and stubbed it out. "No smoking while on duty, Private. All those regular military types are watching us. Time to be professional."

The man stared down his nose at her. Pretty easy to, since he was a good foot taller. "Damnit, girl! You know how expensive those things are? You get a tiny bit of rank and you think you're better than me? I was a real specialist back in my Army days." He yanked out his pack from a shoulder pocket to light another. Sophie ripped the case from his giant hand and tossed it into the truck. Laughing, he effortlessly pushed her out of the way and went to retrieve his precious.

With the black Humvee blocking the real soldiers' view, she followed closely behind him. As soon as he turned around, she cupped a handful of his nuts and squeezed. Hard. She didn't like to fight dirty, but he had body armor on over his solar plexus. While he wrestled with his stomach over not puking, she put a knife to his throat.

"I got these stripes by killing a marine during the street fighting. You don't look tougher than a marine. This isn't the regular Army, big boy. No enlistment contracts. You're free to go whenever you've had enough. But while you're here, you will respect my rank or I'll bury you. Might piss off the Lieutenant, but the worst he could do is fire me. So, are we cool?" Only when his eyes showed sincerity did she release her grip and pull the blade back.

"This is stupid shit, Jamal. If you have a problem taking orders from a woman, then don't think of me as a girl. Think of me as your worst fucking nightmare!" She slapped him on the back.

"You're a stupid brute sometimes, but a good fighter most of the time. I respect that. Now, let this shit go. Let's get back to work. We won't talk about it again." She turned her back on the suddenly quiet big mouth, just in time to see their militia lieutenant coming around the front of the vehicle.

Like a good officer, he pretended not to have seen anything. "Hey Kampbell, we've got a new mission."

"When and where, sir?" She kept one critical eye on her squad even while talking to him.

The LT grinned wide. He was ex-military and amazed at the quality of some of these amateurs. With a little time and proper coaching she'd make a great leader. In a perfect world, the platoon sergeant would be responsible for developing her. In their far from perfect organization the LT was both platoon leader and platoon sergeant. Similar to being a single parent. There just wasn't the time to do everything that needed doing.

"Sacramento doesn't like having all their eggs in one basket. They're suddenly in a hurry to get these things scattered. We're going to move some of the bombs back to secure homes in California." He lowered his voice.

"I don't want to freak anyone out, but I think it's only a matter of time before the Air Force, the real one out East, levels this whole place. Despite the lies the base headquarters are feeding them they must be guessing by now that things aren't kosher here."

Sophie didn't look worried, just curious. "Do you think they'd really do that, sir? There are hundreds of bombs here. Wouldn't an air strike cause the biggest nuclear explosion ever?"

"Nah, detonating a nuke accidentally is impossible. I was talking with one of the NBC specialists over there earlier. Fire, shock, explosions, etc…that just destroys the delicate arming mechanisms. The rougher you are on a nuclear device, the less likely it is to go off. They've had bombs on planes that had mid-air collisions without a problem. Even had one in a bomber back in the Cold War days that crashed into the side of a fucking mountain without a detonation. No, it's not the nukes I'm worried about. It's *our* fragile little asses that aren't so hardy."

He looked up like he expected to see B-52's at any moment. The sight of four friendly F-16's circling high above should have been reassuring. The protective cover only reminded him why they needed it. Well, it was an officer's job to worry like an old woman and a sergeant's to get things done.

"So, we'll be escorting the packages? There never was much time for convoy training, but we'll do the best we can, sir." Sophie didn't wonder about planes and strategy, just about who would make the best driver.

The LT shrugged. "Even easier than that. They're moving out in three convoys. Heading north, south and west. We got lucky. Our platoon goes with the west bound team; the quickest way home.

The Guard will carry the weapons in their 5 tons. They'll provide the real security with those light armored cars of theirs. Our job is simply traffic control. We'll move in two sections. One ahead and one behind the convoy. We're responsible for blocking intersections and clearing lanes through traffic jams; that type of stuff."

He tossed her a short-ranged, encrypted, military issue squad radio. The militia's privately bought models were better, but she pretended to be appropriately impressed. "Here's a gift from our Guard partners. I'll take the first section and you'll be leading the second. If there's anything wrong you can talk straight to the regular troops. I know it's a major responsibility, but you're the best I've got for this mission." He searched her young face for any hint of uncertainty or self-doubt. How frightening that he found none.

"Ok, Sophie. But we need to be on the same page. Nothing can slow this party down. Our orders are to make sure we don't stop for any reason until we're at, well, wherever we're going. They won't even tell me the final destination." He waved at all the armed people around them. "Sometimes I think there's no more trust left in the world!"

Thirty miles away and almost ten high, a Global Hawk launched from Texas loitered in lazy circles. Even at that distance, the $120 million drone's classified sensors could still read the name tags of the specks crawling around the desert base below. Positively identifying the slick, 12 foot long silver bullets they were cramming into the back of trucks was child's play.

*

Joint Task Force North
Fort Bliss, Texas

"Without a doubt, sir. They're preparing to move 'em. All our HUMINT and SIGINT are in agreement."

The White House liaison staffer shook his head and stole some random colonel's chair. "You have to call off the strike, General. If the B-61's are outside the bunkers, God knows how much radiation would be released. We'll have to try something else."

The Air Force general still struggled to fathom just how far discipline had broken down. An entire wing going over to the enemy…nothing like it had ever happened in Air Force history.

"Negative. The bombers will stick to the plan and sanitize the area. Even if it only slows them down, that's enough. I've got a Special Forces task force en route to retake the base. Delta Force and Green Berets will secure the bunkers, and a battalion of Army Rangers will take care of the rest. We just need to hold these bastards in place until then."

This suit was the same one the president sent to keep an eye on the doomed Florida airborne operation back in January. He was here now because of his "extensive experience" coordinating with the military. The general hated him almost as much as the rebels. This kid who couldn't tell the difference between a Bradley and an Abrams was the president's eyes, ears and mouth to the Armed Forces. It's a crazy world.

"General Lyon, did you not hear me? I understand these things can't detonate; you people have been talking about that for hours. Still, it's about the public relations damage of playing with such fire. The president cannot run the risk of even trace amounts of radioactive material being spread about the base."

"Listen up, son. We know what we're doing. The big HE bombs will hit specific command and control facilities far from the nukes. The cluster bombs will blanket the ammo area, true, but they are small explosive devices. Dangerous to people working around there, but most unlikely to damage one of those warheads. We'll carry on as planned." He turned his back on the civilian and focused on receiving updates from subordinates.

The bureaucrat couldn't wrap his mind around this insubordination. In his world, political connections equaled rank. "General, you are out of line. I gave you a direct order. This is an extremely important operation. If you aren't going to cooperate, then I will relieve you and find someone else that will. Damnit, man. Don't you have any honor?"

The suit was the type that thought having his chauffeur hit the brakes too hard a violent altercation. A wet stain spread down the front of his pants when the general grabbed him by his $500 tie and dragged him out of his chair. The general waved his free hand at the security detail.

"Airman! Get this fucking little shit off of my base, right now! Honor? What the hell do you know about that? I was dodging flak over Baghdad while you were having your diapers changed by the maid. I will obey a direct order from the president personally, but no longer from any of the vampires he surrounds himself with. No wonder these rebels prefer to fight than serve you people."

***

Bombing Vegas

Jamming a GPS signal is disturbingly easy. The satellites might have been high tech, but they communicate via old fashioned radio waves. Since, even at their closest, the sats orbit 22,000 miles away from the receiver, that signal is not terribly strong. Even a weak transmitter broadcasting on the same frequency only a few miles from the target can effortlessly drown them out. Car thieves have been using cheap handheld jammers, bought anonymously over the internet, to outwit expensive GPS based antitheft devices for years. It was scandalous how long it took the military to copy them.

Except for the circling friendly fighters, nothing showed on the radar screens up in the Nellis control tower. Nothing at all. Not a single civilian plane, big or small, was airborne within a 50 mile radius. A quick call to their counterpart civilian air controllers at the international airport scared them the most. The FAA had grounded all flights in or out of the city and setup a no fly zone around the base; without any explanation. Just a firm order with no expiration time. No one from the government bothered calling the base to inform them. Not a good sign.

The base commander fidgeted. He was always the decisive type, for a senior officer. There wasn't any point in scrambling more fighters. The only four pilots he could positively count on were already airborne. The tolerance of his people was, to put it mildly, nearing its limits. Sending up the rest of the squadron might just be giving the enemy reinforcements. He paused at the E-word thought. So strange, but it felt right.

He still had one card up his sleeve though. Some of his staff had an interesting plan to jam all GPS signals in a 20 mile radius. Normally, he never would have considered the idea, since it was such a huge threat to all the civilian aircraft around. Thanks to the Feds, they now had an opportunity…and the desperate need to try it.

He had a space operations team at the base; primarily staffed by contractors. As long as their paychecks kept coming, their loyalty wasn't such an open question. They were pretty motivated about the idea of reprogramming some of the airfield's powerful radio transmitters to override all military and civilian GPS bands in the vicinity. The job was theoretically straightforward, since they had all the hardware, software and codes necessary, but it had never been tried before.

The chance to do something truly new, to turn a radio antennae and computer into a weapon, guaranteed the loyalty of the civilian technicians more than the promised bonuses. Forcing them to stay on duty at the base during the eventual airstrikes helped guarantee high quality work as well.

There are ways around this jamming, of course. The military sinks a lot of money into R&D every year. Not all of it is siphoned off by unscrupulous, overbilling contractors. Every now and again, all that money spent yields useful products. Each of the $2 billion B-2 bombers closing in on Nellis was equipped with state of the art anti-jamming equipment. Despite all that electronic fire power aimed at them their instruments were not affected at all. That's why they didn't have the slightest idea what the enemy was trying to do.

While the bulk of the Air Force's aircraft were properly shielded, no one ever thought to also protect the GPS guided bombs they dropped. Putting $50k electronic countermeasures onto something you were going to blow up anyway was an expense that even those extremely generous congressmen on the Armed Services Budget Committee thought a tad wasteful.

After the infamous Nevada strike, the Air Force would get all the funding they needed to upgrade their ordinance. But that came later. It wouldn't do much to save the citizens of North Las Vegas today.

The great thing about GPS guided weapons isn't how accurately they can be dropped–a 2,000 lb bomb gives a lot of room for error. What is revolutionary is how far away they could be deployed from. You can stand off miles and, thanks to GPS controlled canards on the rear of the death sausages, still be sure the package will hit within 5 meters of the target.

Somewhere over the Hoover Dam, four stealth bombers unleashed their payloads from 50,000 feet high and almost 15 miles away. A mix of 24 large HE and cluster bombs arched towards the rebellious base below. With their GPS guidance shut off, the suddenly "iron bombs" made no corrections for atmospheric conditions or ballistic wobbling. In short, with every mile they fell, they missed their programmed targets by hundreds, sometimes thousands, of meters.

Cold War-era air raid sirens screeched all over the base. The rebels scurried to shelter in the sturdiest structures they could find: the partially buried ordinance bunkers. None appreciated the humor of hiding in a bunker packed with explosives to survive the bombs coming towards them. At first. Once they heard faint blasts safely in the distance did they start joking again. The comedy respite ended abruptly when somebody pointed out they came from the west. In town. For some reason, out here in the middle of a sprawling desert, this military base jutted right up against civilian areas.

One great big bomb slammed into a Wal-Mart less than half a mile from the base's main gate. The cheap corrugated tin roof of the sprawling shopping Mecca wasn't sturdy enough to trigger the point fuse. The bomb didn't detonate until it struck a shelf full of flat screen TV's. 2,000 pounds of high explosive turned the entire electronics department into a crater and destroyed the building from inside out. Scores of satisfied shoppers and minimum wage earning associates were either vaporized or shredded apart by millions of cheap Chinese made chunks of plastic shrapnel.

A bit to the north, a cluster bomb sprayed hundreds of ball bearing packed death canisters over an elementary school. With class being out and all the kids at home, due to the self-imposed national crisis, that hit should have counted as a lucky break. Would have been too, if the school wasn't also being used as a polling station for the referendum. In typical monkey fashion, dozens of people rushed out into the parking lot to see what all the booms in town were about…just as hundreds of small booms erupted around them. Even worse, this polling location had a number of reporters doing exit interviews. Some survived with their cameras intact.

Across the country pundits, politicians and other crazy people had their self-righteous rants interrupted with "breaking news" from out West. Washington maintained an impressively firm "no comment" line, hoping to avoid any mention of loose nukes. Their silence was far more incendiary than any rhetoric.

The first network to seize the initiative in this information vacuum got to define the narrative—that of a preemptive airstrike on a potentially rebellious state. Anti-Fed talking heads hopped up and down in their seats at the live footage of unarmed rebels being slaughtered, regardless of which way they were voting. Pro-Fed commentators, already a sinking majority, found themselves even further divided. That dwindling minority still preaching calmness and negotiation pretty much realized it was time to shut up and pick a side.

*

Check

"What a fucking joke!" General Lyon threw down his binoculars only to quickly snatch them up again. A battalion of Army Rangers waited helplessly in C-130's on the Briggs Army Airfield because of a handful of Texas Rangers. Black and white SUV's blocked their runways and kept 400 of his best men out of the fight. Of all the problems he had, this was the easiest to fix. Or should have been, at any rate.

Even after kicking out the president's pet idiot, the Pentagon, under obviously intense White House pressure, demanded he do nothing to engage these intruders. Something about a political solution in the works. Politics, at a time like this! Couldn't those fucks in Washington see the country was at war?

They had a couple of months to work out a political solution. Negotiation now should be confined to prisoner exchanges. The most important Special Forces operation since the Syrian chemical weapons seizure—derailed by some cowboy hat wearing amateurs! He could, and should, sweep these dozen or so poorly armed civilians aside without breaking a sweat.

He gripped the radio mic, keyed to the Ranger commander, so tight his knuckles turned white. Discipline and obedience to orders made a last stand against the massed forces of common sense and outrage. Just before he unilaterally declared war on Texas, one of his intelligence officers reported.

"Sir, we have some new developments. It looks like they are changing their plans." He redirected the general's attention back to the digital map screens.

"SIGINT believes, and two friendly human sources on the base have corroborated, that Sacramento charted some commercial flight out of the private airport in Vegas. The Hawk also clearly shows the rebels preparing to move out with several truckloads of nukes in one big convoy. Looks like the airstrike spooked them, even if we didn't hurt them much." He recovered from the shock caused by the unprecedented airstrike failure enough to be embarrassed.

The Rangers were suddenly irrelevant. Even if he got them airborne now, it'll take at least two hours before they could hit the base. He reviewed what assets he had handy. Dicey as it was, he only had one logical option to choose.

"Redirect the SF boys to the airport. First and foremost, we need to get physical control over those nukes. Then we'll figure out a way to extract them. We have to work with what we have, for now."

This isn't the mission to retake Nellis they ran through so many mockups and trained all morning for, but whatever. That mixed SF team were real pros and damn good at adapting on the fly. The only serious worry was air cover, or the lack of it, to be precise. Only a few F-15's escorted the strike team. Every Air Force base in Nevada's neighboring states either no longer responded to orders or were under siege. The planned reinforcements in Texas were also apparently out of the equation, thanks to the fucking politicians. For obvious reasons, no Air National Guard unit in a thousand miles of Nellis could be trusted.

"Find those guys some air support from somewhere as fast as possible, but send them in anyway."

His operations officer said a silent prayer as he sent America's finest on practically a suicide mission.

Two states west, and just a few miles short of the Nevada border, four specially modified Blackhawk helicopters finished their midair refueling at the same time the new orders came in. Their four plane fighter escort roared ahead to find and distract their rebel counterparts.

The troops in the slow moving choppers hashed out some quick changes to their plan, but other than that they didn't worry. Most grabbed a catnap. It might be a long night. Command always wet their pants over these "Big Missions," but it was just another job to these guys.

*

And Mate

The president clearly learned from his previous mistakes. When the governor of Texas called his office he was put straight through. Never mind that the ultra-conservative show horse on the other end was an old political foe. Right now he longed for the days when a political fight meant just name calling. Back when "blood on the floor" was cute hyperbole.

"What can I do for you, Governor Berry? I hope there is a rational explanation for these peculiar reports I'm receiving." The president's voice managed the right balance of stern authority but willing tolerance. It must've had some effect, since the other man's deep drawl nearly disappeared as he so carefully tried to articulate his hastily prepared speech.

"Mr. President, it is my duty to inform you that the Texas Legislature is meeting in an emergency session in response to the Federal Government's recent combat operations in Nevada. With the imminent threat to Texas civilians so great, I have been forced to take action to defend our citizens. As long as the military situation remains fluid, we cannot allow federal forces to stage offensive operations from Texas soil. The risk of involving our state in open conflict with other states' militaries is too great."

The president listened to enough of that nonsense. "What do you mean, 'Texas soil,' Governor? Last time I checked, Texas was a part of the United States. I'm warning you, now is the wrong time to play that old secessionist stunt card of yours."

"Mr. President, I assure you, we stand behind the Stars and Stripes and loyal to her constitutionally chosen government. But with that being said, you're rushing headlong into civil war and Texas is on the front lines. This may seem like a minor strategic problem way over there in Washington, but it sure looks like the end of the world from where we're sittin'."

The president turned his back on the room full of advisors. "I can see your point, sir, but now you must understand mine. You need to remove your people from federal property with all haste. Refusing to fully support federal forces in limited circumstances is one thing…actively hindering our troops is an act of treason." He wondered if he'd pushed too hard.

Instead of cursing or denials or even threats, he just heard a long pause in response. Eventually, his longtime critic surprised him.

"Sir, look, I respect what you're doing. These people want to destroy America as we know it and rebuild it in their image. They need to be stomped out, and the sooner the better; before they gain any further traction. Heck, if I was in your shoes, I'd be just as aggressive. But I'm not in Washington trying to hold the country together. I'm down here in Austin trying to keep my state in the Union. That's hard enough to do. You know that you personally, and the Federal Government in general, don't have a lot of supporters in the Lone Star State.

People down here are terrified. We're trying to stay as neutral as possible, but everyone's convinced California and company will hit back against us for your action. The legislature can't allow that. If I stand in the way, I'll be impeached by the end of the day. Who knows what type of nut would take over in the current political climate? Please understand my position, sir."

The president was far from understanding, but with the most populous state in the Union going AWOL and the 3rd most populated under martial law, he needed to walk a thin line to keep the 2nd largest state on his side. He shook his head trying to wrap his mind around this whole "sides" thing. Way too late for "might have been's."

"What do you propose then, Sir? Your people are putting American soldiers in jeopardy by standing in our way. This isn't politics as usual–you need to pick a side. The hottest places in hell are reserved for those who, in times of great moral crisis, maintain their neutrality."

A bit of the governor's drawl crept back. "Now you're quotin' the Bible to *me*?"

The president could only laugh with frustration. "Dante actually–not important. Look then; what do you propose to do? You have five minutes to convince me with hard actions, not just talk, that Texas is part of the solution and not part of the problem."

"Sir, I wouldn't of called ya' up if we didn't have a plan. We're still polishing the details, but here's what we know will pass both state houses here and in Oklahoma. First–"

The president's voice held a razor edge, but he kept any worry out. "Why do you assume they will follow your lead? The Oklahomans had the sense to reject the referendum. I don't see them signing a suicide pact with Texas. Don't take me for a fool, Governor."

The Texan tried not to gloat about the card up his sleeve. Tried and failed. "The vote missed by less than a one percent margin; if you'll remember. Mr. President, perhaps you should check on Tinker Air Force Base. The Sooners threw in their lot with their cultural kin, not with some East Coast elites."

The President bit off a sharp rebuttal. Several of the uniforms around him hung up their phones and nodded. This insanity is even more contagious than he assumed. He let the cowboy finish. Buy some time to think.

"As I was saying, sir, Texas and Oklahoma have no desire to war with anyone. However, we are not so naïve as to ignore the conflict around us. We will continue our membership in the Union–we are still Americans, after all. But there are two major caveats.

First, no federal forces will be allowed to originate combat operations against so-called rebels from our lands. So much as a single bullet fired across our border and it's a deal breaker.

Second, all Texas and Oklahoma military forces, both Guard and irregulars, will be independently commanded. We will comply with your Federalization order and our troops will fight with honor and distinction to defend the borders of the United States from internal or external threats. But to make things clear from the start, none of our people will participate in offensive operations into any 'rebellious' state.

In short, sir, we will defend the United States against any armed aggression, but will not help you wage a war in order to expand your powerbase. The formal declarations will be sent to Congress tomorrow but, out of respect, I wanted to give you a summary ahead of time."

"Respect you say…sir, I don't know where to begin pointing out all the fallacies in your position. You are not leaving me many peaceful options to mitigate this crisis. I am finished threatening and warning. This game ends now. Maybe we *should* take our chances with a new governor."

Fear edged the governor's voice as much as outrage, but all the president heard was his anger. "Sir, with all due respect, you don't have a leg to stand on. These threats don't hold any water. Don't bite off more than ya' can chew. If we're going to be on the front lines, by God, then it'll be on our terms. And on our eastern border, if need be! You wanna' play a cowboy, Mr. President? That's fine, but we aren't going to be the Indians!"

Yet another state leader hung up on the President of the United States.

*

Trouble

"I just don't understand why all the fuss over these Goddamn nukes! We can't use them anyway. One of the Air Force guys told me they've all been deactivated remotely. Washington flipped a switch and *poof*! The insides are dead. Now they're so much expensive, radioactive scrap metal. He called it a Permissive Action Link or something. There's just no point to all this crap anymore."

Nobody liked that perspective. This was The Big Mission. Everyone was counting on them. The driver gave his 2 cents.

"Maybe, but once we get these things back to Cali them lab coat wearing types will figure out a way to fix 'em. Once we got a real deterrent the East will have to back off and quit fucking with us." Most of the crew nodded at his more hopeful prediction.

Mr. Know-it-all, with a flourish of borrowed knowledge, had a response even to that.

"I doubt it. They say bypassing one of these PAL's is like performing a tonsillectomy while entering the patient from the wrong end. We'd have been better off sneaking into Texas and stealing a bunch of tanks. We could put them to a lot better use than these damn bombs.

"Here, for the sake of argument, let's say you're right. Somehow, the bright boys figure out a way to rearm these things. What then? We aren't crazy enough to use them in America, inside either border, I mean. And Washington knows that. We'd look ridiculous and desperate threatening to nuke the East Coast over which government you should pay taxes to. As for those East Coast assholes, they want to take over the country, not destroy it. You know what I'm saying? Who the hell is cold blooded enough to ever fire a nuke in this so-called war?"

Jamal reached into the front passenger seat and clapped the quiet woman on her shoulder. "I bet Sophie would! She'd nuke 'em all and have the war over by dinner. This gal has got more balls than all the brass in Sacramento combined!" Either from fear or respect, or both, but ever since their "wall to wall" counseling session he'd been loyal as a puppy.

Sophie kept her poker face on. She had her own ideas, but now wasn't the time. It was time to be a buzz kill NCO. "Nukes or guns, the tools don't matter. There's still plenty of killing left to do. Plenty of Feds and sympathizers willing to dish it out our way too. So, quit the gossiping and scan your lanes. Those Fedefucks want their toys back real bad. You saw what they did in town. Imagine what they'd do if they knew exactly where we were."

With the escort mission almost over everyone was too relaxed. Not a good thing. She reached for the radio mic and reminded the other two Humvee crews in her section to cut the chatter, stay alert and watch their AO's. The men in the other vehicles marveled at how she could possibly know they were screwing off. Uncanny, that woman.

Her gut had better timing and more tactical awareness than any of the professional soldiers around the FedEx cargo plane behind them on the tarmac.

Special Forces operate in small groups well behind enemy lines. To pull off the crazy things they do, surprise is their biggest advantage. Once surprise is gone, shock is their next most powerful weapon. When all else fails, overwhelming firepower is used to steamroll the enemy into rapid submission. In this case, the federal SF team descending on McCarran International Airport had all of the above advantages.

The National Guard element was nearly finished loading the last of one hundred 12 foot long nuclear bombs into the chartered freight plane. Even though all other flights were temporarily grounded, no one paid much attention to the sound of helicopter blades whooping closer. After all, an airport is a big and loud place. Everyone sure heard the four armored M1117's suddenly explode, however.

The Californian brigadier general in charge of this nearly successful operation stood in the cargo bay of the plane, personally overseeing the loading. He dashed from window to window to watch his armored outer cordon disappear under a deluge of Hellfire missiles.

He caught quick glimpses of the Blackhawk helicopters making high-speed, low altitude passes around him.

These weren't the boring utility model either. Those apparitions of death were the so-called "Battle Hawk" mod. A dreadful hybrid of a transport and attack helicopter. Every few seconds a salvo of 70mm rockets or a hundred rounds from the 7.62mm mini-guns would ripple out…from each bird. And there were four of them running a deadly circle around him.

He hollered into his squad radio for all elements to return fire or get into cover in the nearby hangers. He had nearly a company out there, but only static answered him. In the 30 seconds it took for him to comprehend the situation, every man further than 10 yards away from the transport was killed.

Sophie and her section, pulling the far outer cordon several hundred yards away, stared open mouthed at the devastation. This was, suddenly, their first real combat mission and it wasn't like anything they had ever heard or imagined. Nearly a hundred well-armed, professional soldiers and some 16 vehicles were not just destroyed…but simply erased from existence.

Impressively, the cargo plane in the middle of the inferno was completely unscathed. By the time the amateurs could comprehend what was going on and wondered what they should do about it, the choppers began deploying their primary weapons–riflemen.

18 Delta Force operators fast-roped down from two hovering helicopters. One team dropping on each side of the plane. In the next 49 seconds, they would neutralize the crew and any surviving guardsmen without taking a single casualty. Including the pilots, since one unwisely picked up a weapon. No big deal. A couple of the Fed troopers were rated to fly this simple freight job, if need be. The other two choppers dropped their loads on the large hangars and warehouses just to the west of the tarmac. 18 more high-speed, low-drag, "regular" Special Forces cleared those structures in less than two minutes.

Sophie's LT figured it out quicker than most. Over the radio came his stern, but reassuring voice: "Alright everybody. Things just got real. We have zero chance to retake that plane. There's no point in even trying to stop them. Stay well away from them and the choppers might not notice you. Looks like they won this round, ladies and gentlemen. Let these people do whatever they want. I repeat, do not engage. Do not do anything to hinder their escape. There's nothing more we can accomplish here. All stations acknowledge, over."

Even as he briefed the platoon, he forgot that not everyone was listening into that radio frequency. His own gunner, for example, didn't hear a word. He was too focused on the enemy helicopters. Those were dangerous machines, alright, equipped with expensive antimissile countermeasures and flown by some of the best pilots in the world.

On the other hand, when hovering in place less than a hundred feet over the ground, they were sitting ducks to his .50 caliber machine gun. He sighted one in and depressed both fire buttons, grinning as smoke poured out of the machine. He was positively laughing when that smoke became fire and the bird spun several times before finally crashing just to the side of the big transport.

He wasn't laughing when another Battle hawk almost instantly identified him, acquired his vehicle in the heads up display and blasted off a laser guided Hellfire. The missile, intended to kill 72 ton super-armored tanks, didn't leave much left of the 2 ton fiberglass and aluminum Humvee. Nor of the five flesh and bone men inside.

Sophie wasn't the most senior or even the most experienced surviving militia NCO after the LT was cremated. But, she was the only person in the platoon with a plan. That gave her all the authority needed.

"All vehicles, dismount, now! Everyone rally at the Reno Avenue business park gate. We'll take these fuckers on foot! Leave your trucks and rally on me!"

*

The only thing more impressive than the whole platoon rallying on her position in less than 10 minutes, without attracting the helicopters' deadly attention, was that they even followed her lead. At least until they were all in one location. When she explained her plan of breaching the warehouses, clearing out the enemy and then besieging the plane, fear quickly overtook discipline.

One of her fellow squad leaders balked first. "Are you fucking crazy? Those are Navy Seals or whatever over there. We don't stand a chance. You heard the LT. I'm not going to throw my life away over this shit." Sophie stepped closer to him and tried to give a pep talk. "No, not another word from you, Kampbell. You're trying to get everyone killed and I'm sure as hell not going to be a part of that."

Jamal came up on the guy from behind with murder in his eyes, but Sophie delivered the fatal blow. She wrenched his rifle straight out of his surprised hands and pointed away from the field. "I will not have you shitting on the memory of our people. Get out of my face, you fucking coward. Move, now! You just resigned. The rest of us have work to do." He stormed off, shaking his head and muttering under his breath.

She probably could have gotten away with shooting him, but the example she set held her fighters in place far better than violence. Punishing the cowardly just wasn't an efficient motivator. A warrior who fears death as much from his own side as the enemy will do his best to avoid contact with either. Eventually, they become as much a liability to friendly's as a threat to the enemy.

Shame, on the other hand, was incredibly effective. The fear of letting down your comrades, of losing that hard won respect, held the fighters firmly in place and guaranteed they wouldn't be following that other guy. Common sense had now been equated to cowardice. It was an ancient trick to spur soldiers into overcoming that paralyzing fear of death. But old tricks are the best tricks.

The Special Forces fellows occupying the warehouse closest to the plane were mildly curious who these new actors were. They wore old style BDU's and not modern digital ACU's, but were decked out in the coolest looking tactical gear money could buy. They rocked the latest super-duper tactical vests and belts with more modular pouches than you could imagine.

Those fancy foreign rifles were brand spanking new as well. Oh boy, did they also have all sorts of expensive optics, laser designators, halogen lights and God knows what else filling up the rail systems! Each one was a "tacticool" running advertisement for Ranger Joe's. They sure must have felt high speed.

Oh, they looked the part, no doubt. But they didn't act it. Their movements as they worked their way towards the building were an imitation of tactical action. Someone had shown them how to bound and stack on entry, and obviously they must've even practiced somewhat, but they clearly weren't professionals.

There was just too much communicating going on. Not just how they kept shouting at each other instead of giving hand signals, but why they felt they needed to. It was evident they didn't have real trust in each other yet. A somewhat organized group, but not really a team yet.

Unfortunately, for these young braves and their insurance carriers, the men they attacked were an elite team. A team that had worked, trained and fought intimately together for over three years. Each member instinctively knew exactly what their partner would be doing, without looking. They shared targeting information effortlessly and without excitement.

Sophie and most of the platoon crouched among maintenance vehicles in the parking lot and provided over watch. Her best squad stacked on a side maintenance door in the middle of that aluminum sided warehouse. How eerie the quietness. She expected, and hoped, the enemy inside would engage as they approached. With her greater numbers and firepower the enemy shouldn't last long–if they could just find them.

Instead, she had to wait for this team to gain a foothold inside before sending in the rest. Her people were trying their best, but motivation is not the best substitute for experience. They spent too long organizing themselves before finally kicking in the door and surging inside…in a tight cluster. Had they lived, they might have learned. Unfortunately, combat doesn't work that way. The first test is often the final exam. Where an F grade stands for being "fucked."

A mini hurricane of gunfire broke loose as soon as the last fighter disappeared inside. Two distinct sets of fire could be heard. One set of disciplined, rapid short bursts and several long video-game style automatic rips. Sophie prayed that at least some of the disciplined fire came from her people. In less than 30 seconds, all was quiet again. She would wait 5 minutes for a sitrep or any other sound from her team. No one ever came outside.

There wasn't much that she could do. Sending in another squad seemed insane, despite every instinct telling her to attack. Letting these fucks escape after losing so many of her teammates was likewise out of the equation. Her equally pissed off surviving fighters were angry when she pulled them back under cover. The hunting fever raged through them all.

Sophie could tell she didn't have much time. Her tenuous hold on authority was at stake here. If she didn't think of something quick, her people would either commit collective suicide through charging in there or simply give up and walk away from the whole damn thing.

Maybe they could breach the building. She did have one Humvee handy. The big jet's turbofans whining to life cut short her internal strategy session. Without warning, the rear guard in the warehouse laid down hellish suppressive fire in every direction. One of her people 200 yards away returned fire from behind the corner of a CONEX shipping container. The enemy casually shot through the aluminum siding and silenced him permanently.

The Battle Hawks that were standing off suddenly came back with a vengeance. They'd taken the time to acquire targets. Luckily, they focused their rockets first against the confused but massing police forces at the gate. She had a brief window.

Sophie slid her helmet back and wiped some of the sweat off. This scorching pavement in the desert baked her mind. What was left of her platoon begged her for a plan without saying a word. What the hell could they do? She was seconds away from ordering a retreat when something changed the equation. "The ramp's down! They're leaving!"

Sure enough, the plane crept slowly along the tarmac towards the airfield. Several SF troops from the warehouse sprinted to catch up. The helicopters overhead went wild, expending the last of their impressive ammo load in burning everything within 500 yards. Now or never.

"Jamal! Let's go! I'll drive the Humvee; you gun. Everyone else, cover us!"

Jamal didn't have a clue what she had planned. Not that it mattered. Her desperate confidence was all he needed. Her team stepped up and did a hell of a job keeping the enemy occupied. Some militia fighter dropped a Delta operator covering his running buddies from the back ramp with a hip shot. They even put a few holes into one of the whirly birds. Didn't crash it, but wounded the copilot/gunner, limiting its effectiveness. The smoke clouds from all the burning vehicles and buildings hindered the target acquisition of the other two choppers.

In all this confusion, Sophie floored her Humvee to catch the fleeing plane. Less than a hundred yards away, she attracted the full attention of the rear guards. They slowly raised the ramp and picked up speed as their last guy jumped aboard. Four more soldiers kneeled on the rising slope and blazed away exclusively at them. She thanked God and her not-cheap paymasters for splurging on the armored windshield.

Still, even that tough bulletproof glass had limits. One tight 3 round shot group after another smashed the see-through armor a foot in front of her face. She could barely see through the kaleidoscope of cracks. Engineering has it limits. Only a matter of time before something got through. The right front tire was already flat and black smoke billowed from under the hood. The engine knocked terribly. 100 yards to go…they weren't going to make it.

"Jamal, get up there and suppressive them! Don't worry about the nukes."

Her gunner unhesitatingly popped his head out of the turret. Insane or not, Sophie had a plan. About 15 rounds rattled off before he stopped; likely a jam. All of the enemy's shooters threw themselves prone. One wouldn't get up again…the guy that had been raising the ramp.

"Great job, Jamal! Keep it up!" Out the corner of her eye, she caught him resting on the hammock-like strap serving as a gunner's seat for long hauls. She reached over and slapped his knee hard. "Quit fucking off and get on that gun!"

Her slap dropped his body back into the cabin. His face made a squishing sound rather than a thud when it struck the radio mount. Several enemy rounds had already split it open. She didn't cry or scream, just gritted her teeth, dropped into the lowest gear and hit the ramp ahead. When it was obvious she'd breached the plane, she didn't hit the brakes.

Instead, she hit the gas.

Her war whoop could be heard even over the grinding and screeching as 190 hp shoved her nearly 20 feet into the cargo bay before the dying Humvee finally gave up the ghost. Her mad driving knocked over two pallets of nuclear bombs and crushed at least one Special Forces operator. Instead of diving out the door, she did the last thing they expected. She lobbed fragmentation grenades out from inside the turret. One to the rear and one to the front.

Then she reached up, with one hand, and blindly fired the remainder of the M240's belt in the general direction of the flight cabin and passenger seating area. She'd hoped to distract them, maybe disable the plane. She had no way to know she just killed or seriously wounded seven people up there in that packed compartment. As busy as Sophie was, she didn't notice the taxing plane pickup speed but also gently curve to the right...away from the runway.

Somebody opened the right side passenger door. She gave him 3 rounds to the neck and face as a hello. Only after his body crumpled did Sophie dismount. With the armored door shielding her back, she stood on the corpse she just made to get a better view. Six more hostiles were behind her. Well, back there, but not in good shape. Fragmentation grenades, while not terribly powerful in the open, are impressive in confined spaces. Every one of those shooters squirming back to their feet had a shrapnel injury and often bleeding ears. They weren't exactly in top form.

Sophie didn't worry about the why or how as she calmly finished them off with aimed pairs. She ducked back into the Humvee to reload when someone opened the door from the other side. Shit. There were just too many of them for her to give full 360° security. She leapt forward and gave the stone faced Delta guy a banshee scream as her final resistance. Instead of a muzzle flash, the whole roof of the plane came apart.

The cargo bay lights went out as an ear-splitting screech filled her head. God's fist punched the Humvee and somehow flipped her face down and butt up into the backseat floorboard. It took a few moments for her brain to pull itself mostly together again. Something had ripped the open armored doors on both sides straight off. Nearly the first two feet of the Humvee's roof was pealed open like a sardine can. Some massive yellow crane stuck in its place.

Sophie's helmet was nowhere to be found. The girl popped her bare, pony-tailed head out of the hole and took a peak into hell. All the shooters that were next to or in front of her were now gone. Well, not a hundred percent true. She could see an arm or leg sticking out of the rubble here and there. Both fuel-packed wings were still intact, but the plane's upper fuselage looked like some giant took an ice cream scoop to it. The miracle of her survival would haunt her for years.

A few SF fellows also survived, for a while. Sophie's quick responding team took out some before she stopped them. "Keep one or two alive. I'm sure the Guard's intelligence guys could learn a lot from them."

Even the choppers above were running. Their fighter escort had finally been finished off. Rebel interceptors from all over Nevada now prowled the area, looking for payback. None of the Battle Hawks would make it back to base.

More friendly Guard troops would arrive within minutes to police up the damaged, but non-leaking nukes. In all the excitement, Sophie had completely forgotten about them. She hugged her survivors, straddled one nuke and flipped a bird in the direction the helicopters flew off.

Miles away, a Global Hawk banked slightly and zoomed in with 128x intensity. The hideously expensive machine would be shot down by Nevada's air defenses within minutes, but for the moment, she streamed back east chilling images. The president was, by now, personally observing the operation in real time. His face held no expression as this girl, only a few years older than his own daughters, tossed all their strategic calculus on its head.

The rebels were now a nuclear power.

A superpower.

Chapter 12
20 March
Capital Building, Tallahassee, Florida

"Mr. Speaker!" The latest congressman to hold that title fielded the question from a reporter his staff already thoroughly screened. "Does this blanket amnesty also apply to the renegade Supreme Court Justices hiding in California?"

There was a good reason the veteran politician was selected for this role. His down home shrug and easy going, youthful grin belied the gravity of the situation.

"It doesn't apply, because they haven't done anything wrong. It is the position of the president and this Congress that they have simply resigned their posts. The Senate has already approved the president's new appointees. We even sent out the old Justices' final paychecks. At least the post office is still loyal out west!" No one laughed at his joke. He quickly changed the subject by answering an unasked question.

"No, of course we do not recognize the legitimacy of this ridiculous, fantasy government in certain states. Nonetheless, the Healing Act is valid nationwide, not just here in Florida. Everyone is being given a second chance."

The same reporter surprised the politico's handlers with a follow up question. "Does that mean, in fact, that you are willing to let people get away with murder?"

He was ready for the trap question. It was the single most divisive issue in Congress today. "Of course not. A soldier fighting for their homeland is not murder. We will evaluate every case individually, but you're missing the key point.

Anyone willing to lay down their weapons and pledge an oath of allegiance to the legitimate Federal authorities will be pardoned for any crime committed in the misguided attempt to overthrow the legally chosen government of the United States."

The poorly vetted reporter lost her professionalism. "I thought the pledge of allegiance was to the Flag, the Constitution, and to liberty and justice for all. When the hell did the Feds get inserted?"

Some of the other reporters laughed nervously, others applauded and a few shouted at the provocative woman to shut up. The Speaker was a real pro, though. Heckling didn't throw him off stride. He kept going as if he hadn't heard a thing.

"That includes everyone who voted for these so-called 'freedom referendums.' Even any member of the military, or civilian government employee, who has taken up arms against our country or otherwise acted against us. It's time to end this senseless fighting. We are all Americans. Let our differences strengthen our land and not tear it apart." With proper dramatic flair, he stopped grinning and stared unflinchingly at the camera cluster.

"With that said, this generous plan is also a limited time offer. Do not test the resolve or patience of the US people. You have 72 hours to come to your senses. After that, any secessionist or terrorist activity will be met with overwhelming military force. Guantanamo Bay has been reactivated for domestic terrorists—don't make us fill it up again."

Gathered behind him on the state's capital steps, a couple dozen stone faced senators, congressmen, generals and admirals solemnly nodded. The cameras panned out for an impressive panorama of the core architects behind the Great Reconciliation Plan presenting a united front. Conspicuously absent were the most hawkish politicians and officers.

It was thought prudent that those opposed to immediate reconciliation be left out of the photo op. If people saw the grinning faces of leaders that advocated nationwide martial law and waging total war against rebel held areas suddenly supporting the Act, its credibility might just be undermined. In this war, imagery and news spinning were as effective as guns and bombs.

On the plus side, zooming out gave the cameras an incredible view of hell on earth. From behind the Capitol, a buzzing grew incessantly louder. The reporters thought the large remote controlled plane cresting the dome and then circling ominously was part of some elaborate power demonstration. The thick cordon of soldiers ringing the perimeter didn't recognize it as part of their inventory. Must be some special model used by all those Secret Service agents protecting the big wigs. The suit wearing bodyguard detail assumed it must be some experimental military job—they'd never seen anything like it before. Novelty alone was enough to worry them.

Even though the drone thing seemed to be slowly gaining altitude and not kamikazing into the crowd, the lead agent decided to get his principals inside anyway. It took a few seconds for him to decide, but before too long the old "stranger, danger" reaction won out.

Had he not hesitated, they probably still would have died. Just as he took the Speaker by the arm a weak bang came from above. He threw himself on the politician, drew his pistol and searched for the threat. The toy plane broke apart in a small explosion about 40 feet in the air. A silvery smoke cloud expanded outwards. Not falling, but spreading almost 60 feet in diameter. A faint wisp of propane filled the gawking onlooker's nostrils a split second before the air itself literally exploded.

Fuel air explosives work differently than the more traditional type. The oxygen in the air is the real explosive. The propane and fluoridated aluminum merely a booster charge. The explosion is also relatively slow, more like a movie. You can briefly see the blast wave coming towards you. Unfortunately, that won't help much to save your life.

The real killer isn't that impressive fireball, but the sledgehammer wave of overpressure ahead of it. That's why so many body armor clad soldiers, standing a hundred yards away, had some of their internal organs punctured. Dead without a single outward sign of injury. Closer into the hellfire, all the air is sucked away to feed the devil's toy. Air is evacuated so fast the lungs are immediately ruptured.

The dignitaries directly underneath the blast spent their last moments alive suffocating from the sudden vacuum around them, even as they were being incinerated alive. The few survivors were so badly burnt and permanently disfigured they'd wish they weren't so "lucky." For the first time in their careers, these statesmen and generals were getting a taste of the shit storm they so easily threw young soldiers into. The stench of overcooked, high-fat human meat and that gut wrenching scorched hair smell would hang over the square days after the bodies were removed.

With the video feed to the drone no longer available, Marcus had to get his after action report streamed over the internet like everyone else. He fleetingly felt regret for the reporters caught in the slaughter, but his sympathy didn't last so long for those ghouls. Where were they when his world ended? His family's lives apparently weren't worth the air time. But these asshole generals and politicians deserve wall-to-wall breaking news coverage?

He felt worse about the loss of the grad student designed remote control drone. What a marvelous machine they whipped up. Reliable and able to carry his 700 pound homemade thermobaric bomb almost a mile from the city park to the capitol building. He honestly felt shame for stealing and destroying it. He'd have to find those young people and make it up to them somehow.

Which would be a little more difficult now. He couldn't imagine himself ever going back to work at the university. The authorities would surely put the pieces together eventually and find out who did this. A distinguished fifteen year career as a respected chemistry professor flushed down the drain. Compared to what he'd lost already, it was of small concern. His revenge wasn't as fulfilling as he'd expected, though. That could only mean he hadn't gotten enough.

On his way back from the state capitol he drove by his old home in Gainesville. The debris was left exactly as it had been that terrible day. Or almost. Someone had removed the aircraft wreckage. The anger at the only monument his wife and daughter would ever have being hauled away like so much trash brought the hate back.

He wasn't even with them that dark, sunny day during the initial invasion of Florida. He was across the street, talking to a pro-Fed neighbor about keeping an eye on the house while they were gone. He'd waited way too long to evacuate his family. Who could've imagined that the fighting would reach so far south? Everyone knew it was supposed to be more or less symbolic resistance. Maybe a short firefight, but then one side or the other must cave in. Instead, the whole world collapsed.

He only remembered his neighbor's open mouth, a bone-rattling roar and then the heat. When he managed to roll over after the explosion, he crawled aimlessly through the black fog so thick you needed a knife to cut through it. Eventually, he reached a clearish space and his heart stopped.

Only the tail fin of an F-22 jutted into the sky from where his garage had stood. Maybe if, by some miracle, Rachel and Jessie had stopped packing the car and were back in the house…it wouldn't have made a difference. The whole property and the neighbors on both sides were one solid wall of flames. The only thing not burning was the tail assembly of that damn jet. A marker from God to show where his family had been taken.

He didn't waste any more time crying down memory lane. The school's ROTC instructor was missing. Supposedly, gone underground and joined the rumored resistance. Through a friend of a friend he made a date for tonight to grab a beer and discuss politics. The way his seatbelt dug into his gut, maybe the middle aged professor wasn't in the best shape. Nor had he ever even touched a gun in his entire life. It didn't seem a promising career change.

On the other hand, the insurgents might just be able to find use for someone that could safely make bombs from a thousand everyday ingredients. And he wasn't just a chemist…he was a damn good teacher.

Shortly before the government announced their humane amnesty plan, an alphabet soup of federal agencies swarmed over the state and hauled off thousands. Rubber stamped warrants or not, it was an old fashioned purge of dangerous characters. Well, they missed the most dangerous person with their *lettres de cachet*: the intelligent man with nothing left to live for except revenge.

***

22 March
DC

"Damnit David, we've been on opposite sides for years, but this isn't some budget showdown. You people can't keep playing these games. You offer blanket amnesty one day, total war the next. We need a concentric and consistent plan to put this country together again. It's time to quit screwing around. We're talking about the future of the Union—the future of democracy!" The president subconsciously avoided the windows in the refurbished Oval Office.

The new Speaker of the House, the hastily appointed replacement to that unlucky post, held up his hand. "For once, you're correct. That's why we can't afford new elections right now. Probably not for a long time to come. You're the best man to handle this crisis. Your resignation will not be accepted." They both pretended like that mattered.

"Meaning I'm the sacrificial lamb? What did I ever do to you? Seriously, you're taking this in the wrong direction. We've lost control. One side has to give in or this division will be permanent. Elections allow everyone to save a little face, as well."

"Damnit, Mr. President! You were right; we were wrong. There, are you happy? When's the last time some Representative sat in your office and told you that? Your term has already been extended for one year by a near unanimous vote, something unprecedented in US history, and now you want to back down?"

After so long fighting uphill, the president struggled to grasp that other politicians could believe in him. As much as he tried to rationalize it, he knew that things had moved way beyond who was sitting in the Oval Office. Too much had changed, and too many people liked the changes. Whether the East or the West or whatever side won didn't matter much. Either way, peace would only be found on the other side of war. Maybe he could speed up that process and make it as painless as possible.

"Ok, but if you're going to stick me with all this responsibility, you're going to give me the necessary authority. No standing around acting innocent and self-righteous when I send American soldiers to fight against other American soldiers. No pretending you had nothing to do with it."

The Speaker didn't even try to act like he had no idea what the president meant. "I understand. That's the main issue I wanted to talk about today." He delved into his bag and tossed the president a binder. There were no aides or advisors in this meeting. "Here's what we've been working on since California went off the deep end. The vote's in the morning."

It didn't take him long to read it all. The resolution was short and vague for a reason.

"My God. I'm surprised this even got out of committee. Maybe you can swing the votes, but the Senate will never accept this. It'll take so much watering down to pass as to be meaningless."

"Give us some credit, Mr. President. This draft was written by a bicameral, bipartisan committee. This is no political game. Its passage is a mere formality." The congressman grinned wide, crossed his legs and threw a flabby arm over the sofa's back.

"Sir, I don't think you really appreciate the new political landscape we're working in. Just like in the Civil War," the president grimaced at the comparison, "our colleagues from belligerent states in both houses have been expelled. Well, they're still physically here in Washington and some of these sad souls wander into session. They aren't recognized to speak and their votes don't count, but they try anyway. You should see how irate they get. The Capitol Police have to kick someone out almost every day! Which is a hell of a funny sight to see." He laughed a little at this one bright spot in the whole disaster.

"Anyway, the net effect of all the chaos recently is 142 representatives and 36 senators have been banned, killed or in the hospital. Since all the rest are terrified, it's breathtaking what we can accomplish. A painful weeding process, to be sure, but incredibly effective."

The president wasn't so excited. "This thing is essentially a domestic War Powers Act. You are authorizing me in advance to basically do anything I want. Or as you so loosely state it: *'to approve and confirm any necessary acts of the President of the United States, for suppressing insurrection, rebellion and domestic terrorism.'* What's the catch?"

"None whatsoever...as long as you win this war."

"So, you all would make me a dictator just to avoid the responsibility of making decisions on your own?" The president shook his head in resignation, not in refusal.

The congressman didn't look half as embarrassed as he should have. "Come on, you know wars can't be led by a committee. We are in dire need of true leadership. Someone to do the dirty, grey area of the Constitution work–the type of terrible decisions that no politician worrying about reelection can make. Plus, let's face it, you are either the most beloved or hated man in this country. No one alive today, for better or worse, can shrug you off as a weakling."

The president said nothing as he wandered away from the sofa and towards his desk. He produced a pack of Newport Menthols from a bottom drawer, took one out and tapped the tobacco far longer than necessary. There was a lighter in there too, but he didn't touch it. He hadn't had a cigarette since the reelection over 4 years ago. Sure, he made a promise to his wife, his kids and to himself, but come the hell on! That was all before this shit popped up. Twirling the cancer stick, he bought some time.

"Let's make it clear from the start, Mr. Speaker, so there are no false illusions. You realize that I'll have to slap Florida under Martial Law, right? It may even be necessary to temporarily suspend Habeas

Corpus and the right to bear arms in much of the country. Hell, for rebel held and occupied lands, the Constitution will be an extremely flexible document. I don't want to do it, God help me I've tried everything to avoid getting this far, but I won't hesitate to use every ounce of power that you give me."

The congressman barely hesitated before answering. "We all know that. It's not something we relish either, but somebody has to assume that role. You're now that somebody."

The president was astonished and disgusted by how easily they were willing to sale out democracy. How effortlessly they put the delicate virtue of a 240 year old republic into the hands of a dictator. All to avoid assuming a little responsibility. Well, it had to be someone. Ending the war quickly and with minimum destruction was going to be tricky, but just maybe he could pull it off. The real challenge was to give that power up when finished.

The President snatched the lighter from the drawer. A moment later he sucked deeply on that delicious, minty tar air. He prayed he was strong enough to give up at least one of these vices eventually.

***

New Game

Donaldson basked in herodom and sunshine on a Cuban beach with thousands of other runaway Florida fighters. They all tried to avoid watching television. They also tried to ignore their leaders always walking around in deep conversation with their Cuban counterparts and some wild eyed man in a Hawaiian shirt.

Out West the population and their leaders slowly woke up to the novel idea that the Federal Government wasn't even close to falling. Despite all the hopeful rhetoric they told themselves. All those fence sitters were finally forced to pick a side. That helped the fledging new government more than the old. Every day brought new regular military desertions to their cause. Often in whole bases with much of their equipment and most of their personnel. Most of the staff, but never all.

More civilians were also migrating west than east. That was far more important than the raw numbers suggested. Someone willing to just pack up, leave their home and strike out for something new is the most loyal and motivated type of citizen you could find. Or fanatical, as some critics pointed out.

So many people, both in America and America 2.0, wondered when the other shoe would drop. The weakness of the central government was a driving force behind the referendums in the first place, but when they didn't fold people got worried. Why weren't they stomping on the West? Crushing these people they so vehemently called rebels?

The baby new government consisted of just 14 states: Alaska, Washington, Oregon, California, Nevada, Arizona, New Mexico, Utah, Idaho, Wyoming, Montana, Colorado, Kansas and Nebraska. Barely a third of the population of the United States, and that was only paper strength. Here in the early stages of the separation, the reality was less impressive. In every state loyal to the new nation there existed vocal and sometimes militant minorities threatening the new system. Some towns and whole counties, especially along the nebulously defined border, were more hostile than the real USA.

Not that the Feds were in much better shape. Their sweeping military advantage existed only in the media's imagination. A large chunk of the Armed Forces, especially air and naval assets, were still deployed overseas. To redeploy them stateside would take weeks. Large losses, particularly in equipment, during the "low intensity domestic operations" in Florida took yet another big bite out of immediately available resources. Garrisoning a tropical land of 19 million hostiles drained even more.

Concerns, well, panic over the loyalty of the various state reserves and National Guard forces ensured they would not be committed to battle any time soon. This paranoia, arguably justified, nevertheless resulted in the United States voluntarily removing half their army from the equation. When you consider the gargantuan defections to the west, from individual soldiers going AWOL to whole brigades assimilating into the new rebel command structure, the military balance between the two sides approached equality.

Besides the lack of military options, the single biggest concern holding back both US governments was political. Or more accurately, no one had a clue what the hell to do. This stuff was all so damn new. Breaking away from the crumbling old government was one thing; figuring out what to do next was something else. Not to mention that, so far, military action hadn't paid off so well. Something the Feds could attest to.

The two sides continually cast about for quick solutions to this incredibly difficult strategic situation, but kept coming up short. Neither leadership camp could accept that the only way to win this fight was to launch a long, protracted land war to subdue and occupy the enemy. A massive, continent spanning war appeared necessary, but also impossible. The politicians couldn't imagine the population of either side stomaching such a war. Of course, a negotiated peace settlement was even more unimaginable.

Unlike the Florida fiasco, the two sides would not stumble into this fight. They'd have to approach the slaughter with their eyes wide open. Every day of political inaction strengthened the cohesiveness of the new nation's military and government while sapping the power of the old. Well, draining power, but not resolve.

The West represented 40% of the American land mass, not something that could be blitzed even if the US military was at full strength. They were no banana republic to be steamrolled in a day's campaigning. A gargantuan buildup would be needed. A generation defining type of expansion to the Armed Forces not seen since the Second World War.

So, with surprisingly little reluctance, that's what the leadership on both sides set out to do. What needs to be done must be done. If it just so happens that billions could be made in the process, well, there's no reason that patriotism can't be profitable.

And it was. Shortly after the new nation's foundation, thousands of Preppers "bugged out." They were ready for the widespread disruption to the financial institutions and trade infrastructure. But civilization did not implode; it was more a sizzle. Sure, for a time, luxury goods were in terribly short supply. New smartphones, fancy cars and overpriced sports jerseys were hard to find at any price. To quite a few Americans, that alone was a sign of the Apocalypse.

But production of the necessary things in life actually increased. When supply is crimped, prices soar. When prices jump everyone becomes an entrepreneur and tries to make a quick buck from the disruption. Before you know it, supply will flood demand. Just like after a devastating hurricane, for example. Bottled water, canned food and fuel for generators are in short supply for a while, but not too long.

When someone in trouble is willing to pay a 300% premium for a gallon of gas, well, then you can't argue the efficiency of a free market. Out of the goodness of their hearts, everyone and their mother fills up a car with whatever aid supplies have the highest profit potential and rushes in from out of state. Those first to market reap the rewards. Those coming later find an oversaturated market.

The Preppers were right about inflation though, but it was distributed fairly evenly. Wages almost matched the price spikes, thanks to the government's rampant money printing. The Federal Reserve pumped an unprecedented, some would say unholy, stream of new dollars into the economy to calm the commodity markets. All they succeeded in accomplishing was fueling the fear more. At least they created bubbles across the board, rather than in any one asset class. They could get away with this without crashing the dollar mainly because of the economic wildfires consuming the rest of the world.

With so much manufacturing slowly, but steadily returning stateside to take advantage of revitalized military spending, the Chinese Yuan became practically junk. You could forget the Euro. Those Europeans responded to the crisis with their typical wishful thinking naivety. Cut government spending even further, except for welfare of course, while drastically hiking the already oppressive taxes.

It didn't take long for the core Eurozone economies, France and Germany, to consume 60% of their gross domestic product with taxes. De facto communism, without at least partially effective central planning. It was impossible for the private sector to expand faster than the tax burden. They'd chewed their legs off to get out of a trap, only to bleed to death later.

By the time populist anti-austerity, anti-globalization politicians took over power, things were beyond repair. In Germany, a distant grand cousin of a once frightening Austrian celebrity would soon be addressing *dem deutschen Volke* as their latest Chancellor. He had some interesting ideas about who was to blame for the disaster and what to do about it. The European Union experiment wouldn't survive the year. That left the US the only safe harbor for vulnerable cash in this worldwide Tsunami, war or no war. The foreign money poured in. Stocks, bonds, real estate–all prospered. But the hottest investments were new arms manufacturer startups.

Making economic recovery even easier, the militarized border existed only on maps. It was just too long and far too new for any side to "secure the border." With all the money to be made, cross-border trade continued the same as always. Sometimes overzealous customs agents made it necessary for trucks to take county roads and avoid the major interstate crossing points, but not always. Most of these "smugglers" operated in plain sight since they had no problem spreading a little of the wealth around to local custom officials and soldiers.

Regardless of the particular arrangements, the sealed border might be the most lucrative in the world. Wheat, corn, soybeans, potatoes–you name it, all these foodstuffs found their way from the wide open fields of the URA to the grocers of New York. There were also no shortages of coal or manufactured goods coming west in exchange. By the truck or trainload, you couldn't stop people from making money. That's the thing in America: Political passion runs deep…but capitalism runs deeper.

*

29 March
Sacramento, California

"Pray tell, General, how did the Feds just waltz into Alaska without a fight? What are we paying you for? One week into the job and you've already lost an entire state! I can't wait to see what you'll do next week."

The head general in charge of the "free" US Armed Forces withered under the fire of this tiny woman. California's Governor Salazar, or the Provisional President of the United Republics of America as she called herself, was not the quiet type. This short, slightly chubby woman had more ambition and drive in her little finger than most of her advisors had in their whole families. Unfortunately, her military experience did not match that passion.

"Well, Ms. President, except for a small contingent in Anchorage, they've only reoccupied the military bases. Bases that we stripped of personnel and equipment to reinforce the border, at your request."

"Spare me the excuses. You're missing the big picture. From a propaganda standpoint, with the capital in their hands, they own the whole place. Do you realize how much work went into getting Alaska on board? All that politicking pissed away by raw military force. Damn if there's not a lesson to be learned there. What are you going to do to retake it?"

"Ma'am, we don't really have any options at the moment. After the surprise federal assault Canada began enforcing their declared neutrality. They've ordered their borders closed to military traffic from both sides. With the Feds having such naval superiority in the Pacific, I don't see how we can risk an amphibious operation either. For the time being, we just have to move on."

"And what about our navy? I thought we captured something like 100 ships? I saw two aircraft carriers just the other day in San Diego. Surely that's more than what the Feds have in Hawaii."

"The paper strength is misleading, ma'am. Combat power is not simply the sum of our weapons and delivery systems. These ships require a vast number of highly trained technical specialists. With our extreme manpower shortages we can sortie only about 50 major vessels. Maybe including one carrier, with a reduced crew complement, if we accept lower overall combat efficiency. Even that small force would strain our limited resources. No ma'am, at best we can scrounge up half the naval assets we believe the Feds could muster."

She wasn't terribly interested in the details. "Fine, then. Alaska will have to wait. What about that scheme in Florida? Have we made any progress?"

The general couldn't help but sigh as he sourly answered: "Mr. Esterline can best field that question, ma'am."

The fledging new government didn't have an official intelligence service yet. The few professional spies and analysts that "came over" were obviously a little suspect. The best they had was this freelancer. You couldn't tell by that expensive suit and slowly graying hair, but this ex-Green Beret had trained and advised paramilitary forces in a half-dozen exotic locales. And that wasn't even the primary qualification on his impressive resume.

Back in his CIA days, they called him a top-notch strategic operations officer. Hell, one referral claimed he was the acknowledged master at waging proxy wars. He manipulated or outright bribed God knew how many Arab and African dictators into launching seemingly random military interventions against extremists. While the official records are sealed for 70 more years, legend has it that with a single well-timed drone strike he once sparked a short but deadly power-struggle war between the original Al Qaida group and their affiliate branch in Yemen.

After abruptly leaving civil service, he joined the private sector as "a troubleshooter, of sorts." Since he was fired in an embarrassing manner back before The Split, and had an obvious axe to grind with his former employers, his loyalty wasn't such a mystery. His sanity was an entirely different question.

"Yes, ma'am. We've rearmed the exiled Florida guardsmen in Cuba. Our negotiations with the People's Republic there have paid off handsomely. The Reconquista will handily liberate Miami. Those few thousand fighters will lead a People's uprising of millions well beyond just Florida. Within a week, I will raise for you fresh armies inside the walls of Rome! Despite the general's skepticism, success is assured."

General Stewart smacked his palm on the polished mahogany round table. He had everyone's undivided attention. "What the hell are you talking about? Ma'am, please tell me you're not actually considering this fantasy? As we've discussed, we need to focus all our energy on building a viable defensive force. That's your only chance to negotiate peace from a position of strength. The last thing we can afford is to escalate things. Especially not with such off the wall stunts like this."

President Salazar appeared genuinely surprised. "General, we are way beyond finding 'a peace we can live with.' I'm in this to win it, and you can bet that the Washington crowd is as well. I want to make sure you're not laboring under any false pretenses—we're at war!

"And in this war, Mr. Esterline has so far gathered us much more success than your dawdling. His maneuverings brought Kansas and Nebraska on board, without even holding referendums. He's why our soldiers are facing off with the Feds across the Missouri River and not in the streets of Denver! With that record, when he speaks, he will be listened to."

For his part, Esterline wasn't smug about the public dressing down the boss gave his uniformed rival. He was so self-assured he didn't need any external validation. Those puckered lips held pity and not spite for the poor general who lacked his brilliance.

Esterline jumped up and buzzed about the room with his usual intensity, shoving printouts into everyone's hand. "As I was saying, there's more combat power over there than you think. Here are the details. I've worked everything out with the Cubans. In exchange for most favored nation trade status and some other direct aid, they will support the liberators with the full weight of the Revolutionary Armed Forces."

Another military man took over for the smarting general. "Um, I'm not seeing much in the way of weight here. A few dozen obsolete planes and even older warships. Where are the troops?"

Esterline grinned knowingly. Or psychopathically, as some critics worried. "That's where our brave Floridian Freedom fighters come in. Come now, we will *use* the barbarians, but we won't repeat Rome's mistake. No foreign fighters on our soil! But we can take advantage of their support to get our people into Miami."

With a flourish he produced his own digital projector and computer. The leadership crowd stared awestruck at the fabulous projections on screen. Crazy or not, you have to admit he believed every word he said. Sincerity always lends a certain credibility.

"If we launch a diversionary attack along the border, where they're expecting us anyway, the Gaul's–I mean Feds–will leave Florida totally exposed. Their occupation forces are scattered all over the state. They aren't ready to meet an external invasion. Practically all of the Air Force and Navy are deployed along the border or in transit to blockade our coast. They are naked. We need to hit now! While they're still weak and disorganized."

More heads nodded than at the beginning. President Salazar carefully studied their expressions. Even a few of the military ones were in grudging agreement.

"Ok, I think we have plan. This is a low risk, high payoff proposition. Unless we come up with something better, it's time to set a date. Can we be ready by next Monday?"

The general knew when he was beaten. Well, at least they'd have the element of surprise. Who in the USA would guess they'd do something so reckless? "Yes, ma'am. We can be. On 17 April, we'll launch our offensive."

Esterline's face held no sense of triumph. He didn't feel any obstacle had been overcome. The outcome of this meeting was never in doubt. His scheme was the best way to go; anyone could see that. He refilled his water glass yet again and let his mind run loose with the million little details to be worked out. No matter who ran the operation, this was still his war.

Chapter 13

1 April

Where the name United Republics of America came from is still shrouded in historical uncertainty. The favorite story claims it was first used in a heated exchange between Ms. Salazar and the president shortly after his emergency term extension. During one of the last conference calls, just before reunification negotiations broke down for the last time, her assistants and their federal counterparts were at each other's throats. She and her rival president ignored the insults and teenager-like threats their staffs traded–mostly.

The president's staffers mocked the concept of a rival government and in particular her status as the legitimate president. In response to the remark that, sure, there were two Americas, the USA and the United Sociopaths of America, she stepped into the debate and coined a new term.

"The first President of the United Republics of America would like to speak to the last President of the United States of America privately." The legitimate sounding URA silenced the president's men. She drew a solid and dangerous line in the sand by showing that they'd moved well beyond legal squabbling and headline grabbing.

The least favorite, though most likely story, claimed the name was a product of some LA advertising agency. The well-crafted result of countless focus groups. It's also possible that both versions hold a little truth.

Origins aside, a name was finally necessary if they were ever going to achieve complete legitimacy. It was getting confusing every time so-called federal officials warned of the dangers from other people calling themselves federal officials. URA authorities vehemently denied they were in any way, shape or form seceding from the Union, even as they redesigned the flag. Those early days were confusing, to say the least.

One unintended consequence of the title adoption is that it gave foreign powers a government to recognize. Not that anyone in Sacramento had sought such recognition. Some back channel feelers were put out, but the initial feedback wasn't reassuring. Formal requests were not sent out to foreign governments over fear of the political embarrassment rejection could cause.

But this didn't keep some traditional enemies of the US from immediately recognizing the newly minted URA as a legitimate nation. Iran and North Korea issued friendly press releases the same day California passed the Freedom referendum. The compliments were accepted by Sacramento with awkwardness. Unsure of the appropriate response to this unwelcomed support, URA politicians did the same as their USA counterparts—they ignored it.

One nation no one could ignore, however, was the People's Republic of China. In a tongue in cheek mocking of the USA's long standing quasi-recognition of Taiwan, they announced their own "One America" policy shortly after the name adoption. While publically stating that there was only one America and one legitimate American government, they chose to remain neutral and not oppose either claimant. This roundabout granting of legal status to the new regime from someone actually important opened the diplomatic floodgates.

Within weeks, most non-NATO member states accepted some variation of China's policy. And China didn't offer just moral support, either. Apparently, in the diplomatic world, there is a huge difference between "not opposing" and "not supporting" something. In less than two weeks a private, nonprofit "Chinese Institute of America" opened in Sacramento.

This new nongovernmental organization graciously offered to perform citizen and consular services, as well as serve as a point-of-contact for trade issues in America. Not in the USA or URA, but simply in "America," according to their website. That this company employed double the staff in their sprawling office park as the official embassy in DC surprised no one.

That the onsite manager of this firm was not a high ranking Chinese bureaucrat, but a high ranking Chinese military officer was surprising, though. Oh, the general resigned his post to work "in the private sector," but the deputy operations officer of the Chengdu Military Region Special Forces doesn't walk off the job without official sanction. As a matter of fact, the company had a strange habit of recruiting almost exclusively from ex-military, intelligence and foreign ministry workers in the PRC. All mundane administrative details were outsourced to some local US company.

Washington's reasoned response to this insult was to return the PRC ambassador's passport. At the urging of Congress, the president reluctantly ordered all PRC missions in loyal areas closed. Two weeks later, a terrified Taiwan received the official recognition from a spiteful US Senate they always wanted...just as all US military forces were being withdrawn from the Pacific. Mainland China's outrage was epic. But who cares, what could they do way over there?

The greatest annoyance for the California led republic was how helpful the PRC's were. In Beijing's eyes, the only thing better than one giant export market like the US were two markets. They were supposedly the communists, but man oh man, did they have a lot of ideas on how to profit from the crisis.

From day 1 they'd been proposing one scheme after another to increase military cooperation between the two countries, in order to strengthen "mutual defense." Proposals to trade military technology fell through when it was clear they had little to offer. Their hopes to sell arms to the provisional government likewise fell on deaf ears.

Never mind that there were good reasons the Chinese government stole weapon designs from the US and not the other way around. The big driver behind the growing military buildup in the URA was as much economic as political or strategic. Too many jobs had already been lost in the economic devastation of the last few months. Sacramento officials tactfully, but firmly made it clear that these new defense contracts would go to domestic sources.

Undaunted, their representatives persevered with one creative scheme after another. The solution they pushed the hardest, though politely rejected every time, involved getting Chinese troops stationed in the new country. With foreign peacekeepers on hand, the USA would never dare attack for fear of starting World War Three. The Chinese seemed genuinely interested in the security of the new government. They were even surprisingly frank about their rationale. A hot war would be a disaster…but an inter-American Cold War would be pretty damn good for business.

To be fair, that last point was echoed by many movers and shakers throughout both Americas.

***

3 April
Fort Myers Beach

Three federal MRAP 4x4 trucks coasted lazily along Estero Blvd. Thirteen soldiers on board scanned their sectors just as casually. Between the stunning view of the Gulf Coast a hundred yards away and the bikini clad girls playing volleyball, they were far from alert. Their "patrol" was more in an armed Baywatch style than the expected wet version of Iraq. Which suited the men just fine.

The lead truck's gunner enjoyed the best view. "Dude, all these years I bitched about the Army sending me to shitty, dusty places. I always hoped we'd invade somewhere with a beach! I just joined the Service too soon."

His driver was equally impressed, but less enthused. "Except that these are fucking Americans, man. I got an aunt who lives in some retirement village around here. How crazy is this shit?"

"What ain't crazy about the military? At least this time the craziness is hot…" Their sergeant lost track of his thought as he admired some hot pants wearing chicks rollerblading past them and waving.

Seemed a lot of people around here had respect for the US Army. Just as many flashed thumbs up at them everywhere they went as glared with unshielded hatred. Of course, the majority in this town didn't seem to give a damn one way or the other. Things were way different farther north, where the real combat took place, but down here, you felt on vacation rather than on duty.

The gunner stuck his head into the truck. "No bullshit, Sergeant, how long you think we can milk this? How long until they send us to the front?"

"Hell if I know. I am but a mushroom; same as you. Kept in the dark and fed shit."

The know-it-all driver already had everything worked out. "As soon as they figure out where the 'front' is. Remember Kansas? They were staging a whole shitload of gear and troops there when the state just upped and joined this 'New America' thing. No referendum, no speech making, just called out their Guard and closed the border to everyone except those Western militias.

Most of the armored vehicles and heavy equipment were surrendered in exchange for allowing the trapped troops to leave unharmed. It was a huge disaster, and all over the real news. We lost, like, a division or so of gear without hardly firing a shot. How do you invade a country that has no fixed border?"

"Yeah, I heard about that. But you forgot about all the guys that didn't leave. Even the liberal news outlets admitted that thousands stayed behind and joined the enemy."

The sergeant's voice cut in with deadly seriousness. "It's best to forget about them. Nothing good can come from discussing this. You hear about these desertions all over the country...but they'll start cracking down on them at some point. I don't mean a slap on the wrist either; I'm talking real bad shit."

The new specialist in the back finally pitched into the conversation. "I know what you mean, Sergeant. In my last unit, they were chaptering people out of the Army left and right. Make one joke that some officer takes the wrong way and you're gone." He snapped his fingers and laughed. "I've never seen anything like it. There used to be no way out of the military once you raised your right arm, and now people have to fight tooth and nail to stay in!"

He suddenly stopped laughing. "At first, I mean, that's all they did. Just kick you out. The day before I was transferred here I heard about some rough shit going down."

Everyone was all ears. "A bunch of guys being kicked out hit up the armory on their last night. Made off with most of a company's worth of small arms and machine guns. No one knows if they went out west or what. Several guys still on active duty were arrested for 'aiding and abetting the enemy.' The colonel even talked about executing the highest ranking one! I transferred out the next day, but I hear the whole base is on lockdown still. No one can trust anyone there."

The driver's voice oozed skepticism. "I didn't hear about that and I read every issue of the Army Times cover to cover."

The sergeant threw up both hands. "A lot of stuff gets conveniently left out of the Times. It used to be pretty good, mostly independent, even if a bit cheesy. In the last couple of weeks though, Christ, it's like some propaganda piece out of World War 2."

"How fucking old *are* you, Sergeant?"

The NCO bit off a comment about being old enough to knock up the driver's mother. He had to get these dumbasses to pay attention. As usual, they weren't taking things seriously enough.

"Listen, I believe him. All the higher ups are nervous as hell and suspicious of every damn little thing. Like I said, you should watch what you say. Speak your mind around me; I don't give a shit. I think you're all idiots anyway, but remember, these are ultra-sensitive issues with the officer folk."

The driver spit out the window. "You are what you lead, boss!"

The NCO reached over the radio mount between them and playfully punched his helmet. "Shit, they're wasting too much money with these new loyalty tests nowadays. What we really need are IQ tests!"

The driver flipped him the bird. "Seriously, Sergeant. Think about it. What *they're* doing is stupid, even by the Army's low standards. Just let these bitches go if they want to puss out."

The new guy was the thoughtful type. "Most of them aren't chicken, really. I know at least one of them pretty good. He was a real badass–got a Silver Star back in Helmand. Just went AWOL and drove back home to Idaho the day they joined California's stunt. He emailed me after he enlisted in their 'Army.' They gave him an immediate promotion to staff sergeant and now he's a damn drill instructor. He has a class of a hundred civilians that he's turning into soldiers. Say what you will about his politics, but he's got guts. That's no pussy."

The gunner hollered down the hatch. "Speaking of pussy, when are we going to get a chance to mingle with the locals, hmm? Try to win some hearts and ass."

"It's hearts and minds, dipshit."

"Believe me bro–I ain't picky about her mind!" Even the uptight new guy laughed.

Their NCO took one last look around the peaceful, idyllic beach island. "Maybe we ought to mosey our way back to the FOB." He radioed the rest of the section.

"Alright, boys, let's head on back to Naples." The horny soldier above him moaned. The NCO grinned and added a quick FRAGO. "On second thought, let's grab a bite to eat along the way and do some 'relationship building' with the natives." The gunner clapped him on the back and hooted.

It didn't take long for the hulking armored trucks to get off the island. After the dense beach district traffic, the two lane causeway heading towards the mainland felt wide open. The convoy crossed a bridge and roared onto an even smaller sandbar called Lovers Key State Park. What a beautiful name for such a terrible place.

A few seconds after crossing the bridge they saw something that made them slam their breaks hard. A 10 foot gator lay sunning itself in the middle of the road. None of these fellows had ever seen one before. This was Florida after all, but still...

Novelty spooks a professional soldier like a break in routine puts a dog on edge. The NCO barked immediately over the radio. "Watch your spacing. Crew served's: give me 360°. Dismounts out and do your 5 x 25's, over."

The convoy took up defensive positions without further discussion. Those soldiers that weren't driving or manning a "crew served" machine gun got out in pairs and began searching for threats. The "5x25" system is, by now, a basic counter-insurgency tactic. One soldier would take a knee and cover his partner. The other man advanced in 5 meter increments, scanning intently his immediate vicinity for signs of IED's, until he got 25 meters away from the vehicle. It seemed incredibly out of place in this vacation retreat, but SOP was SOP. No matter how ridiculous.

Even after each element reported clear and any possible moment of surprise had clearly passed, their section leader still felt uneasy. He personally approached the gator and cleared the surroundings. No telltale signs of anything. Only after his gunner scanned the full perimeter twice with the vehicle mounted thermal set did he begin to relax. The hi-resolution imaging equipment was top of the line. Even in broad daylight it could penetrate through the thick bush on both sides of the road and find anything lurking nearby. No one was around for at least a hundred meters.

"Is the Warlock still on?" shouted the section leader.

His gunner back in the truck made a quick check of the vehicle's electronic signals jammer. The manufacturer claimed that this big green box created an impenetrable "bubble" of electronic jamming within a 300 meter radius. The entire electromagnetic spectrum, except for those bands used by friendly radios, was thoroughly denied to the enemy and any radio-frequency command detonated IED's. From cell phones to garage door openers, nothing was supposed to get through. It even worked, more often than not. What more could you hope for with technology?

"Roger. Full strength and not actively intercepting anything."

Maybe he was overreacting. This wasn't freaking Afghanistan, after all. Let the dumbasses take a few pics with the gator. "Alright, get your damn photos, but stay alert."

Despite his standard issue gruffness, the sergeant figured it was pretty damn cool too. He took photos for his guys while still throwing one eye on the Mangrove trees around them. He couldn't quite put his finger on the problem, but something puckered his asshole. A car horn honked behind the convoy.

"Keep them back! No one passes us until we're done. You know the drill."

At that point something clicked. The whole time they were playing there, not a single vehicle had come from the opposite direction. They were just so used to the traffic parting for them that no one thought twice about why no oncoming cars came their way. After so long stopped here…that couldn't be an accident.

The gunner who swept the entire area with his thermal sight paid no attention to the heat signature from the gator. It never crossed his Minnesotan mind to wonder why a cold blooded reptile would have a warm belly.

One of the soldiers, the bravest, if not the brightest, poked the mini-dinosaur with his rifle. "This gator is dead," he announced with authority as he also lifted the tail.

"Contact 12 o'clock–get down!" The explosion drowned out everything the NCO screamed after "contact." Not that hitting the deck does much good when a 50 pound artillery shell, surrounded by hundreds of BB's packed in a bag inside the gator's belly, blasts off at your feet. It took hours to police up all the tiny pieces of the two guys that stood over the gator.

The bomb even shredded the NCO diving to the ground 5 meters away. His body parts were mixed in a bag with his men. They would need DNA testing to sort it all out.

The troops in the high speed "Mine Resistant, Ambush Protected" armored trucks were unscathed. But all that advanced armor did little good if you were dismounted. They'd always feel a little survivor's guilt after nearly every man outside the vehicles were killed or to some degree wounded.

Several hundred yards away, blocking the other bridge on the far end of the island, a couple of exceptionally well-armed policemen didn't jump when they heard the blast. Instead, they hopped back into their squad car and tore off back to the mainland, away from the explosion. The piled up traffic could finally go ahead.

A few minutes later, a report reached the occupation headquarters in Orlando. An aide stuck a black flag pin into a wall map of Florida. The colored pin represented location and type of lethal insurgent attack. This was the first entry on the map, but far from the last. The board would be full by the end of the month.

***

15 April
A hot spring

So many politicians on both sides accepted the arms buildup as an end in and of itself. In their world, power and influence are products of your perceived strength. Wasn't a large and well-equipped military the same thing as having strong poll numbers? Holding strategic points surely the same thing as having powerful political connections.

You weren't expected to ever use those muscles; just having huge biceps should keep you from ever getting into a fight. Your impressive appearance alone should be able to bend people to your will. Most of the time, things worked out like that. However, if you look too tough, then people get worried. And scared people aren't the most rational.

Never mind the psychological nonsense involved–the arms race was good for business. So many people were poised to make a hell of a lot of money by tripling the size of the current military. A lot of people needing jobs, a lot of arms makers needing more business and a lot of politicians needing campaign contributions. All of this led to a lot of bullshit.

From the West to East Coasts, dying manufacturing hubs found a new lease on life. Maybe pumping out more tanks and artillery than trucks and industrial machinery, but hey, it's all still capital goods. Most importantly, it's all solid profit on the balance sheets.

*

The economic disruptions of the last few months removed the most important safety valve in US/China relations: being major business partners. Competing nationalistic and ideological differences could be held at bay and defy the historic odds, so long as both sides worked towards a shared purpose. Without the common goal of making a quick buck, these two extremely ambitious peoples were inevitably going to butt heads. The only thing surprising is that it didn't happen earlier.

China had their back against the wall. Their biggest export market was trying its hardest to rebuild a real manufacturing base at the same time demand from the rest of the world slumped in the worldwide economic crisis. A young, new Chinese middle class watched their jobs disappear as fast as their hopes for a better future. After getting a taste of the high life, of all the luxuries and security a bit of money could provide, they'd be damned if they'll meekly go back to sustenance farming.

One foreign firm after another closed their Chinese operations and reinvested back in America. Starting in the 70's, this economic realignment took two generations in the US before an entire middle class lost their jobs to China. Imagine if those fundamental changes all happened in just one year? And that the good jobs weren't being replaced with at least low paying positions in a bourgeoning service industry. If the good (ish) life was simply yanked away and sent overseas almost overnight? Millions of Chinese workers didn't need to use their imaginations; they witnessed the painful tragedy destroying their lives in real time…and they were pissed off. Naturally, the people looked to their leaders for salvation.

To call the Politburo of the People's Republic of China communists is not accurate. They have one belief, only one goal to strive for: staying in power. They are pragmatists first and foremost. Communism, capitalism, democracy, etc…these labels mean little to them. To the leadership caste, all these ideologies are mere fashions to be either embraced or crushed, depending on the mood of the masses. If the majority of the population were to convert to Scientology, then Tom Cruise would be installed as premier overnight. They'd do whatever it takes to protect their comfortable place in the world

So, when facing the greatest internal unrest since Tiananmen Square, it was no surprise they looked outward for options. When the US snatched Alaska back into the Union with a lighting airborne strike, Chinese outrage rivaled that of the URA. More importantly, the PLA was in a position to back up their rhetoric with hard action. The oil and abundant natural resources in Alaska were merely bonuses. The real prize would be the fighting itself. Nothing pulls the people together like an external war. The threat from "the others" is always good for a lot of mileage.

Similar logic dictated the forcefulness of the US response to any foreign intervention, but they had an additional factor in their strategic calculus. Everyone kept sticking their nose into the US's problems. The whole world thought they were entitled to a say in America's future. The most forceful of which were France and Russia. Both pushed hard to setup UN peacekeepers along the URA/USA border. The Administrations on each coast pretty much decided how they would respond to any direct foreign interference ahead of time. The only question was who would be the test subject?

Despite all the secrecy the Chinese tried to maintain, mainly out of habit, there was little surprise when their fleet finally sailed out of Guangzhou late at night. In the age of satellite surveillance, they didn't waste time trying to obfuscate their route once at sea. Watched by the world, they made a beeline for the Bearing Straight. One sternly worded diplomatic protest after another by the United States was either stalled or simply ignored.

Logic backed up that Chinese arrogance. All USN ships and aircraft had long since been pulled out of the Western Pacific. They also presumed far too much on their solid relations with the URA. Not once did anyone in Beijing try to coordinate with them, but just assumed they would help distract the US defenders. The enemy of my enemy is my friend, right?

Never before had the PLA projected so much power so far from the mainland. Indeed, just to assemble and place the flotilla steaming non-stop towards the Gulf of Alaska took nearly everything the country could muster. Thirty of their best transport and support ships, including a few commercial ones pressed into service, were escorted by thirty of their most modern warships. Only thirty escorts because they were all the somewhat advanced long-range combat vessels seaworthy in the entire fleet.

Despite major logistical challenges, the Chinese put together an impressive show. The centerpiece of the armada was the *Liaoning* short-deck carrier–China's only real aircraft carrier, bought cheaply from the Ukraine years ago. They'd spent a fortune renovating and modernizing her. If not carrying any helicopters and loaded down exclusively with fixed-wing aircraft, she could launch all 46 J-11 multi-role fighter bombers China owned, some of the best jets in their inventory.

In addition, all 24 ultra-modern SU-35 fighters China had bought from Russia, flown by the best pilots in the PLAF, circled directly overhead to furnish even more air cover. It took every single midair refueling tanker in their inventory to keep them on station, but it was worth it to make the USAF think twice about interfering in their business.

Nearby, two commercial freighters, converted at great cost to serve as amphibious assault ships, rounded out the mobile air wing. Between them, they could sortie 60 helicopters for the initial attacks to augment the scores of hovercraft and old fashioned landing ships. It was no D-Day armada, but still more than enough firepower to get the job done.

The whole point of all this heavy metal was to deliver the fleet's human cargo: 18,000 of China's best marines, Special Forces and airborne troops. The cherry on top of the cream of the crop. According to their intelligence, they would easily outnumber US occupation forces by at least 3 to 1, and probably match them in quality. Between Canada's diplomatic stubbornness and URA forces tying the USA down, once the airfields in Alaska were secured, they could likely reinforce their bridgehead faster than the Americans.

Those ships, planes and troops here represented a tiny fraction of China's complete strength, but the forces involved came from the only fraction that mattered. On paper, the People's Liberation Army was a 2 million man behemoth. But not all men are created equally. The vast majority of that military consisted of poorly trained and educated conscripts armed with obsolete equipment. Worthless in a modern war against a foreign power, but dangerous internally.

Merely a fraction of that horde were a qualitative match for Western militaries. Only a small core of loyal professionals were properly trained and armed with the nation's most modern weapons. It was this same irreplaceable elite the PRC committed to their little game of Risk. "Never gamble with more than you can afford to lose," sounds like a Chinese proverb.

The ships in the fleet packed themselves together much closer than necessary for modern naval combat. All their surface-to-air missiles and fighter escorts were compacted as densely as possible, in order to provide maximum protection from US airstrikes. That was the only real threat, since what was still loyal of the US Pacific Fleet operated much further south, trying to blockade the West Coast.

According to their satellite intel, not a single US naval vessel patrolled within 400 miles. It's possible a US submarine or two lurked undetected nearby. They could hurt the force, but had no real chance of stopping them. Against all odds, they caught the US with their pants down.

The Chinese admiral commanding the invasion drank in the freezing air from the bridge. His historic mission cruised 800 miles northeast of Attu Island, which the Japanese briefly overran during the early days of WW2. The Gulf of Alaska still beckoned 100 miles east, and their target even further, but he could barely suppress his excitement. Even the Japanese, at their most powerful, weren't able to get so much combat power so close to the US mainland. He checked his watch again.

They'd begin launching their first softening up airstrikes in just a couple of hours, as soon as dark finally set in. These 14 hours of sunlight up here in the Arctic Circle were a pain in the ass. In the meantime, he wanted to enjoy his fighters swatting this incoming American reconnaissance flight out of the sky. He raised his field glasses along the azimuth his radar people suggested. How unbelievably arrogant of the round eyes to toss just two small fighters against his fleet. Well, time to educate the barbarians.

Despite his vantage point, he didn't see much of what happened. The initial sunbursts from both cruise missiles blinded him before he could comprehend what hell was being unleashed upon them. A few moments later, as he nearly had things puzzled out, the blast wave reached his carrier.

He dived inside the armored bridge reflexively; not that it helped. A freight train of overpressure tore away the entire top-heavy control castle of the ship and chucked it playfully into the sea. Only a few twisted girders remained. Dozens of expensive aluminum planes and hundreds of highly trained personnel on the flight deck were simply erased from existence.

The flashes from the twin 176 kiloton nukes, exploding exactly 3 miles apart and 25,000 feet high, were seen all the way across the Bering Strait in Russia. Partly because they were looking for them. Moscow, like every other nuclear capable nation on earth, received about 5 minutes advance notice of the attack. Never a good idea to spook your nuclear equipped neighbors.

Both nukes were intentionally detonated at high altitude, so called "air bursts," in order to reduce fallout. Every hi-tech plane orbiting the fleet either disintegrated or was forced to ditch in the frigid blue below. However, only 5 of those 60 ships were actually sunk outright. An AEGIS knock-off cruiser and a giant roll-on/roll-off transport full of marines directly beneath the blasts were practically vaporized. Three small destroyers not too far away also capsized, but everything else stayed afloat. Seaworthiness aside, the fleet was utterly destroyed. Forty more ships, including both aircraft carriers, were so badly damaged above the waterline as to be left floating derelicts. The few lightly damaged vessels and the even rarer unscathed ones, such as submarines, rushed in to pick up survivors. A noble but fruitless gesture.

Modern warships are not the steel-clad floating fortresses of old. Such ships might have given some protection from the radiation. The thin aluminum vessels employed nowadays provided little more safety from the gamma and neutron rays than the skin of the crew inside.

Any of those sailors, airmen or troops in the core of the fleet blessed enough to survive the twin nuclear detonations already received lethal doses of neutron radiation in the initial brief pulse and God knew how many gamma rays from the intense local fallout. It might take minutes or it might take days, depending on how well shielded they were, for the radiation poisoning to overcome them, but their end was never in doubt. They were dead men walking.

Deadly men walking, when they were rescued by the relatively "clean" ships further from ground zero.

Radiation poisoning is rarely incurred immediately. It's the regular exposure to non-lethal doses that adds up to painful death. Most of the rescue ships pumped in thousands of gallons of radioactive sea water and sprayed it all over the place in self-destructive attempts to put out the fires. Others received their final dosage of contamination by immediately throwing those they saved into the ship's showers. Flushing radioactive ash into the ship's water system did not help things.

The Chinese naval command never bothered performing extensive NBC training before. Let alone invest in advanced decontamination equipment. Such a scenario was pure fantasy; they had far more pressing threats to address. During the long trip back to port thousands would die because of this oversight.

By the time the remnants of the armada eventually limped back to within sight of the mainland only 5 packed ships were still afloat. All the others had been loaded with the daily wave of fatalities and scuttled. After 10 days of unfathomable hell, the scabby and mostly hairless survivors cheered weakly to gaze on home again. Constantly updating higher command of their plight paid off. The first rescue ships approached them still 50 miles from the coast.

Those coastal defense vessels launched two Silkworm ship-to-ship missiles into each contaminated vessel without so much as a "good bye" over the radio. Several helicopters thudded overhead to machine gun any survivors in the water. From the perspective of what was left of the Chinese government, this embarrassing little incident was finally over. Time to move on with their much bigger problems.

Once committed to repelling any foreign invasion with nuclear weapons, the US planned to go whole hog. Forces were staged to follow up the attack on the fleet with a first strike on China's small nuclear arsenal. Many heated debates were held in the White House and Pentagon over that issue. The traditional wisdom made it clear that, with nuclear arms, there was no room to half ass things. There is no scalable option in nuclear war. Either don't employ the strategic weapons in the first place, or hit first and hit hard against all of the enemy's counterattack ability. Anything less is naïve and dangerous.

Of course, in typical fashion, the USA decided on a compromise. Nuke the invasion fleet and eliminate China's only nuclear equipped ballistic missile submarine with a conventional strike– all as a warning. An American P-3 patrol plane casually took care of that last task off the coast of the Philippines seconds after the detonations. The Chinese boat operated 500 feet deep, with her captain convinced they slipped out of the South China Sea undetected. At least until their sonar reported splashes from two air dropped torpedoes.

The final touch to this strategic compromise, tacked on almost as an afterthought, involved punishing some of China's senior leadership. Synchronized with the nuclear strike, the East China Sea suddenly gave birth to 36 cruise missiles. A North Korean patrol ship spotted the smoke trails originating from the open ocean, but since they were all heading northwest, it wasn't their problem. They didn't even report the incident. Who wanted to be the bearer of bad news in a dictatorship?

None of the three American attack submarines would ever be caught, though everyone knew they were operating in the area. A fourth sub, which lobbed twelve more missiles towards a target in Shanghai, likewise escaped. With the best of the PLAN deployed out of theater the Chinese had limited options to hunt them all down. Their 2nd string naval forces weren't exactly chomping at the bit to take on the best of the US Navy.

Shanghai had little to do with the overall campaign, but one target in the suburbs represented an opportunity Washington couldn't pass up. If you're already hitting the Chinese mainland, why not the headquarters and main support facilities of China's frustratingly effective cyber warfare unit?

The US wasn't so stupid as to believe they could destroy the internet with bombs. It was just that they had no equivalent response to China's thousands of organized hackers and cyber terrorists. In line with America's standard operating procedure, they proceeded to bomb the shit out of anything they didn't understand. You could argue the attack was crude and totally out of proportion, but you can't argue its effectiveness.

The rest of the Tomahawks soared at wave and then tree top height nearly 500 miles towards Beijing. Almost an hour later, cruise missiles slammed through the roofs of more than thirty targets. Each penetrator warhead violated the upper floors of the doomed structure and spurted its 1,000 lb HE load deep inside the packed buildings.

Only two of the targets, a senior PLA leadership bunker and an admin building, were clearly military targets. The others wrecked seemingly random political offices, private residences and a few commercial sites. Regardless of how the attack looked, the US just killed or severely wounded more than 50 of the PRC's top bureaucrats, generals and businessmen (in China, the last two were often the same).

The blast wiped out a hundred more faceless, but valuable assistants and advisors, further hampering the effectiveness of the surviving leadership. Not a single elected PRC official was harmed. The goal was to decapitate China's real leadership, not to kill symbolic targets. Only three out of seven members of the Politburo Standing Committee were killed though; the rest weren't where intelligence claimed. As things turned out, that was okay. Those three deaths opened up more than enough opportunity for ambitious younger men.

Before ambulances and fire trucks even arrived on scene, the NSA briefly took over all digital radio and television stations across the country. Perhaps most devastatingly, they managed to hack every ISP's filters and unblock all internet sites in China. Millions of young, educated Chinese read Western news and history uncensored for the first time in their lives.

Adding yet more fuel onto the fire, the US president's pre-recorded short speech went out to millions across the People's paradise to explain what happened. His popular persona, even overseas, patiently detailed why the US struck back and promised to end all hostilities, as long as no PLA personnel crossed the International Date Line. Millions in China, who bought into their country's propaganda about how incredibly dangerous that American president was, found his proposal reasonable and generous.

In the People's Republic, you can't just "write your congressperson" or sign a petition. There was only way to get the attention of their insulated leadership: on the streets. Not by protesting, but by dragging those old men out into the open.

His speech was deadlier than any nuke. With the most loyal and dangerous core of their military gone, dozens of their most dynamic leaders killed and the already restless masses taking to the streets, the country's ultra-centralized government imploded. Succession of leadership is always the Achilles heel of authoritarian regimes.

The People's masters might have handled an orderly transition of power better if they weren't under such unprecedented pressure. Within hours, a military coup brought some order to the political chaos. Until it was followed by a populist counter-coup, which then sparked a counter, counter-coup from the Ministry for State Security and…well, things were confusing for a while.

Historical records from this early anarchistic period are skimpy and unreliable, but what's certain is that within weeks this cycle of violence plunged China into a full-fledged civil war. If you can call a war between at least 6 different sides civil. The conflict with the US petered out almost immediately since neither side could effectively hurt the other without resorting to nuclear weapons—and the mutually assured destruction that would entail. Eventually, a snobbish Russia helped broker an armistice.

The domestic effects of this mini-war on Americans were also striking. Some hardliners in Washington hoped that the slaughtered Chinese would serve as a terrifying example to these URA fanatics. They were half right. The moderates did get scared. Scared right into the arms of the extremists who'd been warning about the Feds' insanity all along. What little support the president still enjoyed in the West was permanently undermined.

On the other hand, except for providing a few more converts to the "freedom fighters" in the insurrectionist South, the victorious and bloodless (to America) war strengthened the president's support among his base in the East. Americans love a winner. US news/propaganda networks relentlessly hyped up the silent role the URA played. Eastern television spun their inaction as culpability in allowing a foreign power to attack the US mainland. What more proof do you need that these people wanted to destroy America?

One unspinable result of the nuclear strikes was eliminating any chance of further foreign interference in the American conflict. All talk of deploying UN peacekeepers, or any type of unilateral or multilateral military intervention, abruptly stopped. Not even America's allies were willing to get too deeply involved with these nuclear cowboys.

For better or worse, the Second Civil War would remain a purely American disaster…or opportunity.

The Beginning

I hope you enjoyed my little tale. Please don't forget to review this book at your favorite retailer. I will gladly send you a free copy of any of my other books you request if you take the time to leave honest feedback. Positive or negative, I am eternally grateful for all feedback from my readers and analyze (I.E. obsess) over them all! Just leave your review and shoot me a private message on any of the following sites:

Facebook: www.facebook.com/operationenduringunity
Twitter Handle: @OpEnduringUnity

To discover other great veteran authors, please visit my free book review blog:
Military and Veteran's Fiction: Sound Off!
Blog: www.rappeters.wordpress.com/

Acronyms/Slang

.50 Cal: M2 .50 caliber (12.7mm) machine gun. Large and heavy, almost always mounted on a vehicle because it requires 3 men to carry the weapon, tripod and just a small supply of ammo.

Has poor accuracy and a slow rate of fire, but its ability to throw a half-inch slug with the force to penetrate a brick wall or light-armored vehicle at over a mile makes it a favorite among all branches of the Service. Barely changed in design since World War 2.

2-oh-3: Single shot, 40mm grenade launcher. Attaches underneath a M16 or M4. Official designation: M203. Usually just called the 2-oh-3.

2-40: M240b 7.62mm medium machine gun. Normally referred to simply as the "2-40." About 10 pounds heavier than the SAW. Just barely able to be carried and effectively used by a single soldier, it's usually mounted on a vehicle or, if dismounted, an extra soldier is assigned to carry the ammo.

3-20: M320 grenade launcher. Fires 25mm "smart" grenades, slowly replacing M203.

AT-4: Single use, disposable bazooka-like weapon. Standard unguided anti-tank rocket used by US Army. Swedish made, it is dirt cheap but reliable. Effective range only 300 meters.

AHA: Ammunition holding area. Ammo dump. When not in the field, anything that goes boom, from small arms rounds to artillery shells, are stored there.

Apache: AH-64 attack helicopter. Fast, armored and heavily armed this craft also boasts a 128x FLIR system. Whether used as scouts, quick reaction fire support, or just flying snipers, the Apaches are probably the most feared and respected helicopter in the world. Primary disadvantage is the relatively short on station time (1-3 hours, depending on mission parameters).

APC: Armored Personnel Carrier. Lightly armored/armed vehicle used for support tasks. Examples: Armored ambulances, mobile command vehicles, transporting combat engineers.

COMSEC: Communications security. Referring specifically to the daily changing cryptographic code groups used by the encrypted radios.

DPICM: Dual Purpose Improved Conventional Munitions. Generic term for a variety of rounds. Essentially means fairly useful against vehicles and personnel.

FRAGO: Fragmentary order. A modification to the original mission plan that doesn't alter the core objectives, just how they should be achieved.

HARM: Radar seeking missile. High-Speed Anti-Radar Missile.

HEMTT: Heavy Expanded Mobility Tactical Truck. An eight-wheel drive, diesel-powered, 10 ton cargo truck.

Humint/Sigint: Human and Signals (electronic) intelligence.

IBA: Standard issue body armor. Each letter pronounced. Stands for the trade name, "Interceptor Body Armor."

Double lapped Kevlar strips give moderate shrapnel protection across most of the upper torso, and with mission-specific attachments the groin, neck, shoulder and upper arms as well.

In addition, 4 "ballistic inserts," made up of special ceramics and a thin steel backing, cover the upper chest/back and lower sides of the rib cage. Providing protection against even armor piercing small arms rounds (usually).

IED: Improvised Explosive Devices. Unfortunately, infinite variety in size, composition, triggering mechanisms, delivery means and concealment methods. Fall broadly in 3 general categories:

<u>Claymore-like</u> (anti-personnel): At its simplest, just a small bomb designed to throw out lots of shrapnel, often direction specific. Sometimes combined with homemade napalm, poisonous gases and/or acids because some people think bombs are just not lethal enough.

<u>Shaped charge</u> (anti-vehicle): Sometimes just a single, large convex copper plate in a tube with an explosive propellant in the closed end. Other times, sophisticated multi-battery arrays of different slugs. Intended to do one thing: hurl superheated armor-penetrating projectiles at close range into passing vehicles. Often kills occupants without destroying the vehicle.

<u>Blast</u> (anti-everything): From a simple artillery shell in a trash bag on the side of the road to multi-ton truck bombs and everything in between. Usually employed against buildings, fortified positions (ex. checkpoints, heavily armored vehicles) or for pure terror purposes.

Tragically, there is no rule stating that an IED can't combine elements of all the above.

IFV: Infantry Fighting Vehicle. Heavily armored and well-armed vehicle intended to not just deliver infantry to the fight, but fight alongside them. Almost always tracked.

Javelin: Expensive and heavy super-bazooka. Fire and forget, it has the options of direct or "top attack" modes. Max effective range: 2500 meters.

Kevlar /K-pod: Nicknames for the standard issue Kevlar helmet.

LZ: Landing Zone

M1 Abrams: 72 ton US main battle tank. Armor made out of laminated strips of steel, special ceramics and depleted uranium making it the most heavily armored tank in the world.

Behind that armor sits a massive, German-designed cannon coupled with an extremely accurate fire control computer allowing a decently trained crew to hit a moving target, while the tank itself is moving, at over a mile. Effective range from a stationary position is unknown, but from Gulf War experience, at least 4 miles.

Also, propelled by a modified F-16 jet turbine engine, making it the fastest moving tracked vehicle on the battlefield.

Basic Armament: 120mm smoothbore cannon (Effective range: 6000m+)

7.62mm coax MG

.50 Cal MG (turret ring)

7.62mm MG (loader)

Bradley: M-2 Bradley. The Army's heavy Infantry Fighting Vehicle. More than a "battle taxi," it's intended to fight alongside the 6 man (9 in a pinch) infantry squad it transports. Crew of 3. Armor several times stronger than that of a M113, but a fraction of a true tank.

Basic Armament: 1x 25mm Bushmaster automatic cannon

1x 7.62mm coax M240B (400m effective range)

2x TOW Antitank guided missiles (2000m effective range)

M-4: An M-16 with a slightly shorter barrel and "collapsible" buttstock. The standard rifle of the infantry and most combat arms branches (Infantry, Armor, Artillery, Combat Engineers).

M113: The Army's generic, turret-less APC. Lightly armored and lightly (if at all) armed. Is essentially a "battle taxi." Quite adaptable, however, with dozens of modified variants. Most commonly used as: transport for front-line, but non-combat support personnel, mortar carrier, armored ambulance, mobile command center. Minimum crew of 2. Unlike most US equipment, it is cheap and easily maintained.

MBT: Main Battle Tank. Extremely heavily armored and armed tank. Does not carry infantry internally.

NCO: Generic term for all sergeants, from E-5 to E-9's. Stands for Non-Commissioned Officer. Each letter always sounded out for some reason. Never pronounced "Nico." They are also never called "Noncoms."

NODs: Night vision goggles. Officially, Night Observation Devices. Pronounced "nahds."

OPFOR: Opposing Force. Mainly called so in training.

OpOrder: Operations Order. General plan.

QRF: Quick Reaction Force.

Reaper drone: MQ-9 Unmanned Aerial Vehicle. The latest, hunter-killer variety of the famous Predator surveillance drone. Can deliver 3,800 lbs of ordinance out to a range of 1,150 miles.

ROE: Rules of engagement. General guidelines for the use of force, usually accompanied by a list of situational specific do or don't shoot. Always prefaced with the disclaimer: *"Nothing in these Rules of Engagement limits your right to take appropriate action to defend yourself and your unit."*

SAW: M249 Squad Automatic Weapon. Standard light machine gun, 5.56mm. Replaced the Vietnam-era M-60. Pronounced simply "saw." Fires the exact same ammo as the M16, but belt fed. Can fire from a standard magazine in a pinch, but that drastically ups the failure to feed rate (jamming).

S-X: The command staff of a unit. Starting at Battalion level and higher, each unit's headquarters staff has 6 "S Shops." Divisions and Corps designations start with G:

– S-1: Personnel and general Administration. Roughly equivalent to civilian HR.
– S-2: intelligence/counter-intelligence.
– S-3: Operations & Training. The largest section. Responsible for turning the commander's general directives into detailed plans and "managing" the battle.
– S-4: Supply & Maintenance
– S-5: Civil Affairs/Psyops.
– S-6: Signal (communications/IT)

TC: Track (or vehicle) commander. Every military vehicle has a minimum crew of 2: driver and track/vehicle commander.

TOC: Tactical Operations Center. Fancy way to say command post.

TOW: Tube launched Optically tracked Wire guided missile. The modern varieties can be guided to their target via remote control out to a range of 4.5 km. Mounted on a tripod or vehicle. Delivers tandem shaped charge warheads (5.9 kg HE) that are able to penetrate at least 16 inches of solid steel.

WILCO: Radio speak for "Will comply." Often used as a way to express displeasure or disagreement with an order without openly stating so.

Made in the USA
Charleston, SC
17 June 2014